Award-winning

Book Reviews Reviewers' Award. She has also won the *CataRomance* Reviewers' Choice Award, been named a TOP PICK author, and has been nominated for numerous other awards.

Brenda Harlen is a former attorney who once had the privilege of appearing before the Supreme Court of Canada. The practice of law taught her a lot about the world and reinforced her determination to become a writer—because in fiction, she could promise a happy ending! Now she is an award-winning, RITA® Award–nominated national bestselling author of more than thirty titles for Mills & Boon. You can keep up-to-date with Brenda on Facebook and Twitter or through her website, www.brendaharlen.com.

Discover more at millsandboon.co.uk

MISS WHITE AND THE SEVENTH HEIR

JENNIFER FAYE

HER SEVEN-DAY FIANCÉ

BRENDA HARLEN

MILLS & BOON

First Published in Great Britain 2018
by Mills & Boon, an imprint of HarperCollinsPublishers,
1 London Bridge Street, London, SE1 9GF

Miss White and the Seventh Heir © 2018 Jennifer F. Stroka
Her Seven-Day Fiancé © 2018 Brenda Harlen

ISBN: 978-0-263-26501-9

38-0618

MIX
Paper from
responsible sources
FSC
www.fsc.org
FSC™ C007454

This book is produced from independently certified FSC™
paper to ensure responsible forest management.

For more information visit: www.harpercollins.co.uk/green

Printed and bound in Spain
by CPI, Barcelona

PROLOGUE

ELSA WHITE STOOD before the window of her stylish Manhattan office adorned with black furnishings and gold trim. It wasn't just any office building. It was a skyscraper owned by White Publishing. And Elsa's office was on the top floor. She enjoyed looking down upon the rest of the world.

From her office window, the people below looked like peons—small and inconsequential. She smiled, knowing she was so much better than them. She had money, lots of money, and a powerful reach. She was forever finding ways to make her presence in publishing even greater—legal or illegal, it made no difference to her.

Elsa moved in front of an oversized gold leaf mirror that hung on the wall next to her desk. She pivoted on her black stilettos this way and that way, never taking her gaze off her image. A smile bloomed on her face. Perfect. Her manicured red fingernail slid down over her ivory cheek. There wasn't a wrinkle to be had anywhere on her flawless complexion. Nor should there be with the massive amount she paid her plastic surgeon.

She tucked a few loose strands of platinum-blond hair behind one ear, leaving the other side of her smooth bobbed hair to hang loose. Perfect.

Knock. Knock.

"Come in." She'd told her personal assistant to send in Mr. Hunter, the private detective, as soon as he arrived.

Elsa continued to stare into the mirror. She never tired of her reflection. How could anyone tire of such beauty? Deciding to reapply her "Wicked Red" lipstick, she retrieved the tube of lipstick from the glass table beneath the mirror.

As she removed the cap from the tube, her gaze sought out the man's reflection in the mirror. "Well, don't just stand there. Tell me what you've learned about my stepdaughter."

The tall man with short, dark hair stood his ground, seemingly unfazed by her snappishness. "She's working in Los Angeles."

"So she's still living across the country. Good. Very good." The farther away Sage White remained from Elsa's empire, the better.

"She's working for *QTR Magazine*—"

"What?" Elsa swung around and glared at the man. He never once glanced away or in any way acted as though he was fazed by her anger. This normally would have sparked Elsa's interest, but right now she was preoccupied. "I thought I got her blackballed from all publishing houses."

"You did, but then *QTR* was drawn into some sort of lawsuit and that's how she got her foot in the door. From what I was able to uncover, the senior Rousseau was forced to step down from the failing company. Before he did so, he put your stepdaughter under an ironclad contract that even the board could not break so long as Miss White showed a steady improvement in the company's profitability."

No longer concerned about her lips, Elsa returned the lipstick to the table. "Why is this the first I'm hearing of it? I pay you good money to keep a close eye on her."

The man's expression hardened. "The deal with *QTR* just happened. They kept everything hush-hush until the contract was signed. Even the board overseeing *QTR* didn't know what had been done until it was too late."

Elsa folded her arms, holding her left elbow up with her right hand. Her long shiny nail tapped on her pointy chin as she considered this new development. She couldn't allow

Sage to become successful. With enough funds, Sage could dig into the past. If she were to unearth the truth, she could send the empire that Elsa had lied, deceived and flat-out stolen tumbling into ruin. And that just couldn't happen.

Elsa had outsmarted that girl since the day her father died. She would continue to do so. The company afforded her the lifestyle she deserved and allowed her to maintain her beauty.

Elsa's narrowed gaze zeroed in on Hunter. She had plans for him. "Tell me more about *QTR*."

"It appears they are in a downward spiral. They are losing shelf space in stores and their online presence is shrinking."

"Oh, good. Very good." Her worries diminished, but she knew not to take Sage for granted. She had too much of her father in her. "Keep a close eye on my stepdaughter. She is not to be underestimated. And she cannot be successful at *QTR*. I will stop her at all costs. Now go." Elsa pointed to the door.

The man hesitated as though disliking being ordered around. Elsa was not used to people standing up to her. She liked being able to bend people to her will. She'd never been able to bend Sage and that was why the girl had to go.

When the man turned to the door, Elsa zeroed in on his finer assets—very fine indeed. Perhaps she'd dismissed him too soon. But by then the door was swinging shut. She would have to scratch her itch another time.

Elsa turned back to her reflection. No one was about to unseat her as queen of this publishing empire. She had nothing to worry about—certainly not the likes of that insipid, happy-go-lucky girl. A headline-worthy failure would ruin Sage's future in publishing once and for all.

Elsa broke out in a cackle.

It was all going to work out perfectly. She would see to it.

CHAPTER ONE

Five months later...

SHE ONLY HAD one more month.

One more month to prove that her plan would work—to keep her job.

Sage White worried her bottom lip. Even though she'd stemmed off the hemorrhaging expenses of *QTR Magazine* and in fact was now turning a small profit, she still had a long way to go to appease the board. She had to prove that her plan to reorganize the magazine would work not only now but also for the long term.

The magazine had been on the verge of shutting down when Quentin Rousseau II reached out to her. To say she was surprised by his call was an understatement. She had interned for him in college. He had been wickedly smart and savvy. He took a liking to her. For two summers, she absorbed every bit of knowledge he'd been willing to impart to her. In those days, the magazine still had some integrity. It was in more recent years that fact-checking took a backseat to the sensational headlines.

Quentin Rousseau II had been good to her—he'd even brushed off Elsa's well-planted lies about her. That had not sat well with Elsa, who swore vengeance. The woman's threats hadn't fazed the senior Rousseau. For that, Sage felt indebted to him.

Still, she had been hesitant about accepting the position. Who wanted to step up to the helm of a sinking magazine? However, the elder Rousseau had given her an incentive—

a big financial incentive—to make this work. But it also came with a deadline—six months to show improvement and a firm plan for the next year.

Now, sitting behind the managing editor's desk, she wondered if she'd made a mistake. For the last four—almost five—months, she'd spent every waking moment trying to secure the future of the longstanding magazine. With not much more than sheer determination and a skeleton staff, she'd done the impossible—turned the magazine's content one hundred and eighty degrees, from sensationalized headlines to meaningful interviews on important topics. The substantial changes were enough to create a bump in the bottom line. In fact, it impressed the board enough to approve a modest increase in funding. This was making it possible for Sage to at last hire a much-needed PA.

She stared down at the next résumé on her desk. She'd put off hiring a PA as long as possible, not wanting to take funds away from more necessary areas. But with tasks piling up faster than she could tackle them, it was time to hire a very capable, multitasking assistant.

The name on the rather lengthy résumé was Trey Renault. He would be the seventh man in a row that she had interviewed that day. She smiled and shook her head. This definitely wasn't a coincidence.

When she'd casually let it slip that her thirtieth birthday was in a few weeks, Louise, the head of human resources, declared that Sage should find a nice guy to settle down with. Sage tried to politely explain that settling down wasn't on her to-do list. She had a lot of other things that needed her focus. A family would have to wait.

She scrutinized each line of Trey Renault's résumé. His education and references were impeccable. On paper, this man was impressive. But he lacked experience in publishing. Would he be a quick learner?

Her phone buzzed. She answered and learned that the

man in question had arrived. She glanced at the time on her desktop monitor and found that he wasn't just five minutes early, he was a full ten minutes early. Oh, a man after her own heart. She told the receptionist to show him back to her office.

Knock. Knock.

Sage stood and smoothed her navy skirt down over her thighs. She then ran a hand over her hair, making sure the long dark strands weren't out of place. She didn't know why she was making such a fuss. It wasn't like she was the one being interviewed.

She came around her desk and opened the door. She had to crane her neck in order to smile up at him. From behind a pair of dark-rimmed glasses his dark gaze met hers, but she was unable to read anything in his eyes. A man of mystery. She was intrigued.

She held out her hand. "Hello. My name's Sage White."

The man's large hand enveloped hers. His grip though firm was not too tight. "*Bonjour.* I am Trey, um… Renault."

A Frenchman. She had to admit, she found his accent sexy. He wasn't so bad himself, in that tall, dark and handsome sort of way. His brown hair was trimmed short on the sides with the top a little longer and a bit wavy. His face was quite attractive, even if it was partially obscured by a full beard and mustache. She couldn't help but wonder what he'd look like after a shave.

"Welcome, Trey." She stepped back to make room for him to enter her office. "Please come in."

His face didn't betray any hint of emotion. Sage closed the door and then turned back to this man who intrigued her more than all the other applicants added together. His gaze moved swiftly around her office as though taking in his surroundings. She wanted to ask what he thought of what she'd done with the space, but she squelched the urge. They had other more urgent matters to discuss.

Once he made his way across the room, he took a seat in one of the two black leather chairs facing her desk. Sage returned to her own chair. She didn't know what it was about this man that had her so intrigued, but there was something different about him aside from the accent—yet there was something familiar, too.

Sage smothered a sigh. She was letting her imagination get the best of her. Trey Renault was an applicant just like the other six bachelors who'd paraded through her office.

The first man she'd interviewed wouldn't so much as shake her hand. He went on to tell her about all of the germs in the world. With his knowledge of illnesses, she started to wonder if he should have gone to medical school and become a doctor.

The second man yawned through the whole interview. She couldn't tell if it was her that had bored him or if he hadn't slept the night before. The third man had definitely woken up on the wrong side of the bed. The scowl on his face seemed to be permanent. He'd complained about everything including his previous employers. The fourth man couldn't stop sneezing. She was beginning to wonder if he was allergic to her.

Bachelor number five was a pleasant change with a nice smile and good attitude, but as the interview went on, she found he'd smile and agree with everything she said. Number six had great looks but it didn't appear he had much going on upstairs.

With the prestigious Cannes Film Festival quickly approaching, which was pivotal to the magazine's future, she had no more time to interview applicants. The truth was they weren't exactly breaking down her door. She had to pick the best of these applicants.

And so far bachelor number seven appeared to be the front runner. Then she caught herself glancing down at his left hand. Yep, another bachelor. Louise had certainly done her homework.

Sage jerked her gaze back up to his handsome face. His chin was squared and his nose straight. But it was his eyes that drew her in with their dark and mesmerizing depths. It'd be so easy to get lost in them. Just like she was doing now.

She jerked her gaze away from him and back to the résumé on her desk. She stared blindly at the paper. With his good looks, he'd definitely make Monday mornings more bearable.

Gathering her thoughts, she welcomed him again. She then started her well-practiced spiel about the highlights of the magazine and an overview of the position requirements. She couldn't be swayed by his good looks. She had a board meeting at the end of the month that would determine her future. And from what she'd heard, her former boss's estranged son had assumed the position of CEO and he'd made it his mission to put the magazine out of business.

Most people didn't even know this son existed. She'd done an internet search and hadn't been able to come up with even a photo of the mysterious son. In this day and age of social media how was that possible?

His mission was to uncover the truth.

Quentin Thomas Rousseau III had persuaded most of the *QTR* board to do away with his father's beloved magazine. However, his father's last act as CEO had been to install a new managing editor. And somehow this woman—a woman with a questionable past—was turning things around for the business. She was reopening doors with vendors that had previously turned their backs on *QTR Magazine*. She'd eliminated the red ink, and if business kept increasing, she'd soon turn a sizable profit. But how? And why save this sinking ship?

Knowing his father had many connections and lots of money to sway people, the only person Quentin could trust to uncover the truth was himself. However, he couldn't just burst through the doors of *QTR Magazine*, announce that he was the new CEO and expect people to open up to him. It meant he'd have to take extraordinary measures.

And then it'd come to his attention that the new managing editor was in need of a personal assistant. That was the moment he'd started plotting his fact-finding mission. It was nothing too far out there. After all, there was a reality show about bosses going undercover in their own companies. Why couldn't he do the same thing?

And finally, he needed an alias. He decided to use the name he'd gained in boarding school. His friends thought his real name, Quentin Thomas Rousseau III was just too uppity. He soon became Trey, meaning "the third." His mother had hated it, but he'd liked having a different name than his absentee father. For this mission, he'd combined his nickname with his late mother's maiden name.

Since he'd initially met with the board of QTR International he'd grown a beard and mustache, which he found itchy, and he'd cut his longer hair super short. To finish the look, he'd given up his contacts and purchased dark-framed glasses. Even his own mother would hesitate to recognize him.

His only problem was that he didn't expect Sage White to be so young. He must have missed her age when he'd done his research. And more than that, he didn't expect her to be such a jaw-dropping knockout. The pictures online certainly didn't do her justice. With her dark hair, fair complexion and vivid blue almost violet eyes, he was sorry that they were on opposite sides of this magazine deal—very sorry.

"Mr. Renault?"

There he went letting himself be distracted. He was going to have to work harder to remain focused when he was around her—if he got the job.

"Oui." He cleared his throat. "I mean, yes."

She gave him a strange look and then in a blink it was gone. "I must admit your résumé is quite impressive."

She leaned back in her chair, looking quite at ease as though she were born to sit there. And perhaps she was at ease, considering her father had been a legend in the publishing industry. But something had gone astray after her father's death and somehow Sage White had been blackballed from the industry...until now. What did his father know about Sage White that he didn't?

Sage sent him an expectant look.

"Merci." He'd worked hard to make sure his qualifications would catch her attention. However, the trick was making sure he didn't appear to be overqualified.

She arched a dark brow as she gave him a pointed stare as though she were trying to read his thoughts. "Why would you want to work here at *QTR?*"

To find out about your special brand of magic. And put a stop to it.

Suddenly finding his mouth a bit dry, he cleared his throat. It was best to stick with as much of the truth as possible. "I've heard you're making great strides in turning the magazine around and I would like to be a part of it."

She nodded as though his answer was acceptable. Then she glanced down at his résumé. "I don't see where you have any experience working in the publishing industry."

He'd noticed that, too, when he was putting together his first-ever résumé. He'd never needed one before since he'd started his own software company while still in college. He'd always been his own boss. In fact, he was used to people answering to him, not the other way around. This arrangement was definitely going to take some adjusting for him. But how hard could an assistant position be?

Still, he hadn't wanted his résumé to be too perfect or it would have been suspicious. Nor did he want it to be filled with too much fiction. And so his work experience was limited to positions within a few trusted friends' companies.

Trey swallowed hard. "Publishing is new to me. But I like challenges. And I'm a fast learner."

Again, she nodded. She sat back in her chair and gave him a serious stare. He couldn't help but wonder if she was deep in thought or if she was somehow trying to intimidate him.

"It sounds to me like you get bored easily," Sage said. "Is that the case?"

How had she done that? Read him so easily? He had to admit that it made him a bit uncomfortable. He enjoyed being a man of mystery. "I…" His voice died away as he desperately sought out some answer to assuage her worries. "I thrive on challenges."

The worry that had been reflected in her eyes faded. "I can definitely challenge you."

Suddenly his imagination veered from the subject of business. In his mind's eye, she was challenging him, but it wasn't with reports or emails; instead it was with her glossy full lips. They were so tempting. And the berry-red hue made them stand out against her ivory skin.

He swallowed hard and drew his gaze upward to meet hers. "Then it sounds like we'll make a great team."

"Not so fast. I didn't say you were hired."

"But you will. You need me." He sent her one of his best smiles.

She didn't appear phased. "I don't need anyone."

"So you're one of those."

"What's that supposed to mean?"

Not about to stumble down that rabbit hole, he said, "You need me, you just don't know it yet."

Sage leaned back in her chair and crossed her arms. If she was trying to look intimidating, it wasn't working. "You have a very odd way of interviewing."

He did? That was quite possible, but he'd gained her attention. She wouldn't forget him.

"I'm the man you need. I'm smart, timely and efficient."

"And not lacking in conceit."

He shook his head. "It's not conceit when it's a fact. Give me thirty days and I'll prove it to you."

He could see by the look in her eyes that he was getting through to her. She would hire him. He was certain of that. This interview had lingered longer than he'd ever imagined and she genuinely seemed interested in him—in his skills, that is.

CHAPTER TWO

HE WAS COCKY. She'd definitely give Trey that much.

But sometimes that wasn't such a bad thing.

Sage always did like a challenge. It was his third day on the job and he'd presented a very big challenge. But of all the candidates, he struck her as a get-it-done type. And that's who she needed on her team right now—if she hoped to continue to turn around this magazine.

An email popped up. Sage was just about to call a management meeting, but the subject line caught her attention: *Elsa White*. That name was enough to send her good mood in a downward spiral. What was her stepmother up to this time?

Sage had always known that her stepmother had outmaneuvered her into gaining control of White Publishing. Sage had been young and naive. She'd wanted to believe that her stepmother wasn't a monster, but reality was much harsher than Sage had been prepared to accept at the tender age of eighteen. It had been that particular birthday when she'd lost her childhood home, her destiny and her naivety. She'd been forced to grow up—it came with a lot of painful life lessons.

She knew that if she was wise, she'd let go of the past and keep moving forward, but she couldn't. She remembered being a little girl and sitting behind her father's large desk at the headquarters of White Publishing. Her father would swing her chair around until she was looking out over the bustling city and he would tell her that one day all of this would be hers. But she was never to take it for granted. As the head of White Publishing, she would have a great responsibility and it went beyond the quarterly results. She needed to be generous, understanding and compassionate with everyone around her.

That had been before he had been bewitched by Elsa. After that, nothing was ever the same. Had her father truly changed his mind about the business and her role in it? It was a question she'd been contemplating off and on for years. Sometimes she thought she knew the answer, and other times she wasn't so sure.

Knock. Knock.

Trey ducked his head inside the door. He looked as though he were going to say something but then he hesitated.

"What did you need?"

"Um…" He stepped farther into the room. "I've sent out that email to the department heads, so I was going to head out to lunch—"

"Already?" She glanced at the time on her computer. A quarter till twelve. She frowned. Did she strike him as some sort of pushover?

"I was in early."

This new role as management was taking some getting used to. For so many years, she'd been the one taking the orders; now she was the one handing them out. But she couldn't let anyone see her discomfort. If she did, she'd lose their respect and it'd be all downhill from there.

"Lunch can wait."

Trey's brows rose. "But I have plans."

"This work needs to be your priority."

Trey opened his mouth, but he immediately closed it.

She grabbed the stack of manila folders from the corner of her desk. In this modern day, they still did a lot of things via hard copy. Going forward, she'd like to automate a number of functions, but for now, like so many other things, it'd have to wait.

Sage held out the files. "I've approved these reports and disbursements. Please see that they get to the appropriate departments."

He stepped forward and accepted the files. "Anything else?"

She refused to let his cool tone get to her. She didn't ask anyone to work any harder than her. "Yes, there is."

And then she began to explain a new report she wanted him to prepare each month analyzing the ad space. Advertising was their bread and butter. She needed to keep a close eye on it and if possible expand the magazine to accommodate a higher frequency and larger campaign. Fashion and cosmetics were their biggest contributors, but she was interested in expanding to other areas such as upscale furniture or designer products.

Trey made notes. "Couldn't you just get this from the advertising department?"

"I could." But she wasn't sure she trusted the supervisor. It was rumored that his work was declining and his lunches were more of the liquid variety. Until she had proof, she was unwilling to act on the rumors.

"Then why don't you?"

She leveled a cold, hard gaze on him. "I asked you to do it, not them."

He at least had the decency to look uncomfortable. "I'll get right on it."

Trey walked away with his tasks in hand. She wondered if she'd handled everything correctly with Trey. She needed to be forceful but not too over the top. Had she pushed too hard?

Second-guessing herself was a bad habit of hers. It was something she'd started to do after her father died and Elsa had found fault with everything Sage did, from the cooking to the cleaning. Sage shoved aside the unhappy memories. There was work to do.

And an email to read.

Sage turned back to her computer monitor and sighed. For every email she'd responded to that morning, there were two new ones. She worked her way from top to bottom. She assured herself that this was her normal routine and not a stalling tactic, but at last, she opened the email from her private investigator.

The first thing to catch her attention was the fact that the investigator was on to something regarding her step-mother. Thank goodness. He was the third investigator she'd hired. The first had taken her money and produced zero results. The second one had been caught snooping around White Publishing. This third man cost her all of her savings and more. She'd bet everything on him. He was her last hope.

But the second thing to catch her attention was that he needed more money. The sizable retainer she'd previously paid him had given her serious pause. It had wiped out her savings and then some. The only way to pay him more was to get the board's approval of her business plan for the magazine's future and receive the bonus stated in her contract.

Knock. Knock.

At five after twelve, Trey returned. "The paperwork has been dealt with and I have your report started. I'm going to lunch." He studied her for a moment. "Unless that's a problem?"

"That's fine."

"Are you sure? Because you're frowning again."

She nodded. When she saw doubt reflected in his eyes, she said, "Seriously, it's not you. It's an email I received."

"That's what the delete button is good for."

She leaned back in her chair. "You don't know how

tempting that is right about now. I have enough headaches. I don't need another one."

"Well, there you go. Problem solved."

"I wish. But deleting the email isn't going to make this problem disappear."

"I take it we're not talking about *QTR*."

She shook her head. "Afraid not. But I can deal with the email later. Go and enjoy your lunch."

"What about you?"

"What about me?"

"It's lunchtime. Remember? You need to take a break and eat."

Was he working his way up to asking her to lunch? The startling realization that she'd enjoy spending a leisurely hour staring across the table at him jarred her. Trey wasn't just any guy. He was her assistant.

She gave herself a mental shake. With the board meeting at the end of the month, she had to stay focused. "I don't have time for lunch today."

"I'm beginning to notice a trend with you."

This was the first personal conversation they'd taken time for since he'd started. The reason she'd chosen him over the other candidates wasn't his dark and mysterious eyes or his potential to be a male cover model. Her reasons were far more basic.

He was smart and cocky—enough so that he'd want to do what it took to make himself stand out in a good way. And that's what she needed. A person ready to hit the ground running. And that's exactly what Trey had done. He'd taken on every task she'd given him—even when it'd kept him here after hours.

She was almost afraid to ask, but she couldn't resist. "What trend would that be?"

"You never have time for lunch or anything else that isn't business related."

Lunchtime was her quiet time. She did eat, but it was always something simple that she could eat at her desk while answering emails and reviewing deadlines.

"It's the way I like it." She'd been working so long and so hard to keep herself afloat that she didn't have time for a personal life. Maybe one of these days when the magazine was back on track and she resolved things with her stepmother. "I need that report completed as soon as you get back."

The truth was she didn't like Trey analyzing her. She didn't want him unearthing her shortcomings. Because aside from his sexy good looks, Trey was astute and not easily won over, which made her want to gain his respect. Did that make her a bad boss? Was she supposed to be immune to the feelings of her employees—even when they were six foot two, physically toned and had mysterious dark eyes?

"Hey, Trey."

Trey nodded and smiled at the passing mail lady. It was the following day and he had yet to complete the advertising report to Sage's satisfaction. Every time he thought he'd nailed it, she changed the criteria. He didn't know if she was trying this hard to make a good impression on the board or if she was trying to make him quit. Either way, she was only delaying the inevitable. Come the end of the month, the board would vote to shut down the magazine.

He honestly never thought when he went undercover that he'd have this much work to do. He thought he'd answer the phone, sort mail and fetch coffee. So far Sage had answered her own phone, the mail provided more projects for his growing to-do list and the boss lady had her own coffeepot. In other words, this job was not the cushy position he thought it'd be.

"Trey, just the person I need to see." Louise, the head of human resources, stood just outside her office door.

He came to a stop. "What do you need?"

"For you to settle a debate." She waved at him to follow her into the office. The older woman with short, styled silver hair sent him a warm smile. Try as he might to remain immune to her friendliness, he liked her.

Something told him this wasn't work related. "I really need to get going. Sage needs this information." He held up the papers in his hand. And for emphasis, he added, "Right now."

Louise shook her head. "Don't worry. This will only take a moment."

He glanced around, finding he wasn't the only one who'd been drawn in. Ron, from subscriptions, was propped against a file cabinet in the corner. He waved and Trey returned the gesture. On the other side was Jane with the short blond hair with pink streaks, but he couldn't recall which department she worked in. She flashed him a big flirty kind of smile. He didn't smile, not wanting to encourage her attention. Instead he gave a brief nod. What in the world had Louise drawn them in here for?

Louise moved to the doorway, checked both directions in the hallway and then proceeded to close the door. She turned to them. "It's come to my attention that Sage's birthday is this month. And I think we should do something for her."

Trey didn't like the sounds of this. He'd come to *QTR* to shut it down, not to make friends. The longer he was here, the harder it was to keep his distance. Just like he knew that Ron loved to surf. He could tell you anything you wanted to know about surfing—even some things you might not care to know. Once Ron started talking, it was hard to get away.

Day by day, the employees of *QTR* were changing from

nameless numbers on spreadsheets to smiling faces with families to support. He hadn't factored that in when he'd devised his plan to put his father's cherished company out of business.

And worse yet was Sage's unflagging devotion to saving the magazine. In the little time he'd been here, he'd witnessed her long hours and her attention to details. How was she going to take it when they closed it—when *he* closed it?

"Trey?" Louise's voice drew him from his troubled thoughts.

He glanced up to find everyone staring at him as though expecting an answer. The only problem was he didn't know the question.

As though sensing the problem, Louise held a plate of cookies out to him. "Go ahead. Take one of each. I need to know which to make for Sage's birthday."

He made a point of eating healthy, preferring fruit to desserts. He'd watched his mother drown herself in food after his father abandoned them. His mother's health problems had eventually spiraled out of control. As he waited for her at a doctor's appointment, he swore not to follow in her footsteps.

Still, Louise had made a point of making him feeling welcome at *QTR*. And it wasn't like one cookie was going to hurt anything.

He took the double chocolate cookie with a swirl of white frosting. "But isn't a birthday cake more traditional?"

Louise sent him a knowing smile. "I've already done some investigating and the birthday girl prefers cookies. And since this is her milestone birthday, she can have whatever she prefers."

"Milestone?"

Louise nodded and placed a couple of other flavored cookies in his hand before moving to Jane. "Yes, she's going to be thirty. I couldn't believe it when she'd mentioned it, but I double-checked her personnel file."

Trey had to agree with Louise. His boss didn't look like much more than a college grad, if that. And he was finding it increasingly hard to concentrate on his work with Sage around. Her beauty was stunning. He just wished that she didn't try so hard to micromanage everything—including him.

He made short work of the baked goods, finding them all quite good. In the end, he voted for the double chocolate cookie. Louise beamed as he complimented her culinary skills.

As he walked away, guilt settled on him. He was about to take jobs away from these people. The *QTR* employees weren't cold and heartless like his father. They were warm, friendly and caring. The exact opposite of his father.

On the way back to his desk more people greeted him with a smile. This was the friendliest office he'd ever been in—even on a Monday morning. It only made him more conflicted about his plan.

CHAPTER THREE

TREY LEANED BACK in his chair, stretched and placed his feet on the corner of his desk. After days of pulling numbers from various sources, the advertising report was officially done—well, at least until Sage gave him yet another adjustment or addition.

Today marked his sixth day on the job and he'd not only completed the report but he'd also managed to cut his workload in half via a combination of macros and a few short computer programs. He was feeling pretty pleased with himself.

He removed the eyeglasses that he hadn't quite adjusted to, closed his eyes and leaned his head back as classic rock music pounded in his earbuds. It was nice to just sit back for a moment and enjoy all that he'd accomplished. After all, he deserved it.

He'd been working nonstop since he'd taken this undercover position. He'd made inroads with the new managing editor, but so far he had yet to uncover her secret to success. Sure she was first in the office and the last one out, but there was more to it. She did keep her office door closed a lot. So what was she up to in there? Were there bribes involved—

His feet were shoved off the desk.

He jerked forward in his seat as his feet hit the floor. His eyes snapped open. Was this someone's idea of a joke? Because it wasn't funny.

And then his gaze met Sage's. Her eyes darkened and appeared almost violet. If it wasn't for the distinct frown on her face, he might have been moved to compliment the striking color of her eyes. But now definitely wasn't the right time.

He straightened up, not sure what to say.

Sage continued to frown as she gestured for him to remove his earbuds.

He'd totally forgotten about them. His full attention had been on his boss. Was it strange that he found her even cuter when she got worked up? Her face flushed. It made him want to pull her into his arms and kiss away her worries. Not that he would ever act on the impulse.

Trey scrambled to pull the earbuds from his ears and then press the pause function on his phone. "What did you need?"

"I've been buzzing you. Didn't you hear?" And then realizing the foolishness of her question, she continued. "There's a red light on your phone. Right here." She pointed it out.

"I was busy."

"Doing what? Taking a nap?"

"Hey, that's not fair. I just finished that report—again. And I needed to rest my eyes for just a moment."

"You finished it?" The frown on her face eased.

He nodded. He reached around her and retrieved the printed and proofed copy from the top of his desk. He still wasn't quite sure of the purpose of this report, but as he handed it over, he noticed Sage's pleased expression.

He hadn't known her long, but in that period of time he'd studied her. She cared a lot about the people that worked for her—except him. They butted heads a lot. He realized that was as much his fault as hers. Thankfully this arrangement wouldn't last too much longer.

He'd also noticed that she held back a lot. Many women he'd dated had been more than willing to share the intimate details of their lives. Not Sage. It wasn't like they were dating. That would never happen. But she never mentioned anything about her life outside these office walls. He found that a bit odd.

"Thank you for this." She started toward her office and then turned back. "From now on, earbuds are prohibited in the office."

He opened his mouth to counter a defense, but the firm line of her glossy lips had him closing his mouth without uttering a word. This was her office—her rules. Even if he didn't see the harm with earbuds. He allowed his employees to use them. His motto was happy workers were productive workers. But the problem was that he wasn't the boss here.

She continued to stare at him. "Aren't you coming?"

"I didn't realize…" His voice trailed off as he scrambled to his feet and followed her.

"I thought you might be interested in the process of deciding on a cover for next week's edition."

She was right. He was definitely interested. Perhaps this was where she sprinkled her fairy dust that made all the vendors sit up and take notice of *QTR* once again. "Yes, I would be very interested."

She gestured for him to follow her into her office. Three large computer monitors sat on a table. She moved to her desktop computer and pressed a couple of keys. Her gaze moved to the monitors, which remained dark. Her fine brows drew together as her rosy lips pursed together. She tried again with the same results.

Computers were his field of expertise. "Can I give it a try?"

She shook her head. "I've got it."

She tried again with the same results.

"I'm pretty good with computers." He moved to her side ready to take over.

He reached for the keyboard at the same time she did.

Their fingers touched. Her hand was soft and warm. And her touch sent a wave of attraction washing over his eager body.

When he raised his gaze, he caught the look of desire in Sage's eyes. But in a blink it was gone and he was left wondering if it had ever been there at all.

She glanced away. "I'll get it. Just hang on."

"You do realize that I'm your assistant, right? So let me assist."

"No. I can figure this out."

"Are you always so stubborn?"

Her gaze met his. "I refer to it as independent."

He shook his head and backed off. He wondered what had happened to her to make her so stubborn and unwilling to accept help.

After flipping through a couple of papers and reading something, she tried again. A triumphant smile lit up her face as the monitors flickered on. "There we go. I hit the wrong key before."

Each monitor displayed a cover of *QTR*. There were different headlines and different fonts. He had to admit that this was all new to him as for so much of his career he'd focused on software development and website design.

"These are the three layouts that my staff has put together for the upcoming week." She gave him a moment to read the headlines. "Now they want me to choose which will have the biggest reach both online and in the supermarket aisles."

He read each headline.

Superstars Go Pink and Blue
Serenaded Beneath the Stars
Singing for Angels

Trey turned to Sage. "They're each different stories?"

"No."

He frowned. He hoped she wasn't going to slip into his father's old ways. Had she decided that responsible journalism was just too hard? Disappointment hit him. He'd expected so much more from her.

He crossed his arms. "Is this a bit of sensational journalism? A tricky headline to draw in the reader and then a story that takes enormous liberties with the facts of the story—"

"Certainly not." She studied him for a moment. "I was hired to put integrity back into this magazine and that's exactly what I intend to do."

"So there's a country superstar in the backwoods?"

"Something like that. There's a charity event in San Diego to fundraise for the children's ward in a local hospital. There's a lineup of celebrity singers from pop to classic to country. The benefit concert will be televised and have a very special audience. The children in the hospital that are well enough will be moved by wheelchair to the outdoor garden area. Others will see it televised live in their rooms and they will also meet some of the performers afterward."

He breathed easier knowing that she hadn't resorted to nefarious means of keeping the magazine afloat. And then it struck him that he was rooting for her. When had that happened?

He gave himself a mental shake. She was getting inside his head with her pretty smile and her good heart. But he couldn't let himself get caught up in her plans as he had his own job to do.

"What do you think?" Her voice jarred him from his thoughts.

"It sounds like it will be a successful event."

"It will. The tickets are all sold out."

"I'm assuming you got a couple." He wouldn't mind helping such a good cause. He could accompany Sage—

unless she already had a date. The thought didn't sit well with him.

"I did." She gave him a strange look. "Is something wrong?"

He shook his head, hoping it would chase away the unwanted thoughts. "No. Will you, ah, need someone to accompany you?"

"The tickets aren't for me. I've assigned a reporter and a photographer."

For some reason that he didn't want to examine too closely, her answer disappointed him. He would have liked getting to know Sage outside of the office. She was a complex person. She had a good heart, but she didn't let people get too close. She was willing to help people, but she refused to be helped. The more he got to know her, the more he wanted to know about her.

Sage stared at the three layouts. "Does one speak to you more than the others?"

"The singing for angels one makes me want to know who is singing and are they really singing to angels."

"My thought exactly." She turned off the other layouts and focused on the one he'd suggested. "I think the headline should be larger."

"Aren't you going to run a photo to go with the headline?"

"No."

"I think you should."

"That's what other publications would do."

"They do it because it works."

Her gaze narrowed in on him. "Are you saying you don't trust my judgment?"

"I'm saying why take chances when a photo will draw the fans?"

She leaned a curvy hip against her desk. "And what

about the readers that aren't big fans of the celebrity? Will they be drawn in, too?"

He shrugged. He hadn't considered that angle. "But what if no one picks up the magazine or opens the digital edition?"

"Nothing is guaranteed."

"Then why take a risk?" He stopped himself, realizing that by playing devil's advocate he was fighting for the magazine to succeed. What was it about being around Sage that mixed up his thoughts?

"Because it's my call." Her tone was firm.

He got the hint. She was the boss and he wasn't. So his opinion didn't count. This gave him pause.

He'd said similar words to his own employees. He hadn't any idea of how those words felt when you were on the receiving end. Going forward, he'd have to listen more and let his employees know that he valued their opinion.

"You've heard things about me, haven't you?" Her gaze met his straight-on. Not giving him a chance to answer, she continued. "I know people talk, but if you think I'm going to let this magazine fold, you've been talking to the wrong people. I know what I'm doing."

Suddenly he realized her response had less to do with him and more to do with her proving herself. The look in her eyes said the opposite of her words. In her blue eyes, he saw worry and doubt.

What was it about him that got to her?

Sage sat at her desk that evening. It was well past quitting time, but she had emails she'd pushed off all day that needed responses.

Besides, even if she went home, she wouldn't be able to rest. Her mind kept replaying her disagreement with Trey. For some reason, he got under her skin. And that wasn't good. She couldn't afford to be distracted.

He was still in his ninety-day trial period. Letting him go at this stage would be quick and painless.

Tap. Tap.

Sage glanced up to find Louise standing in the open doorway. "I thought I'd find you here."

"Am I that predictable?"

Louise nodded. "You need a life beyond these office walls."

She would, just as soon as she reclaimed the legacy that Elsa stole from her. Until then, she had to keep working at *QTR* and earn her bonus in order to pay the private investigator. Someday this all would end.

"You looked like you had something serious on your mind when I walked in." Louise took a seat. "Anything you want to talk about?"

"It's Trey. I'm not sure he's going to work out."

"Really?" There was genuine surprise in Louise's voice. "I thought he was easy on the eyes."

He was. That was one of the problems. And when his hand had lingered on hers, her stomach had dipped like she was riding a roller coaster.

"He, um...doesn't do things the way I expect them to be done."

"But he does them?"

Sage grudgingly nodded. "And he has this habit of disagreeing with me."

"So you want someone who agrees with everything you say?"

"No, but he's..."

"He's what?"

Distracting her—making her think of her sorely lacking social life. "He's still on probation and I just want to make sure he's the right fit."

"As shorthanded as you are, can you afford to be picky?"

Louise was right. The Cannes Film Festival was later

that month, and if they were fortunate enough to get passes, she needed someone reliable to help with it. And on top of being sexy, Trey had proven he was reliable.

She sighed. "You're right. There isn't time to find a replacement."

"I think he'll surprise you."

That's what she was afraid of.

His feet pounded the asphalt.

His muscles burned in that satisfying way.

His lungs strained to pull in more oxygen.

And Trey never felt more alive than when he was pushing his body to the limit. He normally made a point of running every morning. Today wasn't normal. His life was anything but normal since he met Sage.

With evening setting in, he continued running—pushing himself. After bumping heads with Sage most of the afternoon, he was filled with pent-up energy. That woman was so frustrating and yet so enticing. He couldn't decide whether he wanted to yell at her or pull her into his arms and kiss her.

He let out a frustrated groan as he slowed to a walk a block from his condo. The sooner he got the information he'd come to *QTR* for, the better. Ever since he'd stepped inside the office, everything had grown increasingly complicated.

The shrubbery next to him shook. He came to a stop. There was no wind to explain the sudden rush of motion. It was probably a squirrel. He was about to move on when he heard a high-pitched whine. Or was it a bark. Could there be a dog in there?

Trey peered closer at the bush. In the long shadows of evening, it was hard to make out a dog in between the leafy limbs. Then the bush moved again.

Arf! Arf!

Trey straightened and looked around to see if someone was looking for their dog. The bush was sitting next to a park, but no one was around. Just then a car turned onto the street. By the time it reached Trey, it was well above the speed limit. He didn't want anything to happen to the dog.

Trey turned back to the bush. Why was the dog in the bush? Had it gotten lose from its leash and gotten scared?

Trey already had enough of his own problems. He didn't need someone else's. But if he had lost a pet, he would want someone to go out of their way and make sure it got safely home.

With a sigh because he knew that he wasn't going to get anything else done that evening, he crouched down next to the bush. "Come here, fella. It's okay. I won't hurt you."

Arf! Arf!

The bark had to be a positive sign, right? Trey hadn't had a dog growing up. His mother said that she had her hands full with him and running the house alone. She couldn't take on a dog, too. As such, he didn't really know much about animals.

He kept his voice soft. "Come on. Come here."

He kept talking to the dog in gentle tones, hoping the dog would trust him enough to poke its head out. He wished that he had some food on him. If worse came to worst, he could run home and grab some food—

The leaves moved again. A little head poked out.

Trey didn't waste any time. He cautiously moved his fisted hand toward the dog, hoping it wouldn't bite him. Instead it sniffed him.

"Good boy." Trey made sure to keep his voice low and steady. "I'm going to pick you up, but you don't have to worry. I won't hurt you. Promise."

And then he swiftly reached into the bush and wrapped his hand around the dog's midsection. A clipped bark signaled the dog's surprise. Before the dog could move, Trey was lifting it to him.

The dog weighed practically nothing. In fact, he could feel the dog's ribs. Its fur was matted and dirty. Sympathy welled up in Trey.

"What in the world has happened to you?"

The dog shook with nerves. Ignoring the filth, Trey pulled the dog against his chest, trying to comfort it. The dog didn't fight him. Trey wondered if it was because the dog at last knew it was safe or if it just didn't have the strength to fight.

"Come on, buddy. Let's get you home and fed."

Trey felt awful that he'd almost kept going. The little dog was desperate for someone to care for it. He didn't know that he was the ideal person for the job, but he would do his best.

CHAPTER FOUR

THE NEXT MORNING, Sage kept checking Trey's outer office. Usually he arrived early, but not today. She checked the time. He still had another fifteen minutes. Why did he have to pick today of all days to sleep late? She had big news to share with him.

After speaking with Louise, she decided that between the exhaustion and the stress, she'd blown that hand-touching episode out of proportion. After all, he arrived at work every day and was never late. He got his work done. What more did she want?

She knew what else was bothering her. This attraction that was arcing just beneath the surface could be a problem when it was just the two of them on the very romantic French Riviera. And this upcoming business trip couldn't be canceled. The future of *QTR Magazine* was riding on it.

She'd just learned that her request for passes to the Cannes Film Festival had been approved. The committee had honored the magazine's long-standing attendance and granted them three passes. One for the photographer and two for people to cover it with interviews.

She would need Trey's help on this trip. The thought of covering the Cannes Film Festival on her own seemed, well, quite overwhelming.

Sage was hoping to make inroads with more stars and perhaps cover more than just their appearance at the festival. She had learned quickly that turning this magazine around was all about making contacts, whether it was a distributor, vendor or A-list actor. It was all about who you knew. And quite frankly, she'd exhausted her very short list of famous acquaintances.

She had just taken a seat at her desk to respond to some emails when she heard a noise. It sounded like Trey. Anxious to finalize the plans, she headed for the door.

"I've been waiting for you. I have news." She stopped in her tracks. A ball of white fur was sticking out from under Trey's arm. "What is that?"

He turned to her. His hair was scattered. His shirt was unbuttoned at the collar and his tie was stuffed in his pocket. "It's more like who is this?"

She frowned at him. "I'm not playing games. Is that a dog?"

Trey nodded. "I can explain—"

"You can't have a dog in here."

"I didn't have a choice."

"You should have left him at home." She glanced around, hoping no one else was nearby. She didn't need everyone thinking that it was all right to bring their pet to work. "Come in my office."

Once they were both…er…all three in the office, she closed the door. This was not the smooth start to the day that she'd been hoping for. And after Louise had soothed her worries about keeping Trey on staff, he pulled this stunt.

"Listen, I know this is awkward." The dog began to wiggle in his arms. "Do you mind if I put him down?"

Sage shook her head. It probably wasn't a wise decision. What if it peed on the carpet? Or worse?

Trey set the white dog on the carpet. She was relieved to see that the dog had a collar and leash. He began to sniff around, taking in his new surroundings. Sage kept an eye on it. She told herself that it was to make sure it didn't make a mess and not because it was the most adorable ball of fluff. When it stopped in front of her and turned those big brown eyes on her, she longed to pick it up and cuddle him. But she just couldn't give in to that temptation. She was the boss. She had to set an example.

She forced her gaze away from the cute pup and back to her assistant. "I don't know what you were thinking by bringing him here, but he has to go. Now. And preferably without anyone seeing you."

"But that's the problem. I don't have anywhere to take him."

"I'd think taking him home would be an ideal solution."

"But he's not mine."

Before she could speak, she felt something cold and wet against her leg. She glanced down to find the dog sniffing her. Her instinct was to kneel down and make friends, but she didn't want Trey to think that whatever he was trying to pull here was acceptable. This was one of those moments when she didn't like being management.

Sage turned her attention back to Trey. "Do you normally bring other people's animals to work with you?"

"I must admit that it's a first."

"And your last."

"If you would let me finish. I can explain this. It's really kind of a funny story." He hesitated. "Actually, it's not funny ha-ha. It's funny as in strange and a bit sad."

She should be upset, but when the puppy looked at her with those big innocent eyes, her irritation melted away. The little white dog with long fur was so cute. No wonder Trey had taken it in.

Unable to resist any longer, she asked, "Can I pet him?"

"Um, sure." Trey's face filled with confusion soon followed with relief. "He's a very friendly little guy."

"Hi." She knelt down and pet him. His white fur was soft, but it was long and gnarled. "You are such a sweet thing. That's great that you adopted a dog—"

"I didn't adopt him. It's more like he adopted me."

Sage straightened. "Say again."

The dog moved and sat at Trey's feet. Its little tail swished back and forth. "I found him hiding in a bush when I was out running last night. He was shaking with fear."

"Aw…poor baby?"

Trey nodded. "He didn't have a collar or any way to identify him. And from the looks of him, no one has cared for him in quite a while. I took him home, fed him and cleaned him up the best I could."

"There's one thing I don't understand. Why did you bring him to work?"

"I didn't mean to. I thought the animal shelter would be open early, but it opens late today. If I could just keep him here until they open—"

"You aren't keeping him?" She glanced down at the little dog that was now leaning up against Trey's leg as though they belonged together. "He seems to have really bonded with you."

"I… I'm not a dog person."

She arched a brow. "Really? Because you certainly seem like it to me and…what do you call him?"

"I didn't name him because I'm not keeping him."

"You can't keep calling him puppy or dog." She turned her attention back to the white puppy. "Come here."

Surprisingly, the dog came right to her. It's little tail swished back and forth. "You certainly are a friendly little guy."

"He's certainly that. Even when he woke me up at 4:00 a.m. to take him outside. He was as happy as could be. Me not so much. I was half-asleep and almost walked into the wall."

She scooped the dog up in her arms. "Is that true? Are you a happy little guy?"

Arf!

Sage couldn't help but smile at the dog's cheery personality.

"Maybe you should keep him," Trey suggested.

"Me? I don't think so. I spend all of my time here at the office." She couldn't resist running her hand over the dog. It was when she touched his front leg that it whimpered. "Is it hurt?"

Trey frowned. "Not that I know of. But he was so dirty last night that I might have missed something when I was cleaning him up."

Sage moved to her desk and set the dog down. "He whimpered when I touched his front right leg."

They worked together until they uncovered a nasty, oozing cut beneath some knotted fur. Sage scooped the dog back in her arms, careful not to touch the wounded area. Through it all, the pup continued to wag its tail.

Trey reached out to pet him. "You certainly are one happy guy."

"That's it."

"What's it?" Trey looked utterly confused.

"His name. We'll call him Happy."

"Really?" Trey's gaze moved from Sage to the dog, whose tail picked up speed. "I guess it fits." Staring at the dog, he asked, "Would you like the name Happy?"

Arf! Arf!

Sage laughed. "I think he agrees."

"I'll take him over to the shelter. I'm sure they'll know what to do with him."

Sage looked into Happy's eyes and she just couldn't let him go to some shelter where he would get lost in the crowd and possibly forgotten about. She had to be sure that he was well taken care of.

"Call the Smith Veterinarian Clinic. Tell them you found a stray and its injured. If they give you any problems, you can mention my name. It might help."

He sent her a puzzled look. "I thought you said you didn't have time for pets."

Busted. "I don't have any pets. But that doesn't mean that I don't have roommates with pets."

Trey's eyes widened and he smiled as though his problems were solved.

"Don't," she warned. "I'm not keeping him. But I want to make sure that he's taken care of. Besides, as I recall, you're the one that found him."

"Okay. Okay. I'll call."

Knock. Knock.

The door opened and Louise stuck her head inside. "Good morning. I…" Louise's voice faded away as she took in the sight of Trey's disheveled look. "Sorry. I just wanted to tell you about some new coffee I picked up last night. But it can wait."

Arf! Arf-arf!

Louise's gaze lowered to the floor. "Well, who are you?"

Arf! Arf!

Everyone chuckled at the dog's response.

"And you're a chatty one, too." Louise walked farther into the room.

Sage turned to Trey. "I've got the dog. Go make the call. Tell them it's an emergency and we're on our way."

"We?"

"Yes. Now hurry up."

Her father always told her that if you wanted something done right to do it yourself. It was a philosophy that she'd taken to heart, much like her approach to fixing *QTR*. And she wouldn't get any work done until she was certain Happy was on the mend.

She impressed him.

And that wasn't an easy thing to do.

Trey couldn't believe how Sage had set aside her work and worried over the pup until it had a proper bath, trim, stitches and antibiotics. Not necessarily in that order. During the examination, the vet had revealed that the dog was chipped. And all of his shots were up to date.

And now as they sat in the car, an awkward silence enveloped them. Trey needed a distraction from thinking about what they were attempting to do—return Happy to the owner that had lost him. And as far as he could tell, the owner hadn't searched for him—at least, not for long.

As he slowed for a stop sign, he chanced a quick glance at Sage. She was fussing over the dog. The dog looked perfectly contented and none the worse for wear after his veterinarian appointment. Either that dog was the most laid-back animal or Sage had a magical touch.

"Did you have pets growing up?" Trey returned his attention to the road.

"I did. All sorts of pets. My father enjoyed indulging me."

"What sort of pets?"

"I had a white-and-black cat named Mittens. And I had a couple of birds—"

"Wait." He slowed for another stop sign. "Are you saying you had a cat and birds at the same time?"

She smiled and nodded.

"But how? Aren't cats supposed to hunt birds?"

"Not Mittens. She found them interesting for about five minutes but then she went on her way."

"Amazing." He shook his head in disbelief. "I take it you're good with animals."

She shrugged. "I had a rat. He didn't like me much. He bit me and hid in his cage."

Trey laughed. "You had a pet rat?"

"What's so funny about that?" she asked with a perfectly straight face.

He subdued his amusement. "Nothing. It's just that you never cease to surprise me."

"I also had fish, a bunny—" she paused as though to think about it "—a hamster and a guinea pig."

"You had a very interesting childhood."

He didn't want to stop driving. This was the first time Sage had let down her guard with him and he liked it. She was a lot different outside the office—more relaxed and much more approachable.

"It was amazing." There was lightness to her voice as she drew upon her memories. "For my birthday, my father didn't get me presents. He said that I got enough throughout the year. Instead he would take me on an adventure. We would visit a different part of the world each year. Those are some of my very best memories. We would explore new cultures and the food—it was amazing. My father told me I didn't have to eat it all, but I did have to sample a little of everything. I was surprised by some of the cuisine that I enjoyed—especially my first experience with sushi."

"Your father sounds like he was a really great guy. You must have loved him a lot." A stab of jealousy dug into Trey. He'd never had a relationship like that with his father.

"I did. My father was the best. He did everything he could to give me a great childhood. The only thing that would have made it better is if my mother had been able to share those experiences with us. But she…she died when I was just a baby."

"I'm sorry you lost her. But I'm sure she's smiling down on you."

"Me, too." Sage lowered her voice. "Sometimes I talk to her. Do you think that's silly?"

Without hesitation, he shook his head. "Everyone needs to talk to their mum now and then."

Sage nodded. "Between my father and my pets, I felt truly loved."

Trey envied her childhood. His was quite different. His mother might have been there physically, but she was quiet and withdrawn after his father left. Trey always wondered if a part of her had died when his father abandoned them.

"You don't want to do this, do you?" Sage asked, interrupting his thoughts.

"Do what? Take Happy back to his owner? The same owner that let him loose and didn't even put up posters for his return or post any sort of notice online—"

"How do you know that they didn't? Did you look?"

He could feel her intense stare as he maneuvered the car down the street. "I might have done a quick search last night while Happy was getting adjusted to his new surroundings."

"I bet you did more than a quick search."

Was she able to read him that easily? He wondered what she made of him. He was tempted to ask, to see how much she got right. The question hovered on the tip of his tongue.

"Stop!"

There was nothing in front of them. He checked the rearview mirror as he jammed the breaks. "What's the matter?"

"This is it."

"What is?"

She pointed out the window at the older home with the front door hanging open and a moving truck in the driveway. Beside the driveway was a wrought-iron post with the street number. Sage was right. This was the place. He'd been so caught up in his thoughts that he'd almost passed it by.

He wheeled the car into a parking spot on the street. He glanced out Sage's window at the stately home. Not too big, but not small either. The outside was stone and the front door was red and arched. The hedges were trimmed. And a for-sale sign was in the front yard.

Arf! Arf!

"Sounds like Happy knows he's home." Sage didn't smile.

So all it took was a cute dog to win her over. He was beginning to wonder if Sage was having second thoughts about returning the dog. All he had to say was the owner better have an explanation for letting the dog loose and not searching for him. It better be a really good excuse.

"Okay. Let's get this over with." Trey exited the car and quickly made his way around to open Sage's door.

Happy was so excited and wiggly that Sage let him down. With his leash on, he led them across the road and up the walk to the open front door. Trey wasn't happy about this. He didn't want to see anything else happen to Happy. The little dog could have died out on the streets. And where was his owner? Moving away without their dog?

Trey was about to ring the buzzer when an older man with gray hair entered the foyer with a big box in his hands. His eyes widened when he saw them standing on the landing. "If you came to look at the house, it's by appointment only."

Didn't the man see the dog? Didn't he care? Trey struggled to keep his temper in check. "We didn't come to look at the house."

As though Sage could tell that Trey wasn't at all pleased with any of this, she said, "We came because we…er… rather *he*—" she gestured to Trey "—found your dog."

"My dog? I don't have one."

Sage bent over and scooped up Happy. "You mean, this isn't your dog?"

Happy licked her cheek and wagged his tail. Trey wondered what it was like to be that happy, even after the one person who was supposed to love and protect you disappears from your life. Trey was not the least bit happy.

"That's my mother's dog." The man set the box down and came closer. "I didn't know what had happened to him.

I thought the people who were supposed to be taking care of him for her had taken him home."

"No." Trey wasn't happy with the man's lack of concern. "He's been wandering the streets half-starved and injured."

The man's hesitant gaze met his before it turned back to the dog. He reached out to pet Happy and a low growl filled the air. Both Trey and Sage turned surprised gazes at the dog. He seemed to like everyone except this man.

"Is your mother home?" Sage asked.

The man shook his head, making his comb-over slide down on his forehead. With a swipe of his hand, it moved back over the bald spot. "She passed on last week."

"Oh. I'm so sorry." Sage looked a bit awkward as though not sure what to say next.

"Will you be taking care of the dog?" Trey asked, not sure the man would do any better than the dog-sitter who originally lost Happy.

The man's brows drew together. "I can't. My apartment doesn't allow pets. And…and as you can see, that dog has never liked me."

Trey trusted Happy's judgment of people. After all, the dog was crazy about Sage. But how could he not be with the way she fussed over him?

"Are you sure?" Sage asked. "He's a really well-trained dog."

"Trust me. He wouldn't be happy with me."

Trey didn't need any reassurances from the man. It was obvious Happy didn't belong with him. "We're sorry for your loss. We'll be going."

Trey placed a hand on Sage's elbow and turned back toward the car.

"What about the dog?" the man asked.

"We'll take care of him," Sage replied with certainty. "Don't worry. He'll have a good home."

And with that they made their way back to the car.

Once they were both inside and driving away, Trey glanced at Happy contentedly lying in Sage's lap with his chin resting on her knee. "Did you really mean that? You know, about us taking care of Happy?"

She shrugged. "It wasn't like we could leave him with that man. Did you hear the way Happy growled at him?"

"Yeah. He sure didn't like the guy. Wonder what he did to the dog."

"I don't want to know. I just want to make sure that Happy is safe."

"Should we take him to the shelter?"

"We can't do that," she said quickly. "You know, because of his stitches. We need to keep an eye on him and make sure it doesn't get infected."

Trey nodded as though he understood, but he didn't. Not really. He was certain there were skilled people at the shelter that could care for Happy, but he didn't say anything. It appeared Happy had won Sage's heart.

Sage had a way of casting a magical spell over the males in her orbit. If Trey wasn't careful, he was going to forget about his real reason for working at *QTR*. And he just might give in to his desire to kiss her.

CHAPTER FIVE

It is no big deal. After all, it is only temporary.

The excuses crowded into Sage's mind as she made a spot for Happy on the couch in her office. It wasn't like they could trust just anyone to make sure Happy didn't chew his stitches. Thankfully he wouldn't have them in very long. And hopefully there would be no need for the cone the vet had sent along with them—just in case.

Happy put his head down between his paws and his eyes drifted closed. He'd had a big day and it was only lunchtime. Trey had volunteered to run downstairs to the restaurant and grab them some food. In this instance, she wouldn't make a fuss over the restaurant's exorbitant prices. That way they could have a working lunch and make up for some of the time they'd missed that morning as well as keep an eye on Happy.

As it was, she still had big news to share with Trey. And this adventure with Happy had shown her a different side of him. She'd admired the way he'd not only taken in a stray dog but also cleaned him up, bought supplies and cared enough to risk bringing him to the office.

Trey cared a lot more for Happy than he was willing to let on. She noticed how he asked the vet all sorts of questions. And then again when he grew protective when they attempted to take Happy home.

As though sensing that she was thinking of him, Trey breezed through the doorway. He smiled at her. "I picked something a little different."

She made a point of having a salad every day for lunch. "What did you pick?"

"Quit looking so worried. I think you'll approve." And then, as though he wasn't so sure, he added, "And if you don't, I'll get you a chicken salad."

She smiled. If she ever thought of having a family, she would want someone like Trey. He was sweet and thoughtful but not afraid to push boundaries when the need arose. He definitely would make some woman a good husband. She could imagine him with a baby in his arms.

She gasped. What in the world had gotten into her? He was her assistant. Not boyfriend material. No matter how attractive she might find him. She had to keep these wayward thoughts at bay. Maybe all the long lonely nights at the office were catching up with her.

"What's the matter?" Trey stared at her. The concern was written all over his face. "Is it Happy?"

"No. He's fine." She swallowed down her discomfort. "Why do you think something is wrong?"

"You gasped."

Oh, yes, that. Hmm... "I just remembered that I have something important to discuss with you and we're running out of time."

He continued to stare at her as though not sure if he believed her or not. Even Happy had lifted his head and was staring at her. She was going to have to work harder at keeping her thoughts in line. And if she did have an errant thought, she would not—could not—react.

"Are you going to serve up that mystery food? I'm starving." She cleared off space on her desk so they could eat there.

Trey quickly served up the food. When he lifted the lid on hers, he said, "It's citrus grilled salmon with rice noodles and vegetables."

She was quite pleased with the selection. "But how did you know that I love salmon?"

He retrieved his lunch from the bag. "Truth?"

She nodded, wondering if Louise had been his source of information. If so, she was going to have to say something. She couldn't have Louise going around sharing all her personal information—no matter how well intended.

"I guessed." He sent her a smile. She refused to acknowledge the way the twinkle in his eyes made her stomach dip.

"Good guess."

"And how's—" Trey nodded toward Happy "—he doing?"

"You wouldn't even know he didn't belong here all along. He's made himself right at home."

"You know the longer he's here, the harder it's going to be to give him up."

She didn't want to think about parting with the dog. "How about we cross that bridge when we get to it?"

Trey looked as though he were going to say something else, but then he nodded in agreement.

After they were halfway through their meal, Sage glanced over the glass desktop at him. "Is your passport up to date?"

His brows rose high on his forehead. "It is."

"Good. I have exciting news. We're attending the Cannes Film Festival."

The lack of expression on his face surprised her. "And you're looking for an escort?"

He didn't have any idea just how appealing that sounded to her. In fact, it surprised her quite a bit. She prided herself on being self-sufficient and not needing someone in her life. After her father's funeral, she'd felt profoundly alone. She'd foolishly thought Elsa would feel the same way and that they could lean on each other. She couldn't have been more wrong.

Her stepmother had taught her that the only person Sage could count on was herself. Being reduced to Elsa's maid after her father's death had been jarring, but then to be kicked out of her childhood home on her eighteenth birthday drove home that lesson. Sage had never felt more alone—more betrayed.

And it reminded her not to get too comfortable with Trey. They'd shared a moment of friendship today as they helped Happy, but it needed to stop.

"Sage? Hey. Hello." Trey waved his hand in front of her face. When she focused in on him, he asked, "Where did you go?"

"Sorry. I just got lost in my thoughts."

"Not happy ones, I take it."

"Was it that obvious?" She really didn't have a poker face.

He nodded. "If you don't want me to go to France with you, I'm fine with that."

"No, it's not that. I was just thinking about my step-mother."

"Thinking about going to France with me makes you think of your stepmother? I'm confused."

Sage shook her head. "Don't mind me. I guess I'm just tired. But in answer to your question, no, I don't need an escort. I do, however, need an assistant to stay on top of things both here and there."

He hesitated.

"Is that going to be a problem?"

He shook his head. "I can handle it."

"Good. We need to find out which Hollywood stars plan to be in attendance and then we have to research what's going on in their world that they might want to talk about—a new house, a vacation, an upcoming film project or a charity. Or whatever is of interest to them."

"So you want to provide a platform for the stars to share with the world something of their choice."

"Exactly. If the celebrity is excited about a subject, it will come across in the article and hopefully the readers will get excited, too."

"And you plan to do all these interviews at the festival?"

She shook her head. "As nice as that would be, it's not practical. We're going to be there to generate connections and set up interviews for a later date."

He stared at her for a moment. "Is that how you've gotten all of those interviews that have changed the entire platform of the magazine?"

"You read them?"

He paused as though considering his answer. "After our interview, I wanted to make sure I was on top of things. So I read a bunch of back issues."

"Including the scuzzy ones that got the senior Rousseau in trouble?"

He nodded. "What exactly happened there?"

She knew some of it and had pieced together other parts, but she wasn't in a position to reveal details. "It was the board's decision to change the direction of the magazine."

He arched a dark brow as though hoping for more information.

"Don't look at me like that. I can only say so much."

"Fair enough." He took another bite of food. A few moments later, he said, "And this trip, it's important to you?"

"It is."

He nodded. "It's been a while since I've been back to France."

"I take it you grew up there."

"I did, but then I moved away."

"You mean for work?"

"Yeah. Something like that."

So she wasn't the only one holding things back. The

part that surprised her was that she wanted to know more about him. She wanted to know everything about him. Maybe this trip to a romantic, seaside town wasn't such a good idea, after all. But it was too late to back out. She truly needed the help. And to tell him that he would no longer be accompanying her would only arouse his curiosity.

He was going home.

Trey worked hard to mask an emotional response. He'd had the house closed up after his mother passed away. He'd moved his business to the States—San Francisco to be exact. But to go home again, it filled him with a rush of conflicting emotions.

And when he did go back—when he faced those painful memories—he didn't want an audience. He wanted to do it on his terms.

"You don't look happy about this opportunity." Sage took a bite of her lunch.

His gaze met her puzzled look. "It's great." He searched for a way out. After all, there were other employees who could accompany Sage. "When did you say we'd be leaving?"

"I didn't. We don't have plane reservations yet. I was hoping you could work on it."

His thoughts immediately turned to the private jet he'd recently acquired. With it, there wouldn't be any problems flying whenever they wanted to. But that was another part of himself that he couldn't share.

"I'll work on it. What day would you prefer?"

"The festival begins next Wednesday." She glanced at her day planner. "I'd say Monday. Tuesday at the latest."

He made a note on his phone.

Just then Happy woke up. He sat up on the end of the couch. He yawned and then shook his head.

Sage smiled. "Looks like someone had a good nap."

Happy jumped down and with his tail wagging ran over to Trey.

"Hey, boy." He pet him. "Looks like you're starting to feel better." Trey lifted his gaze to meet Sage's. "Thanks for letting him stay here with us."

"What's the point of being the boss if you can't bend the rules every now and then?" As though Happy sensed she was talking about him, he moved around the desk to visit her. "But of course when you're all better, you'll have to stay home."

Arf!

Trey laughed. "I don't think he agrees."

And then a thought came to him—a way to get out of traveling with his beautiful boss, who made him forget his mission and made him long to take their relationship to a much more personal level.

Trey cleared his throat. "I really should stay here with Happy. With his condition—" which wasn't that serious but it could have been "—Happy shouldn't be left alone."

"Does someone need a babysitter?" A familiar voice came from the doorway.

They both turned to the door to find Louise standing there with a stack of files in her arm and a smile on her face. Happy ran over to her. His tail moved so fast that it was nothing more than a blur of motion. Louise knelt down and fussed over the dog. He stood up, pressed his paws to her knee and licked her cheek.

"I think the answer to your problem just walked in the door." Sage smiled at Happy's antics.

The dog sure had won over Sage. He hadn't had as much luck with Sage. The woman was stubborn and resistant to any sort of help he might offer. Which just made the idea of them going on this trip together a very bad idea.

"I'm sure Louise has other plans," Trey said.

"Plans for what?" Louise straightened and stepped farther into the room.

Before Trey could say anything, Sage launched into an explanation about the trip. Instead of looking put out by the idea, Louise smiled. She liked the idea of dog-sitting?

"I wouldn't mind watching over the little fella," Louise said as though she could read Trey's thoughts. "Would you like that Happy?"

Arf! Arf!

Sage smiled. "Good. Problem solved. Thanks, Louise."

"Yes," Trey said, still trying to accept the inevitable. "Thank you. If I can ever repay the favor just let me know."

There was an ominous twinkle in Louise's eyes when she said, "I will."

He didn't even want to consider what it might mean for him. Something told him that it wouldn't be as simple as picking up coffee or donuts. No, Louise was a sharp lady. When she called in that favor, it would be something meaningful.

"Before I go," Louise said to Sage, "I was wondering if you had the profit and loss statements for the past five years?"

Sage gave Louise a strange look. "Why would you want those? Isn't human resources enough for you? You want to expand into accounting, too?"

"Heavens, no. I ran into Ralph in the hall."

"Ralph, huh?" Sage had a funny tone in her voice and a goofy smile on her face.

Trey had obviously missed something. But it was better that way. The more he got involved in their lives, the harder it'd be when it came time to close the magazine.

"It's not like you think." Louise's voice lacked its normal tone of conviction. "We're friends, is all. I've been married already. And so has he."

"And now you're both widowed. Why not keep each other company?"

Trey chanced a glance at the unusually quiet Louise. For the first time, he witnessed the bold and forthright woman blush. Maybe Sage was on to something.

Avoiding eye contact, Louise said, "Like I'd started to say, Ralph stopped to speak to you and found your door closed. I told him I'd ask you for the documents when I spoke to you."

"Is this for the upcoming audit?"

Louise shrugged. "You're asking the wrong person."

"I wonder why Ralph thinks I'd have those statements," Sage stated, opening and closing desk drawers as though searching for the missing documents. "You'd think those would be kept in the accounting department."

"Mr. Rousseau liked to be in control of everything," Louise supplied. "Have you looked through those file cabinets?" She gestured toward the wall-to-wall line of four-drawer file cabinets.

Trey couldn't help but think that it sounded like his controlling father—always wanting things his way. And when his mother refused, his father didn't care to compromise and just up and left them—left him. The man didn't even give them a backward glance.

Sage turned to Trey. "I hate to give you this task, but could you go through those file cabinets and see if the P&L statements are in there. It's really important that we do well on this audit."

He nodded and set to work. The metal file cabinets were old and the papers inside them were even older. Drawer after drawer, file after file, he searched. And then he opened a drawer that lacked any papers. He was about to close it when a photo caught his attention.

Trey was drawn to the image. It was a photo of himself when he was two or three. He reached for it. The fact that his father had it…should it mean something to him? A spark of hope ignited. In the next breath, he acknowledged that it had been discarded in an old file cabinet. That should be all the answer he needed.

"I see you've found Mr. Rousseau's photos," Sage said from behind him.

Photos? There was more than one? He peered back in the drawer to find his parents' wedding photo and one of him as a baby.

"They were on his desk when I got here. I think he left them because he thought he'd be back once the lawsuit quieted down. I considered messengering them to him, but I didn't want him to read anything into the gesture like I was pushing him out—not after everything he's done for me."

His father had these photos on his desk? But why? Was it for show? That had to be it. No other answer made sense.

"I thought he was estranged from his family?" Trey returned the photo of himself to the drawer. As he did so, he found himself curious about his parents' wedding. Had they been happy at the beginning? He withdrew the framed photo. His father had been smiling like he didn't have a care in the world and Trey's mother…he'd never seen her look happier.

A lump formed in the back of Trey's throat. If they'd been this happy at the start, was he the reason the marriage fell apart?

"I don't know the details." Sage's voice reminded him that he wasn't alone. "I just know that he talked highly of his son."

Highly? Really? Trey found that so hard to believe. Trey took one last look at the photo. His mother had been so radiant and full of life, nothing like the woman his father had left behind. The broken, lonely woman that Trey had tried to care for.

Trey returned the photo to the drawer. He choked down

the rising emotions and closed the drawer, warding off the unhappy memories of his childhood.

"Would you like me to help you search?" Sage offered.

"I've got this." He kept his back to her, not wanting her to read into the expression on his face. "Besides, don't you have a meeting with circulation in ten minutes?"

Sage glanced at the clock. "You're right. I totally forgot."

"No problem. That's what I'm here for."

She grabbed her digital tablet and rushed out of the room.

He was actually grateful for a little time alone. It would give him a chance to shove all those unwanted memories to the back of his mind.

He had no idea why his father had all those photos, but it wasn't because he loved his family. No one that loved their wife and child walked away.

That's why Trey had avoided any sort of committed relationship. He didn't want to be like his father and realize too late that he wasn't cut out to be a family man. No child deserved to be discarded like he'd been.

CHAPTER SIX

ELSA STOOD IN front of her gold-leaf-trimmed mirror. With a finger, she lifted one brow and then she did the same on the other side. Then she drew back her cheeks. It was time for some Botox. She would schedule an appointment for this afternoon.

She picked up her compact and powdered her pointed nose. Perhaps she should do something different with her hair. But then again, why? Could it look any better? It was hard to improve on perfection.

Knock. Knock.

"Come in." It was about time Mr. Hunter arrived for their meeting. He was already ten minutes late. She did not have room in her life for tardiness. Time was money.

The door opened and the hulk of a man stepped inside. "Sorry I'm late. Traffic was snarled."

"I don't care about the traffic. What have you learned about my stepdaughter?"

The man was younger than her. He was tall, dark and in her opinion modestly handsome. Perhaps if she wasn't in such a rush for information, she might enjoy a little alone time with him. But right now she had to deal with her stepdaughter—the girl gave her nothing but a headache.

"Hurry up," Elsa said, anxious to know what Sage had been up to now.

He lifted his digital tablet and consulted his notes. "She's still with *QTR*, but she's on probation. She has to show the board a marked improvement and a solid strategy for the future by the end of the month. And it appears Rousseau's son is taking over the business as CEO."

"A son? I didn't know he had a son. Get me as much information as you can on him." She couldn't have Sage being successful. That wouldn't do. But first she had to gain information and then she'd formulate a plan. "And how did my stepdaughter look?"

"Beautiful." The man's eyes lit up and he smiled as he recalled Sage's image.

Elsa's back teeth ground together. Her gaze narrowed in on the man. "How beautiful?"

"She has grown into the most stunning woman." His voice had a sense of awe in it, which only compounded Elsa's frustration. He rubbed his squared jaw. "She turned heads wherever she went. People seem to fall under her spell whenever she smiles at them."

"She used to do the same thing to her father. She'd smile and he'd do whatever she wanted. He didn't care that as his wife my needs should have come first. It was always all about that brat kid."

"There's something else you should know. Sage is asking questions about you and this company."

The breath caught in Elsa's throat. She knew this day was coming. Once Sage had the means, she would come after Elsa. The girl had to be stopped once and for all.

Elsa turned to the mirror and stared into it. That girl was always trying to ruin everything for her. With an angry groan, Elsa lifted her arm and sent her metal compact crashing into the mirror. Glass shards fell to the floor. If she didn't stop her stepdaughter soon, Sage would have enough clout and money to reveal the truth about how Elsa ascended to CEO of White Publishing. And that could not happen.

Heedless of the mess, Elsa turned to Hunter. Perhaps she should have been paying closer attention to her stepdaughter. She wouldn't make that mistake again. "Do you have someone watching her now?"

"No. You didn't say you wanted twenty-four-hour surveillance—"

"Do I have to spell out everything for you?" she shouted. Her anger and fear bubbled to the surface.

The man's face masked his emotions. "She's leaving for the French Riviera in the morning. Would you like me to follow her?"

Elsa arched a dark brow. "For the Cannes Film Festival?"

Hunter nodded. "From what I gather, she's shorthanded and handling the event herself. Well, herself and her male assistant."

Elsa turned her back to the man. Perhaps it was time she had a face-to-face meeting with her stepdaughter. It was time to remind Sage of her proper place in this world—cleaning floors and washing dishes.

"We're both going."

CHAPTER SEVEN

A GENTLE RAIN tap-tapped on the car windows.

Trey leaned back against the seat, wishing the raindrops could wash away the past hurts. He stifled a deep sigh. The truth was that he would rather be anywhere but here. The only consolation was that they'd be staying at a hotel instead of venturing to the château with its abundance of painful memories.

All of Cannes was blanketed in the darkness of night. With the lull of the car engine and the rhythmic tapping of the rain, Trey struggled to keep his eyes open. He'd never learned to sleep on airplanes. And with his seat being separate from Sage's, he'd read a spy novel for most of the flight.

The lights of the city sparkled and glistened in the rain like fine jewels. It was only fitting because his hometown was a treasure on the French Riviera. If only it didn't hold so many painful memories.

He wondered what his mother would think of his plan to bring down the magazine. Would she cheer him on? Or would she be disappointed that he couldn't let go of the past?

Sage pressed a hand to his arm. "Are you okay?"

Trey pushed away the troubling thoughts. "Of course. Why do you ask?"

"Because we've arrived at the hotel and you haven't gotten out of the car."

He glanced out the window at Cannes' finest hotel. When he was a child he imagined this place was a palace and a rich king lived within its walls. Other times, he would pretend his father lived there, taking care of important business, and that one day he'd return home. But in truth, his father never stayed at this hotel that he knew of and his father never came home.

Trey choked down the unwanted rush of emotions. "I think I'm just tired. I can't sleep on planes."

"I guess we have that in common because neither can I."

"Then let's get checked in and we both can get some rest."

He alighted from the car and asked her to get their room keys while he saw to the luggage—all six pieces of it. One piece was his and the rest belonged to Sage. Thankfully some of the suitcases had wheels. How long did she plan to be in France?

Inside, Sage was at the registration counter. From across the lobby, he couldn't hear what was being said, but Sage was talking with her hands and that was never a good sign. Maybe it was a communication problem.

He picked up his speed, hoping to smooth out the situation. He came to a stop next to Sage. "Is there a problem?"

She turned to him with a distinct frown on her face. "I suppose the fact that they gave away our rooms and they have nothing else available could be considered a problem." The frustration in her voice was unmistakable as was the exhaustion written all over her face.

"Let me see what I can do." Perhaps the exchange of French and English had created a miscommunication. He really hoped that was the case. "Did you make the reservation?"

"Yes. But they have no record of it."

"Don't give up just yet."

Sage let out a yawn that spurred Trey into action. But after speaking with both the desk clerk and the manager, they still didn't have any unoccupied rooms for the duration of the festival.

Trey knew with the festival taking place that there wouldn't be any vacancies anywhere in Cannes. There were stories of A-list actors sleeping on the beach because when there's no room available, there's literally nothing available.

Trey had an alternative, but he didn't like it. There was his family's château. He still had a skeleton staff looking after it. He didn't want to keep the place, but he couldn't bring himself to sell it either. It made no sense, but that seemed to be a recurring theme in his life.

He withdrew his phone from his pocket and signaled to Sage that he would be right back. He'd made his housekeeper aware that he was flying in. She was anxious to discuss some issues concerning the château. He told her that he'd stop by when he had a free moment. He'd made it clear he didn't plan to stay at the château so he had no idea what condition the house would be in. On top of that, he didn't know how he'd explain any of this to Sage.

Just take it one problem at a time.

She'd made a mess of things.

Sage mentally kicked herself for not verifying the reservations. She'd meant to, but then she'd gotten distracted.

When Trey returned from making a call, she asked, "Did you come up with alternate lodging?"

"There's nothing available. The city is filled to capacity with festivalgoers."

"Oh." She'd really been hoping his phone call had been productive. "I guess I could do an internet search and start calling them. Maybe I'll get lucky and someone will have a last-minute cancellation."

Trey sighed. "Or you could just come home with me."

"Home? With you?" She sent him a strange look. "I know you're tired, but we're in France not California."

"I know that."

"Then how can I go home with you?"

"Okay, it's not actually my home, but you do recall that I'm from France, right?" He smiled.

Was he inwardly laughing at her? "I didn't forget. The accent gives you away."

"Listen, this banter might be more fun if I wasn't so tired." Before she could dispute the claim, he continued. "My head is pounding, so how about you just agree to come with me?"

It was one thing to stay in the same hotel in separate rooms, but it was much more intimate to share a house. "Are you sure about this?"

"Quite frankly, no. But we can't sleep in the lobby of this hotel."

She hated to admit it but he was right. And she was so tired.

Trey didn't wait for her response as he turned to the door. With the luggage in tow, he headed for an available car. She couldn't help thinking that this was wrong. She knew by the look on his face that taking her with him was the last thing he wanted to do.

There was something growing between them. It was something she didn't want to examine too closely. Though she had a lot of friends, she didn't let anyone get too close. It hurt too much when they betrayed you.

She'd had a boyfriend after she'd finished college. Charlie had been a blond-haired, blue-eyed hunk of a man. At first, she'd resisted him, but every time he'd walked into the coffee shop where she worked in the evenings and on weekends, he flirted with her until he gained her trust. Looking back on that time still hurt.

Charlie had said all the right things—done all the right

things, from flowers to fancy dinners. She'd thought at long last she was no longer alone in this world. She'd let down her guard and confided in him about her hopes, dreams and fears.

And then she'd gotten her first official editorial position working for a well-known publisher. It wasn't her beloved White Publishing, but it was a highly sought after position.

She was all set to start in two weeks. And then everything went sideways. Suddenly the company withdrew their job offer with some flimsy excuse about a mix-up.

And then she caught Charlie in a lie followed by a strange text message on his phone. Once confronted by a furious Sage, he confessed to being hired by Elsa to spy on her. And that Elsa was behind the lies that cost her the job. Her stepmother had smeared her name in the publishing world.

There was only one reason her stepmother would still try to hurt her—the woman had a deep dark secret. That day, Sage got all the confirmation she needed that her suspicions about Elsa were true. She was certain Elsa had lied, cheated and thieved her way to the top of White Publishing. And now Sage would do whatever it cost to out her conniving stepmother—including sacrificing a personal life. That was the day Sage hired her first private investigator.

Once they were in the car headed away from the bright lights, Trey said, "Don't worry. Everything will work out."

She turned to say something, but in the glow of the passing lights she caught his dark, mesmerizing gaze. The words stuck in her throat. Every time he looked into her eyes, she felt as though she were going to drown in his dark brown eyes.

Her pulse quickened and she wondered what it would be like to kiss him. Before now, they'd always been at work where there was a constant string of people in and out of her office. There was no time for indulging in a kiss.

But tonight, all bets were off. She assured herself that exhaustion was playing with her mind. As she continued to stare at him, she knew she wasn't alone with these wayward thoughts.

Though she hadn't dated many men, she did know when they were interested in her. And Trey was interested. Still, there was one more complication—they worked together. And crossing that line would come with a host of complications.

With a sigh, she leaned back against the leather seat. She just needed some sleep. Tomorrow things would be much clearer.

"We're here." Trey's voice lacked any enthusiasm.

She looked out the window at the impressive château. No expense had been spared in its design or in the landscape that was illuminated with lights lining the drive.

"You said this place belongs to a friend?" She couldn't help wondering what sort of friends Trey had. Obviously they had deep pockets.

"Um…yes." He got out of the car before she could ask any further questions.

As she continued to stare at the château, she wondered about Trey. She craved to know more about him. Who were these friends? Did he have lots of friends? Did he travel overseas often? The questions were endless. Every day there was something new that she wanted to know about him, but she kept stuffing the questions down. It was better if they didn't get to know each other that well—at least, that's what she kept telling herself.

She'd gotten so lost in her thoughts that Trey had time to round the car and open her door for her. She stepped out, glancing around at her new surroundings when a new worry came to her.

"Are you sure your friends won't be upset about you bringing me here without checking with them first?"

He shook his head. "Trust me."

She wanted to trust him. And that surprised her. It'd been a long time since she'd felt that way toward a man.

Trey led the way to the front door. As she followed, a dreadful thought came to mind. Sage swallowed hard and tried to push off the troubling thought. But it wouldn't leave her in peace.

The question that had hovered at the back of her throat refused to be smothered. "Is this your girlfriend's home?"

There was a distinct pause. "I don't have a girlfriend."

It shouldn't have mattered to her, but there was a great sense of relief in his answer. "Your friend must trust you a lot. This place…it's magnificent from the outside. I can't imagine what the inside must be like."

He didn't say anything as he opened the door and stood aside for her to enter. She stared in awe. This place was more than magnificent. It was jaw-dropping, mouth-gaping striking. The foyer was spacious with a gleaming tile floor and stone walls that rose high above her head, forming a dome with a crystal chandelier suspended in the center.

She turned to say something to Trey, but he had stepped back outside to retrieve their luggage from the car. She went out to help.

Trey frowned when he saw her in the rain. "What are you doing out here? You're going to get soaked."

The rain had picked up since they'd arrived just moments ago. But that wasn't enough to deter her. She wasn't used to anyone waiting on her. Since her father died, she'd been the one waiting on people—till she took on the managing editor job at *QTR*. But it was all still so new to her.

It was raining too much to argue. Soon they both had the luggage inside the château. Thankfully she'd packed for all occasions and had a raincoat. She slipped it off and looked around for a place to put it. She couldn't imagine ruining anything in the fancy house that looked more like a museum.

It reminded her of her childhood home in a way. It, too, had been impressive, but her parents had decorated it in a way that was beautiful but comfortable. This château was more a showplace than a home.

She turned to Trey. His face was pale and etched with deep lines that bracketed his eyes and mouth. It was like he'd aged ten years since they'd arrived. What had caused such a reaction?

"Here." Trey held out his hand for her coat. "I'll take it."

He promptly slung it over a chair in the corner. Then he added his coat.

"You can't do that." She rushed over to the chair to retrieve her coat.

"Why not? I'll hang them up tomorrow when they're dry."

"But the chair—"

"Is fine." He sent her a puzzled look. "Why are you so worried about a chair?"

"Because this place—it's like a museum. I don't want to ruin anything and have your friends upset with you." And then she decided to state the obvious. "I can see how worried you are. It's written all over your face."

"There's nothing you can do to this place that will cause a problem. Just relax." He moved to the bottom of the sweeping staircase. "Would you like something to eat? Or should we call it a night?"

The meal on the plane hadn't been much and it had been a while ago, but right now exhaustion was winning. "How about we sleep and then eat?"

"Works for me." He headed up the grand staircase. "There are a lot of bedrooms. You can have your pick as we're the only ones staying here."

"This is an awfully big place just for the two of us."

Maybe staying here wouldn't be so bad. There would be plenty of space and they wouldn't end up on top of each other. And then realizing her wording could be construed in an intimate way, she inwardly groaned. Thankfully she hadn't vocalized her thoughts.

"Is something wrong?" Trey gave her a strange look.

She shook her head. "I'm just tired."

Walking up the flight of steps took considerable effort. She stifled a yawn. She really needed some sleep. She'd be able to think more clearly in the morning. Her head hung low. Right now, she just had to concentrate on putting one foot in front of the other.

At the landing, she bumped right into Trey. Only an inch or two apart, she lifted her head. His brown eyes searched hers. Her heart slammed into her throat, blocking her next breath. If she were to lift up on tiptoes and he were to lower his head, their lips would meet. And at long last, she would know if his kisses were as hot as she imagined.

After all, this was the French Riviera. She couldn't think of a more romantic spot on earth to give in to her fantasy. The pounding of her heart drowned out all of the reasons that this was a bad idea. Maybe Louise was right. Maybe she needed more in her life than work.

And then Trey turned away. He cleared his throat. "There are four rooms to the left and four rooms to your right. Pick whichever one suits you."

"Are you sure? I mean, I don't want to be a bother."

Trey didn't say anything for a moment as though he were lost in his thoughts.

"Trey, what is it?"

He shook his head. "Nothing that can't wait until the morning."

"Are you sure?"

He sent her a smile and nodded.

She started down the wide hallway and stepped in the first bedroom. It was decorated in reds and whites. A large bed sat in the middle of the room with a white comforter and matching pillows. She moved to the bed and sat down. She immediately sunk into the mattress. Wow. Talk about a soft mattress. Not exactly her idea of comfort.

The next room held black and white decor with a red accent. The room was beautiful, but the bed was the exact opposite of the other room. When she sat on the edge, the mattress barely moved.

She caught the amusement in Trey's eyes as she made her way through the rooms.

"Are you just going to follow me around and smile?" She frowned at him.

"I'm just wondering if any of the rooms are going to be up to your standard."

"I'm not normally a picky person."

He nodded, but his eyes said that he didn't believe her.

"I'm not," she insisted as she entered the last bedroom.

She came to a sudden halt. This room was different from the others. There was no striking decor. No fancy pillows or remarkable paintings on the walls. This room, for the lack of a better word, was plain. While one wall was brick like much of the house, the other walls were a smooth plaster in a warm cream color. And the artwork on the walls were photos of different French landscapes.

A large oriental rug stretched out over the hardwood floor and extended under the king-size bed. The bed faced a set of French doors that were slightly ajar, letting in the fresh sea air. And overhead were exposed beams running the length of the ceiling. She never would have put this room in the same group as the others as its atmosphere was so different—so relaxed.

But the telling sign was in the mattress. She walked

over to the bed and sat down. It wasn't too soft or too hard. It was perfect.

She smiled. "This is it."

Trey's brow arched. "Are you sure? This room isn't as nice as the other ones."

"That's one of the things I like about it. And the bed is perfect." Then realizing that he might have been planning to stay here, she said, "Unless you were planning to sleep here."

"No." He said it rather quickly. "I'll just grab your things."

"I can get them."

He shook his head. "Tonight you're my guest."

She was so tired that she didn't have the energy to argue with him. If he was that anxious to carry all her suitcases upstairs, more power to him.

In the meantime, she'd just lean back on the bed and rest for a moment. It had been such a long, long day or was it two days now? She wasn't sure with the long layovers and the time change.

Maybe she'd just close her eyes for a moment...

Of all the bedrooms, why did she have to pick that one?

Trey frowned as he struggled to get all five of her suitcases up the stairs. The woman really needed to learn how to pack lighter. He didn't think he owned enough clothes to fill five suitcases. Okay, so maybe they were planning to be here for two weeks, but there was such a thing as a laundry machine.

At the top of the steps, he paused. It was a good thing he exercised daily. He rolled the cases back along the hallway to the very familiar bedroom. The door was still ajar.

"Sage, it's just me." He would have knocked but his hands were full trying to keep a hold on all the luggage.

There was no response. Maybe she'd decided to explore the rest of the house. Or perhaps she was standing out on the balcony. It was one of his favorite spots to clear his head.

But two steps into the room, he stopped.

There was Sage stretched across his bed. Her long dark hair was splayed across the comforter. He knew he shouldn't stare, but he couldn't help himself. She was so beautiful. And the look on her face as she was sleeping was one of utter peace. It was a look he'd never noticed during her wakeful hours. If you knew her, you could see something was always weighing on her mind. And he'd hazard a guess that it went much deeper than the trouble with the magazine.

Though he hated to admit it, he was impressed with the new format that she'd rolled out for the magazine. Instead of it being a trashy rag, it now had integrity and, at times, it was a platform to promote social change for the positive.

But he wasn't ready to back down on his campaign to close the magazine's doors. None of it changed the fact that to hurt his father in the same manner that he'd hurt him, the magazine had to go. It had been Trey's objective for so many years. He never thought he'd be in a position to make it happen—but now as the new CEO of QTR International, he was in the perfect position to make his father understand in some small way the pain his absence had inflicted on him.

Trey's thoughts returned to the gorgeous woman lying on his bed sound asleep. She was the innocent party— the bystander who would get hurt—and he had no idea how to protect her. The only thing he did know was that the longer he kept up this pretense of being her assistant instead of the heir to the QTR empire—the worse it was going to be when the truth finally won out—and it would. The truth always came to light—sometimes at the most inopportune times.

The burden of his secret weighed heavy on his shoulders. He moved quietly in the room, placing the luggage in the corner. And then he turned back to Sage. It'd been a long time since he'd had a woman in his bed. And this time he wouldn't even have the pleasure of joining her.

Although, there was no way she could sleep in that position with her feet dangling off the edge of the bed with her high heels still on. Should he wake her? He glanced at her face. She looked so contented.

He moved quietly across the floor. He knelt down next to her. His hand wrapped around her calf, enjoying the smoothness of her skin. And then realizing he was letting himself get distracted, he slipped off one shoe. She never missed a slow, steady breath. He then repeated the same process with the other leg.

Somehow he had to get her legs on the bed without waking her. Apparently she was more wiped out than he'd imagined. As he settled her comfortably on the bed, all she did was roll away from him. Her summer dress rode high up on her creamy thigh and suddenly his mouth went dry.

Turn away. Forget it. She's off-limits.

His mind said all the right things, but the rest of him was tempted to wake her—to see if she was as attracted to him as he was to her. The devil and angel played advocates in his mind. After all, she didn't know who he really was. But it wouldn't be right to start things under a false premise, no matter how casual it might be.

He draped the soft fabric of the bedspread over her. And then he noticed that a few strands of hair had strayed across her face. He should just leave her be, but his fingers tingled with temptation. He reached out and ever so gently swept the hair back. And then he turned and headed for the door.

CHAPTER EIGHT

SAGE AWOKE SLOWLY.

She was warm but not too warm. And the bed was soft but not too soft.

And best of all, she was wrapped in very strong, capable arms. She opened her eyes and gazed into coffee-brown eyes. Her heart fluttered in her chest. She didn't know that she could be this happy.

Trey smiled at her as his fingers stroked her cheek. His thumb traced over her bottom lip, sending a bolt of desire through her core. The truth was that she'd never get enough of him. Trey was everything she'd ever dreamed about—and more.

Her hand reached out to him. Her palm pressed against his bare chest. She could feel his heart. It was still pounding with need. Her fingers inched up his muscled chest until her hand wrapped around his neck, pulling him closer to her.

As she scooted closer to him to press her lips to his, he disappeared. Her hand landed on the empty spot in the bed. Where had he gone? Her gaze searched the room but it was empty. Once again she was all alone.

"Trey! Trey!"

The next thing she knew she was being jostled. "Sage, wake up. It's a dream."

Her eyes blinked open. "Trey?"

"Yeah. It's me." He sent her a reassuring smile. "It was just a nightmare. Do you remember what it was about?"

She remembered every delicious detail and it was certainly no nightmare. And she also remembered that, in the end, he'd left her. Just like the other people in her life.

She shook her head. "It's a blur." She glanced down, finding herself still dressed in the clothes from yesterday. "It looks like I fell asleep on you last night." And then she realized how that sounded as heat rushed to her cheeks. "I, uh, must have been more tired than I thought."

"No problem."

Her gaze moved to the man who starred in her very hot dream. Her face grew warmer. Why did Trey have to be the man of her dreams? Now how was she supposed to act professional around him knowing she secretly desired him?

Don't make a big deal of it. He can't read your thoughts. Just act normal.

She took in his smart-looking suit. "It looks like you're all ready to face the day."

"I've been up for a while." A serious expression came over his face. "Sage, we need to talk."

Oh, no. What exactly had she said in her sleep? She didn't want to know. Nope. Not at all.

She scrambled to climb out of the other side of the bed. "Sorry I'm running late. Just let me grab a quick shower and I'll be ready to go."

"You don't have to rush—"

"Sure, I do." She moved to her suitcases, which were waiting for her in the corner of the room. "We have to get our badges."

"We have all day."

"It can be a long wait since they have to take our photo. Besides, this is a good day to catch some people before they get caught up in the movie premieres and the parties."

He arched a brow. "How would you know?"

She shrugged. "I attended the festival with my father. It was a long time ago, but I still remember parts of it. And one of those memories was waiting in line at the Accreditation Centre. I take it you've never attended?"

He hesitated. "I've attended the festival."

"Then you should know we have a lot to do today."

"If you say so." Trey moved to the door. "I'll get us some breakfast."

"Just coffee for me."

"You need more than that since we'll be walking to the festival." When she sent him a surprised look, he added, "A lot of the roads will be closed. Walking will be our fastest option."

"Okay. I'll be down in a few minutes." If she could just get them away from this very cozy setting and into the public, things would smooth out. And hopefully Trey would forget about her calling out his name and whatever else she'd said in her sleep.

"We'll see about that."

Before she could say another word, the door snicked shut. Alone again. She sighed. She looked at all of her luggage. Perhaps she had brought a lot of clothes but she knew she had to dress smartly. So her roommates had loaned her a few dresses, creating an extensive, all-event wardrobe.

Her and her two roommates routinely shared clothes. On a tight budget, it made clothes go a lot further. But if she could keep *QTR* on its upward swing, her finances wouldn't be quite so strained. Of course, her latest private investigator looking into her stepmother was taking a large bite out of each paycheck. She'd instructed him to look under every rock until he found what Elsa was hiding.

Sage placed a suitcase on the large bed and opened it. With her arm full of dresses, she moved to the wall of closets and found half of them filled with men's clothes. It must be the owner's. Thankfully there was enough room for her things.

Not wanting to keep Trey waiting much longer, she didn't bother with the other suitcases. They could be dealt with later.

* * *

He never expected to hear Sage calling out his name in her sleep.

Trey had no idea what to make of it.

Her tone hadn't been one of passion. Instead there had been an urgency to her voice. So if she was having a nightmare, why would she cry out to him? It was just one more thing for him to ponder about his beautiful boss.

They had just collected their photo badges and were standing outside the doors of the Cannes Exhibition Centre. Sage was pleased to find their badges were marked with a red dot containing the letter *R*. It granted them access to red-carpet screenings.

Trey may have grown up in Cannes, but he'd never been that involved with the festival. So, much like Sage, he was figuring it out as they went along.

People strolled by in stylish clothes. Some were famous, others weren't. All smiled brightly when there was a camera pointed in their direction.

He glanced over at Sage as a smile lit up her face. She wasn't wasting any time trying to save her…er…*his* magazine. He didn't like that they were on opposite sides of keeping the magazine. Still, he couldn't help but applaud her resilience.

"Hello." Sage stepped forward and held out her hand to the female lead in an upcoming action film. "I'm Sage White with *QTR Magazine*—"

The young actress immediately withdrew her hand. "I can't talk to you. I've heard about your magazine."

"But you don't understand—"

"I understand enough." The young woman turned and walked away as fast as she could on those five-inch heels.

Sage turned a worried gaze in his direction. He didn't know what to tell her. His father had done quite a number on the magazine—taking it from stellar reporting to the depths of heresy. They were lucky his father hadn't put headlines of UFO sightings on the cover.

The magazine had been in Trey's family for generations. Each generation had made their mark on it. Way, way back in the beginning, the magazine had started here in France.

A few generations later, it had been relocated to the States. New York to be exact. But then Trey's great-grandfather had moved it to Los Angeles. He was a big fan of John Wayne. But when it came time for Trey's father to put his mark upon the publication, it was all about profits. It didn't matter how he got them. He'd taken the Rousseau name and dragged it through the mud.

And now it was up to Trey to put an end to it all. But perhaps Sage's idea for the magazine wasn't a bad one—but would anyone even give her a chance? As time went by, she didn't get past a greeting before people moved on.

"Perhaps we should try again tomorrow," Trey said, feeling bad for her. "When people aren't in such a rush."

"I can't stop now. I haven't even gained one new contact."

He'd give her a gold star for effort. "But it's only the first day of the festival. People are still getting settled in. There are still ten more days to go."

"I know. But I had a goal to gain at least one good contact per day. You don't understand how important this is." Sage started walking.

Trey kept pace with her. "Maybe you're putting too much pressure on yourself."

She cast him a sideways glance. "You don't believe that, do you?"

He did believe it, but he also knew she wasn't in the mood to hear his observations right now.

He reached in his jacket pocket and pulled out a small envelope. "Perhaps this will help."

She had to admit that she was very curious. "What is it?"

"I've secured us an invitation to the Red Heart Gala tonight."

"You what?" Her mouth gaped. "But that party is totally exclusive. I heard some of the stars couldn't even get invitations."

"See. The problem with them is they don't know the right people." He sent her a big smile.

"And who might that be?"

"I don't know if you can be trusted with this highly sensitive information. If it leaks out, I might lose my source." He winked, letting her know that he was teasing her.

"I swear no one will hear from me. Now spill."

"It's Maria."

"Maria?" It took her a second to figure out who he meant. "You mean, Maria—that works at the château?"

He laughed. "Yes. The one and the same."

"But I don't understand."

"Maria is a part of the housekeeper network. If you need something, her group can definitely pull it off. They are amazing and highly resourceful."

"I'm totally impressed. These tickets are highly sought after. Anyone who is anyone will be there."

"And that's why we'll be there."

"You mean to try and gain some interviews?"

He shook his head. "Not tonight. It will be all about enjoying yourself and just soaking up some of the atmosphere. No stressing. No worrying. And no working."

"But—"

He held up a hand, stopping her protest. "There are no *buts*. Those are the rules or we don't go."

"I still have one *but*."

He didn't want more problems. "What is it?"

"But I don't have a red dress to wear. I have black, blue, turquoise and deep purple but no red." When he sent her a puzzled look, she said, "The dress code is red, except for the men. Black tux is mandatory. You do have at least one tux with you, don't you?"

He nodded. "I made sure of it before we left LA."

"So that just leaves me with nothing to wear."

Trey told her about a couple of local dress shops. They agreed to meet up later at the château. As soon as she walked away, he reached for his phone to call ahead and tell them to charge him for anything Sage picked out. But then he paused. How would he explain that to Sage since he hadn't found the right time to tell her about his true identity? He slipped his phone back in his pocket.

The evening was amazing.

Sage and Trey had walked the red carpet and posed for a photo. Trey explained that even though they weren't famous, the photographers made money selling the photos back to the people. Sage had to admit that she would be buying the photo—most definitely. She never wanted to forget this amazing experience.

She never imagined she'd be in the same room with so many stars. It was dizzying trying to name all the celebrities. And the fact that she was speaking with them as though she were one of them—well, it was a night she'd never forget.

The hotel where the gala was being held was the same one where she was supposed to be staying. The architecture was stunning. Marble pillars supported an intricately designed ceiling. And one crystal chandelier wouldn't do for this ballroom. Instead, there were at least a dozen. This place was fit for royalty.

She glanced down at her deep-red full-length gown, wondering if she was dressed appropriately.

Her visit to the boutique let her know that she couldn't afford anything in the store, even if she had maxed out her credit card. But the salesgirl, having noticed the distress written on Sage's face, told her about a little out-of-the-way shop where secondhand dresses were sold for a fraction of the original price.

It was where Sage had found this off-the-shoulder, figure-hugging gown with a daring slit up her left thigh. It didn't fit exactly, but a few strategically placed pins in the bodice held it in place. And luckily, she had a pair of black stilettos that paired perfectly with the dress. She actually felt like Cinderella at the ball. Did that make him her prince?

Her heart fluttered in her chest. The most handsome man of all was the one holding her in his very capable arms. She lifted her head and stared up at Trey as he guided them around the dance floor.

"Are you enjoying yourself?" Trey's voice broke through her thoughts.

"I am. I don't think my feet have touched the ground since we arrived." She leaned in closer. "Did you see the jewels people are wearing?"

Trey smiled and nodded as they practically floated past the white marble columns surrounding the dance floor.

"Look at that." She pointed at the enormous chandelier made up of thousands of crystals. "I love how the light dances off it. Now that is flashy."

A smile lifted his lips and smoothed the lines on his face.

"What are you smiling about?"

"You. I've never seen you so..." He hesitated as though searching for the right word.

"Awestruck? Impressed?" Then she moved her hand, stroking her fingers down over his soft beard. "Captivated?"

His dark eyes lit up as though her touch awakened a part of him. His gaze dipped to her lips. Her pulse quickened. She had a feeling this night was just getting started.

She couldn't turn away. My, he was handsome. So handsome and sweet that her reservations about trusting him slipped from her mind. Tonight, they were no longer boss and assistant. Tonight, he was just Trey—a devastatingly handsome escort with a twinkle in his eyes. And she was just Sage, his date. So was there any reason not to let down her guard and treat him as she would any man who caught her eye and dazzled her with the most amazing night?

The lyrics from the next song wrapped around them. Their bodies swayed gently to the tune. As her body brushed against the hard plains of Trey, the breath caught in her throat. Every nerve ending in her body was stimulated.

In that moment, with his hand pressed lightly to the bare skin at the small of her back, she couldn't think of any reason not to give in to her desire. She stopped dancing. She lifted her chin and their gazes caught.

Questions reflected in his dark eyes. His mouth opened to say something, but nothing came out. The next thing she knew his head was lowering toward hers and she was lifting up on her tiptoes. When their lips met, it was like a powerful jolt of electricity zapped through her body.

She had never felt this way with any other man. Trey was unique in so many ways. And she never wanted this magical night to end.

His lips moved slowly over hers. His touch was soft and teasing. A need grew within her. She wanted more of him. All of him—

The band stopped. A round of applause filled the room, jolting both Sage and Trey back to reality. With great reluctance, Sage pulled back.

Her lips tingled as Trey led her from the now-empty dance floor. She had no idea where they went from here, but she was anxious to find out.

They spent the rest of the evening mingling, dancing

and sipping bubbly while eating the most delicious hors d'oeuvres, but sadly there was to be no more kissing.

Sage was surprised at her eagerness to taste him once more and was disappointed that Trey didn't feel the same. Because as soon as they arrived at the château, Trey mumbled something about needing to send an email and he disappeared, leaving her alone with her thoughts.

She'd messed up. She knew it. Crossing that line between them was a mistake. Going forward, she was going to have to do better.

CHAPTER NINE

THE NEXT MORNING Trey knew he had to say something to Sage about the kiss. He'd seen the confused look in her eyes when he'd backed off and when he'd made a quick exit after they'd arrived home.

It wasn't that he didn't want to follow that kiss up with more—a lot more. The problem was that Sage didn't know the "real" man she was about to get involved with. And if they were about to start something, even casually as he didn't do commitments, then she deserved all the facts.

After watching his parents, he didn't believe in living happily-ever-after. Love was fleeting at best—at worst it crushed people. Either way, he refused to end up on the losing end like his mother.

And this morning, Sage was acting differently—cooler. They had just finished breakfast and headed for the festival when he decided to lay everything on the line.

"Sage, we need to talk."

"I know. We were so busy with the festival yesterday that I didn't get to touch base with you about the audit prep work. Is it all coming together?"

"Yes. But this isn't about the audit—"

"Good. I'll check my emails when we head back to the château to dress for this evening's movie premiere."

"Sage, wait." And then realizing how abrupt that sounded, he said, "Please. What I want to talk about isn't work—"

"Stop." She quit talking and turned to him. "I know

that I crossed a line. It was wrong of me. It won't happen again."

"Sage, if you'd let me speak."

"No. Just let it go. Please. It was just a lapse of judgment. It didn't mean anything." When he didn't say anything, she continued. "I just got caught up in the excitement of the evening."

So he'd misread the situation? Good. They could get back on track.

"So how about we get to work," he said, wanting to end this awkward conversation.

"We're okay?" Her gaze searched his.

He nodded. "Let's go."

They continued toward the festival. Trey shoved aside the awkward moment with Sage. It was best not to dwell on it. But still, a strained silence lingered between them.

When they reached the Grand Theatre Lumière for the morning showing, Trey excused himself to get them both coffee. The truth was that he needed a few moments alone to gather his thoughts.

Meanwhile, Sage had zeroed in on a young actress and planned to go introduce herself. He hoped it went well. Wait. There he went again, wishing for Sage to succeed. Was that really what he wanted?

The line at the café was long. Fifteen minutes later, Trey stepped up to the counter. He ordered espresso for himself and a vanilla latte for Sage.

He was on his way back when he spotted a tall, slender woman approaching Sage. The woman had her back to him, but she was much taller than Sage. In fact, the woman was almost as tall as him. Her willowy figure was draped in a snug black dress. Her platinum-blond hair was cut short and not a strand was out of place.

He paused near one of the large pillars outside the theater. If this woman happened to be an actress or person of interest, he didn't want to interrupt Sage's chance to nail down an interview.

He could only hope this was the break Sage had been hoping for. It would be a good way to ease the tension between them. And then they could go home and what? He'd reveal the truth of his identity to her?

How exactly would that go?

She'd most likely fire him. And that would be the easy part. The other part—the one where there is pain and possible tears in her eyes—well, he wasn't so sure that he was up for that.

He moved a little closer. Neither of the women appeared to notice him.

"Sage, my dear, what are you doing here?" The older woman's voice held an icy tone. "Shouldn't you be off cleaning floors or some such thing?"

This woman knew Sage? And then the woman turned, giving Trey a full view of her face. It was Elsa White.

His body tensed. He wanted to move to Sage's defense. But at that moment, Sage's gaze met his and she gave a slight shake of her head, warning him off.

Standing on the sidelines was not a position he was used to taking. When it came to caring for his mother, he may have been young but he'd stepped up, making sure she made her doctors' appointments and took her medicine. But Sage wasn't like his mother. Sage was strong and more than capable of taking care of herself.

Sage's face instantly hardened. There was absolutely no sign of that famous smile that she shared with everyone. "Elsa, I didn't expect to see you here."

Trey couldn't have been dragged from his spot. If Sage needed him, he'd step up. But he wasn't the only one to notice the exchange. These two women were oblivious to the observers. Right now, their sole focus was on each other.

His gaze volleyed between them. There was so much

tension arcing between these women that it could light up all of Cannes. To say there was no love lost between these two was an understatement.

"You shouldn't be here," Elsa said. "You don't belong."

"I'm right where I need to be. Shouldn't you be in New York plotting your next devious deal?"

Anger lit up Elsa's eyes before they narrowed with an evil glint. "I don't have to be in New York to do my plotting. You are out of your league here. You best be on your way little girl."

Sage squared her shoulders and lifted her chin. "I'm not a child anymore. Your scare tactics no longer work on me."

"Oh, dear, you misunderstand me. I'm not trying to scare you. I'm warning you to get out of my way before I roll right over you."

And with that the older woman turned and strode away.

Sage stood there for a moment as though gathering her thoughts. Trey approached her. He really wanted to question her, but he knew now wasn't the right moment. She would open up to him when she was ready and not a moment sooner.

Sage began to walk and he fell in step beside her. She was quiet for a moment. She didn't stop until they were at an overlook. The morning sun danced upon the water. The multitude of yachts looked like toy boats from this distance. But Trey's attention was on Sage and what he could do for her.

She paused at the railing. "I'm sorry about that. I seem to be making a habit of apologizing to you."

He handed her the latte. "Don't be sorry. You didn't do anything wrong."

"I'm sure you're wondering about that woman back there." Sage continued to stare straight ahead, not giving him a chance to look into her eyes.

"It's okay. You don't have to talk about it." He meant

it. Even though he was curious, he had never seen Sage so upset. It was best to let the subject rest.

"You're right. I don't want to talk about her." Sage glanced at him. Determination reflected in her gaze. "But I have to."

"Okay. I'm listening."

She took a sip of her coffee. "Elsa is my stepmother. My mother died when I was young. And for many years, my father and I were alone. Then one day my father tells me that he met someone. I was genuinely happy for him. I knew how lonely he was without my mother."

"It couldn't have been easy for either of you."

"His relationship with Elsa could only be described as a whirlwind romance. At first, Elsa was friendly. It wasn't until much later that I realized it was all a show—at least where I was concerned. I never figured out if she cared about my father or if he only constituted a ticket to a better life. I hope she truly loved him because he must have loved her."

"Why do you say that?"

"Because growing up, he used to take me to the office of White Publishing and he'd tell me that one day it would be all mine. He said it was my legacy. And then when he unexpectedly died of a heart attack, the will was read and the company and house…" She paused as though to rein in her emotions. "It all went to Elsa. I was gutted. I… I felt so betrayed."

"How old were you?"

"I was sixteen. I went from private schools to public. I lost all my friends. And when I wasn't in school, I was cleaning the house. Elsa got rid of the staff, saying that we had to tighten the purse strings as the business was in trouble." Sage turned to him with sadness reflected in her eyes. "You don't want to hear all of this."

"I do, if you want me to."

"For my eighteenth birthday, Elsa kicked me out. At the time, my shares of White Publishing were worth pennies per share. Not having a cent to my name, I was forced to sell her my shares in order to eat. To this day, I regret that decision. When I signed those shares over, I handed over any right to my legacy. But at the time, I was so young and scared. I didn't know how to take care of myself. I learned really fast."

"I wish I had known you then."

"Why?" She eyed him suspiciously. "Would you have ridden up on your white horse to save me?"

He shrugged. "I don't ride horses, but maybe a white car."

She didn't laugh at his attempt to lighten the mood. "I didn't need someone to save me. I needed to save myself. I needed to learn that even without my father's money, I would be all right. I learned a lot about myself in those years."

"But you shouldn't have had to."

Sage turned to face the sea. "Maybe I did. I'll be the first to admit that my father spoiled me. I had no idea how much so until I had to feed myself and put a roof over my head. In that manner, Elsa did me a favor."

"Don't go giving that woman any compliments. She's pure evil."

"Maybe. But I learned that I'm stronger than I ever thought. I worked for a maid service throughout college. With a full-time job, it took me five years to earn my degree, including taking summer classes. It wasn't easy, but I did it. Now, I won't give up until I have White Publishing back."

He had a feeling that his smiling, beautiful boss was plotting something and it worried him. He'd heard Elsa was not a person to be crossed. "Sage, what are you up to?"

She shook her head. "It's nothing for you to worry

about. Everything is going according to plan. By the way, I just landed an exclusive interview with Starr. Isn't that great?"

"Yes, but don't underestimate Elsa."

Sage's eyes widened. "How do you know about my stepmother?"

"Everyone has heard the rumors of Elsa White. She's notorious in the business and not in a good way." He stared deep into Sage's eyes, imploring her to heed his warning. He'd dealt with his own share of powerful enemies. "Just keep your eyes open."

"Trey?" a male voice called out behind him. "Trey? Is that you?"

With the greatest regret, he pulled back from Sage. He knew by coming to the festival that he would likely run into someone he knew. But with his quiet social calendar, he didn't think there would be many people that would recognize him.

He mouthed, *I'm sorry*, to Sage.

Her normally bright eyes dimmed. "I... I need to get back to the festival and circulate." She glanced over his shoulder at the person approaching. "Don't rush on my account."

He turned to find his childhood friend. They'd been roommates one year at boarding school, but then Sam had moved away. Trey had always wondered what had happened to him.

"I thought that was you." Sam strode up to him all smiles, just as Trey remembered him.

"It's good to see you."

They started with a handshake that ended up in a hug and a clap on the back.

Trey pulled back. His gaze quickly scanned the crowd, searching for Sage, but she was nowhere to be found. He really needed to straighten things out with her.

"So what has you here?" Sam asked.

"Work."

Sam glanced at his press badge. "You decided to work for your father?"

It had been no secret in school that no love was lost between him and his father. When family days rolled around, he was the only one who had no family show up. His father was too involved with his precious magazine and his mother never felt up to traveling. As far back as he could remember, his mother never felt well.

"Something like that." Anxious to turn the conversation away from himself, Trey said, "How about you?"

"I'm producing films."

Trey thought back in time. "You always did have a flair for acting."

"Yeah. But it appears that I'm better behind the scenes."

Trey thought of how he'd turned into an actor with Sage. It had all seemed innocent enough in the beginning. But now that he'd gotten to know her—to kiss her—it all felt wrong.

When he confessed that he was out to destroy the magazine she'd been working so hard to rebuild, she would hate him. But was he at a point where he could just let go of the revenge that he'd been plotting against his father since he was in boarding school?

CHAPTER TEN

THE DEEPEST, DARKEST night had settled upon Cannes.

Elsa stood on the balcony of her deluxe suite enjoying the inky blackness. She lifted her second glass of cognac to her lips and took a healthy sip. The heady liquid hit the back of her throat and burned as it went down. She smiled.

So far her time in Cannes had been utterly boring—well, there was that run-in with Sage. That had been slightly amusing. It would have been more fun if the girl had grown a backbone.

Elsa recalled how Sage had always thought the world was made of rainbows and butterflies. Elsa expelled a frustrated sigh. Whoever thought a kind word or smile could open doors? Only Sage. That foolish, foolish girl.

Knock. Knock.

She moved to the door. Her long, silk robe fluttered around her legs as she crossed the room. Elsa yanked the door open to find Mr. Hunter standing there in a dark suit. The top buttons of his shirt were undone, giving her a glimpse of his chest. Not bad. Not bad at all. His hair had been cut and styled. He really was rather handsome.

Why hadn't she noticed this before? Perhaps the alcohol was skewing her perception or maybe she'd never been so bored and anxious for something to amuse her. Yes, Mr. Hunter just might serve a dual purpose this evening.

But first, they had to get business out of the way.

"What have you learned about my stepdaughter? Has she heeded my warning? Is she leaving?"

"No. She's still here. And I have learned something very interesting."

The way he said the words sparked Elsa's interest. "Is it something I can use against her?"

"I think it is."

Elsa smiled. This man was getting more attractive by the moment. "Come here and sit with me on the couch." She sat down and patted a spot next to her. Once he was seated, she leaned in close to him and inhaled his spicy aftershave. Mmm… He smelled divine. Tonight was definitely looking up. She traced a manicured nail over the slight stubble on his cheek, down his neck and then played with the few hairs on his chest—his very firm chest. "What delicious information have you uncovered?"

Hunter cleared his throat. "Well, it appears her assistant isn't actually her assistant after all. But I don't think she knows it. In fact, I'm certain she doesn't."

Elsa undid a button on his shirt. "If you make this good, I promise you'll receive a bonus you'll never forget."

Hunter's dark eyes met hers. There was the fire of desire burning in them, which only excited Elsa more. She loved when she could control people, whether it was in the office or in bed.

She leaned forward, pressing her lips to his. There was no gentle foreplay. There was hunger. Need. And lust. And he was going to do just fine for scratching her itch.

She pulled back. "Now explain your cryptic remark. Her assistant isn't really her assistant. How is that possible?"

"For some reason that I don't understand, the man acting as Sage's assistant is really Quentin Thomas Rousseau III."

Elsa leaned back on the couch. Her mind was racing a mile a minute. "And you say Sage doesn't know his true identity?"

Hunter shook his head. "Not as far as I can tell."

"Very interesting." So what was the young Rousseau up to? Was he going to be an asset to her plans? Or had he fallen under Sage's spell like so many men before him?

"I need all the information you can find about the young Rousseau. Is there anything else I should know about?"

"Actually, Sage just landed a most sought after interview with Starr."

This news darkened Elsa's mood. She got to her feet and moved to the drink cart to refill her cognac. She took a mouthful of the fiery liquid and swallowed. Her gaze lifted to the mirror that hung over the drink cart. Elsa stared at her beautiful image. Usually it made her feel better, but not tonight. As she smoothed an errant strand of hair behind her ear, she couldn't help but think of her stepdaughter. Maybe the girl had grown more of a backbone than she'd originally thought.

"This interview, will it help her magazine?"

Hunter nodded. "Definitely. From what I gather, it should be a cover spot."

Still holding the glass of cognac, Elsa's hand tightened around the crystal glass. How dare that worthless girl try and beat her in her own arena. Elsa was the queen of publishing. There was no room for Sage.

Elsa caught her image in the mirror. For a moment, she looked older—second best. Anger pumped through her veins.

Elsa turned to Hunter. "I want you to set up an appointment with the actress before her interview with Sage. I don't care what she has planned. Tell her to cancel it."

Hunter's dark eyes widened as though to complain about not being her secretary. But as though he sensed the danger in disagreeing with her at that moment, he said, "I will go take care of it now."

"Not yet." She strode toward him in her stilettos. "I have something else in mind for you."

She had to do something with all of her pent-up energy or she would explode. When she reached him, she placed a hand behind his head and pulled him down to her lips.

And tomorrow—tomorrow I will deal with Sage. She will not win. Never!

CHAPTER ELEVEN

THREE DAYS OF being brushed off by celebrities.

But today would be different.

Sage had the feeling everything was about to change and she chose to believe it was going to be in a good way. She might not have gotten much sleep after attending a party until the wee hours of the morning, but she felt as though she could conquer the world.

And then there was Trey. Try as she might to forget the kiss and his reaction, it was there with her every day, lurking in the shadows of her mind. But there had been no mention of it and things were getting back to normal.

It was best that she centered her thoughts on work. It always brought her comfort. Tomorrow was her big interview with Starr. She'd already arranged to have the photographer meet them. And just so she didn't miss anything in her notes, she was going to have Trey record the session. It was all going to work out and this interview was just the beginning. Today she hoped to secure another interview. It was the only way to keep the magazine alive.

She was due for some good luck. Taking a positive attitude, she was singing a tune as she came down the stairs at the château. Not finding Trey inside, she made her way to the veranda. Trey was sitting there reading something on his phone while drinking a cup of coffee.

As soon as he saw her, he put his phone down. "Did I just hear you sing 'Heigh-Ho'?"

She couldn't help but smile. "You must be hearing things."

He sent a disbelieving look. "I know what I heard."

Trying to change the subject, she asked, "Are you ready to set off to work?"

He gave her another funny look. "I am."

She couldn't help but notice how dashing he looked in a pair of dark slacks and a white dress shirt with the top buttons undone and the sleeves rolled up. It was then that she noticed his watch. It was a designer watch. She'd noticed it before and assumed that it was a knockoff. A very good knockoff.

Trey got to his feet and rounded the table to pull a chair out for her. "But you're not. I'll just have Maria bring out your breakfast."

She was about to protest, but then reconsidered. Perhaps a bite to eat before the interview would be helpful. "Thanks."

"No problem."

In just a couple of minutes, he returned with an apple in his hand.

"Is that all you're eating?" She hated the thought of Maria going out of her way to cook for just her.

"Relax. I already ate."

"Oh." She eyed up the bright red apple. "You must really like apples. You seem to always have one on hand."

"They're a sweet snack and travel easy. You should try them."

"I eat apples."

He arched a disbelieving brow.

"Okay, not very often. Since when have you come to know my habits so well?"

"Since we've been working practically nonstop to get the magazine turned around."

Just then Maria came onto the veranda with a covered dish and a large glass of fresh squeezed orange juice. As Sage ate the delicious food, she realized that staying here

at the château reminded her a lot of her childhood. There
had been glamorous travels to the farthest ends of the earth
and her spacious childhood home had been complete with
a full staff that were more like family than hired help. But
most of all, she'd been able to relax and enjoy herself.

"What are you thinking about?" Trey asked once Maria
departed.

Why not be honest with him? No matter what she
wanted to tell herself, they were much more than coworkers. Friends? Possibly. But somehow it felt like more. She
knew that reading anything into their relationship was
dangerous. For all she knew Elsa could have planted Trey
in her life. It wouldn't be the first time that her stepmother
had done such a despicable thing. But there was something
about Trey—a genuineness that made her want to trust him
with her deepest and most profound secrets.

She set aside her fork. "I was thinking that I haven't
been this relaxed since…since before my father married
Elsa."

Trey didn't say anything. Instead he settled back in his
chair as though letting her open up to him at her own pace.

She averted her gaze out to the sea. "After my father's
marriage to Elsa, the changes to the household didn't happen all at once. In fact, in the beginning Elsa couldn't have
been nicer and Father had been so happy. All those years
of loneliness were behind him. But when my father trav-
eled for business, Elsa started to change. Things in my
room started to disappear."

"She stole from you?" Trey's expression was one of
astonishment.

"When I called her out on it, she was all apologetic. She
claimed there was a charity drive and she didn't think I
would mind donating a few items to the underprivileged.
Of course, looking back now I realize this was all for my
father's benefit. She was so cunning and devious that, in

the end, she had me feeling guilty for wanting my possessions back—including the last gift from my mother—a porcelain doll."

Trey's expression hardened. "Is it all right if I hate your stepmother on your behalf?"

Sage shrugged. "I struggle with that emotion every time the woman interferes in my life, which was quite often over the years. But to hate her would consume me and hurt me, not her. Instead I feel bad for her that she is such a miserable, spiteful person."

Trey's mouth gaped slightly. "You feel sorry for her?"

Sage nodded. "Not like I want to help her or anything. I still think she has a lot to answer for, but sorry as in I'm grateful I can see the good in life, unlike her, and I'm not consumed with revenge or whatever drives her."

Trey leaned forward, resting his elbows on the table. He reached out and placed his hand on hers. His thumb gently stroked the back of her hand, sending goose bumps racing up her arms and setting her heart aflutter.

His voice was low and gravelly when he said, "Have I ever told you how amazing I find you?"

Right now, with him touching her, she was having problems stringing words together. "Me?"

"Yes, you. It seems like no matter what life throws at you, you find a way to keep going—to keep smiling."

Just then she smiled. She didn't mean to. It just happened. And then her gaze caught his and her heart vaulted into the back of her throat. If there hadn't been a table between them, she was certain she would have thrown herself into his arms.

And how would Trey react? Would he push her away? Or would he draw her close. With his hand on hers, her signals were getting confused.

"Sage, there's something we need to talk about."

"Is it about the interview?"

"No. It's about us."

Her stomach sunk to her designer heels. Why did he have to bring up that subject now? Had he been able to read her thoughts?

"Now's not a good time." She pulled her hand away from his, hoping the distance would clear her thoughts. "I just realized that we don't have long until the interview." She pushed aside the rest of her breakfast, having lost her appetite.

"Go ahead and finish eating. We have time."

She shook her head as she washed down the eggs and toast with a big sip of juice. "I want to be early. We need enough time to cover everything without rushing." She lifted her trusty black leather notepad from the table. "I have a lot of questions planned."

"And what would you like me to do?"

"Don't forget to record the session. I don't want to miss anything. You downloaded the app to your phone, didn't you?"

He nodded. "And don't forget to get her to authorize the recording."

"I have the legal release with my questions." She felt like she was forgetting something. "Was there anything else?"

Trey paused as though to go over everything in his mind. "Not that I can think of. Are you ready to go?"

She nodded. "You know, as much walking as we do, I need to start wearing sneakers and carrying my heels in a backpack."

"Do you want to change?"

She was very tempted, but she also knew they weren't the only ones trekking around Cannes. She needed to look her best at all times—or at least until she secured a few more interviews. Maybe after those she could let down her hair so to speak.

* * *

The sunny streets of Cannes were filled with some of the best-dressed people in the world. There were actors and actresses from action movies, romantic comedies and dramas. After almost a week of this, he was getting a lot more adept at matching names with faces. He wouldn't admit it here, but he wasn't much of a moviegoer. He was probably the only one in this large mass of people.

He walked with Sage back to the hotel where the Red Heart Gala had been held—where they'd kissed. He wondered if Sage was remembering their steamy lip-lock.

He'd never had a chance to explain why he'd pulled away. There'd always been a reason why it hadn't been the right time, but the truth was he'd been dragging his feet—delaying the inevitable.

In the elevator, he turned to her. "After the interview, we'll have that talk."

Her gaze averted his. "Okay."

Soon the truth would be out there and it wouldn't be weighing on him. He just didn't know how Sage would react. Would she understand that in the beginning he hadn't set out to hurt anyone?

His thoughts ground to a halt as they stepped off the elevator and approached the suite.

Trey knocked on the door.

There was no answer.

He glanced at Sage. "This is the right suite, isn't it?"

She referenced her notes. "It's the room number she gave me. Try again."

He knocked once more, louder this time.

At last the door swung open. A frazzled-looking young woman peeked her head through the crack in the door. This was not the actress. It must be her assistant. The woman's gaze moved from him to Sage and then back to him. She wasn't exactly the friendliest assistant as she had yet to say a word to them.

"Hi." He used his friendliest smile in spite of her. "Miss White is here for her interview with Starr."

"That won't be possible." The young woman attempted to close the door in Trey's face.

He was too quick for her and put his shoe in the way, bringing the swinging door to an abrupt halt. "Not so fast."

The young woman glared at him. "Move."

"Not until you tell us what is going on here. Miss White has an appointment."

"Yeah, well, things have changed. The appointment is canceled."

Sage stepped around Trey. "I don't understand. The other day Starr was anxious for the interview. Why did she change her mind?"

The young woman glanced over her shoulder as though to see if anyone was listening. "She's just signed an exclusive contract to sell her biography to be released simultaneously with her movie next year. All her promo is now monitored."

"But our agreement was prior to her contract." Sage had the look on her face that said she wasn't going to back down easily.

There were voices inside. The voices were growing louder as if they were approaching the door. Before he saw her, Trey knew the source of the problem.

The door swung wide open and Elsa appeared. She smiled but it wasn't a normal smile. It held a hint of deviousness. And her dark eyes sparkled with evil. The woman gave him a bitter taste in the back of his mouth. All he wanted to do was get Sage far away from the woman.

"Come on," he said. "Let's go."

"Yes, go." There was a note of glee in Elsa's voice. "There is nothing for you here."

Sage's face hardened. Her gaze narrowed in on her step-mother. "You had absolutely no interest in Starr until you knew I had plans with her."

"You did?" Elsa pressed a hand to her chest and feigned an innocent look. "Oh, my." The over-the-top theatrics made it obvious that Elsa had been targeting Sage. "You should pack up and go home."

Trey went to step up to the woman and let her know exactly what he thought of her. Words popped into his mind that he never thought he would ever say to a lady, but then again Elsa was anything but a lady.

Sage grabbed his arm and held him back. She glanced at him with a warning reflected in her eyes. "I've got this." She turned on Elsa. "I don't know why you think you have to lash out at me at every turn. You know, I feel bad for you."

"Bad for me?" Elsa's eyes widened in surprise. "Honey, I'm the one that is about to walk away with this year's up-and-coming superstar. You should feel bad for yourself—always on the losing end of things."

"I might not have gotten the interview, but I have something more—my self-respect and the ability to smile. You, however, don't even know what it's like to be happy. Do you?"

Frown lines bracketed Elsa's face. If looks could kill, Sage would be nothing but a black singe on the red carpet. "Oh, yes. You think you can stand up to me now that you have Quentin by your side. But even he is no challenge for me."

"His name is Trey."

"Really? My mistake." Elsa's voice took on a deeper, more deadly tone. "Or perhaps it's yours. You always were the naive child, wanting Daddy to take care of everything."

Sage turned to him. "Trey, tell her." There was pleading in her eyes that tore at him. "Tell her she's mistaken."

He wanted to do that for Sage. He would have done any-thing to spare Sage this agonizing moment, but it was now out of his hands. It was long past the time for the truth.

As the pain reflected in Sage's eyes, Trey's chest tight-ened. Every muscle in his body grew rigid. Everything with Sage was spinning out of control and he was helpless to stop it. He, the man with all the answers, didn't know how to keep Sage from being hurt.

He turned to Elsa.

How could one woman be so evil? So malicious?

The look of triumph sparkled in Elsa's eyes. His hands clenched at his sides. Why did she want to hurt her step-daughter so badly?

The last thing he was going to let the woman do was stick around so she could gloat. "You've done your dam-age, now crawl back to whatever rock you slithered out from under."

She smiled at him, making his skin crawl. Elsa stepped up to him. She gave his body a lingering glance. "Aren't you a feisty one? We could have a good time together."

"Go."

Elsa sighed. "Such a pity." She moved on to Sage. "This isn't over."

"I didn't think it was." Sage lifted her chin. "We are just getting started."

Elsa let out an evil cackle. "We'll see about that." She glanced back at Trey. "As for you, Quentin Thomas Rous-seau III, I'm not sure you're as much of a challenge as your father."

His gaze sought out Sage. Her eyes reflected the shock and disbelief. He wished he could tell her that Elsa was lying, but he couldn't. Elsa had done what he should have done long ago.

Sage's mouth opened but no words came out. Her gaze moved from Elsa to him.

"Oops. There I go again, letting that cat out of the bag." A toothy grin lit up the woman's face. "I'm sure you two must have things to discuss."

Elsa cackled as she swept past them and headed for the bank of elevators. Trey waited until Elsa was out of earshot before he said, "Sage, I can explain."

It was too late. The damage was done. It was written all over Sage's beautiful face. The disappointment and distrust reflected in her eyes sliced through his heart.

"I don't even know what to call you anymore. Quentin? Thomas? Trey?"

Trey stood tall, ready to face what he'd done. "You can call me Trey. It was my nickname in boarding school."

"Fine. Trey, I have just one question." Her shiny gaze never wavered from his.

He already knew the question, but he wouldn't take away her right to ask it. He owed her that much and more.

"Go ahead." He thought he was ready for her words. He was tough. He was used to facing life alone. And he never thought this relationship, whatever title you wanted to hang on it, would last.

Sage leveled her shoulders and lifted her chin. "Was everything we shared a lie? Were you secretly laughing when I opened up about my past?"

That wasn't the question he'd been anticipating. He thought she'd want him to confirm that he was indeed Quentin Thomas Rousseau III. But she'd jumped ahead. She was already questioning everything they'd ever shared.

"No. It wasn't a lie."

"And the château? Is it yours?"

"Yes."

"Everything was a lie."

"No, it wasn't. Please believe me."

"I don't."

As he looked into her eyes, he could see that he'd already lost her. She'd already closed him off and relegated him to the list of people in her life that had hurt and betrayed her.

The guilt piled on him. He needed to say so much, but before he could figure out where to begin, Sage turned her back on him, and with her chin held high, she walked away.

He'd hurt the kindest, most generous person he'd ever known. He didn't deserve to be forgiven, but he wanted her forgiveness as much as he needed oxygen.

How did he convince her that these growing feelings were very real indeed—more so than he'd ever thought possible?

CHAPTER TWELVE

SHE WOULD NOT look over her shoulder.

She would not.

Sage's heart ached as she walked away from Trey or Quentin or whatever he wanted to call himself. She'd thought at last she found someone that she could trust. Someone that would be a true friend. She couldn't have been more wrong.

Why hadn't she seen it? It was all right there in front of her if she'd had been thinking with her head instead of her heart.

There was his Rolex watch. That was no knockoff. It was the genuine article. And now that she thought of it, he did bear a slight resemblance to his father. And there were his fine clothes including more than one tux. Those definitely didn't come from a secondhand shop like her red gown.

The elevator deposited her on the ground floor. She didn't waste any time heading for the door. She should shove aside all these tangled emotions and work. It was her reason for being in France. But the lump in her throat would keep her from speaking to anyone.

She walked straight out the front door and kept walking with no particular destination in mind. All the while, she continued to think of the telltale signs of his deception. His résumé, it had been too perfect. She wondered which things he had told her were the truth and which were the lies. She shook her head. No, she didn't want to know. It'd only make it worse.

The more she thought of Trey, the faster she walked. Her vision blurred, but she blinked it back into focus. Why in the world had she thought he would be different?

Here she was trying to report on facts for the magazine and she couldn't even get the facts right in her own life. If people knew how gullible she was, they would never trust anything she published. And she couldn't blame them.

Trey probably laughed behind her back, thinking how easily he'd been able to deceive her. But why do it? Why try to fool her?

That last question dogged her the rest of the way back to the château. She tried every conceivable answer, but none of them made sense. What did he hope to accomplish by playing the part of her assistant?

She shook her head, trying to chase away the taunting questions. She had other matters that needed her attention. Once in her room, she grabbed her phone and started calling every hotel in Cannes. With the festival in full swing, she was hoping that there would be an early checkout.

Call after call, she learned there were no rooms in Cannes...anywhere. She sighed. She didn't want to give up on her plans for the magazine. She was running out of time before the next board meeting where she had to present her plan for the restructure and sustainability of the magazine.

She needed caffeine. It would make her feel better. And maybe some chocolate. But first the coffee.

She had just reached the bottom of the stairs when Trey came through the door. His face was drawn and his hair was scattered as though he'd been raking his fingers through it. Was it wrong that she took some comfort in the fact that he was unhappy that his plan had been ruined?

His gaze met hers. "Sage, we need to talk."

"I think we said everything we need to say." She turned

to head to the back of the house. And then on second thought, she turned back to Trey. "There is one thing."

"What's that?"

"You're fired."

With the tiniest bit of satisfaction, she turned and walked away. She still didn't understand his motive. She knew Elsa was not above blackmail or other devious motives. But Sage just couldn't believe Elsa was behind Trey's actions. She'd seen Trey's reaction to Elsa. They definitely weren't working together.

So what was going on?

Fired.

As he watched her walk away, the word echoed in Trey's mind. It was a first for him. Having been his own boss since college, he'd never been in this position. And even though he was the CEO, the fact that Sage felt the need to fire him pricked his ego.

But what was bothering him most of all was the fact that he'd hurt her. Sage had been nothing but good to him. Looking back now, he realized his excuses for not telling her were because he knew once the truth was out there that Sage wouldn't look at him the same way.

He hadn't wanted to lose the close connection that they'd developed. It was new and fragile. It was a connection unlike any other he'd ever experienced in his life.

He should go after Sage. If the problem festered, there would be absolutely no chance for him to repair the damage. He still wasn't sure they could ever recapture what they had. Which was what?

They worked well together, but this thing between them went deeper. But how deep? He wasn't the commitment type. He supposed he'd gotten that from his father.

He didn't want to end up in a relationship like his parents. They never divorced, but they never lived together after his father walked away. He never understood why they'd remained married. What was the point of marriage?

He gave himself a mental shake. He didn't want to get caught up in the ghosts of the past. Right now, he had enough problems in the present. When it came to Sage, nothing was easy. And now he had to make amends—no, he *wanted* to make amends. There was definitely a difference between the two.

He started walking. He didn't know what he was going to say to her. Was there anything he could say that would convince her that they could still work together until the end of the festival? The fact that she was still at the château had to be a good sign, right? And then he remembered the festival and the lack of accommodations. It worked out for him.

At last, he caught up to her on the patio. "Sage. We need to talk."

She didn't even turn to look at him when she said, "We've said everything. There's nothing left to say."

"You might have said everything, but I didn't." He moved to stand in front of her. She averted her gaze, but that wouldn't deter him. "Sage, I'm sorry. I never meant to hurt you."

Her gaze met his. "What did you think was going to happen when you deceived me? That I'd never find out?"

"In the beginning, I didn't even consider how my plan might hurt others. I was after information and working as your assistant was the best way to gain unbiased information. I never factored in the people I'd be working with."

He could see the wheels of her mind spinning. "What information?"

"Can we sit down and talk?" He didn't want to make it easy for her to walk away when she heard something she didn't like.

Sage hesitated. Then she made her way over to a bench. "I don't know why I'm doing this."

"Because you need answers. You want to know why a CEO would go undercover in his own company."

"I do. So tell me. But don't think it will change anything between us." There was a firmness in her voice.

He knew it would take more than this talk in order for Sage to forgive him. But it was a start and that had to be enough…for now.

"Let me start at the beginning. How much do you know about my father and the trouble he got the magazine into?"

She shrugged. "Not a whole lot."

And so Trey revealed to her how his father had in recent years gone with the easy, sensational headlines and played it loose with the truth. And he'd gotten away with it until he started writing a string of fabricated stories about Deacon Santoro. The movie star had threatened a lawsuit that would put the whole corporation in jeopardy. At last, they settled out of court for a nominal amount and the removal of Trey's father from the business, but the settlement also included changing the editorial content. And that's where Sage came into the story.

"That explains the past, but it doesn't tell me why you entered my life," Sage said.

"With my father stepping down from the company, I was in line for the CEO position. It was my chance to do what I'd always wanted."

"What's that? Run the magazine? And I got in your way?"

Trey shook his head. "No. I never wanted any part of the magazine."

"But why?"

"Because it's all my father ever cared about. It wasn't me or my mother. It was *QTR*. And I just wanted him to know what it's like to lose something he loved."

Sage gasped. "You want to destroy *QTR* to get even with your father. But what about all the history? That magazine has been in your family for generations."

"Seven generations to be exact. I am the seventh heir. And I thought the last."

"You thought? You've changed your mind?" There was a note of hope in her voice.

He turned to look directly into her eyes. "You are a very passionate woman. When you get excited about something, it shows in your face, your voice—it's infectious."

"And that's how you now feel about the magazine?" Suspicion reflected in her eyes.

"I didn't at first. I thought you were crazy for wanting to save that dying rag. I couldn't imagine what you saw in the magazine to drive you to save it."

"And now?" Though the glint of suspicion still showed in her eyes, there was also the spark of curiosity.

"And then I started working with you. It was then that I saw what the magazine could be—what good it could do."

"This all sounds too convenient. Why should I believe you?"

"You shouldn't. Not after what I've done. But I wanted you to know that you opened my eyes to the potential of *QTR*."

"And if the future of the magazine were just up to you?"

"I'd continue to help you rebuild it. But it's not up to me. I'm just one vote on the board. And there is some staunch opposition."

"I guess you'd know since you were one of them."

He nodded. There was no denying it. "But if my mind can be changed, so can theirs."

"But not without a plan for the upcoming year. I need a solid production schedule. And now between the bad reputation of the magazine and Elsa's conniving, I don't have anyone on the calendar."

"You still have time."

"No, I don't. I'm leaving tomorrow. I'm flying back to California and putting this whole miserable experience behind me."

The thought that he caused her to give up hurt him more than he thought possible. He refused to give up—on the magazine and especially on setting things right with Sage.

"Don't go." The words passed his lips before he could think through the ramifications.

"Why? So you can lie to me some more?"

"I'm not lying to you. Things can never be the same again, but I will prove to you that I can do better—that you can trust me."

"With us being on opposite sides of the magazine?"

"I told you I've changed my mind."

"And you expect me to just believe you? Would you have ever told me the truth if Elsa hadn't outed you?"

He lowered his head. "I tried to tell you several times. There was always a convenient excuse to put it off. It just never seemed like the right time. We were getting along so well and I... I didn't want to ruin what we had."

"You certainly did that."

He scratched at his beard. "I know. And I'm sorry."

"At least your father must be happy that you changed your mind about the magazine."

"He doesn't know."

"But why not?"

"My father and I aren't close. In fact—" he paused because it still hurt for him to admit "—I don't know him at all."

"You don't?"

He shook his head. "My father left my mother when I was three years old. He said he couldn't run his magazine from France."

"Why didn't your mother go with him?"

"She said her life was in France. And that she would never fit into his world any more than he fit into hers."

"That's so sad."

Trey shrugged. "I think there was more to the story, but my mother died before she told me the whole truth. She didn't like talking about my father."

"It must have been tough being the child of divorced parents."

"That's the thing, they never divorced. In fact, my father showed up at my mother's funeral. He tried to reach out to me but I told him it was too little, too late."

"And that's it? You haven't spoken to him since?"

Trey turned to Sage. "Why do you sound so surprised?"

"It's just that any time your father spoke of you, he always had such glowing reports."

"He talked about me?" Trey found that hard to believe. Anxious to turn the spotlight off himself, Trey realized this was his chance to learn more about Sage. "How do you know my father?"

"We initially met when I interned for him during the summer of my junior and senior years of college."

"You must have made quite an impression on my father."

She shrugged. "I'm not so sure it was that as much as he thought when he hired me that he would be able to control me."

Trey smiled. "I'm guessing you set him straight."

"I did. And he wasn't too happy about it, but by then there was nothing he could do." She turned to him. "But he does care about you. Remember those photos of you and your mother? He really did keep them on his desk. A person doesn't do that unless they care."

Trey shook his head. "He doesn't. I can assure you of that. He made it clear when he left."

Sage reached out and placed her hand over his. "I don't

know what went wrong between your parents, but I'm telling you he never stopped caring about you. Maybe you should talk to him. Hear his side—"

"No." Trey got to his feet. "That isn't going to happen."

"I don't have to tell you that if you pass up this chance, you might not get another. I lost both of my parents and you lost your mother. This is your chance to get answers."

Trey turned to her. He didn't know how things had gotten so turned around. He was supposed to be apologizing for his deception, but somehow they were now delving into his past. And he had to put a stop to it.

"I don't need answers." There was absolutely no hesitation in his voice. "I don't want that man in my life. I'm fine on my own."

Her gaze studied him for a moment and then there was a glint of sympathy. "Everyone needs somebody."

The truth poked at his heart, but he refused to acknowledge it. "What about you? I don't see you going out of your way to draw people into your life."

"Really? Are you so sure about that?"

He paused. That wasn't the answer he'd been expecting. Where was she going with it?

He pressed his hand to his sides. "Okay. Who have you let into your life?"

She arched a fine brow. "You, for starters."

It was true. She had let him in. She'd told him about her past and about Elsa. She'd shared so much with him and he'd let her down.

"And there are my roommates, Lisa and Ann. Louise, at the office, is like a mother hen. And I've gotten to know everyone at the office. We're like one big, dysfunctional family."

Everything she'd said was true. Because it wasn't the traditional sense of a family, he hadn't recognized it as such. But she was right; she took what she had and made a support system for herself. It was more than he had done. Suddenly he felt so alone in this world—it was a staggering moment—much like what he'd felt at his mother's funeral.

And when they left Cannes, he knew Sage would return to her makeshift family with their laughter, teasing and closeness. He, on the other hand, would return to San Francisco where he spent hours in solitude working on his newest security software. And when he was at the office, people kept their distance because he was the boss—not a boss like Sage.

And there was his father. His father might mistakenly think Trey's change of mind about the magazine meant he changed his mind about him, but nothing could be farther from the truth. His father would never again have anything to do with the magazine or QTR International.

If Trey had his way, Sage would stay on as managing editor. But would she agree after what she'd learned?

His gaze met hers. "I just wanted to tell you that I'm sorry. I never meant for things to work out like they have."

And with that he turned and walked away. Too much had been said that evening. He needed to clear his head. Those things Sage had said about his father…they couldn't be right. His father had more than thirty years to be a part of his life and he hadn't done it. Perhaps he'd just been putting on a show for people.

Sage was such an optimist. He knew she wanted him to have a relationship with his father—something she would never have again. But she had to understand that their fathers were very different men. It was never going to happen for him.

CHAPTER THIRTEEN

WHAT TO DO?

After a restless night, Sage was up early. Her conversation with Trey kept rolling around in her mind. Logic told her not to believe him—that he wasn't to be trusted. But her heart said the feelings and emotions they'd shared had been genuine.

Her phone buzzed. She glanced at the caller ID, finding it was her private investigator. She immediately answered. "Have you learned something?"

"I'm on to something big," the man said.

"Tell me."

"It's not complete and I want to be sure before I give you the information. It might take me extra time. Are the added fees going to be a problem?"

Yes. She was giving him every single cent aside from her rent and food. She thought of the money she was going to use to fly home early. The airline wouldn't switch the return portion of her ticket and so she'd have to purchase a new one. But in the light of day, things with Trey didn't appear so dire. If she stayed, it'd save a lot of money.

"Miss White?"

"No. It won't be a problem." She needed answers and she'd do whatever it took to get them.

"Okay. I need a few more details and then I'll give you everything I've collected. I think it's what you're after."

And then a thought came to Sage. Part of her told her not to do it, but a louder voice in her head said it was better to know the truth. "Did you uncover any information regarding Trey…er… Quentin Thomas Rousseau III being involved with Elsa?"

"No. He's not."

The answer came so quickly that it surprised her. "Are you sure?"

"One hundred percent positive."

It didn't get any more certain. "Thanks. Keep digging into Elsa's past. There's something there that she doesn't want us to know about." And with any luck it would be the key to Sage regaining her legacy.

She ended the call knowing that staying here with Trey or Quentin or whatever he wanted to call himself wouldn't be easy. Could she avoid him? Not likely since they were sharing the house. There had to be some way to coexist for a little longer.

Trey refilled his coffee for the fourth time the next morning.

He'd tossed and turned most of the night. Before sunrise, he'd climbed out of bed. He needed to think about something besides how bad he'd screwed things up with Sage.

A glance in the bathroom mirror showed proof of his bad night. But as he scratched at the irritating beard, he realized there was nothing stopping him from shaving. In fact, there was no reason not to put in his contacts. At last, he could get back to being himself. Although there were a couple of changes he wanted to keep—his nickname and the shorter hair.

After his shower and shave, Trey paced back and forth in the kitchen in his bare feet while a new pot of coffee brewed. He yawned and stretched. It'd been a long time since he'd pulled an all-nighter.

"Mind if I come in?"

The sound of Sage's voice had him turning. "Sure. You don't have to ask. You are always welcome."

She openly stared at him.

Had he nicked himself shaving? "What's wrong?"

"You. I mean, you look so different." She continued gazing at him. "Is this how you normally look when you're not pretending to be an assistant?"

"I am sorry about that." He could tell by the stony look in her eyes that his apology didn't sway her. "Yes, this is me except for the hair. I used to wear it longer, much longer. But I'm liking this shorter style. It's a lot easier to deal with. What do you think?"

She shrugged and moved past him toward the freshly brewed coffee. She poured herself a cupful. He noticed that she didn't offer to get him any. It was to be expected.

He wondered what it'd take to get them past this awkward spot. There had to be a way because the future of the magazine was at stake. But more than that, he wouldn't let Sage lose and Elsa win.

Now, he had to prove to Sage that they made a great team and together they could fend off Elsa. "We're going to have to work together if we're going to defeat Elsa."

"This is my fight." Her voice was firm.

"It's our fight. Yours and mine."

She gave him a strange look. "Why would you take on my stepmother?"

"You mean besides the fact that I hate the way she treats you?"

Sage nodded.

It was time he laid out the truth—a truth that even he found surprising. "Because of you, I have found an appreciation for *QTR*." Her eyes widened but she remained quiet and so he continued. "You've shown me what it could be. I like the idea of using it to show the good parts of life. The news these days is so full of depressing topics that

I'd like to be a part of showing the world the positive side of life. And I'm thinking my ancestors would have liked the idea of their magazine being an instrument for good."

"You mean there's something good that has come from all of this?"

"If you're referring to my attitude toward keeping the magazine, then yes."

"And then you can hand it down to your son—"

"No, that isn't going to happen. I'm not going to put a child through what I experienced growing up."

"You don't need to. I've known both you and your father. Yes, there are some similarities but you are very different people. I could see you being a loving, involved father—"

"Sage, stop. It isn't going to happen. I want to see the magazine survive. Nothing more."

A frown settled on her face.

"Stop looking at me like I just ran over your teddy bear."

"It's not you. It's just that the future of the magazine isn't up to me or you. There's the board to contend with and I have a meeting with them at the end of the month to determine whether the magazine continues or is closed down. And right now, I do not have a compelling calendar to show them. If I don't get some big names to grace the covers, they'll be sure to close us."

"You forget that I'm the CEO. I have sway over that board. We'll compile a winning calendar of interviews. And as for Elsa, we'll beat her at her own game."

"How? I thought about it all night and haven't come up with anything except locking her in her hotel room. Or better yet, stuffing her in a suitcase and putting her in the cargo hold of the first plane bound for the States."

Trey laughed. "I didn't know you had such a devious mind."

Sage still didn't smile when she said, "Oh, trust me. I have my moments."

"Anything you care to share?"

"Not yet."

Well, he had to admit that he was intrigued now. There was so much more to Sage than her sunny smile and friendly personality. Beneath her beauty was a strong businesswoman that wasn't afraid to go after what she wanted. He was looking forward to this battle with Sage by his side.

But the most important thing to him was putting the smile back on Sage's face. He had stolen it away and that acknowledgment dug at him. If it was the last thing he did, he would make Sage happy again—even if it meant exiting her life after *QTR* was secure.

He was going to step up his game.

He was no longer an observer.

Trey had signed on to fight for the magazine and that meant thinking outside the box.

They'd just finished watching the premiere of a French film that made a statement about caring for those with mental health issues. It was very powerful. He wondered if Sage knew the language or if she was taking advantage of the subtitles. He wouldn't know because their communication so far that day had pertained to business only—nothing personal.

Outside the theater, a mass of photographers were snapping more photos of the stars. One photographer told Trey and Sage to pose. She didn't want to, but Trey coaxed her into it. He casually placed his arm around her waist. He longed to pull her closer, but he resisted the urge.

As soon as the photo was taken, Sage pulled away. She immediately set to work talking to any performer who would listen to her.

The more he observed her, the more he knew that there

was no stopping her. Just like now, as they stood outside the theater, she was doing her best to make connections. One by one, people turned away from her. Trey wanted to go up to them and tell them to quit being so rude, but he knew Sage wouldn't appreciate the gesture nor would it help their situation.

Sage was a strong woman who didn't need anyone to take care of her. Her strength and determination impressed him. She didn't turn the magazine around with backdoor deals. She didn't pay people off. She didn't make outrageous promises. She did absolutely nothing wrong.

Sage turned the magazine around with integrity, smarts and kindness.

Kindness. Who would have figured?

She was kind to people, found out what they were passionate about and then agreed to get on board to further their pet projects. It was a win-win for everyone.

Now how did you stop something that was so good?

"Trey, this isn't working." Sage frowned. "Everyone sees the name of my publication and turns away. Or worse, they tell me what they think of *QTR*. And it's nothing I would repeat. Maybe I should propose to the board that we take on a new name."

Trey shook his head. "The reputation my father put upon the magazine will follow you, even through a name-change."

"Then maybe I should take off my badge. At least then people will give me a chance before they reject what I'm offering."

"You need your badge to give you access to the festival events, but…" He paused to give this some thought.

"But what?"

She'd been on to something. He just needed to think for a moment.

"Trey. Speak."

"Maybe you need a different approach."

"You mean instead of being up front about the magazine I represent?" When he nodded, she said, "Even though it's clearly printed on my press badge?"

He hadn't gotten this far in business without cutting some corners or playing a little subterfuge. If people got to know Sage without the curse of *QTR* hanging around her neck, both literally and figuratively, they would see that she would never sink to the level of his father.

And then he realized what they needed to do. He looked at the worried expression on her face and couldn't wait to replace it with one of her bright, contagious smiles.

"Come with me." And without thinking, he took her hand in his.

Her hand felt good wrapped around his. It was like they were two pieces of a puzzle and they fit together. He made a point of zigzagging through the crowd of smartly dressed people.

When they'd cleared the crowd of people, Sage withdrew her hand. "Where are we going?"

"You'll see."

"I'd rather know. I really need to get back there and try to make some sort of connection, even if I have to hang a sign around my neck that says *QTR* has changed."

He smiled at her as he led her toward Cannes' elite shops. "You're on the right track."

"I am?" She sent him a puzzled look. "We're going to make a sign?"

He chuckled. "Nothing quite so obvious."

"Now you have me intrigued. What exactly are you up to?"

"I told you, you'll see soon enough. Just enjoy the sunshine and the walk." He resisted the urge to take her hand back in his.

Soon they arrived at the shopping area. Now he just had to find the right shop.

"If you would tell me what you're searching for, I could help."

At that moment, he spotted it. "No need. I found it."

They crossed the street and approached the exclusive jewelry store. "We're here."

"Here?" Sage glanced at the showroom window and then back at him. "You want to go jewelry shopping now?"

He shrugged. "It seemed like a good idea at the time. Come on. Let's have a look inside."

Without waiting for her to protest, he opened the door for her. Sage hesitated, but eventually she stepped forward.

He knew what he was looking for. He passed by the gemstones, the sparkling diamond rings and the designer watches. And then he stopped in front of a glass case.

A young woman with a blond ponytail and navy blue dress stepped up to them. "Is there something I can show you?"

Sage leaned closer and whispered, "What are you doing?"

"Trust me." He stared in the brightly lit glass case. His gaze skimmed past gold chains and paused at a bunch of large pendants. There were flowers, animals and other artistic shapes. "What's your favorite color?"

"Red. A deep wine red."

He glanced around until he found a silver filigree flower pendant that was accented with rubies. It was large and it was beautiful. It would do.

He pointed to it. "That one."

The young woman removed it from the case. "Would you like to try it on?"

He gave Sage a quick glance. She was still frowning at him. He turned back to the saleswoman. "That's okay. We'll take it."

With a frustrated sigh, Sage turned for the door.

He knew in this type of store that prices wouldn't be marked on the jewelry. You didn't come in here unless you could afford the precious gems. And right now, he'd pay anything to make things right with Sage. But he knew this necklace wouldn't buy him forgiveness. It wasn't why he'd purchased it.

Once he'd paid for the necklace, he joined Sage on the sidewalk. "I was worried you wouldn't wait for me."

"If you bought that for me, take it back. You should spend your money on someone you care about."

"I care about you." The words popped out before he could stop them. Was that true? Did he care about her? Now wasn't the time to evaluate his emotions. He had to correct his slipup. "You know I care about you getting the magazine turned around."

She continued to look at him as though not sure she believed him. Finally, she glanced away. "You know you can't put that through on an expense report, right?"

"I know. It'll be fine. Trust me." He reached inside the fancy bag and withdrew the black velvet box. "Let's try this on."

Sage continued to mutter about how foolish this was, but once the necklace was on her, she quieted down. "It covers part of my badge."

"The important part. The magazine's name."

She sent him a puzzled look, which was quickly replaced with a smile. "You want people to notice the necklace instead of the name of our magazine."

"Exactly. First impressions are so important. There's time later for telling them that you represent *QTR*."

She smiled at him. "I knew there was a reason I hired you."

"As I recall, I predicted you would hire me because I was the best."

"The best, huh?"

For a moment, things were easy and fun between them. And the way she smiled at him made him want to lean in and kiss her. He knew that wasn't possible, but it didn't make him desire her any less.

He cleared his throat. "We should get back to the festival and see if this beauty helps you land an interview or two."

"Or three," she added. As they started to walk side by side, she said, "I'll pay you back for this."

He didn't say anything, not wanting to ruin this moment of easiness. He'd missed the laughing, smiling Sage more than he thought possible. This was a start, he just had to build on it—show her that she wasn't wrong about him.

CHAPTER FOURTEEN

SAGE FINGERED THE beautiful pendant.

It felt strange to be wearing a piece of jewelry purchased by Trey. She knew it was purely a strategic move and that there weren't any emotions tied to it. But every time she looked at it, her heart beat faster.

"Hey, where'd you go?" Trey stared at her across an umbrella table where they'd been enjoying a light lunch.

"I was just thinking I shouldn't be sitting here. I should be circulating and putting your plan to work."

"You don't have to push yourself every minute of the day. Sometimes you need to just enjoy yourself."

"I will once I accomplish what I came here to do."

He looked at her like he didn't believe her. "You've accomplished a lot in the short amount of time since you've been at *QTR*."

"And there's so much more to do." Her gaze moved over his shoulder, landing on an A-list actress. Her last two movies had been box office hits.

Trey pulled up the notes he'd made about the actress's past films, upcoming ventures and interests. He read off the information to Sage. Armed with the information to make this hopefully a successful conversation, Sage stood up.

"Good luck," he said. "If you don't need me, I'm going to do some mingling. I'll text you if I get something."

Her gaze kept straying back to the actress, making sure she didn't get away. When she glanced back at Trey, she said, "I'll see you back at the château."

She moved away quickly to catch up with the actress.

You can do this. They'll like your idea. You just have to get them to listen.

"Hi." Sage smiled as she approached the young woman. "Aren't you Abigail Wright from the movie *Visitors from Beyond*?"

"Why, yes, I am." The young woman smiled at being recognized from one of the films being played here at the festival. "Did you enjoy it?"

"I did."

They went on to discuss the film for a couple of minutes. Perhaps Trey had been right about the beautiful piece of jewelry. So far it had been her lucky charm.

The actress's gaze strayed to Sage's badge, which was still obscured by the pendant. "I see you are with the press."

"I am. And I would love to interview you." She was thankful Trey had researched the actress's professional background as well as her volunteer work. "I know you've done some volunteering to build houses for those less fortunate."

The actress's face lit up. "I have. It's a really great venture."

"Perhaps we could frame the interview around the volunteer work you've done and then segue into your films."

"I would like that. What outlet are you with?"

This was the moment of truth. *"QTR Magazine."*

The young woman paused and Sage prayed she wouldn't change her mind about the interview. At last, the actress gave Sage her contact information and they agreed to a time and location.

Sage couldn't tell if the actress was too new to the business to know about the scandalous past of *QTR* or if she was so hungry for attention that she didn't care. Either way, it had worked out for Sage.

One interview down, more to go. And it was thanks to Trey. He was the one that thought of the lovely piece of jewelry to camouflage her true identity. She hoped one day soon those tactics wouldn't be necessary. She wanted *QTR Magazine* to be synonymous with integrity. But for now, Trey had earned a few points in his favor.

Sage adjusted the pendant over her pink press badge, straightened her shoulders and lifted her chin. Steadily putting one foot in front of the other, she headed for the group of people gathered outside the Debussy Theatre.

She worked the crowd like a pro. Agents exchanged business cards with Sage, giving her a sense of optimism. No, it wasn't a firm date for an interview, but each card represented an open door. And she planned to march through those doors.

She'd just approached Johnny Volt, an action movie superstar, when Elsa materialized out of nowhere. Trying to ignore her stepmother's looming presence, Sage said, "It's so nice to meet you."

Sage and Johnny shook hands and exchanged pleasantries.

This was her chance to turn this casual conversation into something more productive. "Mr. Volt—"

"Please, call me Johnny."

"Okay. Johnny, I've heard a lot about your movie releasing in August. It's projected to be a box office hit just like the first one. I was wondering if you'd be interested in a magazine cover and a feature article."

"What magazine are you with?"

"Excuse me." Elsa took that moment to interrupt. "I'm Elsa."

Sage smothered a groan. She would not give Elsa the satisfaction of seeing how her interruption bothered her. Still, it annoyed Sage how the woman descended upon them mid-conversation and announced her name like she was one of those celebrities that only went by their first name. Did she really think she was that big of a name?

"If you'll excuse us," Sage said in a restrained tone, "we were in the middle of a conversation."

Elsa turned back to Johnny. "Before you agree to anything with *QTR*, you'll want to hear what I can offer you. It'll far surpass anything they can do."

Johnny glanced at Elsa with disdain. "You heard her. We're talking. Privately. Now if you'll excuse us."

Elsa's deep-red lips gaped. It would appear that she was not used to being dismissed. Sage struggled to keep from laughing at the horrified expression on Elsa's face when Johnny turned his back to her.

"Is she gone yet?"

With a loud sigh, Elsa turned on her five-inch heels and walked away.

"She is now." Sage stopped herself from apologizing for her stepmother. In the past, that's exactly what she would have done. But not now. She may share her last name with the woman, but she wasn't family. And Elsa's actions were no reflection on her.

"I would like to hear more about what you have to offer. Can I have your phone?" Johnny held out his hand.

She couldn't believe that *the* Johnny Volt was not only talking to her, but he was also going to put his number in her phone. With a slightly shaky hand, she gave him her phone.

He quickly typed in his information. "Give me a call next week and we'll set something up." He returned the phone. "But now I have to go. It was good to meet you."

After Johnny disappeared into the crowd, Trey approached her. "I saw Elsa and got concerned. What did I miss?"

"I'd say that good won out over evil."

Trey laughed. She loved the sound of his laugh. It was

deep and warm. Her gaze caught and held his longer than necessary.

It would be so easy to forgive and forget, but she couldn't. She knew the price of trusting someone and then having them turn on you. Trey already proved he was someone she couldn't trust. She wouldn't make the same mistake again.

Using every bit of willpower, she glanced away. She refused to let down the wall around her heart. He'd already had his chance. That's all he got—but her heart didn't agree.

He had to do more.

The following afternoon, Trey had given a lot of thought to how he could make amends with Sage. He knew nothing he did would undo the past, but he wanted to show her he was better than that—he wanted to prove it to himself.

He'd let himself get so caught up in evening the score with his father that he hadn't realized the price it would exact from those around him.

He needed to get back to being himself.

He needed Sage to trust him again. And the pendant had been a start, but he wanted to do something extra special—something to put the spark back in Sage's big, beautiful eyes. And he had the inkling of an idea that just might do the trick. But he couldn't do it alone.

It was midway into the afternoon when Trey decided to make his departure. They had just arrived outside the Grand Theatre Lumière. The red carpet was in full action with celebrities in designer gowns, sparkling gems and black tuxes. When a celebrity stepped onto the carpet, camera flashes lit up the area. There were so many cameras that it was blinding.

Sage leaned close to him to speak over the crowd. "Did

you see George? Oh, look, there's Uma. This movie is going to be amazing."

He loved hearing the enthusiasm in Sage's voice. Day by day, things were getting better between them. Though he wished the process was faster, he was grateful they'd made it this far.

He leaned close to her ear, catching the sweet scent of jasmine. He lingered for a moment, breathing in her intoxicating scent. When someone bumped into him, it jarred him back to his senses.

"Would you mind if I went back to the château for a bit?"

Concern filled Sage's eyes but in a blink it was gone. "Sure. I've got this. I got caught up in the fact that people are starting to talk with us. But when I mention an interview or a cover, they shy away."

"You'll nail it. Just give it time. The festival seems like a really big crowd, but it's really rather small when it comes to passing information. Once it gets around that you are so nice and have integrity, they will view *QTR* in a different light."

She looked at him with skepticism. "I don't know about that."

"Trust me." The words were out before he realized that was the exact wrong thing for him to say to her. "Forget that. Trust yourself and believe that you can do this."

As he walked away, he realized his campaign to win back Sage's friendship and perhaps her trust had to be many pronged. The first would be celebrating her birthday, which was quickly approaching. It landed on the next to the last day of the festival. And it wasn't going to be any birthday party. He had something very special in mind.

And the other idea was to deal with Elsa. He knew that Sage thought she could handle her, but he had to do something to help. That woman, she just couldn't get away with the way she treated Sage.

He would see about getting his group of online friends, aka hackers, to lend a hand. He'd never needed their help before, but they owed him for various things in the past. This was his time to collect. He needed to know everything about Elsa and all the things she didn't want other people to know—including her questionable acquisition of Sage's family company.

He strode quickly to the château. He needed to speak with Maria, his housekeeper, before she left for the day. She had been with him since he was a boy. In many ways, she was as much a mother to him as his own mother.

As soon as Trey entered the house, he headed for the kitchen. It was Maria's favorite room. She'd told him that numerous times over the years. And he had to agree with her. It was spacious, modern and had the most terrific view of the sea. It was one of the reasons he'd held on to the place.

"Maria." He entered the kitchen and came to a stop. He glanced all around, but she was nowhere to be found. "Maria?"

He started walking through the house looking for her. After covering the ground floor, he was starting to suspect she'd completed her work early and had gone home. He supposed he could phone her, but he'd rather go over the details in person.

He reached the top of the steps when the door to Sage's room opened. Maria stepped into the hallway. When her gaze caught him standing in the hallway, she jumped and pressed a hand to her chest.

When she spoke, it was in French. Though she also spoke English, she preferred her native language. "You startled me." She smiled at him. "I didn't know that anyone had returned."

"Sorry, it's just me."

"Can I get you anything?"

"I could really use your help."

Her eyes widened with interest. "Certainly. What do you need?"

"I need your help planning a birthday party for Sage. If you could take care of coordinating the food and staff, I'll take care of the invitations."

Maria smiled. "You really like her, don't you?"

He hesitated. Until now, he hadn't even admitted to himself about his growing feelings for Sage. For so long, he'd tried holding her at arm's length, but somewhere between rescuing Happy and the Red Heart Gala she'd broken through his barriers.

He wanted to believe that this was the beginning for them. He wanted to believe they could write a different story than the unhappy one his parents had lived.

"I... I do care about her. But I've really messed things up."

Maria patted his arm and sent him a sympathetic look. "Did you apologize?"

He nodded. "But it was more than an apology could cover."

"Give her time. Keep showing her that you care. She'll come around."

"I hope you're right."

"Of course I am. Who could resist that smile?" She patted his cheek. "Now, you'll need to give me a menu so I can get started shopping."

"About that, I have some very specific ideas to run by you."

Together they entered his office and they plotted out a birthday party that would be unlike any other.

CHAPTER FIFTEEN

THE FESTIVAL WAS nearing the end.

Late Thursday afternoon, Sage stared at her production calendar for the magazine; it still had noticeable gaps. For all their efforts, she still couldn't secure all the necessary interviews. And without a rock-solid plan, the board would vote against her. She was starting to wonder if this was a lost cause.

But if the magazine failed, it meant she wouldn't be able to keep up her payments to the private investigator. And she knew if he were taken off the case now, she would probably never get this close to uncovering Elsa's lies again.

And then there was Trey. She should be happy that the closing of the magazine meant he would be out of her life, but try as she did to dislike him—and she did try hard— there was something about him that made her want to forgive him. Had she forgiven him? Perhaps. But did she trust him? That was another story.

Knock. Knock.

"Come in." Sage looked up from the desk in her room.

The door swung open and Trey appeared. "I was wondering if you might be interested in an early dinner here at the château before we leave for the party."

"That sounds perfect. I just need to finish this email."

Trey nodded in understanding. "There's also something I'd like to discuss with you. Can you meet me downstairs when you're finished?"

She nodded and he left.

That was strange. She'd noticed the serious tone in his voice. In fact, his whole face wore a serious expression. What had happened? Or did he have another secret to reveal? Her heart sank. Was there something else he'd been lying to her about?

She turned back to her email, but it suddenly didn't seem like such a priority. She couldn't dismiss her worry. What if it wasn't Trey? What if Elsa was causing more problems?

Deciding she could finish the email later, she closed her laptop. She hurried downstairs. If her stepmother was causing problems for Trey, she would…she would do something. She just didn't know what that something would be. Messing with her was one thing, but messing with someone she cared about was quite another.

Sage came to a stop on the bottom step. Did she care about Trey? Her heart started to pound. The truth was she *did* care about him. She probably shouldn't, but her heart had won the battle over her head.

"Sage, there you are." Trey stepped in front of her. He didn't smile, not a good sign. "I thought you had an email to finish?"

"It can wait. This sounds serious."

"We can talk out on the veranda."

He waved for her to lead the way. She held her tongue until they were standing on the private balcony. But then she turned to him. "What is it? What has Elsa done now?"

His eyebrows rose. "How do you know it's her?"

Sage didn't but it was so much better than the alternative. "Call it intuition."

"Your intuition is right. I heard from one of our distributors today and they said they are discontinuing distribution of *QTR* to their supermarkets."

"What? But why?" And then realizing she already knew

the answer to her own questions, she said, "Elsa. Of course. Did they say why?"

He shook his head. "They were very short and to the point. So I took it upon myself to make inquiries with a couple of our other distributors. It seems Elsa has been making the rounds."

Sage sat down before she fell down. Her whole world felt as though it were crumbling around her. "This can't be happening. That woman won't stop until she puts me in the ground. I probably wouldn't even die in a manner that would please her."

"Hey, it's not that dire. I was able to talk to all of the other distributors and keep them on board. So we're only down one."

"For now, until Elsa finds another way to stick it to me via the magazine." Now that the shock had worn off, anger was taking over. Sage got to her feet and started to pace. "If only I had a way to stop her."

"I might be able to help you."

"What? But how?"

"You know how I'm into computers and security software, right?" She nodded and he continued. "In my business, you get to know the best hackers because I need them to break into my software in order for me to make it stronger."

"So you hire criminals?"

"Pretty much. Hey, if the government can hire them, I can, too. It helps keep them out of trouble."

"But I have a feeling you've turned them back to their illegal activities."

"I'm not admitting anything. All I'll say is that I have a handful of trusted computer experts, and if there's anything in cyberspace to stop Elsa, they will find it. She has no idea what sort of war she has started." Trey looked so proud of himself that she hated to say anything. But he must have read it on her face. "What aren't you saying?"

She sighed. "I had someone do the internet thing and they couldn't turn up anything."

"They weren't looking in the dark corners these guys will be searching. I'm not saying they will, but they could look on her very own computer. That is, if they wanted to."

"I'm sure they will." She wanted to trust Trey. But he'd already let her down once. What would stop him from doing it again?

"Talk to me, Sage." The hopeful look faded from his face. He stepped up to her and reached out, taking her hands in his own. "I know I hurt you, but I promise it won't happen again. If we're going to beat Elsa, we have to work together."

He was right. They were stronger together. She'd been working on taking Elsa down by herself for the past year, but there still wasn't enough to make Elsa relinquish her hold on her family's company.

She stared deep into Trey's eyes. Inside her a war raged—to trust him or not. Having access to all of *QTR*'s files, he had the ability to hurt her. But he hadn't. Nor had he walked away after his cover was blown. He seemed genuinely interested in saving the magazine.

Maybe it was time to give him the benefit of the doubt.

Sage inhaled a deep steadying breath and then she slowly blew it out. "I also have someone digging into Elsa's web of lies. He uncovered small things, but nothing that would stand up in court and prove she didn't belong at White Publishing."

"This person, do you trust him?"

"Let's just say I trust him as much as I trust anyone who makes their living out of spying on people. So far he's proven himself reliable." Now for the latest development. "And he's on to something big."

* * *

Had she forgiven him?

It was so hard to tell.

Trey stood on the deck of the luxury yacht surrounded by celebrities in their finest attire, but he only had eyes for Sage. She was the only star in his eyes.

Her black clingy dress emphasized her curves and made it difficult to concentrate. And the thigh-high slit that gave him glimpses of her bare legs—

He halted his thoughts. He had to maintain a cool, nonchalant attitude. He couldn't risk making a move and scaring her off.

For the life of him, he couldn't read her. She said and did all the right things, but it still felt like there was a distance between them—a wall he wasn't able to scale. It made sense. Sage had been hurt repeatedly in the past. She had learned to armor herself. And he'd foolishly let her down. If only he could undo the past.

Trey forced a smile to his lips as he sidestepped the dancing couples and approached Sage. He carried an umbrella drink that all the guests were raving about. "Here you go. This drink comes highly recommended."

She accepted the orange drink topped with a pineapple chunk and a maraschino cherry. "Where's yours?"

He shook his head and held out his club soda. "I'm driving tonight."

"We didn't drive here. We hired a car, remember?"

He smiled. "I must have been distracted by this gorgeous brunette sitting next to me."

Sage arched a fine brow. "Are you flirting with me?"

"Do you want me to be?"

"That's not fair. You answered a question with a question." She sipped at her fruity drink. "Mmm… They are right. This is amazing."

"And you are changing the subject."

He turned away from all the people and stared out over the water as the Mediterranean sun hovered over the horizon splashing the sky with brilliant shades of orange and pink. Summer had come early to Cannes. And it felt good to be out here on this impressive yacht. Perhaps he'd purchase his own.

"It's a beautiful sunset, isn't it?" Sage asked.

He glanced her way. "Very beautiful indeed."

Her gaze caught his. "You weren't talking about the sunset, were you?"

"No, I wasn't." Suddenly feeling a bit warm, he downed the rest of the club soda.

Her big blue almost violet eyes stared up at him. He longed to pull her in his arms and kiss away all of her doubts. No other woman in his life—and there had been a number of them—had this profound of an effect on him.

The sea breeze swept past them, sending the long wavy strands of Sage's hair fluttering. A few pieces clung to her cheek. It was instinct for him to reach out and swipe the strands off to the side. But as his finger made contact with her smooth skin, it was like a switch had been turned on inside of him. His bottled-up attraction was released and his only thought was how soon they could be alone.

Trey struggled to fight off his pent-up longings. He was a sworn bachelor. He shouldn't care if things didn't work out with Sage. In any other scenario, he would have cut things off by now and moved on. But he couldn't walk away from her.

And if he stood here much longer, he might give in to his desire to pull her into his arms and taste her sweet kisses again and again. It was as though gravity was drawing their bodies closer together.

As though Sage could sense the direction of his thoughts, she took a step back. "The movie screening should be starting soon. It's almost dark."

Disappointment assailed him. "It is." Glancing down, he noticed his empty glass. "And I could use another cold drink. How about you?"

"I'm good. Thanks." She placed the straw between her glossy lips and sucked.

Watching her do such a simple act got to him. It conjured up other more heated thoughts. He needed to walk away and clear his head. He needed more than a cold drink—he needed a cold shower or a dip in the Mediterranean. Although, he didn't think their superstar host would appreciate him diving off the edge of the yacht in the middle of a party. But then again, it would make this party the highlight of the festival.

Trey was in no hurry to get his drink. It was just as well as there was quite a crowd at the bar. This time he requested ice water. Maybe it would cool him down.

With his icy drink in hand, he moved off to the side. When he glanced back to where he'd left Sage, the spot was empty. His gaze scanned the area and then he spotted her dancing with some man that he'd never seen before.

The man was holding her awfully close and the look on her face wasn't a happy one. Trey set aside his unfinished drink and moved toward the dance floor. He paused at the side, not sure how Sage would feel about him storming in and dragging her away from this man. But that's exactly what he wanted to do.

When her gaze caught his, she mouthed, *Help me.*

That was all the encouragement he needed. He wove his way past the other couples and stepped up to Sage. "Excuse me. Can I cut in?"

Before the man could say anything, Sage said, "Yes. I do owe you a dance."

The man frowned at both of them before he relinquished his hold on Sage and stormed off. Trey took her in his arms. He loved the way her slight form felt next to him.

When her head leaned close to his, he got a whiff of her jasmine scent. He breathed in deeper.

"You know," he said, "the last time we danced together, it didn't go so well."

"That was your fault. You rejected my kiss."

"I didn't reject you. I would never reject you."

Sage pulled back to look into his eyes. "Then what would you call it?"

"I didn't want things to get complicated. Not before I told you my true identity."

She blinked. "That's why you pulled away?"

"It's the honest truth."

He could sense something shifting within her. As they continued to dance, it was like she was digesting this bit of news and figuring out where it left them. He wanted to ask, but he decided not to push his luck.

Tomorrow was her birthday and he had a couple of surprises planned for her. Hopefully it'd be enough to finish tearing down the wall between them. For now, holding her close would have to be enough.

CHAPTER SIXTEEN

THE EVENING WAS still a mystery.

Sage had the French doors leading to her private balcony open, letting in the sea breeze. Below her room was the pool and gardens, but tonight there were white tents scattered about lit up with torches. It appeared Trey was throwing her a birthday dinner.

She had to admit she was anxious to find out what he had planned. She was quickly learning he had a flair for the dramatic. But then again, she wouldn't be opposed to a private candlelit dinner.

Her heart thump-thumped at the memory of how Trey had held her close on the yacht. He'd have kissed her, if she'd let him. So why hadn't she?

As upset as she had been with the way he entered her life, she now knew he hadn't set out to hurt anyone, except maybe himself…and his father. But Trey had changed. He was beginning to see that family and legacies meant something—they meant a lot.

She wanted to believe they could make a new start. Ever since he'd bought her the stunning pendant, the walls around her heart had started to fall. His encouragement, unwavering support and constant attention had shown her that she wasn't wrong about Trey. He was an amazing man.

Sage put the final touches on her hair that she'd swept up and back with one smooth curl trailing down her back. She quickly put on the dangly earrings she'd borrowed from her roommate. She stepped back from the mirror to get an overall look at her appearance.

It was a sexy, daring fluff of violet material otherwise known as an amazing dress. She turned in a circle in front of the mirror. The organza fabric practically floated around her.

She felt like one of those stars that walked the red carpet. This dress wasn't an ordinary dress. It was from a big-name designer who she always watched on the award shows to check out his latest designs. Little did she know that one day she'd be wearing one.

And then there were the heels. They made her heart pitter-patter every time she looked at them. They were a deep purple satin with a closed toe. Small crystals bordered the opening. A thin strap wrapped around her ankle.

Earlier today, Trey had escorted her to the boutiques in town. He insisted on getting her a birthday gift. She'd tried on almost every dress in her size. She'd also tried on matching shoes because the saleslady insisted. And, well, what woman could pass up wearing the most stunning pair of heels.

In the end, Sage insisted the dress was more than enough of a birthday gift. The shoes were just too much. But when she'd returned to the château, she'd found the boutique had delivered not only the dress but also the shoes. Trey obviously had selective hearing. She should insist they be returned, but shoes were her weakness. Did that make her a bad person?

A knock at her door had her rushing over to answer it. She pulled it open, ready to thank Trey for his tremendous generosity. However, when she took in his still-damp hair styled to perfection and his black tux, the words stuck in her throat. This man could definitely wear a suit with his broad shoulders, muscled chest and slim waist. Oh, yes, he looked like a star.

"You are breathtaking." Trey's voice jarred her from her thoughts.

"Thank you. I was just thinking the same about you."

"What?" He acted all innocent. "You mean this old thing?"

She laughed. "That old thing looks like a million dollars on you."

A sexy smile lit up his tan face and made his eyes twinkle. When he looked at her that way, her heart raced. He made her feel like she was the only woman in the world for him. "Why, thank you, ma'am." He held out his arm to her. "Shall we?"

She glanced back in the room, feeling as though she'd forgotten something. And then she realized what it was, her press badge and the pendant. She'd been wearing both for so many days that it felt strange not to have them on this evening.

She turned back to Trey. "Yes." As they were nearing the top of the steps, she said, "You really went out of your way. But you shouldn't have—"

"Yes, I should. I love to make you smile."

She stared deep into his eyes. "All you have to do is be with me to make me smile."

"I feel the same way." He moved his free hand until it was covering the hand she had tucked in the crook of his arm. He stared deep into her eyes. "This evening is for you. Now let's get the princess to the ball."

He wasn't serious? Was he?

"Trey, what have you done? You didn't actually plan a ball, did you?"

His face beamed. "Just a little something to say happy birthday."

"Thank you for this memorable day, these fabulous clothes and shoes. You're like my fairy godmother."

He shook his head. "I'd rather be your prince. I'm not much into wearing the tiara and dress thing."

She laughed. "Whatever you want to call yourself, I think you're wonderful."

"I think the same thing about you, too." He released her hand from his arm. "Now get going."

"But aren't you coming, too?"

"I'll be right behind you. But the belle of the ball needs to make her big entrance."

That meant there were people downstairs. She glanced down at the landing, but she didn't see anyone. Perhaps they were waiting out on the patio.

"Trey, tell me what you've done."

"You'll have to go see for yourself."

Her heart raced in that nervous, giddy sort of way. It tickled the back of her throat. And she struggled to suppress a nervous giggle. For so long now, she felt as though she'd had the weight of the world upon her shoulders. But this magical trip to France had her feeling so much lighter—so much more optimistic about the future.

Maybe it was all just a rosy illusion. Maybe she had too much sun and bubbly. Or maybe it was having Trey in her life. Either way, she couldn't be happier.

She held on to the rail as she made her way down the steps. She wasn't so sure she trusted her knees to hold her up. And with the other hand, she clutched the long skirt of her designer gown. She almost expected flashes to go off, like they had at the red-carpet movie premieres. Not that she was anyone special. She was a nobody, living a fairy tale.

Two steps from the landing, she stopped and glanced over her shoulder. Trey was still standing at the top, where she'd left him. He gestured for her to head into the living room.

She turned to find the double doors leading to the living room closed. They were never closed. So her surprise must lie within. Her heart leaped into her throat.

Willing her legs to cooperate, she successfully stepped onto the marble floor of the grand foyer. She started for the living room when the doors swung open and a bunch of smiling faces appeared.

"Surprise!" The house echoed with their happy voices.

A smile immediately pulled at Sage's lips. He'd planned a surprise party for her. She was so touched. No one had done anything like this since...since her father was alive. Her vision started to blur with tears of joy. She quickly blinked them away and thanked everyone.

The next thing she knew Trey was by her side. She turned to him. "You threw me a surprise party?"

He nodded, looking a little worried. "You like it, don't you?"

She sent him a huge, ear-to-ear smile. "I love it. Thank you."

His heart swelled with a warm sensation.

Trey brushed aside the unfamiliar feeling. There was no time to analyze it now. At this moment, his full focus had to be on making Sage happy. That was the entire point of this evening.

If it was at all in his power, he would do whatever it took to make it up to Sage for his deception. Decisions have consequences. He thought he knew that—he thought he understood—but then he'd made a big decision and the consequences turned out not to be his alone to shoulder. He wondered if his father ever came to the same conclusion.

Trey halted his thoughts. Their two scenarios were not the same. His father walked away from his family for a business. Trey hadn't walked away from Sage. He wanted to think that somehow they could start over. Was that even possible?

He turned to her. His gaze lingered, taking in the dazzling sparkle of her eyes and the smile on her beautiful face. In that moment, he was filled with the notion that anything was possible if you wanted it bad enough. And he wanted Sage to be happy—with the night and with him. He wanted to be close to her again. He wanted her to bestow her sunny smile on him. He wanted all of her. Period.

And tonight was his chance to dazzle her, spoil her and just plain make her happy. So far it appeared to be working. Just wait until she found out what else he'd planned, including a very special present.

He cleared his throat. "I remembered what you told me about your father taking you on a trip for your birthday and I wanted to do something to honor that."

"Trey, what did you do?"

A hush fell over the crowd as all eyes were on them.

"Don't go getting too excited. I know we have to remain here in Cannes until the end of the festival and then return to California for the board meeting, so I thought I'd bring some of the world here to you." He took her by the hand. The crowd parted, clearing a path for them into the dining room. It had been cleared of furniture and replaced with a very long buffet with a white linen tablecloth. "Here you'll find cuisine flown in from around the world."

Her mouth gaped. Her gaze moved from him to the food and then back to him. "You really flew all of this in for me?"

"I did."

"No one has ever done anything so thoughtful for me." And then her eyes shimmered with tears.

Panic clutched Trey. Tears weren't good. Tears were out of his realm of control. They made him uncomfortable.

"I… I can make it all go away," he said out of desperation.

She blinked the tears away. "Go away? Never. I love it." She leaned forward and gave him a hug. It was brief, but it was a bridge that he hoped to build upon. "I'm sure all of your guests are hungry. I know I am."

"But you don't look happy. And this is your birthday. You should have whatever makes you happy."

"Okay, then…" She hesitated as though considering what would make her happiest. "For tonight, I want to pretend that all of that nastiness with Elsa and the thing with you never happened. I want to pretend the magazine isn't in jeopardy and, for the first time since my parents died, all is right in the world."

That was a really steep wish, but she was the birthday girl. "Tonight you will be a princess. And your wish is my command." He bowed and waved toward the table.

A smile bloomed on her face. She walked over to the table. He joined her and explained the menu. *Pho* and *goi cuon*—noodle soup and spring rolls from Vietnam. Moussaka and baklava from Greece. Polenta and meatballs from Italy. And the list went on, with treats from the Philippines, Japan, India, Spain and more.

Sage turned to him. "I could never eat all of this. But I'm going to give it my best effort."

He laughed. "That's a plan."

Once she filled her plate to the point of having absolutely no room left, she turned. There was no one behind them. She glanced to the crowd of finely dressed guests.

"Please, everyone, eat. Don't let this culinary miracle go to waste."

Everyone smiled and wished her happy birthday. Then they all got in line.

Trey led her out to the torch-lit balcony where linen-covered tables awaited them. The centerpieces were hurricane lamps that created a warm glow. He pulled out her chair and then he took the seat next to her.

"Thank you for this. It's amazing." She took a bite of the tiramisu from Italy.

"You don't have to keep thanking me. I wanted to do it."

"Really?" Her gaze searched his. "Or were you just trying to appease me?"

"There's nothing to appease. Remember? You wished away our past?"

Her eyes widened. "So I did."

"I really did enjoy doing this for you. It was a challenge finding all of the restaurants that were willing to ship food via air. It takes home delivery to a whole new level."

"It does. But…" She took another bite of tiramisu. "Mmm…it was so worth it."

"I'm glad you approve."

"Approve? I'm floored. This is the best birthday present ever."

"You misunderstand. This isn't your present."

"It's not?" She sent him a puzzled look.

"No. This is just your party. I have something special for your gift."

"I don't know how you could plan anything more special than this. You've already done too much."

"Seeing you smile made it worth it."

And then they set to work savoring all the delicacies. Trey couldn't take his eyes off Sage. She practically glowed with happiness.

Tonight there were no worries about his father or the magazine or trying to be someone he wasn't. Tonight he was Trey, Sage's escort. And his only concern was to keep that smile on her face for as long as possible.

Sage pushed away her plate. "I am stuffed."

"Then we'll have to dance off some of those calories."

"Dance?" Her eyes opened wide. "I don't think I can move. The seams on my dress might split."

"I highly doubt it. You didn't eat that much. And you have to make room for these." Just then Maria arrived with a platter of cookies. "These were flown in from LA."

Sage gave the tray a once-over and then her mouth lifted into a big smile. "Are those Louise's double chocolate cookies?"

He nodded. "She wanted to do something special for your birthday."

"I love those cookies." She reached out for one.

"I thought you were stuffed."

A guilty smile lit up her face. "I have a little room left."

"Don't worry. Maria will make sure you have plenty of leftovers."

"Happy birthday, ma'am." Maria left her a couple of cookies and then took the tray away.

Sage's gaze met his. "Tonight is like a dream."

"Enough of sitting out here. It's time to go join your party." He got to his feet and held his hand out to her. "And I think it's time for your present."

She placed her hand in his and got to her feet. She stood mere inches from him and lifted her chin until their gazes met. "Whatever it is, take it back. I just can't accept anything else. This is a night that I will never, ever forget."

In that moment, he was tempted to pull her closer. He ached to feel her soft curves nestled against him. He longed to taste her sweet lips again. If only he hadn't messed things up.

Still, her entire mood tonight was so different—so relaxed. Would she let him kiss her? Or would she shove him aside?

The truth was he couldn't take the risk. This was Sage's night. He wouldn't do anything to ruin it. He'd just have to push aside his desires and focus on keeping Sage happy. That was the important part.

"Trey?" Her voice was soft, like it was floating on the gentle sea breeze brushing their skin.

He took a step back as he gave himself a mental shake. "I can't take back your present."

"Did you go and get it personalized?"

"Not exactly. But it was definitely chosen just for you."

"Okay. You have me curious now. What did you get me?"

"Come this way." He presented his arm to her.

She gave him a leery look as she complied. They walked into the house. He was suddenly having second thoughts about his surprise. Sage had said that she wanted to forget about the magazine—about the looming deadline with the *QTR* board. And his gift for her would be a reminder of all that.

But it was too late now. He already had all the wheels in motion. He could only hope she would like it.

"Ladies and gentlemen." He waited a moment for silence to descend over the room. "Thank you all for coming. I hope you've gotten plenty to eat. If not, we have lots of extras. This evening is just getting started. There will be dancing in the other room and the bar is open. And it's now time for the birthday girl to find out about her gift."

Trey turned to Sage.

"All these wonderful people are friends and neighbors. They've come here tonight not only to wish you a happy birthday but also to present you with a gift."

Sage stood there looking as though she was not quite sure what to make of what he was saying. He liked being able to leave her speechless. Perhaps he'd have to work on doing it more often.

"These friends are all renowned in their fields. Some are in entertainment. Some are in fundraising. Others are in research or fashion. They have a great many talents. Some live in Europe year-round. Others split their time between here and the States. And they've all agreed to give you an interview and heads-up for their upcoming social engagements."

Sage's mouth gaped as her gaze moved around the congested room. And then realizing that her mouth was hanging open, she forced her lips together. "Thank you all. I don't know what to say. I am stunned and so grateful to all of you for making this the most amazing night of my life."

Trey smiled. And the night was only getting started. He was looking forward to holding her in his arms and guiding her around the dance floor.

CHAPTER SEVENTEEN

THIS HAD TO be a dream.

There was no way the evening had been real. Now that the guests were gone and the lights had been dimmed, Sage knew she should go to sleep, but she was too wound up.

The pieces needed to create a path to her future had fallen into place. Thanks to Trey. Those guests hadn't just been random people. They were all remarkable, from actors to athletes to prizewinning authors to world movers and shakers. They all had diverse and intriguing stories to tell. And she planned to give their voices a platform from which the world could hear them.

"Come dance with me," Trey coaxed.

"But we can't. There isn't even any music."

"We don't need music." Trey took her in his arms.

Their bodies swayed together as though they were made for each other. Sage's cheeks grew sore from smiling so much. She didn't know it was possible to be this happy.

"This the most perfect birthday. Thank you."

"I'm glad you enjoyed it."

"Enjoyed it doesn't even come close to describing how I feel right now."

A waiter went to pass them with a tray full of dishes. Trey stopped him and asked for two glasses of bubbly. They resumed dancing while the waiter sought out the requested bubbly.

Sage slipped off her heels and moved across the floor in her bare feet. Trey twirled her around and dipped her. It was like a scene right out of a black and white movie where she was the leading lady. Best of all, Trey was the leading man.

The waiter came to a stop next to them with a tray of bubbly. Trey took two flutes and handed her one.

He gazed into her eyes. "Here's to the most beautiful birthday girl."

"And here's to the perfect date."

They clinked their glasses together and then sipped at the champagne that tickled Sage's nose. He took the glass from her hand and set it aside. He took her back in his arms and stared deeply into her eyes. "I wish I could make you smile like this all of the time."

"Who says you can't?" She was flirting with him. It was dangerous but she couldn't stop herself.

A smile lifted his very tempting lips. "And what would I have to do to make you smile all of the time?"

Maybe it was the bubbly or the exhaustion as it was now the wee hours of the morning, but she felt a bit daring. She lifted up on her tiptoes and leaned into him.

She whispered, "This would keep me smiling."

She pressed her lips to his. He didn't move. He stood perfectly still. She wasn't even sure that he was breathing.

Oh, no. Had she read too much into the evening? What if he rejected her? She hadn't thought this through. Panic consumed her and she froze.

And then his lips moved over hers. His touch was gentle yet stirring. Her heart thump-thumped. He gripped her waist, pulling her snug against his firm chest.

She wanted to see where this kiss would lead them, but there were still questions—nagging questions. How could she trust him when there was still so much left unsaid between them?

The conflicting emotions within her tempered her desires. They had to talk first. The good stuff was going to have to wait. The last time she'd totally trusted a man, he'd lied to her. She couldn't have that happen again—not when she cared so much for Trey.

It took all her effort to brace her hands against his muscled chest and push. Her gaze immediately met the unspoken questions reflected in Trey's eyes.

"We need to talk," she said above the sound of her pounding heart. And then realizing that her hands were still on him, she lowered them to her sides.

"Maybe it can wait till later. I had something else in mind for now." He sent her a playful smile.

"This is serious." She couldn't let herself get sidetracked. She didn't want to have regrets later.

The smile disappeared from his face. "What do you want to talk about?"

"You."

His brows rose. "Okay. What do you want to know?"

"I want to know if there are any more secrets."

"No, there aren't." He stared deep into her eyes. "I never meant to hurt you. When I first thought up the idea of going undercover, I didn't take into consideration all the people I would have to lie to. I deeply regret it."

"But why didn't you tell me later on? When things started to change between us?" She really needed to know—to understand.

"I meant to but it never seemed like the right time." He raked his fingers through his hair. "I... I was afraid you would hate me."

"Were you going to let the lie just go on and on?"

He shook his head. "I'd planned to tell you, the same day that we ran into Elsa."

"And she ruined your plans?"

He nodded as he reached out, taking her hands in his own. "If I could go back and do things different, I would. I swear."

There was something different about Trey tonight. He

was—she stared at him—he was filled with remorse. The weight of what he'd done showed in the lines now etching his handsome face. Lying to her—to everyone at the magazine—hadn't come easy and it had cost him. That knowledge brought her comfort.

But she'd also witnessed a different side of him while in Cannes. He was a team player and he was willing to put himself out there to make her happy. And he'd changed his mind about his legacy.

She could understand how hurt he'd been after his parents split up. Losing a close family dynamic is traumatic and then for Trey to think his father hadn't cared about him would have colored the way he'd looked at the world.

"Do you promise to be honest with me from now on?"

This was the deal breaker. She couldn't have someone in her life that she couldn't trust.

He stared straight into her eyes and, without blinking, he said, "I do. I swear it."

"That is the best birthday gift." She leaned in and kissed him.

This time he was the one to pull away. He turned and flipped off the lights. "Let's go upstairs."

He held his hand out to her and she placed her hand in his. Together, they ascended the staircase. Quietly they made their way down the hallway.

Outside her bedroom, he kissed her lightly on the lips. "Happy birthday."

When he turned to walk away, she said, "Don't go."

Trey hesitated. "It's late. And—"

"Don't go."

He reached out. His thumb gently stroked her cheek. "I want you to be sure about this—about me."

"I am. You made a mistake and you've tried to make amends. I forgive you."

"You do?"

She smiled and nodded. "It's in the past. This is a new beginning for us."

Sage opened the bedroom door and led him by the hand inside. Trey closed the door behind him. And then he was holding her in his arms.

"Are you sure about this?" he asked.

"I'm sure about you and me. It's going to be a perfect night."

Sage lifted up on her tiptoes and pressed her lips to his. This time there was no hesitation—no butterfly kisses. In the darkness, there was hunger and desire.

Her heart pounded so loud that she could no longer hear anything else. The only thing she knew was that she was no longer alone. Trey had filled in the cracks in her heart.

And tomorrow—

She cut off that thought as she fell back against the bed. With his lips teasing hers, there was no room for thoughts of tomorrow. There was only the here and now. And Trey. That was enough.

CHAPTER EIGHTEEN

EVEN BEFORE HER eyes were open, Sage had a smile on her face.

This was going to be the most wonderful day. How could it not be after such an amazing night? From the birthday party that topped all parties to Trey's heartfelt apology to winding up in his arms all night long.

Her hand ran over the sheets and found the spot next to her empty and cold.

Sage's eyes fluttered open. She scanned the room, finding herself all alone. She wasn't sure what to make of it. Was Trey just anxious to get on with his day? Or did he regret their evening together?

She rushed through her shower and dressed. She was just putting on her makeup when the door swung open. There stood Trey with a tray of food in his arms.

"Hey, sleepyhead, I thought you'd still be in bed after being up most of the night." He smiled at her.

At last, she could take an easy breath. Everything was going to be all right. They were going to be all right. She smiled back.

"I couldn't sleep the day away. Tomorrow is the end of the festival."

"And you want to get out there and line up more potential interviews?"

"Actually, thanks to you, the magazine's calendar is filled. So I thought I would take these last two days to soak up the atmosphere and just relax. We could have a perfectly relaxing afternoon together."

"That sounds very tempting, but I'm going to have to take a pass. I hope you have a good time."

"Wait. What? Why aren't you coming with me?" She was hoping they'd spend the day together.

"Because while we've been concentrating on lining up star-studded interviews, the work back at the office has been piling up. And I need to get to it."

"Oh." Disappointment welled up in her. "You mean your software business."

"That, too. But I was referring to the magazine. Remember, as far as everyone knows, I'm still your assistant."

"But you aren't. You don't have to do that stuff. I can handle it."

"What you can do is walk this way." He led her out to her own private balcony. He placed the food on the table and then turned to her. "Now, sit and eat. And then go have fun."

"But without you?"

"I promise I'll work as fast as I can and then catch up with you."

"I could stay and help. We'd get it done twice as fast."

He shook his head. "I've got this. But if you'd like, I could have Louise start lining up applicants for you to interview when you get back to California."

"But won't she find that strange, considering she doesn't know who you really are?"

He lowered his gaze. "I was going to tell her. I figured that way by the time we get back to LA everyone in the office would know the truth."

It would be best coming from him. "Go ahead and tell her. But I don't know about lining up applicants. With the board meeting coming up, it might be a pointless endeavor."

"Stop worrying. With all the progress you've made, there's no way they'll shut down the magazine. It's going to be the crown jewel of QTR International." He leaned forward and gave her a quick kiss like it was something they did every morning.

And then he was gone. She sighed. She knew he was still trying to set things right between them and that just made her—what? The feeling was just bubbling beneath the surface. It was a word that she'd never used in connection with anyone—until now.

She loved Trey.

She smiled—truly smiled. She couldn't remember the last time she smiled this much. And it was thanks to him.

Now it was her turn to do something special for him. And she knew exactly what it would be. She grabbed her cell phone and scrolled down until she found the number for Quentin senior. Her finger hesitated over the send button. If Trey had been able to learn to appreciate his family's magazine, maybe there was hope for him to forgive his father.

She pressed Send. The phone started to ring.

This was a chance for all of them to have a fresh start.

It was the final evening of the festival.

They were invited to the swankiest gala and Trey was anxious to escort Sage. Tonight would be their grand swan song. He knew when they returned to California that they'd have to contend with their jobs. His would take him back to San Francisco while her position kept her in LA.

Sure, they'd stay in close contact at first. There'd be phone calls every day and weekends together. But he knew from past experience that the phone calls would slowly trickle off and the weekend getaways would grow farther and farther apart.

It wasn't what he wanted, but it was all he had to offer her. But for tonight, they could pretend their future together was rosy. Because try as he might, he'd come to care for Sage more than he'd ever cared for anyone. And he didn't know what to do with all these new feelings.

He straightened the tie to his tux, buttoned his jacket and then headed for the bedroom door. It was time to pick up his date. He couldn't wait to see what she was wearing this evening. Between the gowns he'd gotten for her and what she'd packed in all those suitcases, he didn't think she'd worn the same outfit twice since they'd arrived in Cannes.

He rapped his knuckles on her bedroom door.

"Come in."

He opened the door to find Sage in a long, slinky silver dress. She was standing with her bare back to him. It was quite a tempting sight. And then there was the way the dress hugged her hips. It was perfect on her.

She turned to him. "You're just in time."

"I am?" He swallowed hard as he took in the front of the dress with its dipping neckline. The back was good but the front was amazing. "I mean, I am. You are a knockout."

She smiled but the smile didn't quite reach her eyes. "Thank you. Are you sure this dress works? I could change into something else." She moved to the wardrobe and swung open the doors. "What color would you like to see me in?"

"Slow down. That dress really suits you. Every guy at the gala will want to dance with you." He walked up to her and pulled her into his arms. "But you'll have to let them know that your dance card is full."

"It is?"

He nodded. "Yes, it is. I intend to spend the evening with you in my arms."

He leaned forward and kissed her. Her lips were so soft and so willing. It would be so easy to just skip the event and stay in for the evening. In fact, the idea quite appealed to him.

But then Sage pulled back. "We can't be late."

"Sure we can." He tried to pull her back to him but she was too fast for him.

She moved to the dresser and picked up a necklace. She held it out to him. "I can't seem to get this on. Could you do it for me?"

"Sure." When he went to take it from her, he noticed a slight tremor in her hands. "Is something wrong?"

She glanced away. "No."

He put the necklace on her and then, putting his hand on her shoulder, propelled her around to face him. "I know there's something wrong."

"Why would something be wrong? It's going to be a perfect night as I'm with the perfect man."

"You're jumpy and not acting like yourself. What's the matter?"

"Nothing." She said it too quickly and avoided his gaze. "Sage—"

Chime. Chime.

He turned to the hallway and then back to her. "I wonder who that could be."

She turned to the mirror and put on her earrings. "Why don't you go see? I'll be right there as soon as I grab my heels."

There was an uneasy feeling churning in the pit of his stomach. He had that feeling before, right before a hacker had decimated his software prototype. He shook off the feeling. He assured himself that nothing was going to go wrong tonight. The worst was behind them. Sage knew the truth about him.

And she was probably just nervous about getting all dressed up and mingling with the rich and famous. It could be a lot of pressure, trying to figure out what to say and how to act.

He assured himself that he was reading too much into

Sage's actions as he walked down the steps. Maria had already answered the door. He could hear her speaking, but he couldn't make out the other voice.

When he reached the bottom step, he paused. There was no one in the foyer. Maria must have showed their guest into the living room.

Maria exited the room and nearly ran into him. Her face was white like she'd seen a ghost. "*Monsieur*, I was coming to get you. I wasn't sure what to do. I hope I didn't do the wrong thing."

"Calm down, Maria. Did someone hurt you?"

She shook her head but her eyes were filled with worry. "It's you I'm worried about."

"Me? But I'm fine." And then he realized she was referring to the presence of their guest. "I've got this. You can go."

"Are…are you sure?"

That uneasy feeling in his gut was now much more like a knot. "I'm sure."

He turned to the doorway. He had a feeling he knew who was waiting for him, but he longed to be wrong. He would give anything for it to be someone else.

His feet felt as though they'd been cast in concrete. A steel band felt as though it was cinched around his chest, growing ever tighter. With determined effort, he put one foot in front of the other. And when he stepped into the entrance to the living room, his worst fears were confirmed.

A man stood facing the fireplace as though looking at the framed family photos. Apparently he hadn't heard Trey's arrival. That was fine with Trey. He needed a moment to figure out what to say to this unwanted visitor.

The man was about his height. He appeared to still have all of his hair, although it was silver now.

There was nothing outwardly striking about the man. Nothing to let on how mean he could really be. Any other person would probably think that he was a nice old man. They wouldn't know the damage he'd caused or the life he'd destroyed.

And Trey knew why he was here. This was Sage's doing. This was why she'd been so nervous upstairs. She knew he didn't want this man in his house—in his life. And yet she'd brought him here anyway.

"You are not welcome." Trey's voice came firm and steady, even though he didn't feel like it on the inside.

His father turned. He didn't say a word at first. It was as though his father was taking in his appearance and sizing him up. "I can see some of your mother in you. That steely determination written all over your face is just like her."

"You have no right to talk about my mother. You lost that right a long time ago."

His father nodded and said in an even tone, "I understand."

Trey couldn't take his father's ambivalence. He wanted his father to be as worked up as he was. He wanted his father to show some sort of emotion.

"What are you doing here?"

"I came to see you. I thought it was past time."

Trey vehemently shook his head. It was never a good time for this man to intrude in his life. "I told you at my mother's funeral that I never wanted to see you again. Why would you think that has changed?"

"I asked him to come." Sage's voice came from behind him.

Trey turned. "You shouldn't have done it. You are meddling in something that you don't understand."

Her eyes pleaded with him to understand. "You only get one go-around in this life. When it's over, you don't get any do-overs. No second chances. Don't miss an opportunity to get back your family."

Trey shook his head. "Sage, you can't make this into the happy family you so desperately want."

"Don't be mad at her, son. She was only doing what she thought was best for you."

He swung back around to face his father. "I'm not your son. You gave up that privilege a long time ago."

Trey turned and started to walk away when Sage reached out and caught his arm with her hand. "Please, just hear him out and then you can go."

"I can't. He has nothing I want to hear. He had almost thirty years to say it. Now it's too late."

His father's voice filled with emotion. "I did try to say it, but your mother...she refused to let me see you."

Trey swung around. "That's a lie. She never would have turned you away. She told me how you wouldn't even take her phone calls."

"You only heard her side of the story. But I have one, too. I came back for you, but she wouldn't let me inside. She said you were at school. Another time she said you were at a friend's house. She always had an excuse to keep us apart. We argued. It seemed like that's all we ever did in the end. And then she threatened to take you away so that I would never find you."

"I don't believe you."

"She did it. She took you and it took me almost a year to find you. You must have been about six at the time. She moved to Paris and stayed in a small apartment."

Trey was about to deny it but then the memories started to come back to him. He'd hated the tiny apartment. It was nothing like the château. It stunk and he wasn't allowed outside to play. He'd missed his bedroom, his friends and, most of all, Maria.

"See, you do remember the move. Your mother wanted to punish me. And her greatest weapon was keeping you from me." His father's eyes grew shiny with unshed tears.

And his voice grew gruff. "When I found the apartment, we had a terrible row. The police were called. In the end, I agreed to keep my distance if she would take you back to the château where I knew there would be people around to see to your safety."

Trey remembered awaking to a ruckus. His mother had told him it was a problem with the neighbors. He had no reason not to believe her at the time. But his father's words were starting to answer some questions.

Was it possible his father wasn't the villain that his mother had painted? Trey's head started to pound. It was just too much.

"I can't do this." Trey turned and walked out of the room.

Sage followed him to the front steps. "Trey, don't go. I'm sorry I invited your father here. I shouldn't have done it. Let's just forget this happened and go to the gala. It'll be the perfect end—"

"Stop." He just couldn't take any more of her looking at him like he was the answer to her dreams. "Ever since the birthday party, you keep saying that everything is perfect now. It's not. I'm not."

"I know you're upset, but we'll get through this together. That's what couples do. They work through the thick and thin."

He shook his head. "We're not a couple."

Her mouth gaped as though his words had stabbed her. He hated to see the pain reflected in her eyes, but it was time to bring her back down to earth before she got in any deeper.

"Sage, I do care about you, how could I not? You are sweet, kind and thoughtful. You would make any man the perfect wife, but not me. I don't fit into your plan for a perfect family."

"That's not true."

"Isn't it? Didn't you bring my father here in order to bring us back together? You want that perfect family that was stolen from you. And you deserve the perfect life. But I can't be part of that perfect picture."

A tear slipped down her cheek. "You can if you want to be."

He shook his head. "I am broken. You just heard me with my father. With those two as my role models, I'd have no chance of making the perfect husband or father. I'm too damaged on the inside. I would never make you happy. You are better off without me."

It took every bit of willpower to turn his back on her and walk away.

"But you do make me happy." The whisper of her voice was carried by the breeze.

He assured himself that he was doing what was best for her.

But it sure didn't feel like it.

CHAPTER NINETEEN

THE TRIP TO the French Riviera had been a complete and utter disaster.

And she had no one to blame but herself.

Sage had been back in Los Angeles for a week now and she hadn't heard one word from Trey. Every time she walked past his empty desk, it was like a nail was being driven into her heart. Sharp and painful.

Today was the board meeting. With Trey being the acting CEO, there was no way he could avoid being in the same room with her. She'd arrived at the meeting with a comprehensive report that she'd worked all week to finalize. It detailed where the magazine had been financially and circulation-wise when she took over. It showed the increase in supermarkets and bookstores that were willing to carry the revamped format as well as their online subscriptions. And then there was the calendar of extraordinary individuals as well as global events that they would be featuring for not one but two years. That last part was mainly thanks to Trey and she felt bad about not being able to thank him.

As soon as the meeting had concluded, Trey stood. The breath caught in her throat as she waited for him to approach her. Instead he turned and left the room without a word to her. Other board members stopped to speak with her. Some had questions about a portion of the presentation and others wanted to compliment her on the work she'd done so far.

Why had she ever thought that bringing Trey face-to-face with his father was a good idea? She knew that Trey had been terribly hurt in the past. She had just hoped that somehow father and son could find a new start—something she would never have with either of her parents.

As she made her way back to her office, she couldn't help but think about Trey's parting words to her: *"I don't fit into your plan for a perfect family."* Was he right? Was she looking for the "perfect" family to make up for the one she'd lost?

She'd never really thought about it. Not until now. There had never been an opportunity for her to consider having a family of her own. Sure, there had been Charlie, but their relationship hadn't escalated to the point of thinking about marriage or a family. At least she could be thankful for that one small saving grace. Because she'd made a total fool of herself by believing all of his lies.

But Trey was nothing like Charlie. And then she thought about how they'd met. Trey had lied to her about who he was and what he wanted. But he'd done everything in his power to make it up to her—to show her that he wasn't that person, that he was better.

And the thing was she really liked the real Trey. She liked him so much that she'd wanted him to have the one thing she couldn't have—a family. She'd been so sure if Trey could open his heart and listen to his father that they could find their way back to each other. And it had been a disaster.

Now, not only was Trey out of her life, but soon Happy would be gone, too. She'd thought about stopping by Louise's office because she was still puppy-sitting Happy. She could really use some puppy kisses and snuggles. Not that he was hers, but in the time they'd spent together, he'd snuck into her heart. But she resisted the temptation. She had to get used to life without Trey or Happy in it.

She walked into her office and came to a stop. There

was Happy with his tail wagging. Her heavy heart felt a little lighter and her downturned lips lifted into a genuine smile.

"Hey there, buddy." She set her belongings on the end of the couch and knelt down.

Happy rushed up to her and lathered her with kisses. She scooped him up in her arms and gave him a hug. She didn't understand what he was doing here, but she was so happy to see him.

"Oh, there you are." Louise's voice came from the doorway.

Sage turned. "Were you looking for me? Or the dog?"

"I didn't know if you'd return after the board meeting. How did it go?"

"It's a closed vote. And it might come down to Trey's vote."

"But I thought you said he was on board with the magazine now."

"That was before."

"Before what?"

"Before I decided to play God with his life."

"Oops. That doesn't sound good." An indecisive look settled on her face. "This sounds like it's going to need some coffee and a Danish or two."

Sage moved to her desk chair, knowing that as the boss she should insist they get to work, but her heart just wasn't in it today. Maybe if she talked to Louise, it'd help clear her head. But something told her neither the talking nor the baked goods would help the ache in her heart.

Louise hurried back into the office balancing a plate of goodies and two coffees. She placed everything on the desk and then took a seat as though settling in for the whole sordid story.

Sage didn't want to get into the painful details, but maybe someone else's perspective would help. She needed someone to tell her that what she'd done hadn't been as awful as it felt—even if it hadn't ended the way she'd been hoping.

And so the words came out slowly at first. The more she talked about her time with Trey, the more she missed him. And then as she spoke, she started to see things differently. She finally understood what Trey had been trying to tell her—she was trying to make him do, feel and say what she wanted.

"I can't believe I didn't see this sooner," Sage said more to herself than Louise.

"Sometimes when you're so intimately involved in a situation, it's hard to see things clearly."

Tears rushed to her eyes. "But I hurt not only Trey but his father, too." She blinked away the tears. "I made things so much worse for both of them. And that's not what I meant to do."

"But you brought them back together. That's more than anyone has done in years."

"That's not a good thing. You didn't witness the tension and the anger that filled the room."

"Did they speak to each other?"

Sage nodded. "But none of it was constructive."

Louise's eyes filled with sympathy. "You did it out of the goodness of your heart."

Happy rounded the desk and put his paws up on Sage's lap. She picked him up and gave him another hug. "Do you think Trey has discarded Happy because of me?"

Louise shook her head. "I talked to him last night. He said he had a few things to take care of and then he offered to pay me for puppy-sitting. Like I would take money for watching that furry ball of love." A big smile filled her face as her gaze landed on Happy. "You and I, we're buddies, aren't we?"

Arf!

A smile tugged at Sage's lips. "If he changes his mind, I'll take him."

"You'll have to stand in line. This little guy already stole my heart."

"I'm sure Trey is missing you." She couldn't resist giving Happy another hug and recalling the way they'd worked together to help Happy. That's when she'd let her guard down long enough to see that there was so much more to Trey than his good looks.

"I'm guessing after everything you told me that Trey won't be coming to the office anymore." Louise's voice roused Sage from her thoughts.

"No. He got all of the information he needed."

"Do you really think he voted against you?"

"A week ago, I'd have said no, but now I'm not sure." She recalled the way he'd taken to the office and how he'd worked so hard to get her a star-studded lineup for the upcoming year. "But then I messed everything up. And now I wouldn't be surprised if he didn't want any reminders of me."

Louise frowned. "I don't think he's vindictive. He struck me as a man with integrity and a solid head on his shoulders."

The dog started to squirm and so Sage set him on the floor. "I hope you're right because it's not just the magazine. It's your job and everyone else that works here."

"And no matter what, we all know that you did your best."

Sage's phone rang. In all honesty, she didn't want to talk to anyone else. She was more than willing to call it a day. But it could be the board with a decision about the magazine's future. When she checked the caller ID, it was someone totally unexpected.

CHAPTER TWENTY

TREY HAD BEEN avoiding Sage.

He didn't think he could face her again until he had everything sorted out. He'd been extremely busy since returning from France.

Ever since he'd walked away from Sage that night at the château, he'd felt as though he'd lost a piece of himself. Sure, he was upset that she'd interfered in his life and brought his father to see him. It was wrong and for a while he'd been really upset with her.

His father had followed him to the States. They'd had another talk. This time his father did most of the talking and Trey did more listening. In the end, his father told him to give Sage another chance. In the little bit of time that his father had seen them together, he said he could tell they had something special.

Trey left that meeting anxious to talk to Sage about what had just gone on between him and his father—their first meaningful conversation. But she wasn't waiting for him at home. She wasn't waiting for him. Period.

And he had no one to blame but himself. She had drawn his father back into his life out of the goodness of her heart. If there was one thing about Sage that was undeniable, it was her desire for others to be happy—even if she wasn't.

And now it was time they talked. He hoped that she would hear him out and, in the end, she'd be happy. He'd hired a team of private investigators to work through the information his hacker friends had uncovered about Elsa's dealings. And he now had incriminating proof that Elsa had stolen Sage's legacy.

And with the board meeting concluded and the official vote taken, Trey jumped in his sleek black sports car and raced across town to the headquarters of *QTR Magazine*. He maneuvered the car through the parking lot. Just as a black town car pulled out from in front of the building, he slipped his car into the vacant spot.

Not so long ago, he would have thought of this as his father's building, but now when he looked at the building, he thought of it as Sage's domain. She'd done miracles with this magazine. He was proud of her.

He rushed to the glass doors and, once inside the lobby, he came to a stop. There was Louise and Happy. He glanced around for Sage, but she was nowhere in sight.

Arf! Arf!

Trey said hi to Louise and then knelt down to pet Happy. Even though the dog was cute, he never would have considered keeping him if it weren't for Sage's fondness for Happy. Keeping a dog was a life-changing event for him. It meant scheduling his life around someone else—putting Happy's needs ahead of Trey's hectic schedule. He wouldn't do something like that for just anyone. But he had to admit he'd grown quite attached to the dog and the woman who'd convinced him to keep Happy.

Trey lifted his head to Louise. "Is Sage in her office?"

"No. She just left."

He straightened. "Left?"

Louise nodded.

Trey felt as though the rug had been pulled out from under him. He thought this was his chance to fix everything and now she'd taken off in the middle of a workday. Was she that upset with him?

Louise looked at him. "Are you just going to stand there?"

"What do you want me to do?"

"I want you to…" She glanced down at the file folder in her hand. When her gaze met his again there was a twinkle in her eyes as though she had all the answers to the world's problems. "Do you remember when you said that you would owe me a favor for watching Happy while you were in France?"

He clearly remembered. And he knew one day that favor was going to cost him dearly. It appeared that day had arrived. "I remember."

"I need you to take this file to Sage. I forgot to give it to her before she left."

His gaze lowered to the thin file folder. "Surely it can't be that important."

"She needs it for her meeting in New York."

"New York?" No wonder Sage appeared a bit on edge. He thought she was angry with the way he'd reacted over the reconciliation with his father. But she'd had other more important matters on her mind. "She's going to face Elsa, isn't she?"

"I can't really say. She swore me to silence."

That told him everything he needed to know. "Give me the file." It was the excuse he needed to speak to her and try to convince her to forgive him so he could accompany her on this trip. "I'll see that she gets it."

"I was really hoping you'd say that. And if you don't make it back for a while, no worries—Happy will be fine with me."

"You mean you'll spoil him some more."

Arf!

"Like I said, we've got this. Just make sure Sage is all right." She held out the folder to him.

He accepted it. "I will, if she lets me."

"You can be persuasive. After all, you talked her into

hiring you, didn't you? Flash her that million-dollar smile, and if that doesn't work, grovel."

"Grovel?" He shook his head. He wasn't one that was used to groveling. But when he thought of living his life without Sage in it, groveling didn't seem like such a bad option. "I'll do whatever it takes." He rushed to the door and then paused to turn back. "Thank you."

"What are you thanking me for? You're the one doing me a favor." She winked at him.

"You're the best."

"Stop with the flattery and get going. You don't want to miss her."

He took off out the door. Thankfully he'd left his car right in front of the building in the no-parking zone. Sometimes rules had to be broken, especially when you realize what an idiot you've been.

He stopped next to his car and searched the parking area for the black town car that had pulled out just as he'd arrived. He was certain it would be long gone by now, but then he spotted it waiting in a long line at the red light. Most of the time that stoplight annoyed him to no end with its long green for the main drag but its five-second green for the parking lot. Today he was thanking his lucky stars because it was just the delay he needed to catch up to Sage.

He took a side exit, avoiding the troublesome light, and followed her car onto the freeway. With the congestion on the roadway, he fell back a few cars. It was no big deal as there wasn't any way to get her to pull over here. He would just follow her to the airport where he could tell her—

A car came flying up beside him. It was a flashy red sports car. It swerved into his lane, nearly sideswiping him before it rushed on.

The sports car surge forward and then it veered to the right, cutting off a car. The car braked and started a chain reaction of collisions. Trey practically stood on his brakes to get stopped in time.

When he looked up, he saw the sports car had swerved across the five lanes of traffic. Brake lights lit up. And then the car struck the fender of Sage's car. Trey watched the accident as if it was in slow motion. The black town car spun around and another oncoming car struck the passenger side.

Trey's heart lurched into his throat.

No. No. No. This can't be happening.

She just has to be okay. Please, let her be okav

By now traffic had ground to a halt in all the lanes. Trey shut down his car and jumped out. He wasn't the only one. Others were getting out to help the passengers in the now-wrecked cars. But the red sports car was nowhere to be found. It must have slipped away on the off-ramp.

He ran toward Sage's car. The driver stepped out. He grimaced as he rubbed his neck.

Trey kept moving until he was next to Sage's door. He eased it open and found her sitting there with her head lulled off to the side and her eyes closed. A trickle of blood trailed down the side of her face.

Trey's chest tightened. This couldn't be happening. It just couldn't be too late to tell her that he was sorry. That he loved her. And he would do whatever it took to make her happy.

"Sage?" No response. "Sage, please open your eyes."

The driver moved around the car to stand next to Trey. "How is she?"

"I… I don't know." The breath caught in his lungs. He needed to see if she had a pulse. He reached out and placed a finger on the side of her neck. Her skin was warm and… there was a pulse. The pent-up breath whooshed from his lungs. "She's alive."

"I called 911. The paramedics are stuck in traffic."

Trey turned back to Sage. "Don't worry. I'm not going anywhere." He gently traced his finger down over her cheek. "I'm so sorry. That's what I came to tell you. And that I love you. I love you so much. Please be all right."

He leaned forward and pressed his lips ever so lightly to hers.

When he pulled back, he noticed her eyes start to open. He reached for her hand and took it in his own. "That's it. Come back to me."

Sage's eyes opened wide. She glanced around until her gaze settled on him. "You love me?"

"You heard that?"

She smiled and nodded. "Just tell me that it wasn't a dream."

"It's definitely not a dream." He stared deep into her blue eyes. "I love you, Sage. With all my heart. I'm just sorry that it took me so long to figure it all out."

"Why did you leave me at the château? Why couldn't we have figured it out together?"

"Because you kept talking about everything being perfect. That's a lot of pressure to put on a person—especially someone like me. I didn't think I could give you a perfect family—in fact, I knew it."

"I'm sorry. I didn't realize the pressure I was putting on you. I was so excited about what we could have together that I didn't think about how your past would color your view of the future."

"And I let the past get in the way of my future—of our future. But thanks to you, my father and I are talking. I'm learning that everything in the past wasn't black and white. I think the truth is somewhere in the shades of gray."

Sage smiled. "I'm so glad to hear that you two are talking."

"I never thought I'd say this, but I am, too."

She squeezed his hand. "I've had time to think about

us. And I don't need a perfect family. All I need is you. I love you." She leaned into him and pressed her lips to his. A kiss had never tasted quite so sweet.

When she pulled back, she pressed a hand to her injured forehead. "What happened?"

"You were in an accident. Don't you remember?"

It took her a second and then she nodded. "I remember some of it."

She started to move around, but the seat belt was still holding her in place.

"Hey, you need to stay where you are until the paramedics get here." He didn't want her to hurt herself further.

"Why? I'm fine." She released the seat belt.

"You have blood on your face. You aren't fine."

"It's just a little cut."

"I'd rather hear an experienced medical professional tell me that."

She smiled at him as the paramedics entered the freeway via the exit ramp. "I never knew you were so protective."

"Only about those I love."

Sage got to her feet. "See. I'm fine."

"You're still going to the hospital to be checked out. Do you hear me?"

"But I need to get to New York. My investigator has important information about Elsa."

"While you get checked out, your investigator and my investigators can put their information together and see if it's enough to take to the police."

Her eyes widened. "You had people looking into Elsa even after our blowup over your father?"

"I never stopped. And I have some other news for you."

"Is it about the future of the magazine?" The smile slipped from her face.

"It is. The board voted unanimously for you."

"They did?" She threw her arms around his neck. "If this is a dream, don't wake me up."

"It's not a dream. I love you and everything is going to work out as long as we're together."

He lowered his head and claimed her lips with his own.

CHAPTER TWENTY-ONE

ELSA STOOD IN front of the gold leaf mirror.

"Beautiful as always." She smiled at her reflection.

Her latest facelift had done wonders to erase the years. Perhaps the doctor had been a bit zealous with how much skin he retracted as her eyes were a little off, but he assured her that she'd look like herself in no time.

The doors to her office burst open. She spun around. A distinct frown pulled at her very tight skin. "What are you doing here?"

Sage stood in the doorway with a smile on her face. For a moment, she didn't say anything. A sickening feeling took hold of Elsa's stomach. It was just like her nightmares. But that couldn't be. She'd worked so hard to keep the truth from Sage.

"It's over, Elsa." Sage stepped into her office.

"I… I don't know what you're talking about." There was no way Sage knew the truth. She was lying. "And if you don't get out of here, I'm calling security. In fact, I'm calling them right now."

As Elsa picked up the phone, Sage said, "There's no need to call them. I have the police with me."

At that moment, two New York City uniformed officers stepped up behind Sage. Elsa took a step back. This couldn't be happening. She refused to lose everything.

"You all need to go," Elsa said as though it would make it so.

"The only one leaving here is you. In handcuffs." Sage was no longer smiling. There was a very serious look on her face. "We've just handed over all of the proof the district attorney needs to prosecute you for fraud, embezzlement and a few other charges. And when they are done with you, the SEC wants their turn to try you for manipulating the company stock price. And don't worry, your buddies at the investment firm are getting their own set of bright shiny handcuffs." A big smile came over her face.

Quentin Thomas Rousseau III stepped up next to Sage. "Didn't you forget something?"

Sage turned to him. "Did I? That's a lot of charges to remember."

He nodded. "Would you like me to say it?"

"Sure."

"Stop." Elsa's stomach lurched. She didn't know which made her sicker, the pending charges or their sickening sweet act. "How did you figure it out?"

Sage lifted her chin and leveled her shoulders. "I took a page out of your book. I hired the best private investigator after I found him snooping through my office."

Elsa's gaze narrowed. "You hired Hunter?"

Sage's smile broadened. "I did. I guess you could say he was acting as a double agent."

Quentin spoke up. "Now what was I about to say?"

Sage elbowed him. "You know, what happens to Elsa after the SEC."

"That's right. Once the SEC is done with you, the IRS wants their turn at you. It appears that you've been hiding assets."

"How could I have forgotten that one?" Sage turned to Elsa. "Looks like you're in a mess of trouble. I just hope you didn't mess up my house too much. That's right. The house is coming back to me now that a copy of the original will has been located."

As the officer placed the cuffs on Elsa's wrists, the reality of the situation sunk in. Elsa glared at her stepdaughter. "Your father always loved you best. He never paid attention to what I needed. It was always Sage this and Sage that. He was never worried about me. I had to take what I deserved."

The officer started to read her rights to her. Elsa took one last look around her precious office. And then her gaze landed on Sage and Quentin as they shared a tender look.

"You will never win," Elsa said as she was led toward the door.

"We already did." Sage leaned over and kissed Quentin.

EPILOGUE

Six months later...

IT WAS FINALLY HAPPENING.

Trey was at last going to have the family that he'd always wanted—and wondered if he deserved.

Sage had taught him to forgive himself—and his father. He glanced off to the side to find his father sitting in the back row of their small wedding. If it wasn't for Sage, he didn't think he would have ever been able to open his heart up to his father. He never would have known the truth—his father hadn't left voluntarily. His mother had pushed him away because she wasn't able to share him with his work. She was an overly insecure person. But his mother had never shared that information with Trey. She'd only said his father had chosen his work over them.

With his father permanently retired, the future of *QTR* was now Trey's responsibility—and Sage's. Not only were they merging their hearts and lives, but they also were merging their companies. They were going to be a dynamic duo, at work and at home.

Trey returned his attention to his almost-wife as Sage repeated her wedding vows. He stared into her eyes, seeing his future. He couldn't imagine choosing his work over her. Nor could he imagine her issuing an ultimatum. Sage enjoyed her work as much as he did. But they both enjoyed their time together. Sometimes it was a balancing act. Some days work won out. But other times, they'd slip away for some alone time—which they would do shortly for their month-long honeymoon.

"You may kiss your bride," the minister said.

Arf! Arf!

They both looked down at Happy, who sat between them wearing his little black bow tie. His tail rapidly swished back and forth. Was it Trey's imagination or was the dog smiling at them?

Trey gave himself a mental shake. He lifted his gaze until it met his wife's. They both leaned in close and he pressed his lips to hers. Her kiss excited him just as much now as it had the very first time that they'd kissed. There was definitely something magical about Sage. And he was so lucky to have her next to him for life.

They turned to the couple dozen people that they'd invited to the small, intimate affair. Standing and clapping were all the people that held a special place in their hearts.

Sage leaned closer to Trey. "Is that your father in the back row?"

"It is. I told him if he didn't have anything planned that he could stop by."

"Really?" Sage sent him an astonished look.

"What? I thought you'd be happy."

"I'm happy he's here, but the way you invited him, it was like asking him over to watch a football game. I would have sent him an invitation if you'd have mentioned that you changed your mind. Now what's he going to think? And sitting in the back row of all places."

Trey turned to his bride and cupped her face. "He's going to think I'm the luckiest man in the world. And he has just gained the most beautiful and kindhearted daughter-in-law. Now give me a kiss."

She lifted up on her tiptoes and he met her halfway. But the kiss was much too short as Sage pulled away. He sent her a puzzled look.

"You'll get more later," she said. "We have guests."

"Promise?"

"I do."

He grinned. He'd never been happier in his life. Something told him with Sage by his side that life was just going to get sweeter.

Outside the church, he held Happy in his arms while Sage gathered the single ladies around. She tossed her bridal bouquet. It tumbled through the air and landed in Louise's hands. The woman's face lit up with a big smile.

Sage leaned into her husband's side. "Looks like there's going to be another wedding."

"What makes you think that?"

"Watch."

As the crowd scattered, Ralph from the accounting department approached Louise. He took her in his arms. She smiled up at him and they kissed.

"I think you're right, Mrs. Rousseau."

Sage smiled up at him. "You keep talking like that and we're going to have a very happy marriage."

Arf! Arf!

He turned to Happy. "You're supposed to be on my side. Us guys, we need to stick together."

Sage laughed and it was the best thing Trey had ever heard. He planned to keep her laughing the rest of their days.

* * * * *

"You'll get more later," she said. "We'll have another—"

"Promise?"

"I do."

She sighed. He'd never been happier in his... horse... there and lay with Lizzy by his side that life was just going to get easier.

Outside the church... behind Harry on his arse, was Suzy gathering the mink jacket around. She tossed her bridal bouquet. It tumbled through the air and landed in Louise's hands. The woman's face lit up with a big smile.

"You turned into her hand... Would be good to be another wedding."

"What makes you think Suzy?"

"Well."

As the crowd scattered, Ralph from the security department approached Louise. He took back his arm. She leaned up at him and they passed.

"Until you realit, Mrs. Rousseau."

Seeing much up in him. "You keep talking like that and we're going to have a very happy marriage."

He turned to Harry. "You're supposed to be on my side. Us guys, we need to stick together."

Suzy laughed and it was the best thing they had ever heard. He planned to keep her laughing the rest of their days.

This book is for the teachers who go
above and beyond to make a difference
in the lives of their students, especially
Robin Meyer, Michelle Sandoval and Lori Faccio.
Thank you for all that you do!

Chapter One

No one would ever describe Jason Channing as a morning person—especially not before he'd had at least his first cup of coffee. And yet, he used to set his alarm for 7:00 a.m. every morning, at which time he'd slap the clock to silence the annoying buzz, drag himself out of bed, pull on a pair of shorts and a T-shirt—or jogging pants and a sweatshirt, depending on the season—lace up his running shoes and head out for his 5K run.

It was a pattern he'd established in high school, when he was a quarterback for the Westmount Mustangs and his coach had insisted that routines and discipline were even more important than talent in building a winning team. Jay hadn't played ball in more than a decade, but he continued to run every morning. And for the past two months, he'd had an extra incentive to hit the pavement: Alyssa Cabrera.

The Southern California transplant had moved into unit 1B of the A-frame triplex sometime near the end of the previous summer. He hadn't paid too much attention to his new neighbor at the time—although he'd done a double take that first day, and that second look had reinforced his first impression of the new resident as a definite knockout. But preoccupation with his fledgling business and his own relationship rules had discouraged him from doing anything more than look.

Until one morning in early March when he'd awakened before his alarm and decided he might as well start his day. He'd headed out for his run at 6:45 a.m., just as Alyssa was returning from hers. She was wearing a hoodie, body-hugging leggings and high-end running shoes that suggested her morning routine was more of a passion than a hobby.

He'd awakened an hour earlier the next morning in an effort to sync his schedule with hers. And though she'd initially seemed wary of his request to join her, she'd consented. So he'd set his alarm for the same time the next day again. And the day after that, because it was a pleasure to spend time with a woman who didn't feel the need to fill the silence with idle chatter. As the days turned into weeks, he found that his daily exercise—even now starting at 6:00 a.m.—had become more of a pleasure than simply a habit.

Aside from those early encounters, their paths didn't cross very often, despite the fact that they lived in the same building. As a math and science teacher at the local high school—that much she'd revealed in between sprints—she worked the usual school hours Monday to Friday, while Adventure Village, the family-friendly activity center he owned, required him to be on-site from early to late Wednesday through Sunday.

Then, completely out of the blue and in the midst of a March blizzard, she'd shown up at his door with a covered dish in her hands. Apparently the unexpected storm that had shut down the town had also canceled a staff potluck at the high school, leaving Alyssa with enough chili to feed twelve. She'd already put a container aside for Helen Powell—the widowed resident of 1A, who was out of town visiting her daughter's family—but she still had more than she could possibly store in her freezer.

As Jason had listened to the explanation of why she was at his door, he found himself mesmerized by the curve of her lips rather than the words she was saying. And when his gaze had dipped lower, he couldn't help but appreciate that her soft sweater and leggings outlined her sweet curves. She wore fuzzy socks on her feet, and the top of her head barely reached his chin, but there was a lot of punch in the petite package.

Since the storm prevented him from going anywhere, he'd invited her to come in to eat with him. He'd opened a bottle of merlot and, as they'd shared dinner and conversation, he'd found himself increasingly intrigued by the beautiful woman he'd never really let himself notice before.

After that night, when they'd sipped wine and listened to the wind rattling the windows, he'd been much more aware of his neighbor—and more cognizant of her comings and goings. But their morning runs had done little to satisfy his growing curiosity about his new neighbor.

"Looks like spring is finally here," he noted, when he met her at the top of the driveway on a Friday morning in early May.

"The last time you said that, we got dumped with six inches of snow only a few hours later," she remarked, walking toward the street.

"No chance of that today," he promised. "The sky is clear and blue."

"So far," she acknowledged.

They turned west, away from the rising sun, and picked up their pace.

"Any big plans for this weekend?" he asked as they transitioned from a brisk walk to a slow jog.

Her only response was a negative shake of the head that sent her ponytail swinging from side to side.

"You're not going to ask if I have plans?"

"I don't need to ask if a man whose nickname is 'Charming' has weekend plans," she noted.

He winced inwardly at her use of the moniker he'd thought—*hoped*—he'd outgrown. "Where'd you hear that name?"

"In the staff room at school."

Of course. Because he'd dated Lisa Dailey, the music teacher, Shannon Hart, the girls' gym teacher and soccer coach, and—very briefly—Taylor Lawson, the office administrator.

"Rumor has it you've broken the hearts of all the single women in Haven and are dating someone in Battle Mountain now."

"Was," he clarified.

"She dumped you already?"

He was so surprised by the question, he stopped running.

It took a few strides before she realized he was no longer beside her and turned back, jogging on the spot until he caught up again.

"She did *not* dump me," he told her.

"You dumped her?"

"We decided that we wanted different things," he said as they continued along their usual route.

"She wanted a relationship and you didn't?" Alyssa guessed.

Her assumption hit a little too close to the truth for comfort. "Renee said that I was too focused on my business and not enough on her."

"And instead of trying to appease her with flowers or chocolates or candlelit dinners, you gave her the equivalent of a relationship pink slip."

"Pink was her favorite color."

She surprised him by laughing. "Then maybe you made the right decision."

"What's your favorite color?"

"How is that relevant to anything?"

"It's a simple question—although also a personal question," he acknowledged. "And I've noticed that you always sidestep personal questions."

"Orange," she told him.

"Why orange?"

"That's an even more personal question."

"Tell me anyway," he urged.

She picked up her pace and turned onto Peregrine Lane, and for a minute, he didn't think she was going to answer.

"Because it's the last color you see as the sun dips below the horizon at the edge of the ocean," she finally responded.

"That's right—you're a California girl, aren't you?"

"Former California girl," she amended.

"Why'd you trade sand and surf for northern Nevada desert?"

She shrugged. "It was time for a change."

"Sounds like there's a story there."

"Did you date Belinda Walsh, too?"

"I don't think so," he said, a little warily.

"She teaches English at the high school," Alyssa explained. "And she looks for hidden meaning in everything."

"That's not a female thing?"

She sent him a disapproving glance. "Belinda was talking to another teacher in the staff room one day, explaining the symbolism in a poem her class was studying. She claimed that the blue curtains fluttering in the breeze were representative of the author's depression. I suggested that perhaps the author just happened to be writing in a room that had blue curtains."

He grinned. "Sometimes a cigar is just a cigar?"

"And sometimes orange is just the color of a sunset," she confirmed, waving to him as she made her way to her door.

Clearly that was all she intended to say about the subject, but as Jay made his way up the stairs to his own apartment, which occupied the two upper floors of the building, he wasn't entirely convinced. In fact, he suspected there was a lot more going on with the sexy schoolteacher than she wanted anyone to know.

He did know that she left her apartment at precisely seven twenty-five every weekday morning to head over to Westmount, and she usually returned home by three forty-five in the afternoon. The only exceptions were Wednesdays, when she monitored Homework Help in the library after school, and the second Monday of every month, when there was an afternoon staff meeting. She didn't, as far as he could tell, date very often—or maybe not at all.

Which piqued his curiosity for two reasons: first, she was a beautiful woman, and second, she was new to Haven. Either of those factors would appeal to most of the single guys in town; the combination would prove almost irresistible. This led Jay to believe her presence at home most nights was a matter of choice. But why?

Was she involved with somebody back in California? Was she nursing a broken heart? Or was she simply not interested in any of the guys she'd met?

It wasn't in his nature to ignore an intrigue, but he didn't like being distracted by thoughts of a woman.

So rather than admit that he was, he pushed all thoughts of her out of his mind and focused on getting ready for work.

Alyssa turned off the water, grabbed a towel from the bar and briskly rubbed it over her body. She knew, without looking at the clock, that it was 7:00 a.m. She knew because she was a creature of habit who awakened every morning at six and had her shoes laced up, ready to head out the door, ten minutes later.

She wasn't a competitive runner—not like her sister, Cristina, had been. But she enjoyed challenging herself to go a little farther, a little faster. After too many years of being told to be careful, to slow down, because she was fragile and weak, she had a lot to prove—if only to herself.

She'd started running three years earlier, just a short jog at a moderate pace, to see if she could. And then she could do a little more—and a little faster. Now she was strong, she was fit and she was determined to live her life on her own terms.

She ran for herself. It wasn't really a secret, but it also wasn't something she'd shared with anyone else.

Until Jason Channing.

Somehow, eight weeks earlier, she'd acquired a running partner she didn't need or want. And despite her less-than-welcoming demeanor at the start, he'd continued to show up, until she'd found herself not just enjoying his company but looking forward to it.

But at the same time, being around her upstairs neighbor also left her feeling a little…unsettled.

Of course, if rumors were to be believed—and in the eight months she'd lived in Haven, she'd discovered that they usually were—he had a similar effect on most of the female population in town. Because not only was he unbelievably handsome and charming, he was educated, motivated and rich. Not that he flaunted his wealth. In fact, it was only through a conversation with Mrs. Powell, the resident of 1A, that she'd discovered he owned the triplex they all lived in.

Still, it had taken her a while to accept that the cause of her unsettled feeling was most likely physical attraction. But what woman wouldn't feel some kind of stirring in her blood when she was around a good-looking guy? And Jason Channing was undoubtedly that. Referred to as "Charming" by the women in town, he was six feet tall with broad shoulders, dark hair, deep blue eyes, a square jaw and an easy smile that never failed to make Alyssa's toes curl inside her running shoes.

So although she couldn't deny that she was attracted, she was thankfully smart enough to realize that he was way out of her league. And that was okay, because when it came to the dating game, she was content to sit in the bleachers and watch others play.

Someday she might be ready to suit up and hit the field, but after so many years of being "coached" by her doctors and parents, she just wanted to call her own plays for a while. Which was why she'd finally moved away from the well-meaning but stifling attention of her family.

Eight months later, Renata Cabrera still hadn't let up in her campaign to get her youngest daughter to come home. Her latest effort, begun when Alyssa was home for the Christmas holidays, had been a reintroduction to Diego Garcia. He was "handsome and single" as her mother had promised, but Alyssa simply wasn't interested.

Unfortunately, Renata refused to believe it, and Alyssa couldn't remember the last conversation she'd had with her mother without some mention of Diego. Most recently Renata had suggested that he might be traveling to Nevada to help his cousin, who lived in Elko and had recently split from his girlfriend, move out of their shared apartment and into his own. Alyssa hated to think that her mother had encouraged Diego to make the trip—or to think that she had any kind of personal interest in him—but she couldn't disregard either possibility.

With her travel mug of coffee in one hand and car keys in the other, Alyssa had just stepped onto the driveway when her phone rang. Only one person ever called her early in the morning, so she didn't need to glance at the display to know who it was.

She unlocked the car door and set her coffee in the cup holder on the console before pulling the phone out of her purse and connecting the call. "*Buenos días*, Mama."

"I'm just calling to remind you that Diego's going to be in Nevada this weekend," her mother responded without preamble.

Alyssa closed her eyes and quietly banged her head against the open door. "I didn't realize those were firm plans."

"Then you weren't listening," Renata said.

"I'm working this weekend," she reminded her mother.

"You're working tonight," Renata acknowledged. "And Diego said he would stop by this Diggers' place so the two of you could make plans for when you're not working."

"I have another job, too," Alyssa said. "And test papers and lab reports to mark this weekend."

"You work too hard," her mother protested. "At the school all day and then a second job at night."

"Only two nights a week," she interjected to clarify the part-time status of her bartending job at the local watering hole.

"If you don't slow down, you're going to wear yourself out," Renata continued, as if she hadn't heard her.

Alyssa didn't bother to point out that her sister worked

a full-time job and then cared for a husband and son when she got home, and nobody worried that Cristina was going to wear herself out. All she said was "I'm fine, Mama."

"You need a break," Renata said. "And I think spending some time with Diego will fit the bill nicely."

"Diego's a nice guy," she began in an effort to appease her mother.

"From a good family," Renata pointed out. "And ready to settle down and start a family of his own."

Which was something Alyssa was definitely *not* ready to do. "Mama—"

"Would it be such a hardship to spend some time with an interesting and attractive single man?"

"Of course not," she acknowledged. "But—" she needed to firmly and finally extinguish any hopes her mother had of striking a romantic match between Alyssa and Diego "—the truth is, I've been seeing somebody here."

Except that it wasn't the truth—it was a blatant lie.

But desperate times called for desperate measures.

"You've been seeing someone?" her mother echoed, not bothering to hide her skepticism.

"That's right," she confirmed.

Lied.

Again.

"And why am I only hearing about this now?" Renata challenged.

"I didn't want to jinx the relationship by talking about it too soon."

But apparently she didn't mind going to hell, which was certainly her destination after she added more falsehoods and untruths to the conversation.

"Well, this puts me in an extremely awkward position, Alyssa," Renata said. "If I'd known about this...relationship…I would not have encouraged Diego to look you up while he's in town."

She didn't bother to point out that Elko was a different town in a different county. "Maybe it's not too late to get in touch with him and recommend he change his plans," she suggested hopefully.

"Unfortunately, it is," her mother said. "He's already in Nevada, so I'm just going to trust that, when you see him tonight, you'll treat him as you would any friend visiting from out of town."

"Of course," Alyssa murmured, her mind once again scrambling. "But now I really do have to go, so I'm not late for work."

"Okay," Renata said. "But don't forgot to call Nicolas next week to wish him a happy birthday."

"I won't forget," she promised, already looking forward to talking to her almost-five-year-old nephew—because although he always told her he missed her, *he* never tried to guilt her into moving back to California. "Goodbye, Mama. *Te quiero.*"

After her mother had said goodbye, too, Alyssa disconnected the call and sighed wearily. "I'm going to hell."

"I'm not a priest, but I'm willing to listen to your confession, if it would help."

She jolted at the sound of Jason's voice behind her, then pressed a hand to her racing heart as she turned to face him. Of course, seeing him now, freshly showered and shaven, her heart raced even faster.

"Sorry to startle you," he said.

"It's okay," she said. "I didn't expect— You don't usually leave for work this early, do you?"

"No," he admitted. "And you don't usually leave this late."

She glanced at the clock display on her phone and winced. "You're right."

"I don't want to hold you up any longer, but I'm curious to hear why you think you're going to hell."

"Because I lied to my mother," she confided.

"A big fat lie or a little white lie?" he asked.

"I told her that I had a boyfriend."

"You don't?"

She shook her head. "No. The last date I had—and I'm not sure it even counts as a date—was the staff Christmas party, December 22."

She'd attended the event with Troy Hartwell, the biology teacher. He'd had a little too much to drink and misinterpreted her level of interest, forcing Alyssa to demonstrate some of the moves she'd learned in the self-defense course her mother had implored her to take before she moved away from home.

"Any particular reason for the dating hiatus?" Jason wondered.

"Not really," she said. "I just have other priorities right now—including a test for my senior calculus class this morning."

Jason took the hint. "Well, good luck with that," he said, moving around to the driver's side of his truck and climbing behind the wheel.

She waved as he drove away, then decided that her mother's ongoing matchmaking efforts meant it was time for her to implement plan B.

Chapter Two

"The warehouse. Eighteen hundred hours. Tonight."

Jay shifted his attention from the spreadsheet on his computer to Carter Ford, his best friend of nearly two decades and now his right-hand man at Jason Channing Enterprises. Carter stood in the doorway of Jay's office, which also served as the staff lounge and lunch room of Adventure Village.

He glanced at the papers spread out on his desk and, with sincere reluctance, shook his head. "It's going to take me forever to sort this stuff out."

"What stuff?" Carter asked.

"Invoices to pay, booking requests to log and emails to answer."

His friend crossed the concrete floor and dropped into one of the visitors' chairs, then lifted his feet onto the seat of another. "Isn't that Naomi's job?"

"It was supposed to be," he admitted, scrubbing his

hands over his face. "Until I realized that we were two months behind on our insurance payments and we missed out on the opportunity to host a corporate team-building exercise for fifty people because the email was ignored."

The missed opportunity was an annoyance; the potential loss of liability insurance could have shut down their business.

"I thought you'd set up preauthorized payments for the insurance," Carter said.

He nodded. "For the first six months, the payments were coming out of my personal account, to give the business a chance to turn a profit. Then the automatic debits were supposed to be switched over to the Adventure Village account, but Naomi didn't send the paperwork to the bank."

Carter swore. "Tell me again why we're giving her a paycheck every two weeks."

"She got her last one today," Jay told him.

His friend's brows winged upward. "You fired your cousin?"

"Yeah."

"Your aunt's gonna be so pissed."

"Yeah," he said again, already braced for the fallout.

But he trusted that, if it came down to a family battle, his father would be on his side. Because Benjamin Channing had been the one to urge Jay to find a job for his cousin at Adventure Village so that Ben wouldn't have to make a position for her at Blake Mining. Naomi had an extensive work history, but she'd never managed to hold on to any job for very long. "And while I'm not opposed to nepotism, I am opposed to incompetence—and that's why I've got to deal with this paperwork," he explained to his friend.

"C'mon, Jay, you can take a break for a few hours," Carter urged.

"Maybe tomorrow night," he suggested.

"It has to be tonight," his friend insisted.

"Why?"

"Because it's our first anniversary."

Though he was aware of the significance of the date and knew his friend was referring to the business, he couldn't resist joking, "So where are my flowers?"

"The shop was out of yellow roses," Carter bantered back. "And I know they're your favorite."

"Tell me you at least got a card."

"Mere words cannot express my feelings," his friend said.

Jay snorted.

"But I'll buy you a beer after paintball tonight," Carter offered. "And we'll toast to year one."

"And account ledgers written entirely in black ink," Jay added, sitting back in his chair.

He believed in working hard and playing hard, and he considered himself lucky that there was a fair amount of overlap between work and play for the CEO of Adventure Village, Haven's family friendly recreational playground.

When he'd bought his first property—two acres of dry, dusty terrain that included an old abandoned shoe factory—several of the townsfolk had scratched their heads as they tried to figure out why he would throw his money away. Few people gave him credit for having a plan; even fewer believed he might have a viable one, especially when he acquired the undeveloped parcel directly behind the old factory.

He didn't talk about his project except with those who'd been chosen to work on the development. Because Jay knew that the best way to create buzz about what he was doing was to say nothing. The less people knew, the more they tended to speculate—and then share their speculation with friends and neighbors, who passed it on to other friends and neighbors.

When Adventure Village opened, he'd hoped all the doubters and naysayers and everyone else would understand that the land he'd purchased was an investment— not just in Jason's future, but that of the whole town. As one of only three cities in all of Nevada where gambling was illegal, Haven saw a steady exodus of residents to the casinos in neighboring areas on evenings and weekends. And who could blame them when there was no action in their hometown?

But now the residents of Haven had another option. And not only were fewer people heading out of town on weekends, there were more people heading *to* Haven from other places.

Jay understood that part of the draw, at least in the beginning, was the newness and novelty of his facility. In a state where most people came to fritter away their money at the tables or in the bordellos, a facility that offered a variety of wholesome physical activities for all ages was an anomaly—and week after week, that anomaly was adding to his status as one of the wealthiest men in Haven.

And that was definitely cause for celebration.

"What's the plan?"

"Assassins," Carter immediately replied, proving that he'd already given the matter some thought. Or maybe it was just that Assassins was always his game of choice whenever they geared up and took to the field.

"Who's in?"

"Kevin, Matt, Nat, Hayley, me and you."

Jay looked at the papers on his desk again.

"You started this business because you wanted to have fun," his friend reminded him.

"Yeah," he admitted. "But I didn't realize that fun could be so much work."

"And that's why you need a break."

"Why can't that break be tomorrow night?" he wondered.

"Because after the game, Kev wants to head over to Diggers' to put his moves on the hot new bartender, and she doesn't work Saturdays."

"Kev has no moves," Jay noted. "And what he thinks is hot is usually only lukewarm."

"You're right about the moves," his friend agreed. "But his description of the bartender was actually 'sizzling.'"

"Now you have my attention."

Carter grinned.

Jay decided the unpaid and undocumented invoices would still be there tomorrow.

Alyssa loved her job at Westmount High School. Teaching was her pride and her passion, and helping young minds understand scientific laws and mathematic formulas was incredibly fulfilling. But despite a full timetable and the prep and marking to be completed outside of regular school hours, when she walked out of her classroom at the end of the day, she found that she had a lot of free time on her hands.

So she'd looked for opportunities to meet people and get involved in the community. She joined a book club, but the required readings and once-a-month meetings did little to fill her empty nights. She tried a pottery class but had more luck throwing her misshapen vessels into the trash than throwing clay on the wheel. She tried to teach herself to knit but got the needles hopelessly tangled— not just in the wool she'd bought for her project, but in the sweater she'd been wearing. As a result, she'd filled most of her empty hours through the long winter binge-watching Netflix.

Then one day, when she was picking up a few groceries at The Trading Post, she overheard Frieda Zimmerman (whose husband was the local mechanic and tow truck operator) tell Thomas Mann (the owner of Mann's Theater) that her niece Erika had run off to Vegas to be a dancer. Alyssa hadn't been paying too much attention to their conversation, but her attention was snagged when Mr. Mann commented that Diggers' was going to be short a bartender. Because that was a job Alyssa had some experience with, having worked part-time at a campus bar while she was in college.

Her parents had acknowledged the value of their youngest daughter gaining some work experience and contributing to the cost of her education, but they hadn't approved of the late hours or the work environment. It was the first time Alyssa hadn't backed down in the face of their opposition, and although the job had been physically demanding, she'd enjoyed the work—and the chance to forget about her studies and everything else for a while.

Even on Friday nights, Diggers' didn't draw a crowd comparable to a college bar in Irvine, but Alyssa was eager for something—*anything*—to fill some empty hours. Duke Hawkins had been wary about hiring a schoolteacher to tend his bar, but as she was the only applicant with any actual experience, he'd agreed to give her a chance. In only a few short weeks, she'd earned regular shifts on Tuesday and Friday nights.

Sunday through Thursday, there was only one bartender on duty, but on weekends, there were two scheduled with overlapping shifts. Alyssa worked from seven until midnight and Skylar Gilmore came in at eight and stayed until closing. Sky was a couple years younger than Alyssa, but she'd been working part-time at the bar since she was of age and was now a master of the subtle flirtation that kept customers coming back without expecting anything more from the woman who filled their glasses.

Everyone in town knew Sky as the youngest daughter of David Gilmore, owner and operator of the Circle G—reputedly the biggest and most prosperous cattle ranch in Nevada. Few people knew that she was working toward her master's degree in psychology. She was also open and warm and funny, and she knew everything there was to know about Diggers' regular customers—and most of the less regular patrons, too.

Sky was the third of four kids. Her older sister was an attorney married to the local sheriff, Reid Davidson. In February, Katelyn and Reid had added a baby girl to their family, and proud Aunt Sky was always ready to pull out her phone and share recent pictures of her niece, Tessa. Liam, the second oldest, currently worked at the Circle G with his father and brother, though he'd recently purchased the abandoned Stagecoach Inn with the intention of renovating and reopening it as a boutique hotel and spa.

This plan had caused some tension with his father, who apparently insisted that Gilmores were ranchers, not innkeepers, which led to Liam spending less time at the Circle G and more at Diggers'—which was how Alyssa got to know him. Caleb, the youngest, seemed content to work on the ranch, though Sky remarked that he hadn't been truly happy since a former girlfriend moved out of town a few years back.

"Liam said to tell you that one of the bulls broke through the fence bordering the south pasture," Sky said when she joined Alyssa behind the bar Friday night.

"Does that mean he's not coming in tonight?"

"He's coming in," her coworker assured her. "But he's going to be late."

"Oh. Okay," she said, though she knew that if he was *too* late, her plan B would fall apart.

"What he didn't tell me," Sky continued, as if thinking aloud, "is why it was so important for him to show up tonight—or why you would have any interest in his plans."

"It's a long story," Alyssa warned.

"We've got time—this place won't get busy for at least another hour."

So Alyssa told Sky about Diego's impending visit to Haven. Ordinarily, she'd have no qualms about spending time with a family friend visiting from out of town, except that her mother had been less than subtle in her efforts to facilitate a romance between her youngest daughter and the nephew of her best friend, and Alyssa wasn't the least bit interested.

"Is he a jerk?" Sky asked.

"No."

"Unattractive?"

"No." Because although she wasn't attracted to him, she could appreciate that he had a certain appeal.

"Unemployed?"

"No," she said again. "In fact, he works as a project engineer in the aerospace industry."

"So why aren't you interested?" Sky wondered.

"Because I don't want to date anyone right now—especially not someone handpicked by my mother for the sole purpose of enticing me to move back to California."

"How does my brother figure into any of this?"

"He had the misfortune of being here Tuesday night when my mother called to tell me about Diego's potential travel plans. And he suggested that the only sure way to stop her from setting me up with someone from home was to tell her I'm dating someone here. So—" she looked at Sky, trying to gauge her friend's reaction "—Liam's going to be my pretend boyfriend tonight."

Her friend's brows lifted. "Pretend, huh?"

"Pretend," Alyssa said firmly.

"Oh," Sky said, sounding disappointed. "For a minute, I thought this story might be as good as the sexy book I stayed up all night reading."

"Maybe I can borrow it when you're done, because the only romance I want these days is in the pages of a novel," Alyssa told her.

"Why's that?"

"Because I like my life the way it is—uncomplicated by the expectations of a man."

"Most men are simple creatures driven by simple desires to eat, sleep and have sex." Sky grinned. "Although not necessarily in that order."

Alyssa's experiences with the male gender were too limited for her to be able to contradict her friend's assessment. Instead, she said, "And I have no desire to cook so that a man can eat, or make up the bed for him to sleep on."

"I noticed that you didn't dis the sex," Sky said, her tone contemplative.

"My experience in that area is limited," she admitted.

"How limited?"

"Let's just say I really don't get what all the fuss is about."

"Then you haven't been with the right kind of guy," her friend said. "And it's probably a good thing you only want Liam to be a pretend boyfriend."

"Now you've piqued my curiosity," Alyssa said.

"I love both of my brothers dearly, but Liam is…" Sky paused, as if searching for the right words to express what she was thinking. "He's not always considerate of a woman's emotions." She smiled wryly. "Sometimes he's not even cognizant of them."

"So if I was going to fall for one of the Gilmore boys, I should set my sights on Caleb?" Alyssa joked.

Her friend shook her head. "Except that my younger brother, though inherently more compassionate, is completely emotionally unavailable."

"Then I guess it's a good thing I'm not looking to fall for anyone," she noted.

"Those not looking are most likely to fall," Sky warned.

"I'm not concerned."

"How long have you been in Haven?" her friend asked as she began to unload a tray of glasses.

"Eight months," she answered.

"How many dates have you had in that time?"

"Two," she admitted.

"Two dates with the same guy or two different guys?" Sky continued to multitask as she interrogated her.

"Two different guys," Alyssa clarified. "Neither of which I wanted a second date with."

"Sex?"

She shook her head.

Sky gave Alyssa her full attention now. "You haven't had sex in *eight months*?"

Alyssa's cheeks flushed. "It's actually been a little bit longer than that." Actually, it had been *a lot* longer than that, but she wasn't ready to admit to her friend that she was a twenty-six-year-old virgin.

"You haven't met anyone in that time who's made you think 'yeah, I could get naked with him'?" Sky asked.

Even as she shook her head again, an image of Jason Channing filled her mind and heated her blood. Whenever she was around her upstairs neighbor and current running partner, *feelings*—unfamiliar and unwelcome—stirred inside her. Those feelings sometimes made it difficult to remember that she was happy living her own life and definitely not looking for romance. And even if she was, it would be a mistake to glance in his direction.

"No," she said in answer to Sky's question.

But then he walked right out of her thoughts and into the bar, and her defective heart skipped a beat.

He wasn't alone. Of course "Charming" wasn't alone on a Friday night. He was with a woman—blonde, beautiful, built. No, he was with *two* women. The second was a little taller, with darker hair, but no less beautiful. A second man followed the second woman, and they headed directly for one of the booths.

A double date, Alyssa guessed.

Then two more guys came in and squeezed into the booth, too.

Or maybe just a group of friends, she allowed.

Alyssa tore her gaze away from them to glance at the clock. Because as nice as Jason Channing was to look at, he wasn't the man she wanted to see right now.

In fact, he wasn't a man she could let herself want at all.

Chapter Three

As Jay made his way to the bar, he watched Alyssa give a smile to her customer along with his change. Her attention shifted, and though it might have been his imagination, he thought her smile widened when she recognized him.

"So you're the one," he said to her.

"The one what?" she asked.

"My friend Kevin insisted that we come here tonight to check out the hot new bartender," he explained.

She automatically glanced toward the table where his friends were seated, suggesting that she'd seen them enter the bar. "Setting aside the accuracy of that description for the moment, I hope he didn't make the suggestion in front of your new girlfriend."

"My— Oh." He looked over his shoulder. "Which one did you think was my girlfriend?"

She shrugged. "Either. Both."

"I'm flattered… I think. But no, Nat and Hayley are friends and employees."

"Is the boss buying the first round tonight?" she prompted.

Although there were servers who circulated around the floor, taking orders and delivering drinks, it wasn't unusual for customers to order directly from the bartender.

"I am," Jay confirmed. "Two bottles of Icky, one Wild Horse, a gin and tonic, one Maker's Mark, neat, and a Coke."

She turned to reach into the beer fridge for the bottles he'd requested, providing him with a nice view of her perfectly shaped backside.

"So what made you take up bartending?" he asked, his attention focusing on the chunky, lopsided heart-shaped pendant that dangled between her breasts when she turned back again.

"Too much time on my hands," she confided, deftly uncapping the bottles.

He lifted his eyes to her face again. "Did you lose your teaching job?"

"Of course not."

"Then what you really meant to say was too many lonely nights," he teased.

"I'm not lonely," she denied, scooping ice into a tall glass. "But I spend a lot of time alone and I thought this would be a good way to meet people."

"How's that working out so far?"

She smiled as she filled the glass from the soda gun. "The tips are good."

He chuckled.

"Aside from that," she continued as she poured the bourbon into an old-fashioned glass, "I've learned there are three types of guys who come into a bar."

"What are those types?" he asked curiously.

"Type one are the regulars who might be genuinely nice guys, but their closest and longest relationships are with the bottle," she explained as she scooped more ice into a highball.

"Type two comes in looking to meet a woman, but he doesn't have any interest in getting to know her beyond the most basic exchange of information for the sole purpose of getting her into bed." She added a shot of gin, then squeezed a wedge of lime into the glass.

"Type three is almost worse." She added the tonic, another wedge of lime and a stir stick. "He seems like a good guy, and he's usually with a girl who thinks so, too, but the whole time he's with her, he's scoping out the area for other females."

"I'd suggest that there's also a fourth type," Jay said. "The guy who comes in for a drink with his friends and maybe to flirt with a pretty girl."

"Maybe," she acknowledged, a little dubiously.

"And then there's Carter," he said as his friend joined him at the bar—ostensibly to help him carry the drinks back to their table.

"Hello, Carter," she said, greeting the other man with a friendly smile.

"For once in his life, Kevin was right," Carter remarked, winking boldly at Alyssa.

Jay shook his head. "Type two," he told her. "Not beyond reform, but risky."

Alyssa nodded as she punched the drinks into the register. "Got it."

Carter scowled. "What does that mean? What's a type two?"

"It means that you're *not* going to hit on the bartender—who also happens to be my neighbor," he said firmly.

His friend's gaze shifted from him to Alyssa and back again. "You live next to this stunning creature and you've never invited me over to meet her?"

"And this is him pretending that he's not hitting on you," Jay remarked as he passed some bills across the counter to Alyssa.

She laughed. "Well, I'm flattered," she said.

"Let me know when you want to be *not* pretend hit on," Carter told her, picking up several of the drinks to take them back to their table.

Jay shook his head to decline the change she offered.

Her smile slipped, replaced by an expression of concern. "Ohmygod."

He craned his neck, looking behind him. "What happened?"

"That's what I was going to ask you," she said.

"What do you mean?"

She lifted a hand to touch his face, her fingers brushing lightly over the stubble on his jaw—and the bruise that throbbed beneath the skin.

"Oh, that," he said, wondering how it was that her cautious touch was so unexpectedly arousing. "Matt caught me with my shield up."

"Huh?"

"Paintball," he explained.

"Boys and their toys," she mused, letting her hand drop away.

His skin continued to tingle where she'd touched him.

Or maybe that was just the bruise.

Yeah, it was definitely the bruise, he decided as he picked up the remaining drinks and walked away from the bar. Because he definitely wasn't letting himself get involved with the girl next door.

* * *

"You calling dibs?" Carter asked when Jay rejoined his friends at their table.

"Dibs on what?" Matt Hutchinson wanted to know.

"Of course I'm not calling dibs," Jay said.

"The bartender," Natalya Vasilek answered Matt's question.

"If anyone's calling dibs, it's me," Kevin Dawson declared. "I saw her first."

"No, you didn't," Carter told him. "Because the 'hot new bartender' is a friend and neighbor of our CEO."

Kevin swore.

"But he's not calling dibs," Matt reminded them all.

"Maybe because he likes and respects the woman too much to talk about her as if she was an object up for grabs," Hayley MacDowell said sharply.

"Whatever Jay's reasons," Kevin insisted, "if he's not calling dibs, *I* am."

"No one is calling dibs on Alyssa," Jay said in a tone that brooked no argument.

Carter tipped his bottle to his lips but kept his gaze on his friend, silently assessing.

Conversation moved on to other topics, including a rehashing of all the highlights of their recent game. As they talked, their glasses and bottles emptied.

"I think Alyssa's the real reason you broke up with Renee," Carter said to Jay when the play-by-play had begun to lag.

"I broke up with Renee because she ranked below my business and my friends on my list of priorities," he replied.

"That might be true," Nat allowed. "But that doesn't explain why you keep looking at the bartender."

He dragged his gaze away from Alyssa.

"And the Master Assassin strikes again," Hayley noted.

"Who's got the next round?" Jay asked, holding up his empty glass.

"I think it's my turn," Hayley said, pushing away from the table.

"I'm out," Matt said. "I've gotta get home to Carrie."

Kevin made a sound like a whip being cracked.

Their soon-to-be-married friend was unperturbed. "Yeah, it's a real drag, being engaged to a gorgeous woman with whom I share mutual interests, stimulating conversation and really hot sex."

"I'll give you a hand," Nat said to Hayley, no doubt eager for an excuse to leave the three remaining men at the table.

When they returned with the next round of drinks, conversation shifted again to more neutral topics.

A short while later, Kevin left with Hayley, because they were headed in the same direction. Then Carter and Nat headed out together. Jay knew that he should make his way home, too. Weekends were the busiest time at Adventure Village, and he had the early-morning shift the next day—including two birthday parties on-site.

But he stayed where he was, sipping his Coke and wondering about the discovery that his neighbor and the hot new bartender were one and the same.

Though pouring drinks kept her hands busy, Alyssa's gaze kept shifting between the clock and the door—and, occasionally, the table where Jason was sitting with his friends. Where he remained after his friends had gone.

Sky bumped her hip. "Should we update our earlier conversation?"

"About what?" Alyssa looked at the clock again.

"Your claim that you have yet to meet someone with whom you want to get naked. Because while you're acting as if you're not watching Jason Channing, he's acting as if he's not watching you."

She shook her head. "Jason's my neighbor."

"That could be convenient," her friend said.

"Have you heard anything from Liam?" she asked, eager to change the topic of conversation—and for Sky's brother to make his promised appearance.

Now Sky glanced at the clock and frowned. "No, I haven't. And I didn't expect him to be *this* late."

The only consolation for Alyssa was that Diego was late, too. Or maybe he wasn't coming. She mentally crossed her fingers that she could get so lucky.

"I'll see if I can reach him on his cell," Sky said.

"Thanks."

She looked at the clock again.

Nine twenty-eight.

Sky shook her head as she tucked her phone back into her pocket before heading to the other end of the bar to refill Gavin Virga's drink.

Alyssa sighed.

"Is something wrong?"

She jolted at the sound of his voice so close, then laughed as she pressed a hand to the heart that was hammering inside her chest.

"I seem to have a habit of startling you," Jason apologized.

"It's okay," she said. "My mind was just somewhere else."

"I can't imagine anywhere more interesting than here," he deadpanned.

She laughed again. "Did you want something to drink?"

He shook his head. "I noticed that you've been watching the door."

"I guess I have been," she admitted.

"Waiting for someone?" He straddled an empty stool.

"Sort of."

"How can you 'sort of' be waiting for someone?"

"Well, there's one person I'm hoping will come through the door and another I'm hoping won't," she explained.

"Now I'm intrigued," he said.

Over his shoulder, she saw a familiar figure walk into the bar and swore under her breath.

Or maybe the curse wasn't as restrained as she thought, because Jason's brows lifted—a silent question that she didn't have time to answer. Because Diego had spotted her, too, and was moving purposefully toward her.

And though Jason hadn't been her first choice, she decided that if she could have a fantasy romance with any man of her choosing, there wasn't anyone more fantasy worthy than her handsome upstairs neighbor.

"I'll explain later," she promised as growing desperation pushed aside both rational thought and common sense. "For now, will you please just go with it?"

"Go with—"

She didn't let him finish the question before she leaned across the bar and kissed him.

If this was "it," Jason decided as Alyssa's mouth moved over his, he could definitely go with it. For now and as long as she wanted, because her lips were soft and warm and seductively persuasive.

He'd be lying if he said that he hadn't thought about kissing her, because she was the type of woman that any red-blooded man would be attracted to. But he also knew that it wasn't always a good idea to act on an attraction—such as when the woman who stirred his blood was a friend, co-worker or neighbor. Alyssa checked off two of those boxes, so no matter how much his hormones sat up and begged for attention whenever she was around—and there was no denying that they did—he'd mostly managed to ignore them.

There was no hope of ignoring them now.

She smelled so good...tasted even better.

And he wished there wasn't eighteen inches of polished walnut between them, so that he could put his arms around her and haul her against his body. He settled for circling her wrists with his hands. His thumbs rubbed over her pulse points, finding evidence that her heart was racing as fast as his own.

"I think that should do it." She whispered the words against his lips before she eased away.

Do what? he wondered, noting that her mouth was moist and swollen from their kiss, her cheeks flushed.

But before he could catch his breath to ask the question aloud, someone spoke from behind him.

"I heard this was a friendly establishment," the male voice remarked. "Do all customers get that kind of attention?"

The color in her cheeks deepened. "Diego...um...hi." Then she seemed to gather her thoughts to respond to his question. "And, uh, no."

"You must be someone special, then," the man she'd referred to as Diego remarked, his narrowed gaze focused on Jay.

"Very special," Alyssa chimed in quickly. "Jason is... my boyfriend."

Though Jay instinctively chafed against the word, the silent plea in her eyes begged him not to contradict her claim. Recalling her promise of an explanation later, he decided to go with it—at least for now.

"And you would be?" Jay prompted the other man.

Alyssa jumped in again. "This is Diego Garcia, a family friend from California."

"Well, any friend of Alyssa's is a friend of mine," he said.

Diego shook his proffered hand, squeezing more firmly than was warranted.

"You're a long way from home," Jay commented.

"I'm visiting a cousin in Elko," Diego said. "And since I was going to be so close, Renata suggested that I stop in to say hi to her daughter."

"And now you have," he said pointedly.

Diego nodded and turned his attention back to Alyssa. "If you're not working tomorrow night, maybe we could have dinner together," he suggested.

"I'm not working," she admitted, glancing at Jay, those melted chocolate eyes pleading. "But—"

"But we already have plans for tomorrow night," he finished for her.

"Plans that can't be changed to accommodate a friend from back home?" Diego directed the question at Alyssa.

"Unfortunately, yes," Jay responded. "You see, it's our three-month anniversary tomorrow and I have a very special evening planned."

"How about lunch, then?" the other man offered as an alternative.

"Sorry," he interjected, though the invitation clearly hadn't been directed at—or even intended to include—him. "But we're tied up for the whole weekend."

"And I'm heading back Sunday morning," Diego admitted.

"Well, I hope you enjoy your visit with your cousin and have a safe trip back," Alyssa said, clearly eager for the man to be on his way.

Jay knew that would probably be for the best, but he couldn't deny a certain curiosity about Diego's connection to his neighbor. And since Alyssa herself was rather tight-lipped whenever he asked her about her previous life in California, he decided that this was too good an opportunity to pass up.

"But since you're here now," he said to the other man, "why don't you let me buy you a drink?"

Chapter Four

*W*hat was he doing?

Alyssa frowned at Jason, silently communicating her annoyance.

She couldn't imagine Diego saying yes, but still—what could have possessed her pretend boyfriend to make such an offer? She held her breath as Diego glanced at his watch, shrugged.

"I wouldn't mind a cup of coffee before I make the drive back," he decided.

"Make that two cups, honey bear," Jason said to her.

Honey bear?

But of course, she couldn't object to his use of the term because she needed his help if her ploy was to succeed. Instead, she forced a smile. "Of course, sugar muffin. I was just about to make a fresh pot—I'll have Geena bring it over when it's ready."

Though his brows lifted, a smile tugged at the corners

of his mouth before he turned away to guide Diego to a vacant table.

"Sugar muffin?" Sky echoed quizzically.

"It was the first thing that came to mind," Alyssa admitted.

"I can't believe you're fake cheating on my brother with someone called 'sugar muffin,'" her coworker remarked.

"Your brother stood me up," Alyssa pointed out in her defense.

"He was late," Sky acknowledged, pretending to be miffed. "And you didn't wait half an hour to throw yourself into another man's arms."

"Actually, I waited thirty-three minutes," she said. "Desperate times and all that."

But even as her words justified her actions, her heart—still racing from that kiss—worried that she might have made a very big mistake.

Sky glanced at the table where Jason and Diego were seated as she continued to mix drinks. "He's actually kind of cute."

"Jason?"

"No!" Sky said immediately. Vehemently. "Diego."

Objectively speaking, her friend was right. But Alyssa was more curious about Sky's reaction to her question about Jason. "Do you have a history with Jason Channing that I should know about?"

Sky shook her head. "Not personally."

"Impersonally?"

Her friend chuckled. "No. It's just that I'm a Gilmore and he's a Blake—or rather, his mother was a Blake."

"I'm still not following," she admitted.

"You don't know about the feud?"

"What feud?"

Sky shook her head, but before she could explain, Margot—one of the waitresses—came up to the bar with an order of drinks for a party table in the restaurant, and Sky turned her attention to filling it.

While she was busy doing that, Alyssa grabbed a bus pan to clear some of the now empty tables.

Jason and Diego were still chatting, and though she was admittedly curious about the topic of their conversation, she wasn't worried. She'd made her point to Diego. Now he could go back to Elko—and ultimately to Irvine—cured of any notion that there was a future for them together.

She sprayed and wiped a table, then turned and found herself face-to-face with her mother's best friend's favorite nephew.

"I wanted to say goodbye before I headed out," Diego said to her.

"Oh. Okay." She tightened her grip on the bus pan as he leaned over to kiss her on one cheek, then the other.

"It was good to see you, even for a couple of minutes, Alyssa."

"You, too." And now that she knew he was leaving, she managed to say the words with a believable amount of sincerity.

Or maybe she was *too* believable, because he tried again. "You're sure you don't have any free time this weekend?"

She glanced at the table where Jason was still sitting, watching them, and shook her head. "I don't know what plans Jason has made—" which was the absolute truth "—but if he says we're booked, we're booked."

"I guess I'll see you in July, then."

The expression on her face must have matched the blankness of her mind, because he smiled, and she realized that Sky was right—he was kind of cute. But she wasn't attracted to him in the least.

"Your parents' anniversary party," Diego reminded her. "I assume you'll be home for that?"

"Oh, yes. Of course," she agreed.

"Then I'll see you there."

She exhaled a long, grateful sigh of relief when he finally turned away and headed out the door—crossing paths with Liam Gilmore on his way in.

Sky's brother glanced toward the bar, his gaze searching. Looking for Alyssa. He found her and was at her side with a few quick strides.

"I'm late," he acknowledged, his breathless tone suggesting that he'd raced to get there.

"It's okay," she told him.

He took the bus pan from her and set it on the table. "You're too understanding," he said. "And I'm so lucky that you're mine."

Then he pulled her into his arms and kissed her.

Sharing a public kiss with Jason Channing had drawn more attention than Alyssa wanted. Now, barely more than an hour later, she was kissing Liam Gilmore in the same bar—with Jason Channing watching!

She pulled away. "Stop. Please."

"What's wrong?"

"What's wrong is that you're making a move on my girl," Jason said.

Liam scowled at the other man. "Excuse me?"

Jason slid an arm across her shoulders. "Honey bear, you said you were going to tell him that you'd finally found a real man."

Liam's eyes narrowed dangerously.

Alyssa stepped between the two men. "Diego was here and you weren't," she explained to Liam. "So I tagged Jason to fill in."

"There was no one else around?" Liam's tone was petulant.

"Only Jason and Gavin Virga," she said, naming the octogenarian ophthalmologist who was a Friday night regular.

"So why'd you pick *him*?" he asked again, glaring at Jason.

Alyssa nudged Liam toward the bar. "Go ask your sister to pour you a beer," she suggested.

He did so, but only after shooting one last narrow-eyed stare at Jason.

"I appreciate you pinch-hitting tonight," she said to Jason. "But now that Diego's gone, you can go, too."

"I haven't paid for the coffee."

"I did."

"Why?"

She shrugged. "I figured it was the least I could do to thank you for playing along."

His gaze dropped to her mouth, lingered. And when his lips started to curve, as if he was remembering the kiss they'd shared, her own started to tingle.

She pressed them firmly together and reminded herself that "Charming" had probably kissed most of the women in Haven at one time or another, and she shouldn't make the mistake of thinking that one spontaneous lip-lock had made any kind of impression on him.

"It wasn't much of a hardship," he assured her.

She picked up the bus pan again. "I've got to, uh, get this back to the kitchen."

He didn't object as she slipped past him.

The dishwasher took the pan from her with a nod of thanks, but Alyssa hid in the kitchen for another minute—just long enough to catch her breath and give her heart a chance to beat normally again.

It was just a kiss.

A kiss that had meant less than nothing to both of them. And yet...

She lifted a hand to her mouth.

And yet she'd felt so much in those few seconds that their lips had been connected. More than she'd ever felt from just a kiss. More than she'd ever felt with any other man.

"Alyssa?"

She started, her hand dropping from her lips as she turned to Sky. "Um, yeah. I'll be right out."

"Actually, I was going to tell you that you could take off early, if you want," her friend said. "Most of the tables are empty now and there are only a few stragglers left at the bar."

"Are you sure you don't mind?"

"I'm sure. And you've had a rather…eventful night already," Sky said, her tone tinged with amusement.

"That's one word for it," she agreed. "But I should talk to your brother before I go."

"Liam's cool—it's the other one who looked as if he was going to pop a vein in his head when he saw my brother kiss you."

"Jason?"

"For a moment, I thought fists were going to fly—and then I would've had to ban my own brother from the bar for a year."

It was a harsh punishment, but one Duke insisted be meted out to anyone who dared to throw a punch inside his establishment. Which might be why, in the eight months she'd lived in Haven, Alyssa had never heard about anyone fighting inside Diggers'—although rumor had it that Doug Holland's bar privileges had been reinstated only at the end of January, a full year after he'd given Jerry Tate a black eye for suggesting that his wife was stepping out. Sky had given Alyssa the background on the situation, explaining that Jerry had clearly been baiting the other man, because anyone who knew Doug's wife knew there wasn't another man in town who would want her.

She followed Sky back out front, surprised to discover that Jason had again taken a seat at the bar.

"I didn't expect you'd still be here," she said, glancing warily toward the opposite end of the counter, where Liam was sipping a beer and chatting with his sister.

"What kind of a man would leave his beautiful girl-friend alone in a place like this on a Friday night?" he countered.

"The kind of man who isn't really dating the bartender," she suggested.

"But that's not what you wanted Diego to think, was it?"

"Diego's probably halfway back to Elko by now," she pointed out.

"Still, I figured I should stick around in case he came back."

"I think—I hope—he finally got the message tonight."

"I wouldn't count on it," Jason said. "You were sending out some pretty mixed signals."

"What do you mean?"

"First you kissed me, then you kissed Gilmore."

She managed a weak smile. "Yeah. It's a good thing that Diego had already left, because that might have been a little hard to explain."

"Try explaining it to me," he suggested.

"I think I'm going to need a glass of wine for that."

"Are you allowed to drink on the job?"

She smiled as she shook her head. "I meant at home—I'm finished for the night."

His brows lifted. "And you're inviting me to go home with you—after only one kiss?"

"I'm offering to continue the explanation someplace

where I can kick off my shoes and put my feet up," she clarified.

He rose from his seat as she made her way around the bar.

"I'd offer to give you a lift home," he said, "but I got a ride with my friends—and they all abandoned me."

"So instead you're asking me for a lift home?"

He flashed his usual bone-melting smile. "If it won't take you too far out of your way."

"Lucky for you, my car has a full tank of gas."

He should have left the bar with his friends.

If Jay had walked out with Carter or Kevin, he wouldn't have ended up kissing Alyssa. Because now that he'd kissed her, he couldn't stop thinking about it—and wanting to do it again.

At twenty-nine, he was old enough to have learned that he couldn't always get what he wanted. But as a bachelor and heir to the Blake Mining fortune, it wasn't a lesson that seemed to apply in his relationships with women. Even back in high school, girls had practically lined up for the privilege of dating him, and he hadn't wanted to say no to any of them.

It had taken some time—and the anonymity that came with being an unknown freshman at an out-of-state college—before he gained some perspective. He no longer hit on every attractive woman who crossed his path, he ensured that any woman he did go out with wasn't under the illusion that a few nights in his bed would lead to a ring on her finger and he'd concluded that certain relationships tipped the scales against personal involvement—which was why he didn't date friends, coworkers or neighbors.

Alyssa was the first woman in a long time who tempted him to break that rule.

Going back to her place—which was only one flight of

stairs below his own—was an effective reminder of the most important reason not to make a move on his neighbor. And still, that reminder didn't completely snuff out the temptation.

"You were going to tell me about your love-struck suitor," Jay said, stepping across the threshold into her apartment.

She'd never invited him into her place before, and he was suddenly conscious of the fact that he was in her personal living space. A passing thought that turned his mind in a direction he was trying not to go. So he stayed where he was, just inside the door, while she crossed through the living room to the kitchen, her heels clicking on the hardwood floor.

"I don't think he's love-struck so much as misguided." She took a glass from the cupboard and removed the stopper from a previously opened bottle of wine on the counter. "And that's my mother's fault." She held up the bottle to show him the label. "Do you want a glass?"

"Do you have any beer?" he asked.

She shook her head. "Sorry."

"Then I'll have what you're having," he said.

She poured a second glass, then picked up both and carried them toward the seating area.

"Are you going to come inside and drink it?" she asked, the hint of a smile tugging at the corners of her mouth and lighting her dark eyes. "Or would you prefer to have it by the door?"

He'd stayed where he was in order to put as much physical space as possible between them, as if that distance might somehow dull his awareness of her. "It's a nice door," he said.

"Similar to the one on your apartment, I'd guess."

"Similar," he agreed as he crossed the floor to join her, though he chose a deep leather chair rather than the sofa where she'd settled. "And having spent some time with Diego tonight, I can tell you that he's more than misguided. In fact, I'd say he's somewhere between seriously infatuated and head over heels."

"What was that about, anyway?" she demanded. "He was ready to turn around and walk out the door when you asked him to stay."

"It was…an impulse," he told her, because he wasn't entirely sure of the reason himself.

"Why?" She lifted her glass to her lips.

He shrugged. "Doesn't the definition of impulse preclude there being a reason?"

"Not necessarily."

"And anyway, you're the one who promised an explanation," he reminded her.

"You're right."

"Am I also right in assuming that what happened tonight is somehow connected to the conversation you had with your mother this morning—the one in which you lied about having a boyfriend?"

She nodded.

"And the reason you lied?" he prompted.

"Because of Diego." She sipped her wine. "No, that's not entirely true. Diego is only the most recent of my mother's matchmaking efforts."

"How many have there been?" he wondered.

"It seems as if there's a new one every time I go home," she told him. "At Thanksgiving it was Tony. At Christmas it was Evan—until she realized no progress was being made there and brought Diego in to celebrate the New Year with us."

"Is your mother a professional matchmaker?"

"No. She's a financial analyst, but trying to find the perfect man for me has become her latest hobby. Or maybe it's an obsession. But it's not because she wants to help me find the perfect guy—she just wants me to find a guy who will convince me to move back to California. And not only is Diego her best friend's favorite nephew, he lives in the same neighborhood as my parents."

"That kind of relative and geographic proximity is a definite red flag," he agreed. "You never want to get involved with somebody that you might run into on a regular basis after the relationship ends, because those encounters can be awkward and messy."

She studied him over the rim of her glass. "On the surface, that sounds like a valid argument—except for one thing."

"What's that?"

"It assumes that every potential relationship is doomed from the start."

"Have you ever had a relationship that didn't end?" he challenged.

"Since I just told you about my mother's efforts to find my perfect match, it's safe to assume you already know the answer to that question."

"There you go," Jay said.

She shook her head. "Just because I'm not in love—and not looking for love—doesn't mean that I don't believe it exists," she told him. "And I'm not going to let some artificial boundary determine who I can and cannot date."

Which prompted him to ask the question that had been nudging at his mind for the past two hours: "Is that why you kissed me?"

Alyssa stared at him, certain she couldn't have heard him correctly. "What did you just say?"

"I asked if you kissed me because you were tired of waiting for me to make a move."

His response did nothing to clarify his question, but only succeeded in flustering her almost as much as the kiss.

"I was *never* waiting for you to make a move," she assured him. "And when I kissed you—that wasn't me making a move, that was sheer desperation."

He frowned. "You're saying that you *don't* want to go out with me?"

"Ohmygod—no!" she said quickly, emphatically.

"By all means, take a minute to think about the question before you answer," he said drily.

She felt her cheeks burn. "I don't need a minute to think about it," she said. "I do *not* want to go out with you."

Okay, maybe she secretly thought he was the hottest guy she'd ever known, but he wasn't at all her type. Not that she had a type—but she was certain that he did. She'd seen him around town with different women on various occasions, and they were all tall, slender and blonde. Alyssa was five feet six inches—when she was wearing two-inch heels—and though she wasn't overweight, she was definitely more curvy than most of the women he'd dated, with dark hair and eyes that attested to her Mexican heritage.

"And seriously, what kind of question is that?" she demanded. "How massive is your ego that you'd think I was looking for an opportunity to get close to you?"

He just shrugged. "A lot of women in this town consider me to be a catch."

"I'm not interested in catching you—or anyone. I don't even want to play the game."

"So I really was just in the wrong place at the wrong time?"

"You really were," she confirmed.

But even as she spoke those words to reassure him, there was a part of her that wondered if she was wrong—and that he'd been in exactly the right place at the right time.

Chapter Five

Jay heard voices in the hall and glanced up when Carter, Nat and Kevin came into the office together the next morning. They had a tray of coffee and box of pastries from The Daily Grind, and he held out his hand for his usual—large, black—desperate for the hit of caffeine to revive his sluggish brain. He peeled back the lid and lifted the cup to his mouth.

"Thanks," he said. "I really needed that this morning—I don't think I managed even four hours of sleep last night."

Carter opened the box of pastries and Jay's gaze zeroed in on the bear claw—at the same moment Kevin snatched it out of the box and bit into it.

"I thought the bear claw was mine."

"Did you?" his friend asked around a mouthful of sweet, fried dough. "It really sucks when someone else moves in and takes something you've had your eye on, doesn't it?"

Jay looked questioningly at his other friends. "Why do I get the impression this isn't about the bear claw?"

"Because it's about Alyssa," Nat said.

"What about Alyssa?" he asked cautiously.

Kevin's only response was to take another big bite of the pastry.

"When we were at The Daily Grind, we heard Megan Carmichael telling Kenzie Atkins that you were locking lips with the new bartender at Diggers' last night," Nat explained.

Jay shouldn't have been surprised. The Daily Grind wasn't just Haven's café and bakery, it was where the latest rumors were always as hot as the coffee.

"It's not what you think," he said.

"You mean you weren't kissing Alyssa?" Kevin challenged.

"I mean that's only part of the story."

"I don't care about the story," his friend said. "It's Lacey Bolton all over again."

"Seriously, Kev? That was twelve years ago," Jay said. "Can you forget about Lacey Bolton already?"

"Can you not see that this isn't about Lacey Bolton but the guy who screwed over a friend for the sake of a pretty girl?"

"The situation is completely different."

"Not from my perspective," Kevin argued. "You put the moves on a girl you knew I've had my eye on for weeks."

"First, I didn't put any moves on her—*she* kissed *me*," Jay pointed out in his defense. "Second, how is it my fault that you don't have the guts to make a move on a girl you've supposedly had your eye on for weeks?"

"I was waiting for the right moment," Kevin said.

"How long were you going to wait?" Jay wondered.

"Until last night," his friend said. "If you remember, it

was my idea to go to Diggers' last night because I knew Alyssa would be working."

"And if you remember, you left the bar without making any kind of move."

"She was busy," Kevin said in his defense.

"That didn't stop Carter from flirting with her."

Kevin glared at their other friend.

"But all I did was flirt—Jay's the one who kissed her," Carter said, eager to throw Jay under the bus.

He could argue again that she'd kissed *him*, but he couldn't deny that there had been kissing. Instead, he said, "Do you want me to apologize?"

"Are you sorry?" Kevin asked.

He thought about the very public and very brief kiss he'd shared with Alyssa and felt desire stir low in his belly. He could tell Kevin that it wasn't quite as steamy as people were saying, but the memory of that innocent kiss had kept him awake half the night. He could lie, but they'd been friends for too long for that option to sit comfortably with him. "No," he admitted.

Kevin shook his head. "You haven't changed at all."

"What's that supposed to mean?"

"It's always been about the score with you. Jay always has to be with the hottest girls, the most girls—even the unavailable girls."

"I was a dick in high school," he acknowledged. "But we're not in high school anymore."

"You don't think kissing Alyssa was a dick move?"

Of course it was, if he'd done it for the purpose of getting between his friend and the girl he liked. But he hadn't. Nor could he deny that his friend's secret crush on the bartender had been the furthest thing from his mind when Alyssa's mouth touched his.

"Okay, it was," he agreed. "But when you were talking

about the new bartender at Diggers', I had no idea it was Alyssa. If I'd known, I would have told you—weeks ago—that I knew her."

"I don't care that you knew her first—you shouldn't have kissed her."

"I get that this is a guy thing," Nat interjected. "You want to beat your chests to figure out who gets the hot girl, but you're overlooking two key pieces of the puzzle."

"What pieces?" Carter asked.

"First, dibs and friendships aside, it's not up to you to decide who gets Alyssa—it's up to her. And truthfully, I don't know why she'd waste her time with either one of you."

"Thanks," Jay said. "That's very helpful."

"Second," she continued, as if he hadn't spoken, "and this point is really for Kevin…I know you think Jay only kissed Alyssa because he knew you had a crush on her, but that's not true."

"How do you know it's not true?" Kevin demanded.

"Because Jay isn't a big fan of early mornings, but he's been the first one here almost every day for the past several weeks."

"He owns seventy percent of the business—he should be the first one here every day," Kevin pointed out.

"I didn't know there was a gold star for being an early riser," Jay said, giving Nat a subtle shake of his head.

Which she, of course, ignored. "You don't get out of bed early for a gold star—you get out of bed early to go running with Alyssa every morning."

"Is that true?" Kevin asked.

"Every morning, Monday through Friday, since early March," Nat informed them.

And Jay silently cursed himself for ever confiding in her about his new routine with his neighbor.

"That's almost two months," Carter said, obviously surprised by this revelation. "And probably the longest relationship you've had with a woman in years."

"So why haven't you asked her out?" Kevin wondered. "Or did you ask and she shot you down?"

"I didn't ask," Jay said. "Because getting involved with Alyssa would violate the proximity rule."

"Getting involved with anyone in this town would violate the proximity rule," Nat remarked.

"You won't ask her out, but you kissed her last night?"

Jay gave up trying to explain. "It didn't mean anything to either of us."

"Or did it?" Nat conjectured.

"You can butt out anytime now," Jay told her.

"Actually, I want to know what Nat's thinking," Kevin said.

"Tread carefully—a woman's mind can be a complicated and dangerous thing," Carter warned.

Nat glanced at him over her shoulder. "*You* can butt out."

Carter mimed zipping his lips.

"Maybe the kiss didn't mean anything to Jay," Nat allowed. "In which case you're completely justified in being pissed at him. But I think you should give him the benefit of the doubt—and the chance to prove that he didn't kiss her to undermine you, but because he really likes this girl."

"How's he going to prove that?" Kevin challenged.

She considered for a minute. "Jay does seem to have a short attention span when it comes to the women he dates, and the two-month mark is usually when he starts to feel suffocated and look for an escape hatch."

"That's not true," Jay denied.

"Name the last girl you were with for more than two months," she suggested.

He couldn't do it—not without admitting that it had been back when he was in college, and then opening himself up to further analysis of his dating patterns and commitment issues. Maybe being cruelly jilted by his high school girlfriend at a vulnerable time had done a number on him, but he hadn't completely closed off his heart—he just hadn't met a woman whom he wanted to let in.

And while Nat clearly wanted to believe that Alyssa Cabrera might be that woman, Jay remained skeptical.

She turned her attention back to Kevin. "So if Jay invites Alyssa to be his date for Matt's wedding—"

"That's not going to happen," he interjected.

"—then he'd have to be with her for another two months, which might make him crazy—and provide some satisfaction for you."

"What if it doesn't make him crazy?" Kevin challenged.

"Then it would mean he really does have feelings for her," Nat reasoned. "And you wouldn't want to stand in the way of that, would you?"

"I don't know—I'll have to think on that," Kevin told her.

"All of this speculation is moot," Jay said. "Because I'm not asking Alyssa to be my date for Matt's wedding."

"Then I guess our friendship means even less to you than the kiss you shared with her last night."

"Come on, Kev. You know that's not true."

"I'll know it when you invite Alyssa to the wedding."

"Seriously? If I invite Alyssa to the wedding, you'll forgive me for kissing her?"

"She has to accept the invitation," Nat said. "And you can't date any other women between now and then."

Kevin nodded his agreement of the terms.

Jay shook his head, even as he recognized that he'd been neatly backed into a corner. "Okay. I'll do it," he finally relented. Because he and Kevin had been friends for a long

time, and because he didn't think dancing with Alyssa at
Matt's wedding would be much of a hardship. "Now if we
can focus on the business of business, there's a group of
fifteen coming in at ten for paintball who will need protective gear, weapons and ammunition."

Carter took the hint—and another doughnut from the
box—and headed down to the pro shop.

"Hayley's going to be here around lunchtime to super-
vise the party room today, but we've got balloons and a
cake coming before then," Jay said to Kevin. "Can you
keep an eye out for that while you're covering mini putt
and the arcade?"

The other man nodded and headed out, leaving Jay and
Nat alone—a situation from which she seemed eager to
escape.

"I should check the—"

"What the hell?" he said, cutting her off.

She folded her arms across her chest. "Actually, I think
the words you're looking for are *thank* and *you*."

"You expect me to be grateful?"

"Yes, because I gave you the excuse you needed to break
your ridiculous proximity rule and go out with the girl
who's piqued your interest more than anyone has done in
a long time."

"I don't need an excuse—if I wanted to break the rule,
I would. The fact that I haven't should tell you that I'm—"

"Afraid?" she suggested.

He frowned. "What am I supposedly afraid of?"

"Having a real adult relationship with someone you
might be capable of genuinely caring about."

"You don't even know Alyssa," he pointed out.

"True," she acknowledged. "But I know you."

"I'm *not* going to thank you for this."

"Yes, you will," she said and walked out the door.

* * *

Alyssa awakened the next day feeling out of sorts—and grateful that Jason went into work early on Saturdays, so she didn't have to face him this morning. She didn't even want to get dressed and head out for her run, but she knew she'd feel better once she was moving and her adrenaline was pumping. She tried to clear her mind as her feet pounded the pavement, but she couldn't stop thinking about everything that had happened the night before—but mostly about the kiss she'd shared with Jason.

She'd kissed Liam, too. Well, technically, he'd kissed her. But in each case, her lips had made contact with those of a handsome Haven bachelor. But while kissing Liam had felt as dispassionate as kissing a male relative, kissing Jason had been a very different experience.

The minute their mouths had brushed, she'd felt nothing but heat. It was as if she was dry kindling and his lips were a match, the strike of which started a slow burn deep in her belly that quickly spread through her veins, singeing her nerve endings and melting her bones.

Of course, after Diego left, Jason had acted as if it had never happened. He'd certainly given no indication that the moment they'd shared had made any kind of impression on him.

If only she could say the same. The truth was, she hadn't stopped thinking about the kiss. One kiss that couldn't have lasted more than a few seconds. Half a minute at most. And yet, nearly twelve hours later, her lips still tingled.

She was supposed to be an independent woman happily living her own life. But in that brief moment when she'd been kissing Jason, she hadn't wanted to be on her own.

She'd wanted to kiss him again.

She'd wanted to do more than kiss him.

How much more she hadn't realized until she fell asleep and dreamed about him. Incredibly vivid and erotic dreams.

Desperately, she tried to shove the memories of those dreams aside. Because her mind was so unfocused, she forced herself to alter her route, pushing herself to go a little farther and a little faster. But she couldn't outrun her memories of the seductive feel of his lips moving over hers.

After she'd showered and had breakfast, she sat down to mark lab reports. As usual, there were some kids who understood the purpose of the assignment, carefully followed the requisite steps and meticulously recorded their findings, and others whose reports looked as if they had put words and numbers into a blender and randomly scattered them on the page. Those took a lot more focus—and patience—as she attempted to decipher where she could give marks.

After breaking for lunch, she finished up the lab reports and then had absolutely no idea what to do with the rest of her day.

The knock at the door came when she was cleaning out her cupboards. She wasn't expecting any visitors, but Helen Powell sometimes stopped by just to check in with her, and Alyssa always enjoyed those spontaneous drop-ins.

She opened the door expecting to see her elderly across-the-hall neighbor—and found herself looking at her sexy upstairs neighbor instead. Her heart kicked hard against her ribs.

"Hi, honey bear—I'm home."

Then his gaze skimmed over her, from the messy ponytail on top of her head to the old T-shirt and leggings and rubber gloves on her hands, and his smile faded. "You're not ready."

She brushed an errant strand of hair out of her eyes with the back of her arm, embarrassed to have been caught looking so unkempt by a man who always looked so good. "Ready for what?"

"Our date."

She eyed him warily. "Have you been drinking?"

He shook his head slowly, clearly communicating disappointment. "I can't believe you forgot about our plans."

"We didn't have plans."

"For our three-month anniversary," he prompted.

"Our *what*?" Then she remembered the excuse he'd made to Diego the night before, to explain why she wasn't free to have dinner with the other man. "Well, considering that our romantic relationship is entirely fictitious, I trust you can forgive me for not remembering plans we never actually made."

He glanced at his watch. "I can forgive you—if you can be ready in twenty minutes."

"You're serious," she realized.

"I am," he confirmed.

She narrowed her gaze. "Last night you accused me of making a move on you—"

"I was wrong," he acknowledged.

"—and now you're at my door," she noted. "Why?"

"Because you are, by your own admission, a terrible liar, and I don't want you to have to lie to your mother when she asks what we did to celebrate the occasion."

"She won't ask," Alyssa told him.

"Is that a risk you're willing to take rather than put down your bucket and cloth and come with me?"

"Come with you where?" she asked warily.

He responded with the same words she'd spoken to him the night before: "Just go with it."

Chapter Six

Jay took her to Adventure Village. It wasn't his usual destination for a first date, but he wanted to show off the business he'd built—and have some fun, too.

"I didn't know there was mini golf here," Alyssa admitted when he handed her a putter and an orange ball.

"We started out with a couple of paintball fields, but we've expanded a lot since then," he said proudly. "Hayley is currently designing a new brochure and working on a marketing plan to showcase our newest offerings."

He gestured to the tee area. "Ladies first."

She set her ball down, then crouched to read the green and assess the break.

"Someone takes her mini golf seriously," he mused.

She sent him a quelling glance. "Quiet in the gallery."

His lips curved, but he dutifully remained silent as she lined up her shot.

Her stroke, relaxed and smooth, had the ball rolling up

and over the first hill, gaining enough speed to climb over the next and then come to a stop less than three inches from the cup. His tee shot went out of bounds, costing him a penalty stroke. She finished the first hole with a birdie, he recorded a double bogey.

And that was pretty much par for the course over the next seventeen holes. He did manage a hole in one on number twelve, while Alyssa aced numbers eight, eleven, twelve and fifteen.

"Well, that was fun," he said when he'd tallied up their scores and returned their putters to the rack.

She laughed. "It really was—or at least more fun than washing my kitchen floor."

"Is that how you usually spend your Saturday nights?" he wondered.

"I don't wash the floor every Saturday night," she said. "Sometimes I do windows."

He chuckled as he slid an arm across her shoulders. "While not quite as exciting as that, we do have an arcade where we could kill some time waiting for our dinner to get here," he said, leading her to another room.

Alyssa immediately zeroed in on the Tetris machine. "Do you ever play?" she asked.

He tapped the leaderboard on the screen, pointing to player name JC12 in the second-place position.

"Who's Ford68?" she queried, noting the name in first place.

"My buddy Carter—the one who was pretending not to hit on you last night." Jay pulled a couple tokens out of his pocket. "Do you want to give it a go?"

"Sure," she agreed.

He slid the tokens into the slot, hit the button to select "2-player game" and stood there, watching with his jaw on the ground, as Alyssa effortlessly decimated level after level of the game.

She was still playing when he went to the main entrance to collect and pay for the pizza he'd ordered.

"Are your hands cramping yet?" he asked when he returned to the arcade after setting their food in the party room.

"A little."

"You want to take a break and have some pizza before it gets cold?"

"I just need two more minutes to move into first place on the leaderboard," she told him.

It took her less time than that.

Jay owned the top spot on a couple other games, but he'd never been able to bump Carter out of the number one position on Tetris. Alyssa had done so without breaking a sweat. And watching her had left him feeling both awed…and aroused.

She could have racked up an even higher score, but she stepped away from the game and shook out her hands, flexing her fingers to restore blood flow.

"I didn't know what you liked, so I got half with just cheese and half with pepperoni," he said, turning his attention to their dinner.

"I like pizza," she said.

He opened the box and turned it toward her. She opted for pepperoni, carefully lifting a slice and setting it on the paper plate he'd given her.

"Regular cola, diet cola, orange soda or water?"

"Orange," she decided.

He retrieved two cans from the fridge, then took his seat across from her and selected his pizza.

"You must have spent a lot of time hanging out in arcades while you were growing up," he remarked.

Alyssa shook her head as she peeled a slice of pepperoni off her pizza. "I spent a lot of time with the Game Boy my parents bought to eliminate my boredom while I waited around in hospitals and doctors' offices."

He paused with his can of soda halfway to his mouth. "You were sick?"

She chewed the sausage, swallowed. "I was born with an atrial septal defect—more commonly known as a hole in my heart."

"What does that mean?"

"It means, in my case specifically, that there was an abnormal opening in the upper chambers of my heart," she explained. "I had three surgeries in the first five years of my life, after which the doctors determined that I was perfectly healthy and could do any and everything that all the other kids were doing."

"That must have been a relief."

"You'd think so," she agreed. "But my parents didn't believe the doctors, which meant I was subjected to numerous ongoing tests in their efforts to get a lot of second and third opinions." She lifted the slice of pizza from her plate. "And that was a pretty heavy topic for a fake first date, wasn't it?"

"If there's a list of conversational topics assigned to specific date numbers, I've never seen it," he told her.

She smiled. "Well, I apologize for dumping all that medical history on you."

"No apology necessary," he assured her. "Though I think I'm beginning to understand why you moved from Southern California to northern Nevada."

"It was actually my sister's idea," she confided. "Not Nevada specifically, but the moving away from home."

"Older or younger sister?"

"Older by three years. Cristina's an executive at Google,

married for seven years to a terrific guy with whom she has an adorable almost-five-year-old son."

"Any other siblings?"

She shook her head. "My parents always imagined they'd have a houseful of kids, but that plan was put aside while they focused on making sure I got healthy."

"I've got a brother and two sisters," he said, shifting the focus of the conversation in an attempt to lighten the mood. "All younger. All a pain in my butt while we were growing up. Actually, they're still a pain in my butt most of the time."

She nibbled on her pizza. "Tell me about them."

"My sister Regan is twenty-seven and an accountant at Blake Mining. Spencer is twenty-five and travels the rodeo circuit as a professional cowboy, and Brielle is almost twenty-four and a kindergarten teacher at a private school in Brooklyn."

"That's a long way from home," Alyssa mused.

"She went to New York City to go to college and decided to stay."

"Do you ever visit her there?"

He nodded. "I've been a few times."

"Is it as fabulous as it looks in the movies?" she asked.

"If towering skyscrapers, bumper-to-bumper traffic and oppressive crowds of people are your idea of fabulous."

She smiled, undaunted by his description. "It's been a long-time dream of mine to visit there someday," she admitted. "To see Times Square and Central Park and the Statue of Liberty. To look out over the city from the top of the Empire State Building, see a Broadway show, take in the exhibits at MOMA and the Guggenheim."

"It sounds as if you've given this some thought," he noted.

"A little," she admitted, then laughed. "Or a lot."

"So why haven't you gone?"

It was a good question.

She'd held herself back from doing so many things because she didn't want to give her parents any more cause for concern. And the idea of her youngest daughter traipsing around the country would likely give Renata Cabrera a heart attack.

"Maybe I will," she said. "Someday."

As if on cue, her cell phone rang.

"I have no idea how she does that," Alyssa muttered.

"Who?" Jason asked.

"My mother." She retrieved her phone from the side pocket of her handbag and showed him the display: Mom calling.

"Are you going to answer?"

"I'd rather not," she admitted. "But if I don't, she'll worry that something happened to me, then she'll call again and again until I do."

"Go ahead," he urged. "I'll just sit here and pretend I'm not listening to your conversation."

She was smiling as she connected the call.

But contrary to his admitted intention to eavesdrop, he pushed away from the table and moved to the other side of the room to put the leftover pizza in the fridge.

Alyssa didn't talk to her mother for very long, and when she tucked the phone away again, she asked him, "What did you say to Diego last night?"

Though she'd attempted to keep her tone neutral, some of the tension she felt must have been reflected in the question, because he responded cautiously.

"I get the feeling that you're looking for something specific, but I honestly don't remember all the details of our conversation."

"Did you tell him that I was the woman you'd dreamed

about long before we ever met, and that you couldn't wait for me to meet your family?"

"That does sound vaguely familiar," he confirmed. "An inspired off-the-cuff performance, if I do say so myself."

"You could have talked about anything else," she pointed out to him. "The Golden Knights' inaugural season, or the expansion of the subdivision on the west side of town, or even the price of tea in China. Why did you have to make up details about our nonexistent relationship?"

"Because Diego wasn't interested in any topic of conversation that wasn't you," he told her.

She shook her head. "I only meant for you to play along *in the moment*, but you took over directing and rewrote the whole script."

"What's the big deal?" he asked, unconcerned.

"The big deal is that my parents are now coming to Haven to meet you."

"Whoa!" Jay held up his hands and took an instinctive step backward, as if that might distance him from the very possibility. "I don't do meeting the parents."

"Believe me, I want them to meet you even less than you want to meet them," Alyssa said grimly.

He should be relieved she was letting him off the hook, but he couldn't help but feel a little insulted by her response. "Why don't you want them to meet me?"

"Because you're not actually my boyfriend," she reminded him.

"Okay, that's a valid point," he acknowledged.

"And now I'm going to have to tell my mother that we broke up and she'll tell Diego, and the next time I see him, he'll want to help me mend my broken heart."

"You don't look particularly brokenhearted to me," he remarked.

She dropped her face in her hands. "How did this happen to me?"

Again, he knew she wasn't really expecting an answer, but he couldn't resist teasing, "Because you lied to your mother."

"You're joking," she noted. "But maybe it's true."

"Are you suggesting that the earth's rotation is dependent on some kind of maternal karma?"

"Of course not. But there's no denying a mother's intuition," she told him.

He thought of his own mother and wasn't convinced. Margaret Blake-Channing had been too involved in her career to know—or even care—what her kids were up to most of the time. In fact, he had trouble believing that she'd been away from her office long enough to conceive and bear four children. Of course, considering that both his parents worked at Blake Mining, it was possible she hadn't left her desk at all—and that was not something he wanted to be thinking about right now. Or ever.

Not that he had any cause for complaint. He'd grown up with a lot of privileges and, though his parents had both worked long hours, Celeste had been there to ensure homework was supervised and proper meals put on the table. But the nanny/housekeeper wasn't a strict disciplinarian, so Jay had never felt the need to lie to her.

"Why do you say that?" he asked Alyssa now.

"Because anytime I've been less than completely honest with her, she's somehow known it."

"Maybe you're just a bad liar," he suggested.

"I am a bad liar," she agreed. "I don't like lying—especially to my parents. And every time I'm even just a little bit untruthful, my mother somehow knows it."

"Give me an example," he urged.

"In my junior year of high school, I was out with my

friends and took a few puffs of a cigarette that was offered to me. As soon as I got home, she asked if I'd been smoking—which, of course, I denied—and then she grounded me for smoking *and* lying."

"She probably smelled smoke on your clothes," he pointed out logically.

"And when my friend Karen swiped a bottle of vodka from her parents' liquor cabinet and we mixed it in our lemonade at the Fourth of July picnic, she asked if I'd been drinking. And there was no way she could smell that because it was vodka."

"How old were you?"

"Seventeen," she admitted.

"So maybe there were other signs that you'd been consuming alcohol," he suggested drily.

"Maybe," she acknowledged.

"So your mother caught you in lies about smoking and drinking, and you think that proves she has some kind of sixth sense about when you're lying?"

"And then there was the time I asked to go to a movie with my best friend—and I didn't tell her that we were meeting a couple of boys there, too. But somehow she knew."

"Isn't it possible that someone saw you at the theater with the boys and told her?"

"Of course," she agreed. "But the point is that she always knows when I'm not telling her the truth."

"So that's it? You've lied to her a total of three times in your life?"

"Four, including the boyfriend thing," she said. "Big lies, that is. There have been smaller ones that she lets me get away with—such as when I tell her that the chicken isn't too dry, or I like her new haircut."

"And maybe she doesn't have a clue that you're being

less than truthful about the boyfriend, and she sincerely wants to meet the guy you've been dating."

"This is all Liam's fault," Alyssa decided. "If he had been there when he said he was going to be, I would have kissed him instead of you."

"So are you and Gilmore…a thing?"

"No," she said. "I told you—I'm not dating anyone and I don't *want* to date anyone."

"Why not?" he asked curiously.

"Because I'm enjoying living my own life."

"Why would dating someone change that?"

"It wouldn't, necessarily, if it was someone other than Diego," she acknowledged. "But if I consented to a friendly dinner with my mother's best friend's favorite nephew, that friendly dinner would lead to casual dating, which would then transition into an exclusive relationship and a ring on my finger."

"You really believe that, don't you?"

She shook her head. "That's why, when my mother called to tell me that Diego was going to be in Haven, I came up with the phony boyfriend plan. But Liam wasn't there and I kissed you, and you had coffee with Diego and now…" She sighed. "It's been nice fake dating you, but now I have to figure out how to explain our breakup to my parents."

"Here's a novel idea," he said. "Why don't you tell them the truth—that you're not dating anyone because you don't want to date anyone?"

She chewed on her bottom lip as she considered her options. "Maybe I could still make this work with Liam." The furrow in her brow deepened. "Obviously I'll have to find out what other details from your conversation Diego passed along to my mother."

"Such as your boyfriend's name?" he suggested.

She closed her eyes and wearily said, "Yeah, that could put a wrench in things."

"You think?"

"Unless—" her eyes popped open again "—I can get Liam to pretend that he's you, just for one night."

"That's not gonna happen, either," he told her.

"How do you know?"

"Because he's a Gilmore."

"And?" she prompted.

"And although my last name is Channing, my mother was a Blake."

"How is that relevant?" she asked.

"You haven't heard about the Blake-Gilmore feud," he realized.

"Nothing more than a vague comment from Sky last night," she admitted.

"It's a long story," he said, "but the gist of it is that the Blakes and the Gilmores came to Nevada to settle the same piece of land more than a hundred and fifty years ago. Rather than admit they'd both been duped, they agreed to split the property."

"So what's the problem?"

"Everett Gilmore arrived first and, having already started to build his homestead, took the prime grazing land for his cattle, leaving Samuel Blake with the less hospitable terrain. As a result, the Crooked Creek Ranch—and the family—struggled for a lot of years until gold and silver were discovered in their hills."

"And now both families are rich," she noted.

"But the animosity persists," he told her.

She sighed. "I know I have no right to ask you for any favors, but if you could just meet my parents—"

Jay was shaking his head before she finished talking. "No."

"It doesn't have to be a big deal," she promised. "Just a quick get-together, maybe throw in a mention about how nice it is to finally meet the parents you've heard so much about and—"

"I've heard nothing about them. I don't even know their names."

"Miguel and Renata," she supplied helpfully.

"Which doesn't change anything," he said. "I don't ever meet the parents of a girl I'm actually dating, so to meet the parents of a girl I've never even kissed…" He shook his head. "Not going to happen."

"Except that you did kiss me," she pointed out.

"No," he argued. "*You* kissed *me*."

Her brow furrowed as she considered the distinction. "How does that make any difference?"

"Honey, if I'd made a move on you, I guarantee it wouldn't have been in a crowded bar on a Friday night with a counter between us."

And even while he was trying to remember all the reasons he wasn't willing to make that move, he found his gaze drawn to the delicate shape and tempting fullness of her lips. The brief kiss she'd planted on him less than twenty-four hours earlier had made more of an impression than he wanted to admit, and stirred desires he couldn't let himself acknowledge.

"Okay, then," she finally relented.

But he could tell that she was still trying to come up with an alternate plan.

"Tell them the truth," he suggested again.

"The truth will lead to me walking down the aisle in a white dress before the end of next summer."

"I'm sure you're exaggerating."

"If you'd agree to maintain this charade long enough to meet my parents, you'd realize I'm not."

"Yeah, that's not gonna happen." But even as he said the words, he remembered the promise he'd made to Kevin and silently cursed his predicament.

He'd planned this outing as a way of breaking the ice with Alyssa, showing her that he was interesting and fun so that she'd agree to go to Matt's wedding with him. It was the price Kevin had demanded for his forgiveness, but the instinctive panic that flooded Jay's mind at the prospect of "meeting the parents" had momentarily pushed everything else aside.

Now that the panic had begun to recede, he was beginning to see that her dilemma could lead to a win for both of them.

"I need to learn to stand up to my parents—I know I do," she admitted. "But as nosy and interfering as they can be, I know it's only because they worry about me."

"How old are you?" he asked curiously.

"Twenty-six."

"Isn't that old enough to be living on your own?"

"Of course it is," she agreed. "But they've always been a little…overprotective."

"Because of the heart thing?" he guessed.

She nodded.

"I don't mean to sound unsympathetic," he said. "But the overprotectiveness is their problem, not yours."

"I know," she agreed, pushing away from the table. "Thank you for an enjoyable evening, but I'd like to go home now and try to figure out plan C."

"Does plan C involve Gilmore?"

"I don't know yet."

"Then let's talk about plans for tomorrow before you do anything too hasty," he suggested.

She frowned. "What plans for tomorrow?"

"I'm free for dinner. And that chili you made the day of the storm was really good."

"You want me to cook dinner for you?"

"I'm going to be working all day," he pointed out as he rose to his feet. "And it sure would be nice to come home and share a meal with my doting girlfriend."

"You've already made it clear that you don't want any part of this."

"Maybe our conversation over dinner will change my mind."

Her gaze narrowed. "You're totally playing me, aren't you?"

"There's only one way to find out, isn't there?"

She forced a smile. "Dinner's at six."

Chapter Seven

Alyssa knew Jason's suggestion that she might change his mind about meeting her parents was simply a ploy for a home-cooked meal. Well, she was ninety-nine percent certain of it.

But if there was even a one percent chance that she might be able to change his mind, she had to take it.

And even if he was playing her for a free dinner, she figured she owed him that much for not exposing her deception to Diego. Plus, she liked to cook, and cooking for Jason gave her an excuse to prepare something she wouldn't generally make for herself.

Of course, that meant a trip to The Trading Post, Haven's all-purpose general/grocery/liquor store. Lizzie Cartwright was working the cash register and, as she scanned the items, immediately wanted to know who Alyssa was cooking the special meal for. She tried to convince the woman that she was just experimenting with a new recipe, but as she paid for her groceries, she could tell that Lizzie didn't believe her.

Still, she'd prefer to be the subject of speculation rather than gossip, and if she told anyone that she was cooking for her upstairs neighbor, the rumor mill would be churning before she got home and got her groceries unpacked. Of course, if she'd been thinking clearly, she would have gone to Battle Mountain to shop and avoided exactly this scenario. But she hadn't been thinking straight since she'd kissed Jason.

Which was another reason she should abandon her plan—or at least her efforts to enlist his help. Because spending time with him and pretending to be infatuated with him could lead to a real infatuation.

She covered the skillet and set it in the oven to keep the chicken warm, checked the potatoes and added the washed and trimmed asparagus spears to the tray. She minced some fresh garlic and warmed it in a small pan with olive oil, then poured the warm oil into a shallow bowl, added oregano, black pepper, balsamic vinegar and fresh Parmesan.

When everything was ready, she touched up her makeup. Just a quick brush of powder to eliminate the shine from working over the stove, a touch of mascara to her lashes and a dab of gloss on her lips. And then she changed her clothes, too.

She hadn't planned to dress up. Just because she'd been manipulated into making dinner didn't make this a date. On the other hand, jeans with frayed cuffs and an old T-shirt were perhaps a little too casual if she expected him to give any consideration to her potential as a girlfriend—even a temporary one. So she pulled on a tunic-style blouse over a long skirt, added a metal chain-link belt and a pair of chunky heels and tried to ignore the butterflies fluttering in her tummy, because this wasn't a big deal. This was just a woman sharing a meal with a man she saw almost every day.

But planning the menu, shopping for groceries and preparing the food somehow made the simple act of sharing a meal feel more like a date.

Except that she didn't date guys like Jason.

He was too good-looking, too charismatic, too self-assured. And definitely too egotistical. She couldn't believe his suggestion that she'd made up the phony boyfriend story as an excuse to kiss him! She was still appalled by the idea.

On the other hand, if even half the rumors around town were to be believed, some women had gone to extreme lengths to get close to one of Haven's most sought-after bachelors. And sought-after bachelors like Jason definitely didn't date girls like her.

So she needed to relax and remember that this was just a friendly meal over which she would make a half-hearted attempt to convince him to go along with her fake dating plan, and he would, ultimately, refuse. At the end of the evening, he would thank her for the meal and say goodnight, then go back to his own apartment without a kiss.

Yes, it would definitely be smart to end the evening without a kiss.

But it wasn't what she wanted...

It was more of a negotiation than a date, but Jay found himself stopping at The Trading Post to pick up a bottle of wine and a six-pack of his favorite beer anyway. Then he made a second stop at Garden of Eden, the local flower shop, where he took too long surveying the array of options before finally selecting a mixed bouquet of mostly orange and yellow blooms.

When he finally got home, he showered quickly, then

realized he'd forgotten to shave before heading to work that morning. He took an extra few minutes to raze the stubble from his jaw and knocked at Alyssa's door at 6:02 p.m.

He exhaled an audible sigh of relief when she answered the door. "Good—you're still here."

She frowned in response to the unorthodox greeting. "Where else would I be?"

"I don't know," he admitted. "But the one morning I was two minutes late for our run, you were at the end of the street before I caught up with you."

"That's because starting out late on *my* run would have thrown off my entire schedule for the day," she pointed out.

He offered her the flowers.

"Oh." She looked at the blossoms wrapped in decorative paper as if she wasn't entirely sure what to do with them.

"Now you say 'thank you' and put them in some water," he suggested.

"Thank you," she said, accepting the bouquet.

"You're welcome."

She stepped away from the door so he could enter.

He followed her to the kitchen, where she bent to look in the cupboard under the sink, emerging with a glass vase that she tipped under the faucet to fill with water.

"This is for you, too." He handed her the bottle of wine when she finished with the flowers.

"You're observant," she commented, noting that the label matched the one on the bottle they'd been drinking the other night.

"I brought beer, too," he said, holding up the six-pack in his other hand.

She took the beer from him and put it in the fridge. "Thirsty?" she guessed.

He grinned. "And hungry. I skipped lunch."

"There's bread warming in the oven and dip on the table."

"Bread and dip?" he echoed dubiously. "That's what's for dinner?"

She chuckled softly. "No, it's an appetizer."

"So what's for dinner?" he asked.

"Chicken marsala with oven-roasted vegetables."

"I guess you know how to make more than chili," he noted.

"I do," she confirmed. "And I like to cook."

"So...if you were dating someone, how often would you cook for him?"

"I don't know." She pulled a tray of bread from the oven, then began transferring the slices to a basket. "It would probably depend on how often he takes me out to eat."

"You're supposed to be convincing me to go along with your boyfriend plan," he reminded her.

She waved a hand dismissively. "That was last night. Today, I've accepted that you're unwilling to be convinced."

"But you made dinner for me anyway?"

"I like to cook," she said again. "Plus, you fed me last night, so it seemed like a fair trade."

She gestured for him to sit, then set the basket of warm bread on the table.

"Do you want a glass of wine or a beer?"

"I'll have a beer—if it won't be an insult to your chicken."

She popped the top on one of the bottles, poured it into a glass and set it on the table already set for two with fancy dishes, gleaming cutlery and linen napkins.

"When I finagled a dinner invitation, I really didn't expect you to go to so much trouble," he told her.

"It wasn't any trouble. I love these dishes and I hardly ever get to use them." She peered into the window of the oven door, checking on whatever was inside. "And I should have asked you last night if you have any food allergies."

"No allergies," he told her as he dipped a piece of bread into the shallow bowl of oil and vinegar and spices.

He popped the bread into his mouth, and the flavors exploded on his tongue.

"This is delicious," he said, dipping his bread again.

She took a slice from the basket, tore off a piece and dipped it. She nodded as she chewed. "It is good."

"You haven't made this before?"

"I've made different variations of it," she admitted. "I often tweak recipes I find online to make them my own."

She opened the bottle of wine, poured a glass.

"Aren't you supposed to drink white wine with chicken?"

"Asks the man drinking Icky," she noted.

He lifted his glass. "Beer goes with everything."

"And this pinot noir pairs nicely with the marsala."

He selected another piece of bread from the basket. "What would you have been eating for dinner tonight if you weren't cooking for me?"

"Probably chicken," she said. "But more likely just baked in the oven and served on top of a salad."

He made a face. "Girl food."

"In case you haven't noticed, I *am* a girl."

"I noticed," he assured her, his gaze skimming over her in a leisurely and thorough perusal. "I very definitely noticed."

She chewed on another bite of bread.

He wondered if the flush in her cheeks was from the heat of the stove or the sexual awareness that simmered between them.

"There's a rumor that Adventure Village is adding a go-kart track to its offerings this summer," she said.

"Are you interested in go-karts or just trying to change the subject?"

"Just making conversation." She opened the oven door, then pulled out the tray of vegetables and the pan of chicken.

"Fingers crossed, the track will be ready by the first of June," he said.

"That should keep you busy through the summer."

"It's keeping me busy now," he admitted.

She arranged the food on two plates, carried them to the table. "Then it's probably a good thing that I've decided to recast the pretend boyfriend role."

He surveyed the plate she set in front of him. The chicken and potatoes looked and smelled delicious, but he was wary of the green stuff.

"I'm not a fan of asparagus," he said, poking it with his fork.

"You've never had my asparagus," she pointed out to him. "Try it."

He picked up his fork and knife and sliced into the chicken instead. "And what do you mean—you've decided to recast the role?"

"I've had a lot of time to think about this today," she told him. "And while I understand now why Liam might have some reservations about pretending to be a Blake—or Channing—especially after your snarky comment the other night—"

"What snarky comment was that?"

"—I think," she continued, ignoring his interruption and his question, "with the right incentive, I can get him to go along with my plan."

Jay scowled. "What kind of incentive are you planning to offer?"

"I don't think it would be appropriate to discuss those details with you."

His brows lifted.

Color flooded her cheeks. "Ohmygod—no! Not... No!" she said again. "How could you even think..."

"You can't blame my mind for going there," he said. "You mentioned an incentive, and that would be a definite incentive."

"Uh...thank you?" she said dubiously.

"It was a compliment," he assured her.

"Well, I only intended to offer to help Liam with a... situation," she said, reaching for her wineglass.

"Heather Cross still trying to lure him back?" he guessed.

"What do you know about Liam's relationship with Heather?"

"Haven't you lived here long enough to know that there are no secrets in Haven?" He popped a bite-size potato into his mouth.

"Apparently not."

"Well, believe me, that's a mess you don't want to get in the middle of."

Alyssa sighed. "I'm running out of options."

"There's always the truth."

"You met Diego," she reminded him.

"And the guy is seriously infatuated with you," he acknowledged.

"My mother's fault," she said. "I've done nothing to encourage him, but he refuses to believe that I'm not interested."

"And you figured shoving another guy in his face would do the trick?"

"Desperate times," she said.

His brows lifted. "That's the second time you've said that you kissed me because you were desperate."

"And because Liam wasn't there," she reminded him.

"Now you're shoving another guy in *my* face," he noted.

"Liam's not 'another guy'—he's the one who was expected to be my boyfriend."

"You mean pretend boyfriend."

"No one was supposed to know that part," she reminded him. "And since you've already made it clear that you have no intention of maintaining the charade or meeting my parents, why are we even having this conversation?"

"I'm reconsidering," he told her.

"Why don't I believe you?"

"I don't know. Maybe you're inherently distrustful."

"And maybe you don't seem like the kind of guy who would be swayed by chicken marsala."

"I wouldn't have thought so, either," he acknowledged. "But this chicken is delicious."

"Thank you," she said.

But it wasn't really the chicken that had made him reconsider his position. Aside from wanting to mend fences with his buddy, her willingness—even eagerness—to turn to Liam Gilmore for help was probably the biggest reason he'd decided to help her out.

Maybe it was petty, but it was true. As much as Jay had never wanted the boyfriend role that Alyssa was offering, he was even less inclined to let Liam Gilmore fill it.

"Of course, I would have some conditions if I was to go along with your plan," he said to her now.

"Such as?" she asked warily.

"A home-cooked meal like this twice a week for the duration of our phony relationship."

"You expect me to cook for you on a schedule?"

"I'm horribly incompetent in the kitchen," he confided. "And eating microwaveable meals gets tiresome day after day."

"I'm sure it does," she agreed.

"Even two good meals a week would help break up the monotony," he said, his tone imploring.

"One a week," she countered.

"Two would benefit you as much as me," he told her.

"How do you figure?"

"Because I'd be saving you from a boring menu of grilled chicken and salads."

A smile tugged at her lips, but she came back with another counteroffer. "Three meals over the course of two weeks."

Though they both knew that he was negotiating from a position of power, he admired her refusal to cave to his demands. "That's acceptable," he finally decided.

She offered her hand, as if to seal the bargain, but he shook his head.

"That's only the first condition," he told her.

"What else do you want?" she asked.

"Reciprocity." He picked up the bottle of wine and topped up her glass.

"You want me to meet *your* parents?"

"Ha! No. I want a date for Matt's wedding."

"Who?"

"Matt Hutchinson—one of the guys I was with at Diggers' the other night."

"When's the wedding?"

"July 14."

"That's more than two months away," she pointed out.

"You plan on dumping me before then?"

"I'm thinking it's more likely you'll meet someone else you'd rather take to the wedding before then."

"How and when would I meet someone else when I'm going to be spending all my free time with my adoring girlfriend?"

"I don't do adoring," she warned him. "And my parents wouldn't believe it if I tried."

"Pity," he said. "But the truth is, a wedding can be a tricky event for a single guy. If he shows up alone, most people think he couldn't get a date."

"No one would think you were incapable of getting a date," she assured him.

"A compliment?" he wondered.

"A fact."

"Going solo also makes a man vulnerable to the advances of the single women who desperately don't want to be at a wedding alone."

"I have no doubt you could fend them off, if you really wanted to," she said.

"I'd rather not have to," he said. "And the problem with asking a casual girlfriend to attend a wedding is that she inevitably thinks the invitation means something more than just a date."

"So you're asking for three home-cooked meals over the next two weeks and the option of a date for your friend's wedding in July," she noted. "Anything else you want?"

He thought about her question for a minute, considering various creative demands to add to his list—most that he knew she would refuse. In the end, he only said, "Dessert?"

Chapter Eight

Alyssa glanced pointedly at his plate. "You haven't eaten your asparagus."

"Green vegetables aren't really my thing," Jay told her.

"Is dessert your thing?" she asked.

His head lifted. "What's for dessert?"

"Strawberry and mascarpone tart."

He looked at his plate again, stabbed one of the spears with the tines of his fork and tentatively nibbled on the end. "This is...not bad," he decided.

"Hardly a rousing endorsement, but I'll take it," she said.

He had another bite. "FYI, for future meals, you can stick to meat and potatoes."

"FYI, in my kitchen, you eat the healthy and balanced meal that's put in front of you or you don't get dessert," she told him.

He finished off the asparagus.

She pushed away from the table to clear his now empty plate along with her own.

"Do you want coffee?" she offered, reaching into the cupboard for dessert plates.

"No, thanks."

But he did want a sneak peek at dessert—and another beer—so he followed her to the refrigerator. "That looks really good," he said as he reached over her shoulder for a bottle.

She bobbled the pan she was sliding off the shelf.

"Easy," he said, catching the bottom of the dish.

"I didn't… I thought—" She glanced at the table, where she'd expected him to still be sitting, then blew out a breath. "Sorry—you startled me."

"I would have been really sorry if you'd dropped that tart," he said.

"I've got it," she assured him.

He took it from her and turned to set it on the counter, but he didn't step away from her. And standing so close, he could see the pulse point at the base of her jaw—and how fast it was beating.

He pushed the door of the fridge closed, forgetting about the beer that had been his reason for getting up in the first place. "I have a confession to make."

"What's that?"

"Even before we sat down to eat, I'd decided to give this fake dating thing a shot."

"Why?"

"Because of the kiss," he admitted.

"The kiss?" she echoed.

"Since that kiss across the bar at Diggers', I've found myself thinking about kissing you again."

"You have?"

He nodded. "It also occurred to me that I've been a

lousy boyfriend if that was our first kiss after three months of dating."

"Except that we haven't actually been dating for three months," she pointed out.

"But if we're going to convince your parents that we've been dating for— Actually, it would be closer to four months by Memorial Day weekend, wouldn't it?"

"I guess it would," Alyssa confirmed, albeit with obvious reluctance.

"Then you're going to have to get used to me kissing you."

"My parents are only going to be here for a weekend," she reminded him. "I'm sure we can manage to keep our hands off one another for that brief period of time."

"What if I don't want to keep my hands off you?" he asked, setting those hands on her hips.

"I thought you wanted dessert," she said.

He could see the nervousness in her eyes, but there was attraction there, too. She might deny that she wanted him to kiss her, but they both knew that she did.

"I do," he said and lowered his mouth to hers.

It was true that he'd been thinking about kissing her again, but he hadn't intended to make a move this soon.

Sure, her dating charade would necessitate sharing some touches and kisses, and he certainly had no objection to getting up close and personal with his sexy neighbor. But he'd expected to be able to exercise some restraint. He hadn't anticipated that being close to her would stir him up so much that he didn't just want to kiss her—he *needed* to kiss her.

He needed to know if her mouth was as soft and sweet as he remembered. The barest touch of his lips to hers confirmed his recollection—and made him want more.

Desire, sharp and needy, clawed at his belly, urging him to take everything she offered.

Her hands slid up his chest to hook over his shoulders, holding on as he continued to kiss her. Her lips parted beneath the pressure of his; her tongue danced with his, following his lead.

Their first kiss had been a teasing and tentative exploration. This kiss, from the first touch of their mouths, was different. More urgent. More intense. And much hotter.

His hand slid around her waist, over her bottom, pulling her closer. She gasped as the evidence of his arousal pressed against her belly, but she didn't pull away. In fact, she pushed her hips against him, making him burn with a desire that he held firmly—and painfully—in check.

When he'd lowered his mouth to hers, he'd been certain that he was in control of the situation. But the press of her soft body against him made him realize how slippery his grasp was on that control. And the soft, sexy sounds that emanated from her throat threatened to break even that tenuous grip.

With sincere regret, he loosened his hold on her and took a careful step back.

Alyssa blinked up at him—confusion and arousal churning in her veins. She drew in a slow, deep breath and willed her rubbery legs to help her remain standing.

"Do you want to talk about it?" Jason asked, after several seconds had passed during which the silence was broken only by the sounds of their ragged breathing.

She didn't need to ask what "it" was. Not while the heat of the kiss they'd shared continued to simmer in the air between them.

"No." She turned away to reach into the drawer for the pastry cutter, tightening her grip on the handle when she realized her hands were trembling. Truthfully, her whole body was trembling, but she had no intention of letting him know it. She sliced into the tart. "Except to say that you can't kiss me like that anymore."

"How do you want me to kiss you?"

She didn't have to look at him to see the smile tugging at the corners of his mouth—she could hear the amusement in his tone. "I don't want you to kiss me at all," she said as she transferred the slice of tart to a plate.

"Liar."

She huffed out a breath. "I'm not denying that there's a certain…attraction," she decided. "But I'm not going to sleep with you."

"I'm not asking you to sleep with me," he told her.

"Well, that's good, then," she said, torn between relief and disappointment as she added a dessert fork to his plate.

"Not because I don't think we could have a lot of fun naked and horizontal together," he clarified. "But because, under the circumstances, having sex would only complicate the situation."

"The last thing I want right now is another complication," she assured him.

He nodded. "There is one more thing we need to be clear about."

"What's that?"

"This phony relationship isn't ever going to lead to anything more, because I don't do relationships."

"I don't want anything more," she promised him.

Because that had been the absolute truth in the beginning. All she'd wanted was a pretend boyfriend to convince her mother that she was settled and happy in Haven—so that Renata would stop trying to set her up with other guys.

But now that she'd spent more time with Jason—now that he'd kissed her senseless—she found her heart yearning for more.

* * *

Alyssa Skyped with Nicolas on his birthday, enjoying a fun—and long—conversation with her now five-year-old nephew, who insisted that she watch while he assembled the Lego set she'd sent to him. His little brow furrowed with concentration as he worked, and she was grateful for the technology that allowed her not just to talk to him but actually see him. It wasn't quite the same as being there, and she missed the feeling of his slender arms around her and the baby shampoo scent of his hair, but the visual connection helped.

She was looking forward to talking to her sister, too. She could always count on Cristina to listen to her woes and offer insightful advice. Not that spending time with Jason Channing was a cause for distress by any stretch of the imagination, but she needed someone to tell her that she hadn't made a huge mistake in the bargain they'd struck.

Except that when Cristina took the iPad from her son, Alyssa was greeted by a barrage of questions about her new boyfriend—because, of course, Renata had already shared the news. In fact, Alyssa wouldn't be surprised to learn that her mother had ended the call with her and immediately dialed her other daughter's number.

"This is the hunky guy who's been your running partner over the past few months, right?" Cristina asked, then forged ahead without waiting for a response. "I so hoped something would click between the two of you."

"You did?" Alyssa asked, surprised. "Why?"

"Because it was obvious from your very first mention that you were attracted to him."

"It was?"

"And shared hobbies and interests always help build a stronger relationship."

"Well, I wouldn't exactly call what we have a relationship," Alyssa hedged. "In fact—"

"I know you're a little wary," Cristina interjected. "And I understand why. But it's past time for you to open up and let somebody love you the way you deserve to be loved."

"But—"

"I know the relationship is fairly new and you probably think I'm jumping the gun, and maybe I am a little," her sister acknowledged. "But I want you to be happy. And, of course, a woman doesn't need a man to be happy, but sharing your life with someone really does have its rewards. And it's such a relief to know that I can stop worrying about you now."

That gave Alyssa pause.

She knew that her parents worried, which was why she tried to spare them the details of her darkest thoughts and deepest concerns. But she'd never held back with Cristina, and she hadn't realized that sharing her doubts and insecurities had caused her sister to worry about her, too.

So when Cristina stopped talking long enough to take a breath and Alyssa finally had the chance to tell her that the relationship with Jason was a charade, she couldn't do it. Instead, she only said, "Now tell me what's new with you."

And for the next half hour, they talked about other things while Alyssa felt the tangled web drawing tighter around her.

Jay was shutting down his computer late the following Saturday afternoon when Hayley poked her head into the room. Kevin had taken the day off to help a friend move, Nat and Carter were throwing darts in the office-slash-lounge and Matt was texting on his phone.

"After back-to-back preteen birthday parties, I could really use some adult company tonight," she said.

"There's a new Daniel Craig movie playing at the local theater," Carter said.

Hayley nodded. "That sounds good to me."

"I'm in," Nat agreed. "But I want food first."

"Matt?" Carter prompted.

The other man shook his head. "I promised to help Carrie work on the seating plan tonight."

"Has she turned into Bridezilla yet?" Hayley asked.

"Of course not," Matt denied. "Though she did ask me to prompt you for the name of your guest for the place card."

"You know my guest," she said. "I told you that Carter and I are going together."

"But you responded with plus-guest on the reply card," Matt reminded her.

"Well, yeah, 'cause I'm not showing up to your wedding without a date."

The groom-to-be looked at Carter. "You responded with plus-guest, too."

"Because I'm going with Hayley," he said.

Matt shook his head. "Carrie was worried about how we were going to split you guys up—because the tables only seat eight, and if you all brought dates, you couldn't be seated at the same table."

"Well, now that problem's solved, isn't it?" Hayley said helpfully.

"Except that Matt and Carrie probably ordered two extra meals for guests who aren't going to be there," Nat—who'd spent six months planning her own wedding for a marriage that didn't last half that long—pointed out to her friends.

"Oh." Hayley looked at Matt, obviously chagrined. "I didn't think about that."

"It's fine," he said.

"Kevin have a date for the big day?" Jay asked.

Matt nodded. "He's bringing Sydney, the girl he's helping move today."

"But don't think that means he's forgiven you for the whole Alyssa thing," Nat warned him.

"There was no 'Alyssa thing' except in his mind," Jay said.

"Note to self—do not seat Kevin beside hot bartender," Matt said, moving toward the door.

"Kevin would probably worry more about Jay being seated near Sydney, in case he decides to steal another girl he's got his eye on."

"I didn't steal Alyssa," Jay said, just a little defensively.

"She's your date for the wedding, isn't she?" Hayley pressed.

"Only because Nat forced my hand." Which was true, and yet not nearly the whole truth.

"And all this time you've been spending with her in the interim—that must be a real hardship, huh?" Carter said.

Of course, it hadn't been a hardship but a pleasure. He sincerely enjoyed hanging out with Alyssa and was grateful that their charade gave him a ready excuse to do so.

"Can we forget about Jay's love life and focus on our plans for tonight?" Nat suggested. "Preferably the food part."

"I'm sick of pizza," Carter said.

"Diggers' it is, then," Hayley decided.

"You in, Jay?" Nat asked.

He shook his head. "Alyssa's making dinner for me tonight."

"This is getting to be a regular thing," Hayley noted.

He shrugged. "She likes to cook."

Nat smirked. "Is that what the kids are calling it these days?"

He shook his head. "Get your head out of the gutter."

"You're not sleeping with her?" she challenged.

"Of course I'm not sleeping with her."

"Why is that an 'of course'?" Carter wondered.

"Because we're only pretend dating."

Nat frowned. "What do you mean?"

"Thanks to your interference, I had to ask Alyssa to be my date for Matt's wedding, in exchange for which I agreed to be her pretend boyfriend when her parents come to town."

Hayley smirked. "You had to bribe a girl to go out with you?"

"We entered into a mutually beneficial agreement."

"I don't think this is what Kevin had in mind," Nat said.

"You mean it's not what *you* had in mind."

She didn't dispute the point.

"Obviously I missed something," Hayley said.

"That's right—you weren't here last week for the big confrontation after Jay kissed the girl Kevin had his eye on and Nat had to play peacemaker."

"Peacemaker or matchmaker?" Jay wondered.

"And now you're going to meet her parents?" Hayley pressed.

"It's not a big deal. Her mom and dad are going to be in town for the long weekend, so I'll spend some time with them, play the boyfriend role, then they'll go back to California and the status quo will be restored."

"And you and Alyssa will just be friends and neighbors again?" Nat asked skeptically.

"Why not?"

She shrugged. "What if all this pretending leads to the development of real feelings?"

"That's not going to happen," he said confidently.

"Maybe not for you," Carter acknowledged. "But what about Alyssa?"

"No worries there," he assured him. "She isn't interested in a real relationship right now."

"I still think you're playing a dangerous game," Hayley warned. "Then again—games are what you do best, aren't they?"

Alyssa seasoned the pork roast with garlic, rosemary and thyme and served it with wild rice and green beans with dried cranberries. She'd considered doing carrots instead of the beans but couldn't resist the challenge of putting a green vegetable on Jason's plate again.

While they ate, he talked about his plans for the grand opening of the go-kart track and his intention to do a test run before the end of the following week. In fact, he was so caught up in his excitement over this prospect, he ate the beans without protest.

After dinner, Alyssa carried the platter of meat and vegetables to the counter to wrap up the leftovers. Jason followed with their plates and cutlery and began loading the dishwasher.

"You don't have to do that," she protested, as she did after every meal they shared. And every time, he insisted on doing kitchen duty.

"It's the least I can do to show my appreciation."

"You're going to be paying with fake love and phony devotion," she reminded him.

"A hefty price," he agreed. "Maybe I should have held out for a couple extra meals."

"Too late now—the bargain's been struck."

He moved away from the dishwasher and opened the fridge, scanning the contents. "Where's dessert?"

"What dessert?"

"You really didn't make anything for dessert?"

He looked so sincerely disappointed, she almost felt guilty for teasing him. "Of course I did," she said. "It's in the oven."

He immediately reached for the handle of the oven.

"Don't." She shoved him back and slapped her hand against the door before he could pull it open. "Letting the heat out will affect the baking time."

He dutifully tucked his hands behind him. "The baking time of what?"

"Chocolate lava cake."

His eyes lit up. "When will it be ready?"

"When the timer goes off."

He glanced at the numbers ticking down on the clock. "Three minutes should be just long enough."

"Long enough for what?"

"To kiss you."

She took an instinctive step back. "Or to finish clearing the table."

Jason shook his head. "That doesn't sound like nearly as much fun."

"Sometimes fun has to wait until the work is done."

"You're right," he decided, returning to the table. "And if I wait until later to kiss you, I won't have to worry about being interrupted by a buzzing kitchen timer."

"I've been thinking about the kissing thing," she admitted.

"I've been thinking about it, too—to the distraction of all else."

"What I was thinking," Alyssa said, determined to take control of the conversation, "is that there's really no reason for you to kiss me. I mean, it's not as if we have to demonstrate our technique to convince my parents that we're dating."

"Maybe not," he acknowledged. "But couples who have been dating for several months are usually pretty comfortable around one another. And aside from that night when you grabbed hold of me and practically hauled me across the bar to kiss me, every time I get close to you, you back away."

"Sorry," she said automatically. "I guess I'm a little protective of my personal space."

"If you expect anyone to believe that we're together, you're going to have to let me in."

She nodded. "You're right."

He watched her, waiting.

She drew a deep breath, as if shoring up her courage, and took a deliberate step toward him.

"I'm not so scary, am I?"

"Of course not," she said.

"So why is your heart racing?"

"It's not—"

"It is," he insisted, lifting a hand to touch the pulse point at the base of her jaw.

"It's just that… Actually, I don't know why my heart's racing," she admitted.

"I think you do know," he said. "You just don't want to admit it."

"Admit what?"

"That the attraction between us is getting harder and harder to ignore."

She swallowed. "But we agreed that we are going to ignore it."

"That would be the smart thing to do," he agreed.

But it wasn't what he wanted to do. For the first time, he wanted to ignore his own rules, take her in his arms and—

The buzz of the timer severed his thought.

Chapter Nine

"I have a confession to make," Jay said when he picked up his fork to dig into the lava cake, dusted with powdered sugar and decorated with fresh raspberries.

Alyssa eyed him warily. "A confession along the lines of 'I'm not a big fan of raspberries' or more like 'I'm on the FBI's most wanted list'?"

"Somewhere in between those options, although definitely closer to the raspberries."

"Okay," she said.

"When you met my friends last weekend, did you sense any…friction?"

"You mean, between you and Kevin?"

"I'll take that as a yes," he said. "Well, me, Kevin, Carter and Matt all played high school football together."

"You've been friends for a long time," she noted.

"We have—aside from a brief period in our junior year when Kevin stopped talking to me."

"I'm guessing there was a girl."

He nodded. "Her name was Lacey Bolton. She wasn't a cheerleader or an athlete—she was just a pretty girl who sat in front of Kevin in English class."

"He had a crush on her," Alyssa guessed.

"And she had no idea he even existed, because she was more interested in school than boys. But Kevin was smart and patient, and he had a plan. He asked for her help with a term paper, and they started to get together for study sessions once a week.

"We all ribbed him about taking it slow, but it was obvious he really liked her and was gearing up to ask her to the homecoming dance."

"I've only been here for one homecoming," she acknowledged. "But I know what a big deal it is."

"Especially to the football players, who are in the spotlight all weekend. Win or lose, they're the heroes. All the guys want to play on the team, and all the girls want to go out with the players."

"You were quarterback," she guessed.

"First string," he confirmed. "But I got sacked in the season opener and went down with an ankle sprain. Gilmore took my place on the roster—and my girlfriend."

"Apparently there's some recent animosity between the Blakes and the Gilmores," she mused.

"Getting dumped was hard enough," he admitted. "Losing Jenny to Gilmore made it that much harder. Not only would I have to sit on the sidelines for the big game, I'd be sitting alone.

"And because I was feeling so crappy about the whole situation, I decided that gave me a free pass for crappy behavior."

"What did you do?" she asked, clearly anticipating something bad.

"I asked Lacey to be my date for the homecoming dance—and she said yes."

She winced. "How long did it take Kevin to forgive you?"

"A very long time," he admitted. "And recently I did something that brought it all back again."

"Made another move on Lacey Bolton?"

"No. I made a move on you."

She looked taken aback by his confession. "When did you make a move on me?"

"Well, technically, you made the move when you kissed me, but Kevin doesn't seem concerned with technicalities."

"You told your friend that I kissed you?"

"No," he denied. "But he was at The Daily Grind when Megan Carmichael told Kenzie Atkins that she saw me kissing you at Diggers'."

Alyssa sighed. "I guess I shouldn't have expected to kiss a guy in a public place and not have people take notice." She sipped her wine. "Do you want me to explain it to…Kevin?"

He shook his head. "I don't think that will help."

"So what was the purpose of telling me the story?" she wondered.

"He'd never admit it, but Kevin's a romantic," Jay told her. "And he seems willing to forgive what he sees as my betrayal if I can convince him that I was motivated by real feelings for you."

"If he's known you for so many years, shouldn't he know that you don't do real feelings?"

He arched a brow.

"Just stating what seems to be a well-known fact," she told him.

"Like I said, Kevin's a romantic. But to prove to him that this isn't another Lacey Bolton situation, I have to date you, exclusively, up to and including Matt's wedding."

"You're serious," she realized.

He nodded grimly.

"The seemingly out-of-the-blue invitation to your friend's wedding makes a little more sense now."

"You didn't believe that I just wanted you to be my date?"

She shook her head. "Guys like you don't make plans with a girl that far into the future, because you're never sure that you'll be with that same girl by the time the event comes around."

"That's a little harsh," he noted.

"Maybe it is," she acknowledged. "But I doubt it's untrue."

"Well, since we have a date two months into the future—and the meeting with your parents before then—we're going to need more practice."

She eyed him warily. "Kissing?"

He grinned. "That, too," he agreed. "But what I meant was just hanging out and being together."

"That's probably a good idea," she acknowledged.

"Do you have any plans tomorrow?" he asked.

She shook her head.

"Good. I should be finished work by three, so we'll plan to leave here around four," he decided.

"To go where?" she wondered.

"It's a surprise."

She narrowed her gaze. "Are you going to make me play laser tag or go rock climbing?"

"Those are both good ideas," he said. "But no—not tomorrow."

He'd already introduced her to paintball, and though she'd been apprehensive in the beginning—perhaps more about meeting his friends than potentially being hit by paintballs—she'd willingly geared up. Nat had given her a quick lesson on her weapon—how to load and aim and shoot—then spent some time with her at the target range before announcing that she was ready to go.

Alyssa had loved the game and, afterward, had shown off the various colorful bruises that were evidence of the hits she'd taken. He'd winced at the blue and yellow blemishes that marred her smooth skin, but she'd been proud of her battle scars. Having been held back from trying new things or pushing physical limits for so many years because her parents had worried—despite the doctors' reassurances—that her heart wasn't completely fixed, she seemed eager to do and try anything. Which, of course, made him wonder if she'd exhibit the same curiosity and eagerness in the bedroom—a prospect that was too torturous to contemplate for long.

Aside from the almost offhand admission that she'd been born with a hole in her heart, her medical condition wasn't something she talked about. And while he understood that the surgeries had happened a lot of years earlier and weren't likely at the forefront of her mind, he'd noticed that she always dressed in a way that ensured any remaining scars weren't visible.

Admittedly curious after the night that she'd bumped Carter from the Tetris leaderboard, he'd done an internet search of "atrial septal defect" and "heart surgery scars." What he'd learned had given him some appreciation for what Alyssa deemed overprotectiveness on the part of her parents, and renewed respect for the woman who had exhibited determination and courage in building a life for herself free of anyone else's restrictions.

"If you're not going to tell me where we're going, can you at least give me a hint as to what I should wear?" she asked him now.

"Whatever you want."

She huffed out a breath. "Could you be any less helpful?"

"Stiletto heels and a very short skirt," he suggested.

"Apparently you *can* be less helpful," she decided.

He grinned. "We're probably going to be outside, so wear something comfortable and appropriate for the weather."

"When you say outside, do you mean in a paintball field?"

He chuckled. "Not this time."

"Oh," she said.

And he thought she sounded almost disappointed.

It was May, but what was "appropriate for the weather" in northern Nevada was very different than Southern California. In Irvine, she would have packed her winter clothes away long ago. In Haven, though the sun provided welcome warmth during the day, temperatures tended to drop quickly and steeply when it went down.

After some consideration, Alyssa opted for a long-sleeved peasant-style blouse over a pair of slim-fitting pants with short, low-heeled boots. She used a light hand with her makeup and added a spritz of her favorite perfume.

Jason greeted her with a quick kiss.

He'd been kissing her a lot over the past few weeks, though the kisses had mostly just been casual brushes of his lips. And he'd been touching her frequently, too—holding her hand, draping an arm over her shoulders or just sitting close enough so that their bodies touched. And if his intent was to get her accustomed to those easy kisses and casual touches, she thought it was succeeding.

Unfortunately, instead of inuring her to the effects, her awareness of—and attraction to—him was growing every day, and she was starting to worry that she might get too used to these casual displays of affection and start to believe their phony relationship was real.

"Are you going to tell me now where we're going?" she asked after they'd been driving for several minutes.

"Twelve-oh-two Miners' Pass."

"That doesn't really answer my question," she noted.

"It very specifically answers your question," he argued.

"Okay—what is at twelve-oh-two Miners' Pass?" she asked.

"A house."

She rolled her eyes. "And do you happen to know who lives at this house?"

"As a matter of fact, I do."

She counted slowly to ten while she watched the scenery pass outside her window, but of course, he didn't offer any more information. "Are you going to tell me who lives at this house?"

"I am," he confirmed. "But not until we're a little closer to our destination, because I don't want you to freak out about meeting my parents."

"I don't freak out," she said, ignoring the knots that suddenly tightened in her belly. "And why am I meeting your parents?"

"It seemed reasonable that if I'm going to meet your parents, I should introduce you to mine."

"This wasn't part of our agreement."

"But it was your idea," he said. "When I suggested reciprocity, you asked if I wanted to introduce you to my parents."

"I was *joking*."

"Well, I didn't know you were joking. And when my mom invited me to come over for a barbecue, I decided that having you there would increase the odds of the afternoon being tolerable.

"That sounded harsh," he realized. "And they're really not so bad. A little pretentious and self-absorbed at times, but generally friendly. Besides, it seemed like a good opportunity to give the boyfriend-girlfriend thing a trial run."

"What did you tell your parents about me?" she finally asked.

"Nothing."

"Did you even tell them that I was coming?"

"Nope."

He turned into a wide stamped-concrete driveway in front of a gorgeous three-story stone-and-brick house, the grandeur of which made her forget—for just a moment—the topic of their conversation.

"I really don't think this is a good idea," she said when he killed the engine.

He exited the truck and came around to open her door, reaching across to unsnap her seat belt when she made no move to do so herself.

"Relax, honey bear. We're just here for a burger. My mom's a horrible cook, but my dad does a decent job with meat over fire."

"I'm not sure I believe you," Alyssa said, ignoring the teasing endearment.

"It's true," a female voice said from behind him. "Our mother could scorch a pot attempting to boil water."

Alyssa stepped out of the vehicle and turned to face a woman who could only be Jason's sister. Average height, slender build, light blond hair, deep blue eyes like her brother's and the same quick smile. Regan, she guessed, since he'd told her that Brielle lived in New York and rarely returned to Haven.

Of course, Alyssa had been doubting his reasons for bringing her here, not the truth of his culinary commentary, but she didn't have a chance to clarify as Jason was already making the introductions.

"It's nice to meet you." Instead of offering a hand, Regan gave Alyssa a quick hug. Then she turned to her brother to remark, "And surprising, because you don't have that blank look in your eyes that Jay usually favors in the women he dates."

"Try to make a good first impression," he said. "Oh, wait—too late."

Regan just grinned, unrepentant, and hooked her arm through Alyssa's. "Come on," she said. "Everyone's dying to meet you."

"But—" She looked helplessly back at Jason.

"I didn't tell Mom and Dad that I was bringing a guest," he noted.

"But you told me," Regan reminded him.

"My mistake, obviously," he noted.

"You know how Mom is about surprises," his sister said. "And if she found out that I knew about Alyssa and didn't tell her, she'd never forgive me."

"You mean she'd be annoyed with you, for all of about thirty seconds."

"I'm a middle child—desperate for approval," she said by way of explanation.

"You're the second oldest and a troublemaker," he countered.

"Actually, I'm 'the smart one,'" Regan told Alyssa, using air quotes. "Jason's 'the stubborn one,' Spencer's 'the slippery one' and Brie's 'the sweet one.'"

Alyssa wondered if her own parents had ever described her and Cristina in similarly generic terms. If they had, she had no doubt what they would be. Her sister was "the perfect one" and she was "the broken one."

But she didn't feel broken when she was with Jason.

When she was with him, she felt not just like a normal person but an attractive and desirable woman. And she knew that regardless of how or when they put an end to their relationship charade, she would always be grateful to him for that.

Jason's mention of burgers implied a casual meal. But apparently dining with Ben and Margaret Channing meant eating off gold-rimmed plates at an enormous table in the formal dining room lit by a chandelier that wouldn't have looked out of place in a hotel ballroom.

"And what is it that you do, dear?" Margaret asked Alyssa as she spooned coleslaw out of a crystal bowl, using a fancy slotted spoon that looked like real silver.

Alyssa added a slice of tomato to her burger. "I'm a math and science teacher at Westmount High School."

"I loved math, hated science," Regan said.

"Even physics?" Alyssa asked her.

"I didn't take physics," she admitted. "My guidance counsellor steered me toward chemistry."

"If you like math—and obviously you do," she said, remembering that Jason's sister was an accountant, "you'd like physics."

"Our youngest daughter, Brielle, is a teacher," Ben said.

Alyssa nodded. "Jason mentioned that she lives in New York."

"And teaches at a prestigious private school in Brooklyn," Margaret confirmed. "In fact, they've already offered to renew her contract for next year."

"That's good news," Jay said.

His parents exchanged a look.

"She loves teaching at Briarwood," Regan reminded them.

"Which would be great, if Briarwood wasn't twenty-five hundred miles away." Margaret shook her head. "We should never have agreed to let her go to New York City."

"We couldn't have stopped her," her husband pointed out. "She was eighteen—and determined to put as much distance as possible between herself and Haven."

"We didn't have to make it easy for her."

"I don't think it was easy," Ben said.

"I mean financially," Margaret clarified. "We paid her tuition and all her living expenses."

"Same as we did for each of our other children."

"Except Spencer," Regan chimed in. "Who decided he'd rather ride bareback than read or write."

"Our youngest son left college to become a professional cowboy," Ben explained to Alyssa.

"At least you know Brie's got great roommates and a nice apartment," Jay pointed out. "Spencer lives out of a suitcase, and more than half the time, you don't even know where that suitcase is."

"But he's been very successful," Margaret said to Alyssa. "After dinner, you should let Jason take you into the den and show you some of Spencer's trophies."

"Yeah, because that's going to score him points with his girlfriend," Regan said mockingly. "Showing her his little brother's hardware."

"Jason won his share of trophies, too," Margaret said, though her defense of her oldest son was a little tepid.

"For throwing a football around," Regan said.

"He also graduated summa cum laude with a degree in business," Ben said. "Which would make him a real asset at Blake Mining."

"Can we possibly have one family meal where we don't rehash the same arguments?" Jason asked wearily.

"I'm sure that degree is one of the reasons he's made

Adventure Village such a success in a short time," Alyssa remarked.

Ben let out a derisive snort. "He bought an empty field where fake soldiers shoot at each other with fake guns."

She could sense Jason seething and reached over to put her hand on his arm. "Paintball might not be everyone's idea of a good time," she acknowledged. "But it's certainly popular with a lot of people."

"Teenagers," Ben said dismissively.

"Who, according to the teachers at Westmount, finally have something to do with their time other than tagging buildings and stealing cars."

"And it's not just paintball," Regan pointed out. "There's also laser tag and a climbing wall."

"And mini golf," Alyssa added.

"It's a fine hobby," Ben finally allowed. "I'm just saying that Jason's time and talent would be put to better use at Blake Mining."

"I worked at Blake Mining for six years," Jay reminded his father. "In the mines, in the lab, in the office—and I hated every job."

"If work was supposed to be fun, it wouldn't be called work," his father said.

"Dessert?" Margaret spoke up quickly to interrupt what was apparently a familiar dispute.

"You made dessert?" Regan asked cautiously.

"Of course not," her mother said, as if the very idea was ridiculous. "Celeste prepared everything we need for strawberry shortcake. I just have to put it together."

"I'll give you a hand," her daughter offered.

"Sorry about the side of family drama served with your burger," Jay said to Alyssa as they drove home from his parents' house.

"I'm not unfamiliar with family conflict," she reminded him. "And while your dad clearly wishes you'd chosen a career in a different direction, your mom seems happy with your choices."

"I don't know if she's happy or just unwilling to express her displeasure, in case I decide to follow in the footsteps of Spencer or Brie."

"Did you ever want to leave Haven?" she asked curiously.

"Sure. When I was a teenager and there was nothing to do, I hated this town and promised myself I'd get out at the first opportunity. So imagine my surprise when I went away to school and discovered that I actually missed it. That got me thinking about why I wanted to leave and what would make me—and a lot more people like me— want to stay."

"And that's how Adventure Village started?"

"I guess it was," he admitted. "Well, the idea plus the trust fund from my grandfather."

He pulled into their shared driveway and parked.

"I'm going to sit outside for a while," he said. "I usually need to clear my head after too much time with my family."

"Three hours is too much time?"

"By about two hours," he confirmed.

"Do you want some company?" Alyssa asked.

"I wouldn't mind."

"Just let me go in and grab a sweater," she said.

"No need," he told her. "I've got one in my duffel bag in the back—it's clean, I promise."

He opened the back door, unzipped the bag and pulled out the sweatshirt. She tugged it over her head.

His lips twitched as he helped her roll back the cuffs to free her hands. The bear logo covered her chest and the hem fell to midthigh. "I guess it's a little big."

"But it's warm." She glanced down at the crest. "My sister went to UC Berkeley, too."

"Where'd you go to school?"

"UC Irvine," she replied.

"You didn't want to go away?" he asked.

"I desperately wanted to go away," she admitted. "But my mom worried about me being too far from the doctors who knew my medical history."

"How'd she react when you told her you were moving to Nevada?" he wondered.

"She wasn't thrilled—and even less so when she realized the nearest hospital was thirty-five miles away and didn't have a cardiologist on staff."

"You weren't worried?"

She shook her head. "No, because I believed the doctors who said my heart is fine. I don't need constant reassurances or reminders of something that happened a long time ago."

Maybe it was the dark. Maybe it was that he knew her better than he had a few weeks earlier and felt comfortable enough now to be able to voice the question that had been on his mind since she told him about her surgery.

Whatever the reason, he finally asked, "Is that why you hide your scars?"

Chapter Ten

Jay felt her stiffen beside him, and he wondered if no one else had ever asked her the question. But after a barely perceptible hesitation, Alyssa said, "I hide my scars because they're ugly."

He scowled into the darkness. "Who told you they're ugly?"

"I didn't need to be told—I've seen them."

But he knew her well enough now to sense that there was more to the story, and he hated to think that anyone had ever made this strong, beautiful woman feel as if she was anything less than that.

"Show me," he said gently.

She immediately shook her head. "I don't think so."

"I know you're probably thinking I just want to get a closer look at your breasts, but that's only part of the reason."

She smiled. "I'm going to change the subject now and tell you that I had a good time tonight."

And because he'd never wanted to make her uncomfortable, he followed her lead. "I did, too—for the most part."

"Does your mom really not cook?" she asked curiously.

"She really doesn't," he confirmed. "I ate a lot of pizza and cold cereal growing up."

She looked so horrified, he had to laugh. "I'm kidding. Not about my mother not cooking—that's the truth. But Celeste, the housekeeper-slash-nanny, made sure there was a hot meal on the table every night."

"We really do come from different worlds," she noted. "And, in my world, morning comes early."

"I should be more aware of school nights when I'm dating a teacher," he remarked.

"Fake dating," she reminded him.

Except that this pretend relationship with Alyssa was starting to feel more real to Jay than anything else he'd experienced in a long time.

After dinner with Jason's family, Alyssa got the sense that something had changed in their relationship. She'd seen a side of him she'd never noticed before, observed some interesting family dynamics and glimpsed vulnerabilities she never would have guessed lurked beneath his veneer of self-confidence. And the more she learned about him, the more she liked him.

Of course, watching him with his parents and sister, she also couldn't help but compare his family to her own. She hadn't grown up with the kind of wealth that was evident in every brick of their home and every designer thread on his mother's back, but she'd never had cause to doubt the love or support of her family.

Which only made her feel guiltier about her deception. And the closer it got to the date of her parents' visit, the more nervous she was about introducing them to her boyfriend. She wanted them to like Jason, though she knew it didn't really matter whether they did or didn't, so long as they believed Alyssa liked him.

And she did.

She was also powerfully attracted to him.

Spending time with Jason, being touched and kissed by him, made her body ache for so much more. Maybe she didn't fully appreciate the pleasures that could be shared by a man and a woman, but she yearned to know. And with each day that passed, that yearning continued to grow.

"When are your parents getting in?" Jason's question drew her back to the present as they hit the halfway mark of their run Friday morning.

"Their flight is scheduled to land just after two o'clock tomorrow afternoon."

"We've got a big event on Saturday, but I can ask Matt to cover for me, if you want me to go to the airport with you."

"No," she immediately responded. "I appreciate the offer, and I know my mother's primary incentive for making this trip is to meet you, but I think it's probably best to limit the amount of time you spend with them."

"You don't think I can be a convincing boyfriend?" he challenged.

"I want to minimize the opportunities for missteps."

"So when am I going to meet them?"

"About ten minutes before we leave to go to The Hide-Away for dinner Saturday night."

"I thought you were going to make a reservation at Diggers'."

"I was," she admitted. "And then I realized that it was less likely we'd face questions from friends and neighbors if we went out of town."

"Well, if we're going into Battle Mountain, El Aguila

would have been my choice," he remarked. "They have the best burritos north of Mexico."

"You only think so because you haven't had my grandmother's burritos," she told him.

"Have you ever been to El Aguila?" he asked.

"I can't say that I have," she admitted.

"Then we'll have to go sometime."

"I'd like that, but…"

"But what?" he prompted.

"I think you're forgetting that, after this weekend, you won't have to be my pretend boyfriend anymore."

"But you still have to be my pretend girlfriend until Matt's wedding."

"The original agreement was simply for me to be your date."

"I like this girlfriend-boyfriend arrangement better," he told her. "But even when it's done, we'll still be friends, won't we?"

"I guess we will," she acknowledged.

"And we'll go to El Aguila," he promised.

"Okay," she agreed. "But right now, we need to kick it up a notch or I'm going to be late for school."

"When you say things like that, I feel like I'm a teenager again. Although back then, the math teacher only *wished* she was dating me."

She sent him a sideways glance. "Really? Because Carter told me you had Mr. Donald for math in high school."

He responded by kicking it up several notches, leaving her in his dust.

But she was laughing.

Before Jason headed to Adventure Village Saturday afternoon, he showed up at Alyssa's door with a six-pack of his favorite brew and a framed photo of himself in climbing gear, hanging off the edge of a cliff. Though he was obviously wearing a harness, the image still made her stomach dip as if she was the one suspended in midair.

She looked from the photo back to the man. "Thank you?"

He shook his head. "Doesn't a woman usually want a picture of her boyfriend around so she can look at it when she's not with him? And his favorite beer in her fridge so that he'll want to stop by for a drink?"

"They're props," she realized.

"All part of the service," he told her.

She tucked the beer in her fridge and put the picture on her desk, beside her computer monitor. She picked up the sweatshirt she'd borrowed and carried it back to the foyer.

"I almost forgot you had that," he admitted when she handed him the freshly laundered and folded garment.

"I wanted to wash it before I returned it," she said.

"Appreciated but not necessary," he told her. "And maybe you should keep it for a few more days."

"Why?"

"Another prop to add to the relationship illusion," he pointed out. "The boyfriend's sweatshirt, casually discarded over the back of a chair."

"My mother would be appalled that I hadn't tidied up before their visit."

"Maybe neatly folded on top of your laundry basket, then," he suggested.

"A much better idea," she agreed, taking back the garment.

"Have you checked their flight status?"

She nodded. "Everything's on schedule."

"So when are you heading out to the airport?"

"In about ten minutes."

"That isn't a lot of time, but I can work with it," he said and hauled her into his arms to kiss her.

He'd kissed her often enough over the past few weeks that she should be accustomed to the feel of his lips on hers by now. But still her heart raced and mind blanked.

Every. Single. Time.

She had no defense against the sensual assault of his mouth. She wanted none.

She only wanted Jason.

And yet he always seemed completely in control. He occasionally did a little tactile exploring while she was being thoroughly seduced by his lips, but always through the barrier of fabric. His ruthless restraint tempted her to abandon her own. To shed not just her inhibitions but every stitch of clothing to feel his hands on her bare skin. His body against hers.

It was almost embarrassing how much she wanted him. So far, she'd managed to resist begging him to take her, but the words echoed temptingly in her mind as he continued to kiss her. The sensual flick of his tongue sent flames of heat licking through her veins, making every part of her burn.

"If I don't leave now, we're both going to be late," he said after he'd eased his lips from hers.

"Late?" she echoed.

That incredibly talented mouth curved. "That's what was missing."

"What?" How was she supposed to concentrate on what he was saying when her head was spinning?

"Now when you meet your parents, you'll look like a woman who's thinking about her man," he said.

Of course, he wasn't really her man, but the whole point of this weekend was to convince her parents that he was. The harder task would be remembering that it was just a game they were playing and not letting him into her fragile heart.

* * *

Alyssa was more apprehensive than she'd expected to be about her parents meeting Jason—not just because she worried that they'd uncover her deception, but because she really wanted them to like him. Renata seemed invested in the idea of her youngest daughter falling in love with Diego, and Alyssa worried that her mother might have already decided she wasn't going to like Jason. Although she believed Miguel was less likely to prejudge her beau, she felt anxious anyway.

Her parents were reserved but not unfriendly, and over dinner, they all chatted easily. Her father seemed sincerely interested in Jason's business and asked all the questions about Adventure Village she knew his own father had not. And when her mother expressed curiosity about the battle that had given the town its name, Jason sketched out a brief history lesson that hit all the important highlights.

Any concerns Alyssa had that Jason might try to oversell their relationship proved groundless. He was attentive without being too obvious and deferential without being submissive. While they were eating, he snagged a mushroom from her plate, as if it was common for them to share food; as they walked across the parking lot, he linked their fingers together, as if the casual gesture was an ingrained habit.

After they returned to Haven and the triplex where they both lived—a revelation that created a furrow between Renata's brows—they sat outside for a while to enjoy the starry night. Jason introduced her dad to "Icky" while Alyssa and her mom each had a glass of wine.

When Miguel said he was tired and heading to bed, Renata, of course, went with him, leaving Alyssa and Jason sitting out on the deck under the stars twinkling in the sky.

He moved closer, putting his arm around her and pulling her against his body.

"What are you doing?" she asked him.

"Snuggling with my honey bear."

She rolled her eyes. "Why?"

He put his mouth next to her ear, as if whispering sweet nothings. "In case they're peeking out the window."

The warmth of his breath raised goose bumps on her skin and heated her blood. "You think my parents are spying on us?"

"I think, if they have any doubts about our relationship, they might be looking for evidence of a deception."

"My mother's interrogation over dinner wasn't very subtle, was it?" she asked, struggling to stay focused on their conversation—not an easy task when her hormones, stirred up by his proximity, were clamoring for action.

"I think I handled her questions pretty well. But I also think, even if they're one hundred percent convinced, they would expect their daughter's boyfriend to take advantage of their absence to steal a few kisses—maybe even cop a feel."

She laughed, as he no doubt intended her to do.

"I'm thinking that this pretend dating thing might be better than real dating," she told him.

"Why would you say that?" he wondered.

"Because it's fun without the pressure and expectations."

"It has been fun," he agreed. "But it hasn't been easy."

"I know you've had to do a lot of juggling of your schedule this weekend," she acknowledged. "And I'm sincerely grateful."

"My schedule was the least of it."

"What do you mean?"

He shook his head. "It's my problem, not yours."

"Except that I dragged you into this," she reminded him.

"I wasn't completely unwilling."

"Obviously we have different recollections of how this all began," she remarked wryly.

"I wasn't completely unwilling *after* the chicken marsala," he amended. "Despite the fact that you made me eat asparagus."

She smiled as she tipped her head back against his shoulder. "You're a good sport, Jason Channing."

"I would have said 'savvy negotiator.'"

"We can go with that," she agreed. "But I think I got the better end of the deal."

"Just make sure you've got July 14 marked on your calendar."

"What's the— Oh, right. Your friend's wedding."

"For which you're my plus-one," he reminded her.

"Only because Kevin backed you into a corner."

But Jay knew that wasn't entirely true.

Maybe Kevin's challenge had been the reason for the initial invitation, but there wasn't anyone else he wanted to take to Matt's wedding. After only three weeks, he was tempted to abandon the pretense. Because this make-believe relationship was more real than anything he'd had in a long time.

Or maybe he just wanted to think that was true, to alleviate any lingering guilt over the fact that he'd kissed the girl that one of his best friends had been crushing on.

Or maybe he was just tempted to think they could make a real relationship work because their fake dating had been, as she'd noted, fun. On the other hand, he suspected it had been fun only because he hadn't been thinking about how to get her into bed. In fact, he'd been trying very hard *not* to think about Alyssa in his bed.

Instead, he focused on the purpose of their charade. It was all about deception: Alyssa wanted her parents to believe she was in a relationship so they wouldn't worry about her living so far away—and so her mother would stop trying to set her up with other guys; and Jay was willing to play along because pretending to be infatuated with his neighbor had seemed the quickest way to earn forgiveness from Kevin.

And so far, it *had* been fun. Except for the cold showers. Those had not been fun, and he'd been suffering through them before bed almost every night—and frequently after running with her in the mornings, too.

But as uncomfortable as it was to stand beneath the icy spray, it was necessary. Because as much as he wanted to explore the attraction that simmered between them, he didn't dare make a real move. If he ever got naked with a woman who was his neighbor and a friend, it would be all kinds of awkward when the relationship ended.

The possibility of a mutually satisfying relationship that didn't end never crossed his mind, because he didn't do happily-ever-after. He didn't even do long-term. Maybe someday, but he wasn't ready to settle down just yet.

But the more time Jay spent with Alyssa, the more he realized he didn't want anyone else, and that realization made him uneasy. Thankfully, her parents were going back to California the next day, and the status quo would be restored.

Jason showed up at Alyssa's door just after lunch on Monday to accompany her and her parents to the airport. She was grateful to have his company for the trip back, not to mention that the action scored major points with her mother. They stood together and watched Renata and Miguel go through the security line.

"That wasn't so bad, was it?" he asked.

"Only the longest three days of my life," she said, waving to her mom and dad as they disappeared from view.

"But at least it's done now and we can go back to our re-spective lives as if this weekend never happened." Her tone was upbeat, but she couldn't deny that the prospect left her feeling a little disappointed.

"Just when I was getting the hang of this boyfriend thing," he lamented.

"You were the perfect boyfriend," she confirmed.

"Handsome? Attentive? Charming?"

"All of the above," she agreed with a smile. "But most important—temporary."

He stared at her. "You really aren't looking for a rela-tionship?"

"Why does everyone seem so surprised by that? Why is it okay for a man to not want to be tied down, but a woman is always expected to want a husband and a family?"

"Are you saying that you don't want a husband and a family?"

"Well, sure I do, someday," she admitted. "I'm just not in any hurry for it to happen."

"In that case, you just might be the perfect girlfriend," he decided.

"Look at us—a match made in heaven."

"Haven," he corrected.

She laughed. "But on a more serious note, thank you, sincerely, for this weekend."

"It's not quite over yet," he noted. "And I'm hungry."

"You need to work on your subtlety," she told him.

He shook his head. "I'm not trying to wrangle another meal from you."

"You're not?" Her tone was skeptical.

"In fact, I was thinking of cooking for you—if grilling counts as cooking," he clarified. "We can pick up a couple of steaks, some potatoes, open a bottle of wine and cele-brate the conclusion of a successful weekend."

"I appreciate the offer," she told him. And she was undeniably tempted, but—

"I don't want to hear any 'buts,'" he said.

She closed her mouth, reconsidered her words and tried again. "However—"

"Nope." He cut her off. "'However' is the same as 'but' just with more syllables, so I don't want to hear that, either."

"What do you want to hear?"

"Something along the lines of 'that sounds like a great idea and I would love to have dinner with you' would work."

"That sounds like a great idea and I would love to have dinner with you," she dutifully intoned.

"That wasn't so hard now, was it?"

"No," she admitted. "I just expected that, after all the time we've spent together over the past few weeks, you'd be grateful to have some space."

He shrugged. "It turns out I don't mind having you in my space."

She put a hand on her chest. "Oh, Jason—you're *such* a romantic."

He grinned. "Let me know if you're going to swoon, so I can get in position to catch you."

"Unless we travel back in time two hundred years, I'm not going to swoon," she assured him.

"Modern women don't swoon?"

"No more than contemporary men solve disagreements with pistols at dawn."

"We prefer paintball at dusk," he acknowledged.

"Speaking of which—are you sure you don't want to head back to Adventure Village?"

"Hmm…let me think about that." He tapped a finger against his chin. "Hanging out with a bunch of sweaty guys or some one-on-one time with a pretty girl…that is a tough choice." He took her hand. "But I choose you."

Chapter Eleven

So they picked up steaks and potatoes. Alyssa threw together a salad with ingredients she had in her fridge and they dined on his deck.

"You were right," she said as Jay emptied the last of the wine into her glass.

"Words a man always likes to hear," he remarked. "But what, specifically, was I right about?"

"I do hide my scars."

"I know that," he said, wondering what had caused her to introduce the topic now. Was she feeling relaxed because the weekend had gone so well? Or was it possible that she'd grown to like and trust him? Or maybe her confession was simply an aftereffect of three glasses of wine. "But I don't know why."

"Partly it's because old habits die hard," she admitted. "My mother always made sure the clothes she bought for me didn't let the scars show. She never made a big deal about them, and I know it's not because she thinks they're unsightly, but because they're a reminder to her that I almost died."

"Is there another part?" he asked gently.

"Mean girls and beach day in my senior year of high school."

"Mean girls are usually mean because they're jealous."

She nodded. "And I was dating Craig Gerber. He wasn't on the football team, but he was class president. Smart, good-looking and extremely popular. Not the type of guy who would ordinarily look twice at me. In fact, we'd been in classes together since junior high, and he didn't even know my name until tenth grade."

"What happened then?"

"I got boobs."

He sighed appreciatively. "Those do tend to catch a teenage boy's attention—and often a man's, too."

She smiled at that. "Well, a result of that hormonal spurt, I was no longer the shy, skinny girl who hid out in the library but the shy girl with the boobs who hid out in the library.

"And one day, Craig Gerber came into the library and asked me to have lunch with him."

"And suddenly you were dating Craig Gerber," he guessed.

"There was nothing sudden about it. I was very shy and more than a little oblivious. And there were so many girls who wanted to be with him, it never occurred to me that he could want me—until he asked me to be his date for prom.

"Of course, I said yes." She smiled, a little wistfully, at the memory. "My mother took me shopping for a new dress and shoes and made appointments for me to have my hair and nails done. That night was everything I had dreamed it could be. We danced and we kissed and we stayed out late.

"Then there was a breakfast for grads back at the high

school the next day, and after that, everyone headed to the beach." Her words were a little more clipped now, as if she was in a hurry to finish the story. "Most of the other girls were sunbathing in their teeny, tiny bikinis, and I was wearing one, too, but with a cover-up. They encouraged me to take off the shirt and catch some rays, but I wasn't comfortable baring so much skin—or my scars—in front of everyone there.

"When I continued to resist, Tiffany Butler accused me of being a prude, and Amie Myers said 'You don't have anything the rest of us don't have.'"

Her gaze dropped away. He wanted to reassure her that he didn't need to hear all the unpleasant details, but he sensed that she needed to tell them, so he remained silent, waiting for her to continue.

"But Amie knew about my scars because we were friends when we were little," she confided. "I'd slept over at her house and she'd slept over at mine, so I thought—" She shook her head, as if berating herself. "I actually thought she was trying to reassure me that the scars weren't a big deal."

He touched a hand to her arm, a silent gesture of support and encouragement.

Alyssa forged ahead. "I hadn't considered that, although we'd been close as kids, we'd grown apart over the years. She was outgoing and popular, and I was not—at least not until Craig Gerber started hanging out with me. And one of Amie's new BFFs was Tiffany, who'd been trying to snag Craig's attention for months and was not happy that he'd asked me to the prom.

"Anyway, encouraged by Amie's comment, I took off my shirt." She closed her eyes, and he knew she was clearly envisioning that moment, that day, and his heart ached for the pain he knew she was reliving.

"I didn't think my scars were gruesome, or even particularly noticeable," she said quietly, "but when Tiffany saw my chest, she screamed—a total drama queen shriek of horror that, of course, drew everyone's attention."

Now Jay was clearly envisioning it, too, and he hated imagining how horrible that experience was for her. If he'd been there... But, of course, he hadn't been. And there was nothing he could do to change what had happened in the past; he could only be here for her now.

"And then she pretended to be embarrassed by her reaction and 'apologized'—" Alyssa put air quotes around the word "—and said that she didn't blame me for wanting to conceal my hideous scars.

"I was tempted to ask about *her* surgery, since we all knew that she'd had a nose job as her graduation present from her parents."

"But you didn't," he said. It wasn't a question. He knew she would never be cruel or spiteful, though he couldn't help wishing that another one of her classmates had made the point.

"No, I didn't," she confirmed. "I just put my cover-up back on."

And had undoubtedly been covering up her scars ever since.

"What happened with Craig?" he asked.

"He was a little weirded out by the scars—or maybe by the idea of someone having a hole in their heart—though he pretended not to be. And when he took me home at the end of the day, he kissed me goodbye without trying to sneak his hands under my top and said 'See ya.' He hooked up with Tiffany before the end of the summer."

"Sounds like they deserved each other."

"Anyway," she said briskly, "that's the story. Since then, I have to really know and trust someone before I let them see my scars."

Jay couldn't blame her for that. On the other hand, she'd been carrying some pretty heavy baggage since high school and maybe it was time for her to let go of it.

"That's your choice, obviously. I just think…"

His train of thought completely jumped the track when he realized that her fingers were unfastening the buttons that ran down the front of her shirt.

She stood up and turned to face him, though she held the two sides of the shirt together, covering herself.

He swallowed. "What are you doing, Lys?"

"Proving that I trust you."

And then she pulled the shirt open, revealing lots of smooth, pale skin and full, round breasts cradled by cups of pale pink lace. All the blood in his head rapidly migrated south.

He swallowed again and reminded himself that she wasn't really baring her body but rather her soul.

He knew where to look for the scar and forced himself to focus on the thin, pale line that ran down the center of her chest, between those perfect breasts.

Perfectly motionless breasts, which clued him in to the fact that she was holding her breath. Waiting.

He finally lifted his gaze to hers and held it for a long moment without speaking.

She moistened her lips with the tip of her tongue. "You're not saying anything," she noted. "You're not shrieking, but you're not saying anything, either."

"I'm afraid to say the wrong thing," he admitted. "I want to tell you that you're beautiful, because you are, but even in my head, that sounds inadequate.

"I want to say thank you, for trusting me enough to take a step that I know wasn't easy for you to take.

"And I feel compelled to suggest that you cover yourself up again now, because I don't trust myself not to strip away the rest of your clothes to perform a close and very personal inspection of your gorgeous body."

Alyssa immediately tugged the sides of her shirt back together.

"Probably a wise move," Jason acknowledged, "though a disappointing one."

Her fingers fumbled as she tried to slide the buttons back through the holes.

He brushed her hands away to take over the task, but he stopped just past the halfway point, leaving the top four buttons unfastened.

Then he leaned forward and pressed his lips to the exposed skin above her breasts.

The kiss was unexpectedly sweet...and began the healing of old wounds deep inside.

She cleared her throat and attempted to lighten the mood. "I'm not going to sit here with my shirt only half buttoned."

"You can button it all the way to your throat if you want," he said. "Now that I know what you're wearing underneath, that's what I'm going to see in my mind when I look at you."

"And look at the time," she said.

"You're not really going to rush off already, are you?"

She nodded. "I've still got some work to do tonight. There's only a couple more weeks of school, then final exams and report cards to write."

Plus, she was starting to have real feelings for her sexy neighbor, so she told herself it was a good thing that the charade had come to an end.

And she almost believed it.

Of course, Alyssa's resolution to put some distance between them wasn't likely to get very far when he showed up to run with her the next day at 6:00 a.m. And every morning after that throughout the week.

But the running was routine for both of them, and the more miles they covered, the more confident she was that they'd returned to familiar—and safe—ground. She had a lot of fond memories of the time they'd spent together— from adrenaline-pumping rounds of laser tag to relaxing dinners in her apartment, from the bells and whistles of the arcade to quiet nights and long conversations under the stars, from casual hand-holding to bone-melting kisses.

She packed those memories away in the back of her mind so that she could focus on living in the present. Unfortunately, that mental exercise failed to alleviate the wanting that continued to churn inside her.

"I picked up a bag of frozen shrimp and some of that twisty pasta when I was at The Trading Post yesterday," he said as they neared the end of their route Friday morning. "I was hoping you might show me how to make the dish you were telling me about."

"You want a cooking lesson?" She couldn't help sounding dubious.

"If you don't mind."

Of course she didn't mind, but she also knew that she shouldn't agree. She was trying to put some much-needed distance between them, and spending one-on-one time in his kitchen was not the way to do that. But instead of refusing his request, she heard herself ask, "Do you have any ingredients other than the shrimp and pasta?"

"What else do I need?"

She shook her head despairingly. "When do you want this lesson?"

"Tonight? Tomorrow?" He shrugged. "Whenever you're available."

"I usually work Fridays," she reminded him. "But Duke

asked me to take the Saturday shift this weekend, so I could do tonight."

"Great," he said, sounding pleased by her response. "My place at seven?"

"Okay," she agreed.

And floated through the rest of her day looking forward to seven o'clock.

When she got home from school, she printed up a copy of the recipe and packed up a box with her sauté pan, pasta pot, colander, spatula, slotted spoon, garlic press, olive oil, canned tomatoes, fresh spinach, onion, garlic and red pepper flakes.

Jason raised his brows at the box when he opened the door.

"You said you had the pasta and the shrimp—I wasn't sure what else I'd be able to find in your kitchen," she explained.

"That was probably a good call," he acknowledged. "Although I did pick up a bottle of your favorite pinot noir and dessert from Sweet Caroline's Sweets."

Her gaze immediately went to the white bakery box on the counter. "What's for dessert?"

"You'll find out after you eat your dinner," he told her.

She smiled, recognizing the reversal of their roles in the conversation. "Okay, let's get this lesson started."

She set the recipe on the counter, then began to assemble the ingredients, faltering when she neared the end of the list.

"I forgot the basil."

"Do you need me to run to the store?" he offered.

"No, I meant I forgot it downstairs." She dumped the bag of frozen shrimp into the colander. "Run cold water over these to defrost them—I'll be right back."

Forty minutes later, they were sitting at the table with their pasta.

"It looks fabulous," Alyssa told him.

"I didn't think you'd let me screw it up."

She laughed. "So why are you looking at it as if you're afraid to try it?"

"Because you put green stuff in it."

"The green stuff was in the recipe," she pointed out, raising her own fork to her lips.

He watched as she chewed, swallowed.

Then she reached for her glass and raised it toward him. "Congratulations, Jason Channing—you cooked a delicious meal and it was not on a grill."

He sipped his wine, then finally sampled the pasta.

"It is good," he said, looking surprised—and a little proud.

They chatted about various topics while they finished their meal, including triple chocolate mousse cake for dessert. After clearing up the kitchen, Jason suggested that they take the rest of the wine onto his balcony.

"This view never gets old," she said, lowering herself onto the cushioned teak sofa beside him. "I wish I'd known about this when my parents were here—my mother would love this."

"Oh…um, that reminds me—she called earlier."

She froze with her glass halfway to her lips. "My mother called you?"

"No, she called your cell—when you ran downstairs to get the basil."

"Oh." She relaxed again and glanced at her watch. "I'll call her back when I go downstairs."

"Actually, she said that they were going to Cristina's tonight and that she'd talk to you tomorrow."

"You answered my phone?"

"Should I have let it go to voice mail?"

"No, it's fine," she said. "And now she can enjoy her visit with my sister without worrying that I didn't answer because I'd fallen and cracked my head open in the shower."

"If that's a real concern, I'm willing to spot you in the shower, honey bear."

She rolled her eyes at the deliberately provocative endearment as she shook her head. "Of course it's not a real concern—it's just one of those scenarios my mother dreams up when I'm not immediately accessible to her."

"Is that a yes or a no to watching you bathe?"

"A definite no," she said firmly.

"Because they say that more than thirty percent of household accidents occur in the bathroom."

"Who's they?" she challenged, reaching for her glass.

He shrugged. "Whoever keeps track of household accidents?"

She shook her head as she sipped her wine.

"During our brief conversation, your mom also happened to mention that it's their thirty-fifth wedding anniversary in a few weeks."

"It is," she confirmed. "Though I'm not sure why she'd mention it to you."

"She, uh, wanted to know if I was going to make the trip to California with you for the big celebration."

"And you told her that, unfortunately, you couldn't take the time away from work," she prompted.

"She caught me off guard," he admitted.

She frowned at his response. "You didn't... Jason, please say you didn't tell her that you would be there."

His gaze shifted away, a sure sign that she wasn't going to like his response. "I couldn't think of any reason not to."

"Work? Family obligations? A previous commitment?" She effortlessly tossed out the possibilities. "Pick one."

"You're right—I should have made up an excuse," he acknowledged. "And maybe I would have, but then she pointed out that it would be the perfect opportunity for the rest of your family to meet me."

"They only want to meet you because they think you're my boyfriend," she reminded him.

"Wasn't that the plan?"

She shook her head, beyond frustrated with him and the situation. "I only wanted you to meet them," she said. "*One meeting* so that my mother could stop worrying—and matchmaking."

"She doesn't seem to be matchmaking anymore," he said helpfully.

"And while I'm grateful for that, you are *not* coming with me to California," she asserted. Because she knew that spending ten days in close proximity to the man she was pretend dating would likely result in the development of real feelings. Especially when she was already fighting a daily battle against the physical attraction between them.

And maybe there were moments that she wondered *what if* she went to bed with him—and found herself tempted and tantalized by the possibilities. But so far, she'd managed to hold out against her own growing desire, because she knew that falling for "Charming" wouldn't lead to anything but heartache.

"I should have found a way to get you out of this," Alyssa said as they crossed the state line into California.

"You didn't get me into it," Jay reminded her.

"If I hadn't kissed you in front of Diego, my parents wouldn't have come to Haven to meet my supposed boyfriend, and they certainly wouldn't have invited you to their anniversary party," she pointed out.

"I like California," he said easily. And while it was true, it wasn't the reason he'd agreed to make this trip.

Not that he'd taken the time to examine his motivations

too closely, perhaps because he wasn't quite ready to admit the truth—even to himself. But he could admit that he wanted to know her better, and seeing Alyssa within the circle of her extended family seemed like the perfect opportunity to gain a deeper understanding of who she was and what she wanted.

"Except that we're not here for the beaches or wineries or amusement parks," she responded to his comment. "We're here for a family event."

"I like your family," he said.

"You've only met my mother and father." She uncapped her bottle of water—because, of course, she'd packed numerous snacks and drinks for the long trip—and sipped.

"And Diego."

"Who is *not* family."

But he was a close friend who had aspirations of becoming even closer to the family—or at least Alyssa. And he was the reason that Jay had decided to spend the next eight days in California with his temporary girlfriend. "Maybe he's not family, but he'll be at the party, won't he?"

"Considering that he lives in the same neighborhood as my parents, we'll probably cross paths with him frequently over the next week," she acknowledged grimly.

"Then it's a good thing I accepted your mother's invitation, isn't it?" he said.

"I'm not denying that your presence serves a purpose for *me*—I'm just not sure what you're getting out of it."

"The pleasure of your company," he suggested.

She rolled her eyes.

"And, since you mentioned beaches and wineries and amusement parks, maybe we can sneak away for a few hours and do something fun."

"We will," she promised. "I'm just not sure that a few hours of fun will make up for more than a week with my family. And considering how hard it was for me to get someone to cover my shifts at Diggers', I'm wondering how you managed to wrangle ten days off work to make this trip with me."

"I'm the boss," he reminded her.

"Of a business that's been operating for just over a year."

"Operating very successfully," he pointed out. "And one of the reasons it's been so successful is that I hired the right people." A vague memory of Naomi flitted through his mind. "At least when I made my own hiring decisions and didn't let myself be influenced by family pressures."

"Sounds like there's a story there," she noted. "And we've still got about four hours until we get to my parents' place."

So he told her about hiring his cousin, at his father's request—and subsequently firing his cousin, the result of which was that his aunt was still not speaking to her brother, which pleased his mother, who'd never been particularly fond of that sister-in-law.

Alyssa chuckled in all the right places, as if she enjoyed listening to him talk. Over the past few weeks, they'd shared a lot of stories and confidences. As a result, he'd occasionally found himself wondering if this was what it would be like if she was more than just a pretend girlfriend, because being with her had given him an appreciation for what it meant to share a life with someone.

He definitely wasn't in any hurry to get married and start a family, but it was nice to have company at the end of the day, someone to share a meal and conversation.

Over the past several weeks, he'd occasionally wondered what would happen if they moved their relationship to the bedroom, but he never let those thoughts linger. Because wanting anything more than what they had would be selfish and foolish.

And if there was one thing he'd vowed he wouldn't ever be again, it was a fool.

What they shared, aside from four children, was a love of making money and the status it afforded them in the community. And maybe that was a harsh assessment, but he didn't think it was an inaccurate one. So was it any wonder that he had doubts about his ability to recognize love, if that was what he was feeling?

He'd thought he was in love with Jenny Reashore, the cheerleader he'd dated for several months in high school. In fact, he'd been planning to tell her he loved her after the season opener in his junior year, but that was the night he got sacked and his attention had been diverted by the pain—and then the pain meds they gave him in the hospital. By the time he'd recovered enough to think about sharing his feelings, Jen had already moved on—to Liam Gilmore!—with no more of an explanation than to say "things change."

Yeah, that had cut to the quick. And maybe the experience had made him wary about opening his heart again, but he didn't believe that he'd been scarred so badly that he was incapable of falling in love. In fact, he'd fallen in love with Melanie Lindhurst a few years later, when he was in college. But he'd never said the words to her, either. And when she'd said them to him, he'd started to panic a little, thinking that love meant marriage and kids, and he was barely twenty years old and definitely not ready to make *that* kind of commitment.

But he was twenty-nine now, and he'd noticed that his friends were starting to pair up with their perfect partners. And as he observed their relationships taking shape, he was beginning to see the appeal of sharing his life with someone—especially if that someone was Alyssa.

Or maybe he just needed a strong jolt of caffeine to banish these unexpected thoughts from his mind.

After a quick shower, he followed the scent of coffee into the kitchen, where Alyssa's grandmother was pouring a cup. When he stepped into the room, Valentina reached into the cupboard for a second mug as she slid the first across the counter toward him. "Cream's in the fridge, if you want it. Sugar's on the table."

"This is perfect," he said. "Thanks."

"I usually enjoy my first cup on the deck with the birds for company," she said. "But you're welcome to join us."

"I'd like that," he said, following her through the sliding door and taking a seat across from her.

"Renata will start breakfast as soon as the others get here."

"Others?" he echoed, having visions of the crowd that had gathered the previous evening for a "welcome home" potluck dinner for Alyssa. The group had been comprised of family and friends, including Lucia, Renata's best friend; Daniel, Lucia's husband; and Diego, the favorite nephew. There had been so many people on hand, Jay hadn't been able to pick out Lucia and Daniel, but he noticed that Diego hadn't strayed more than ten feet from Alyssa all night.

Not that she'd seemed aware of or bothered by the other man's presence, but Jay had been both.

"Just Cristina, Steven and Nicolas," Valentina said in response to his question.

"Oh," he said, relieved by the mention of only Alyssa's sister, brother-in-law and nephew.

She smiled as she lifted her mug. "Are you wishing now that you didn't let Alyssa talk you into making this trip with her?"

"Truthfully, she tried to talk me out of it," he confided.

"But you came anyway," she mused.

"I wanted to meet her family." And to remind Diego that Alyssa was with someone else, but he didn't mention that reason to her grandmother.

"Speaking of family," Valentina said, wincing as a car door slammed. "That sounds like Nicolas now."

Not half a minute later, the side gate swung open and the little boy came racing across the grass. "Abuela, hi! Are pancakes ready?"

She rose to her feet and he launched himself at her, wrapping his slender arms around her middle. She stroked an affectionate hand over his hair. "We were waiting for you to get here before we started breakfast."

"I'm here!" he announced.

"I see that."

"And the rest of the neighborhood knows it now, too," Steven said, an obvious commentary on his son's volume.

"You're early," Valentina noted, glancing at the time display on her Fitbit.

"Mom made the mistake of mentioning pancakes to Nicolas last night, and he woke up with them on his mind this morning," Cristina explained.

"It was all we could do to hold him off until eight," her husband confided.

Nicolas looked up at Jay. "D'you like pancakes?"

"I love pancakes," he said.

"Me, too," the boy told him. "Gramma puts 'nanas and choc'late chips in mine sometimes—they're my fav'rite."

"Sounds yummy," he agreed.

"Well, let's go tell your gramma we're here," Cristina suggested, nudging her son toward the house.

Steven went with them.

"And that's the end of our quiet morning," Valentina said with no regret in her tone.

Before Jay could respond, another figure walked through the gate that Alyssa's sister had left open, and his sunny mood turned dark.

"*Buenos días*, Diego."

"*Buenos días*, Abuela," he said, bending down to kiss each of her cheeks. Then he nodded at Jay. "Good morning."

He returned the greeting.

"We're just about to cook up breakfast," Valentina said. "Do you want to join us?"

Jay was glad to see the other man shake his head, declining the offer.

"Thanks, but I ate already. I just stopped by to pick up the casserole dish my mother left last night."

"I'll get it for you," she said.

Nicolas raced out of the house as his great-grandmother was going in. "Bacon's cooking!" he announced. "And Gramma promised to put 'nanas and choc'late chips in my pancakes!" Then he noticed Diego and asked, "Are you going to have breakfast with us?"

This second invitation made it clear to Jay that the other man wasn't just an occasional visitor to the Cabrera house but a frequent guest at their table.

"Not today," Diego responded.

Cristina, never far from her son, set a coloring book and box of crayons on the table, then pulled back a chair for Nicolas to sit.

"Can I help with anything?" Jay asked her, hoping for an excuse to avoid conversation with Alyssa's not-so-secret admirer.

"We've got plenty of hands in the kitchen," Cristina said. "But if you could keep an eye on Nicolas—and keep him out of the kitchen—that would be extremely helpful."

"I can do that," he agreed.

"Thanks," she said, already heading back inside again, leaving Jay alone with her son. And Diego.

The other man didn't waste any time on small talk but bluntly said, "I want you to stop seeing Alyssa."

"I'm sure you do," Jay noted drily.

"She's…fragile," Diego said.

"No, she's not," he argued. "Maybe you want to believe she's fragile so you can tell yourself you're looking out for her, but Alyssa is one of the strongest people I know."

"That doesn't mean she won't be hurt when you toss her aside."

"You're making a lot of assumptions about a relationship—and a man—you know nothing about," he chided.

"Tell me you're serious about wanting a future with Alyssa and I'll back off," Diego said.

"Of course I'm serious about wanting a future with Alyssa," Jay said, and he realized that though he was only repeating the words the other man had told him to say, they weren't untrue.

He did want a future with Alyssa. Maybe he wasn't quite ready to think about putting a ring on her finger, but when he thought about the weeks and even months ahead, he didn't want to imagine his life without Alyssa in it.

The other man scowled. "I don't believe you."

"I don't care what you believe, it's true," he insisted.

"The longer this goes on, the more heartbroken she's going to be when it's over."

"You'd love that, wouldn't you? Because then you could be there to help her pick up the pieces."

"I will be there to help her pick up the pieces," Diego said. "And to show her what it really means to be loved. And when she's ready, I'm going to marry her."

"I hate to destroy this little fantasy world you're building," Jay said, not regretful at all. "But she's not going to marry you."

"How do you know?"

"Because she's going to marry me."

With those words, the arrogant confidence was wiped

from Diego's face. For the first time, the other man looked uncertain. "You didn't... You haven't..."

The stammered response gave Jay a minute to gather his thoughts and correct his course. Because he was clearly on a course that needed correcting.

But Diego's bold assertion had put his back up, and he'd spoken without thinking. Now he had the opportunity to backtrack, at least a little. To suggest that they'd discussed marriage in vague and general terms but eliminate any implication of an actual engagement.

Except that when he opened his mouth to respond, he heard himself say, "Yes, I did. I asked Alyssa to marry me."

"You asked her to marry you?" Diego echoed, his voice hollow.

"And she said yes," he said, because if he ever proposed to a woman, he expected that she would say yes. And because his mouth was apparently a runaway train that his brain didn't know how to stop.

Valentina chose that moment to return with the casserole dish. Diego took it from her with barely a murmured thanks, then left through the side gate again, and Alyssa's grandmother went back inside.

Jay breathed a sigh of relief, confident that he could contain any fallout from that conversation.

Until he remembered the little boy sitting at the table, whose wide eyes confirmed that he'd heard every word.

After the long drive from Nevada and the emotional reunion with her family, Alyssa had fallen into bed exhausted, but sleep had not come easily. And when she'd finally slept, she'd dreamed about Jason.

It was almost seven thirty by the time she dragged herself out of bed. She tied her hair into a ponytail, pulled on a pair of shorts and a T-shirt, laced up her running shoes and slipped out the side door. She'd been tempted to detour downstairs, to see if Jason was up and wanted to go running with her, but she could only imagine how her mother would react if she knew her daughter was knocking on a boy's bedroom door. So she resisted the impulse and headed out on her own.

She did her usual 5K route and returned to the house feeling more like her usual self. After a quick shower and a change of clothes, she was ready to face the day—and her family. Because everyone was gathered around the table for breakfast—not just her parents and grandmother, but her sister, brother-in-law and nephew, too—no doubt lured here by the promise of Renata's pancakes.

"Nicolas just told us the news," Renata said when Alyssa lifted the pot of coffee to fill the mug she'd taken from the cupboard.

She looked from her mother, who was beaming with barely constrained joy, to her nephew, who was busy shoveling pancakes into his mouth, then at the others. Her father nodded, as if in approval, though of what she had no idea; Cristina and Steven were both grinning; Abuela's dark eyes sparkled.

"News?" she echoed blankly.

"He overheard Jason and Diego talking," Valentina said excitedly.

"I can't believe I had to hear it from my grandson." Renata took the lead again. Despite the admonishment of her words, she sounded gleeful rather than disappointed. "Why didn't you tell us last night?"

"Tell you what?" she asked cautiously, lifting her mug to her lips as Jason came in from the deck.

His lips curved when he saw her, but the smile was a little too quick and wide to be natural, and her uneasiness grew.

"That you and Jason are engaged," her mother replied.

Alyssa choked on her coffee.

She looked at Jason, expecting to see the panic that filled her heart reflected in his expression.

Instead, he continued to wear that fake smile as he slid his arm around her and drew her close to his side.

"We didn't say anything because it's still unofficial," he explained. "As you can see, I haven't even had a chance to get a ring yet."

Alyssa didn't know how or why Jason had mentioned marriage. She only knew that she had to rein in the topic before her mother started pressing them to set a date for a wedding that wasn't ever going to happen.

Though her brain was still scrambling to put the pieces together, she felt compelled to say something. "Plus, this week is about celebrating your anniversary," she hastened to add. "And the last thing we'd want to do is steal the spotlight."

"But this is the best news," Renata insisted. "And there is no greater gift to a parent than knowing that her children are loved."

"We should have champagne to celebrate," Miguel decided, obviously caught up in the moment.

"It's 9:30 a.m.," Alyssa pointed out to her father.

"Mimosas, then," Renata said, immediately on board with the plan.

"I'll get the champagne," Steven said, because he knew his in-laws always had a couple chilled bottles in their wine cellar.

"Is that bacon?" Jason asked, eyeing the platter of breakfast meat on the table.

"And sausage and pancakes," Valentina told him. "Come. Eat."

Of course, Jason didn't need to be asked twice.

Alyssa reluctantly joined her "fiancé" at the table, but she only toyed with her food. Even the coffee she'd wanted was now churning uneasily in her tummy. And that was before she had to paste a smile on her face and sip champagne and orange juice as she accepted the best wishes of her family.

After everyone had eaten their fill and the champagne bottle was empty, Alyssa requested a private word with Jason.

She hooked her arm through his and led him outside, all the way to the back of the property, where she could be certain their conversation wouldn't be overheard.

"What was that all about?" she demanded. "Why would you tell my five-year-old nephew that we're getting married?"

"I didn't tell Nicolas anything," he denied.

She dropped her face into her hands. "How— Why—" She drew in a breath and tried again. "How did this happen?"

"He was being a dick."

She frowned. "Nicolas?"

"No," he immediately responded. "Diego."

"I think you need to start at the beginning."

"I was having coffee with your grandmother when he showed up to pick up a dish his mother left here last night.

"Anyway, Valentina went into the house to get it, and as soon as she was out of earshot, Diego confronted me about our relationship. He accused me of playing with your emotions and said that the longer this went on, the more heartbroken you were going to be when it was over, leaving him to pick up the pieces."

"And you responded to that by telling him we're getting married?" she asked incredulously.

He shrugged. "I needed to say something to convince him that he was wrong about our relationship."

"Except that he wasn't," Alyssa reminded him. "Our relationship is a sham."

"I didn't think you wanted me to admit that."

Of course she didn't. But now the lies were getting so much bigger than she'd anticipated, and she felt as if the whole situation was spiraling out of her control.

"Maybe it's time to tell them the truth," she suggested. "We should go back into the house right now and admit that our relationship was a lie from the beginning."

"And then where will I sleep tonight?" he wondered.

She looked at him questioningly. "So what are we going to do?"

"We're going to play this out."

"You can't be serious," she protested.

"If you tell them the truth now, Diego will be back here with a ring before sunset."

"I can handle Diego," she said with more confidence than she felt.

"If you really believed that, our first kiss never would have happened," he pointed out.

"I didn't believe it then," she acknowledged. "But I do now."

"While I appreciate your willingness to blow the cover off our cover story, what purpose would it serve at this point? Besides, it's only for seven days."

"I can't believe you want to maintain the charade of an engagement."

"Pretending to be your fiancé for a week isn't really that much different than pretending to be your boyfriend."

"You don't think so?"

"Only five more days until the big party," Alyssa said to her mother the next morning when she found her in the kitchen, cracking eggs into a bowl for breakfast.

"And we've got a little bit of a problem," Renata said.

"What kind of problem?"

"Tia Deanna and Tio Carlos have decided to come for the celebration. And, of course, they're bringing Selena and Sofia, too."

"Why's that a problem? Aren't you looking forward to seeing them?"

"Of course I am. But we're running out of places to put everybody."

"There are plenty of hotels nearby," she pointed out.

"I can't ask them to stay in a hotel," Renata protested. "They're family."

"So where are they going to sleep?"

"Well, Deanna and Carlos will take the room downstairs, and the girls could squeeze into your room."

"If they're in my room, where am I going to be?"

"In the guest room at Cristina and Steven's place."

"And Jason?" she asked.

"In Nicolas's room."

"Nicolas has bunk beds," she reminded her mother.

Renata nodded. "But the bottom bunk is a double."

With a double-sized comforter that matched the twin—both covered in cartoon dinosaurs. "I assume you've discussed this with Cristina?"

"It was her idea," Renata said.

Alyssa sighed. "I'll tell Jason to pack his bag after breakfast."

"I'm so sorry about this," Alyssa said as Jason drove toward Cristina and Steven's house a few hours later.

"There's no need to apologize," he told her.

"You're going to be sleeping in a bunk bed," she said again in case he hadn't been listening the first two times.

"Which seems to bother you more than it bothers me,"

he pointed out. As long as he had a soft place to lay his head, he wasn't going to complain.

"One dinner a month for the rest of the year."

He turned his head to look at her. "Huh?"

"I owe you big-time for this," she acknowledged. "And a few more home-cooked meals might come close to balancing the scales again."

"Do you have any understanding of how a negotiation works?" he wondered aloud.

"This situation is a lot more than you bargained for," she noted.

"Or maybe you're looking for an excuse to continue spending time with me," he teased.

"You really need to do something about your low self-esteem," she commented wryly.

He shrugged. "I'm not going to turn down your cooking and your company. I was just wondering if there was something more going on here."

"There's nothing more going on here," she assured him. "And now that I think about it, why should I feel responsible for this situation?"

"That's what I'm trying to figure out," he said.

"I'm rescinding my offer," she decided. "Because if this is anyone's fault, it's yours."

"How is this in any way my fault?" he demanded to know.

"If you'd just said that you were busy this week and regretfully unable to attend the party, we wouldn't be in this predicament."

"You're right," he acknowledged. "And you'd be here on your own, free to bask in Diego's attention and affection."

"Okay—the extra dinners are back on the table."

"Well, not yet," he noted. "But I'll count the days."

"You should also hope no one else decides to show up

for this party," she said. "Or we might get bumped out of Cristina and Steven's house, too."

"Welcome to chaos," Cristina said, greeting them from the front porch.

As soon as Alyssa reached the top step, she was folded in her sister's embrace. "I'm so glad you're here." When Cristina released her, Jason was given the same welcome. "And happy to see you again, too."

"Thanks for taking us in," he said.

"Our pleasure," she said, opening the door and gesturing for them to enter. "Steven is in the backyard. He went out to light the grill as soon as Mom called to say you were headed over. Nicolas is with him, because he's been bouncing off the walls all day, eager for 'Tia Lyssa' to arrive.

"Why don't you go out with the men and give Alyssa and me a chance to catch up?" Cristina suggested.

"Sure," he agreed. "Just tell me where to put our bags."

"Oh, just drop them right there for now," Cristina said.

Jason set the bags on the floor as directed.

"I didn't think to ask Alyssa if you were a beer or a wine drinker, but Steven has both outside."

He took the hint and headed toward the doors that were opened onto the back deck.

"I know playing musical beds isn't really convenient, but now we get some one-on-one time without the rest of the family eavesdropping on our conversations."

"You're assuming we have something to talk about that would be worth eavesdropping on," Alyssa said.

"Hello?" Cristina dragged her into the family room and over to the sofa, sitting close to her. "I want the inside scoop on your sexy fiancé."

"What do you want to know?"

"Everything. When? Where? How?" Cristina grinned. "The why is obvious for anyone to see."

Alyssa couldn't blame her sister for having the same visceral reaction most women—including herself—had when they first set eyes on Jason. She just wished Cristina wanted to talk about something, *anything*, other than Alyssa and Jason's phony romance so that she could stop compounding the lies she'd already told her family.

"You know the when, where and how we met," she reminded her sister.

"But not about the engagement."

"Because I didn't want to make a big deal out of it," she said, and that was kind of true, too. Although the bigger truth was that there had been nothing to make a big deal about. "And because nothing is official."

"Maybe you don't have a ring on your finger yet," Cristina said. "But it's obvious that you're both wildly in love."

The only thing obvious to Alyssa was that Cristina wanted to believe her little sister was going to get the happy ending she'd always dreamed of for her. Unwilling to burst her bubble, she only said, "And yet, Diego doesn't see it."

Cristina waved a hand. "Diego doesn't want to see it because he's been in love with you since you were fourteen."

"What are you talking about?"

"The summer Diego's family moved to California, they stayed with Lucia and Daniel while their house was being built," Cristina said.

"I remember that," Alyssa told her.

"Do you remember that Diego had trouble making friends?"

"He was shy."

"So were you," her sister pointed out. "But we were out walking one day, and you saw him dribbling a soccer ball around the yard by himself and invited him to come to Scoops with us."

"You're not honestly suggesting that an ice-cream cone changed his life."

Cristina shrugged. "I've been married for seven years and the male brain is still a mystery to me. But the day after our trip to Scoops, he told me that he was going to marry you."

Alyssa lifted a brow. "He was fifteen. What fifteen-year-old boy talks about marriage?"

"Again—male brain, mystery," her sister said.

"Well, that was twelve years ago," Alyssa pointed out.

"True. But when he saw you again at New Year's, he told me that you were even more beautiful than he remembered and that he was finally going to tell you how he felt about you."

"I didn't even realize he was the same guy," she admitted. "I just knew he was yet another potential future husband Mama was putting in my path."

"She really misses you and wants you to come home," Cristina said.

"She worries about me and doesn't believe I can take care of myself," Alyssa countered.

"That, too," her sister acknowledged. "And I always thought her concern was a little over the top—until Nicolas had to have his tonsils out. A common and minor procedure compared to open-heart surgery, but scary as hell when it's your kid on the operating table."

Alyssa touched a hand to her sister's arm. "I'm sorry I couldn't get back here for that."

"You have your own life to live. And the teddy bear you sent to keep him company in the hospital? He doesn't go to sleep without it."

Alyssa smiled at that. "I wanted him to know I was

thinking about him. And since we're on the subject of Nicolas and sleeping, don't you think it makes more sense for me rather than Jason to bunk with my nephew?"

"Probably," Cristina agreed. "If anybody was going to be bunking with Nicolas."

Alyssa looked at her blankly.

"That's just what I told Mom," her sister explained. "But there's also no way I'd make you or your fiancé sleep in a bunk bed, especially beneath a five-year-old kid who snores worse than Abuela.

"I may be an old married woman now," she continued, "but I remember what it's like to be young and in love." Cristina winked at her. "And recently engaged."

"So where are we going to be sleeping? I mean, where is Jason going to sleep, and where am I?" Alyssa clarified, because the original question sounded as if she expected to sleep *with* Jason.

Her sister's response, "In the guest room," implied the same thing.

And Alyssa realized any hope that a seven-day engagement wouldn't change anything between her and Jason had just taken a major hit.

Because the guest room had only one bed.

Chapter Thirteen

Jay enjoyed hanging out with Alyssa and her sister and brother-in-law; he was understandably a little wary around her nephew. Aside from the fact that Nicolas had announced the phony engagement to the whole Cabrera family—because apparently telling a five-year-old that something was a secret was a surefire way to get him to shout it out—the little guy did everything at warp speed and full volume. But it was apparent to Jay that the boy adored his Tia Lyssa—and that the feeling was mutual.

For dinner, Steven grilled chorizo sausages that were served with corn on the cob and red rice. The wine and beer flowed freely as the adults enjoyed the warm summer evening, and Nicolas, finally dressed in his pj's with his teeth brushed, climbed into his aunt's lap and fell asleep with his head against her breast.

Watching the boy, Jay experienced an unexpected tug of something he recognized as envy. And how crazy was that—to be jealous of the kid just because he was snuggled close to the soft curves of Alyssa's body?

Yeah, their engagement was a lie. In fact, their whole relationship was a sham. Every part of it, except for his growing attraction to her.

"I should take Nicolas in to his bed," Cristina said, though she didn't look eager to move from the sofa, where she lounged with her head on her husband's shoulder.

"Can I do it?" Alyssa asked.

"Of course," her sister agreed. "Just don't wake him, or he'll be up until midnight."

Alyssa rose easily from her chair with the little boy in her arms.

Jay had observed her interactions with Nicolas for the past several hours. He'd watched her pushing miniature cars around and shooting Nerf darts at a target and using hand puppets to act out a story. In everything she did, she was easy and natural with the boy, and Jay knew she'd be a great mother to her own kids someday.

He got up to open the sliding door for her, and she smiled her thanks as she passed through it.

"Oh, Nicolas dropped Teddy," Cristina said.

"I've got it," Jay said, scooping the stuffed bear from the ground beside the chair where Alyssa had been sitting.

"Thanks," she said. "He doesn't go to sleep without it, and if he wakes up and can't find it, his screams will wake up everyone else, too."

He followed the direction Alyssa had gone and found her tucking the blankets around her nephew in the boy's room.

Jay handed her the bear, and she slipped it under Nicolas's arm.

"I thought I should see where I'm going to be sleeping." He spoke quietly, not wanting to wake the boy.

"Well, you're not sleeping in here," Alyssa responded in a whisper.

"I'm not?"

"No." She kissed Nicolas's cheek, then tiptoed out to the hallway. He followed. "My sister put us in the guest room."

"Guest *rooms*?"

She shook her head. "One room. One bed."

Warning lights flashed in his brain: Danger! Danger!

"You didn't object to that arrangement?" His voice was still low, but there was no mistaking the desperation in his tone.

"What was I supposed to say?" she asked him. "Cristina thinks she's doing us a favor, because what newly engaged couple wouldn't want to snuggle up under the covers?"

Only a short while earlier, he'd been envying Nicolas's proximity to Alyssa, with no expectation that he would soon be getting just as close to her. Closer even. Behind closed doors. Alone.

He swore softly.

She just nodded.

"How big is the bed?"

She led him down the hall to another room, nudged open the door and turned on the light.

"Not big enough," he responded to his own question.

"I'll bet you're wishing now that you'd never offered to make this trip with me," Alyssa remarked.

"Not true," he denied. "Your grandmother's tamales alone were worth the drive."

She smiled at that. "There are moments when I'm really sorry I got you into this mess," she confided. "And other moments when I'm so grateful you were there when Diego walked into Diggers' that night, because I'm not sure Liam would have been such a good sport about this."

"Yeah, that's me—a good sport," he said drily.

"You have been," she insisted.

"It hasn't been without benefits," he reminded her.

"Anything aside from my grandmother's cooking?"

"I would give up her tamales for one of your kisses," he said.

"I saw you chow down on those tamales," she noted.

"They're probably the second best thing I've ever tasted." And though he knew he was playing with fire, Jay pulled her into his arms and kissed her.

And yeah, her mouth was the most delicious thing he'd ever tasted. But instead of satisfying his hunger, he found himself wanting more. Needing more.

His hands slid down her back and over the curve of her bottom, drawing her closer. She lifted her hands to his shoulders, holding on to him as he deepened the kiss. Lips parted, tongues dallied. Desire pulsed through his veins.

A light tap sounded on the partially open door and she practically leaped out of his arms.

"Lys? Are you in there?"

"Yeah." She wrapped her fingers around the knob and yanked the door open wider. "I was just, uh, showing Jason where we were going to be sleeping."

"I didn't mean to interrupt," Cristina apologized, her eyes twinkling. "I just wanted to make sure you have everything you need and to say good-night, because Steven and I are heading to bed, too."

"Oh. Um…yeah. I think we've got everything. Thanks."

"Okay." Cristina kissed her sister's cheek. "Good night." Then, her gaze shifting to Jay, she added, "To both of you."

"Good night," he replied.

"Oh, and lock the door," she advised. "Nicolas is an early riser and he doesn't always remember to knock."

Then she pulled the door firmly closed from the outside, leaving Jay and Alyssa alone.

* * *

They danced around one another as they took turns in the bathroom to get ready for bed.

Alyssa brushed her teeth first, then quickly changed out of her clothes and into her nightshirt while Jason was in the bathroom. When she'd packed for this trip, she'd included her favorite sleeping tee, because she hadn't anticipated that anyone might see her in it. If she had, she might have chosen something that was longer than midthigh—or packed a robe.

Instead, she made do with the covers, ensuring she was under them before he climbed into bed. She lay on her back, her gaze fixed on the ceiling, when he came out of the bathroom. She felt the mattress dip as he lowered himself onto the other side, then he switched off the lamp, plunging the room into darkness.

She shifted, trying to move closer to the edge on her side. But the bed seemed to dip toward the middle, wanting to pull her in the same direction. She shifted again, fighting the worn springs and gravity.

"Could you stop wriggling around for five minutes?" Jason asked through gritted teeth.

"I'm sorry," she said sincerely. "I'm not used to sharing a bed."

"I'm not in the habit of sharing a bed, either. Or not exclusively for sleeping purposes," he clarified.

Which substantiated the rumors that Charming knew how to please a woman, but he didn't do relationships. And even though she was aware of all the reasons it would be a mistake to fall for him, it was getting harder and harder to remember why she shouldn't fall into bed with him. Especially now that they were already there, and her body was intensely aware of his.

"So, how is this going to work?" she asked.

"You're going to close your eyes and go to sleep."

"Oh, okay," she said sarcastically. "Because I haven't tried *that* already."

"Well, try again," he suggested.

So she closed her eyes and imagined that she was alone.

But she could feel the heat of his body and hear the sound of his breathing, and her imagination decided that it preferred to go in a different direction, taunting her with the suggestion of rolling toward him rather than away. Tempting her to imagine those strong, talented hands moving over her body, stripping away her panties and nightshirt, caressing her bare flesh. Touching and teasing and—

Her eyes popped open again in a desperate attempt to banish the fantasy playing out in her mind, making her blood heat and her body yearn. She drew in a slow, deep breath, exhaled.

"I'm used to sleeping in the middle," she confided.

"Me, too," he said. "So obviously that's not going to work for either of us."

Another few minutes passed, the darkness silent and tense, before she ventured to ask, "Do you usually sleep on your back or front or side?"

"How would I know?" he asked her. "I'm sleeping."

The fact that he couldn't see her roll her eyes in the dark didn't stop her from doing it. "What position are you usually in when you wake up?"

That question he answered without hesitation. "Reaching out to silence the damn alarm."

His terse response made her smile, even as she knew it was going to be a very long night.

Alyssa drifted off before he did.

Although sleep didn't come quickly or easily to either of them, Jay sensed the gradual relaxation of her body as her breathing became slow and even. Eventually, his did the same.

He was pretty sure he'd fallen asleep facing the wall, because he remembered deliberately turning onto his side, away from her. Because even when he'd been on his back, with his temporary fiancée on hers, he could see her in his peripheral vision. Even under the covers, he'd been aware of her breasts rising and falling with each breath.

And all he could think about was how perfectly those breasts would fill his hands, how arousing it would be to hear her breath hitch when he brushed his thumbs over her nipples. Even those relatively innocent thoughts had aroused him unbearably, and he'd been grateful she was sleeping, so she couldn't see the sheet tented over a certain part of his anatomy.

But although he was certain he'd fallen asleep facing the wall, he woke up with his arms full of soft, warm female, Alyssa's head tucked under his chin, her hair tickling his throat. He breathed in the scent of her and felt his blood stir.

He loved her softness and her curves. Though he'd heard her grumble about a stubborn seven pounds that refused to be shed, he thought she was perfect.

And right now, her perfect breasts were crushed against his chest. One of her perfect legs was flung over his. And her perfect mouth was only inches from his own.

Just go with it.

The four words that she'd spoken to him at Diggers' echoed in his mind. Tempted him.

Of course, she'd been tempting him for weeks now. And the more time he'd spent with her, the harder it had been to resist the temptation—even before he was forced to share a bed with her.

But he was trapped in a web of lies, tangled in so much deceit that he wondered if he'd ever get free. He couldn't blame Alyssa. She'd only wanted a pretend boyfriend for a weekend. He was the one who'd been goaded by his friends to prolong the charade. He was the one who'd raised the stakes of the game—stupidly, perhaps selfishly, but willingly—believing that if Diego couldn't respect that Alyssa had a boyfriend, surely he'd back off in the face of an engagement.

And why did he even care what the other man believed or did? Jay wasn't one of those guys with a hero complex and Alyssa certainly wasn't a damsel in distress. In fact, she was one of the strongest, bravest women he knew. So how had he found himself in this predicament—in bed with a woman who made him ache and whom he didn't dare touch?

He decided it was Gilmore's fault. Though he wouldn't admit as much to Alyssa, her willingness to turn to the other man had been part of his reason for stepping up to the plate. Because he hadn't liked the idea of his sexy neighbor playing out this charade with his high school nemesis— especially considering that he'd lost a girlfriend and his job as starting quarterback to the other man already. So Jay had jumped into this game with no preparation and little hesitation.

Still, he could have backed out at any time before Alyssa's parents made the trip to Haven. And when Renata called, he could have easily made an excuse as to why he couldn't come to California.

Summer was the busiest season at Adventure Village, and everyone else was working extra hours to cover his duties. But he wasn't worried about not being on-site. He trusted Carter to stay on top of everything and to let him know if there were any problems, and his partners were as invested in the success of JC Enterprises as he was.

But the truth was, when Renata mentioned the anniversary celebration, he hadn't been looking for a reason to say no. In fact, he'd been eager to say yes, to have an excuse to spend more time with Alyssa. And *that* was worrisome.

He'd dated a lot of women in his twenty-nine years, although none for any significant period of time. Nat had been right about that. After a few weeks, the shine of any new relationship inevitably began to dull, and he started to withdraw.

He was all about having fun in the here and now, and most of the women he dated wanted the same thing. A couple of his former girlfriends had accused him of being spoiled and selfish, and they probably weren't wrong, but he'd had no desire to change who he was.

Until now.

Until he'd somehow found himself more deeply involved with Alyssa than he'd ever intended.

He hadn't yet decided whether he should blame Nat or thank her—as she insisted he would do—for the situation he found himself in.

His instinct was to pull back from these feelings that were new and unfamiliar, but he didn't want to pull away from Alyssa. Being with her—whether running in the early hours of the morning or sitting under the stars late in the night or anything else at any time in between—just felt right. When he was with her, he wasn't just happy but content, and he couldn't ever recall feeling that way with a woman before. Even after eight weeks of various activities and countless conversations, there was still so much he didn't know about her, so much he wanted to learn.

Was he falling for her? Or had he already fallen?

Was this love?

Or was it just the sexual attraction that simmered between them messing with his head?

Yeah, that made more sense. Because of the terms of their agreement, she was strictly off-limits to him. And forbidden fruit was always the most tempting. So if he wanted to stop fantasizing about getting naked with her, he was going to have to get naked with her.

It made perfect sense to him.

Of course, there was no way it was going to happen in her sister's house. The first time he made love with Alyssa—because his own proximity rules notwithstanding, he no longer doubted that it was going to happen—he wanted to ensure they had complete privacy without the risk of any interruptions.

But damn, it was torture to be so close to her and not be able to touch her the way he wanted to touch her.

Alyssa shifted in her sleep, sighing softly.

Looking up at the ceiling, he silently cursed his friend. Of course, Nat would laugh her ass off if she could see him now, cuddling in bed with a sweet, sexy woman he couldn't allow himself to be intimate with. Not here. Not now.

And not for any of the five more nights he'd be sleeping with Alyssa in this bed.

He almost wished he'd been assigned to the bottom bunk in her nephew's room. Or the sofa in the living room. Hell, even the floor of the garage would be easier than this.

"You're killing me, Lys."

His words, muttered through gritted teeth, failed to penetrate the cloud of slumber that continued to envelop her, because she only snuggled closer.

Her breasts rubbed against his chest, the friction causing her nipples to pebble beneath the soft cotton of her nightshirt. A shirt that had ridden up during the night, so that her legs and the sweet curve of her bottom—barely covered by silky panties—were exposed.

Thankfully, he'd had the forethought to bring a pair of pajama pants and a T-shirt. At home, he slept only in his briefs, but he didn't think that was the best choice for her parents' house. Sharing a bed with Alyssa, he was doubly grateful for the extra clothing barrier between them.

"Lys?" He tried again.

"Mmm." Her eyelids fluttered open. "Oh." Her sleepy eyes widened. "Um…"

"I guess we both ended up sleeping in the middle, after all," he said when she didn't seem able to complete her thought.

"I guess we did," she acknowledged, her cheeks flushing prettily.

She eased back and attempted to extricate her limbs from his. Her thigh grazed the front of his pants and her breath caught.

"You're…um…" Her words trailed off again.

"Aroused?" he suggested drily.

She nodded, the color in her cheeks deepening.

"That's what happens when a guy wakes up with a sexy, half-naked woman sprawled over him."

She quickly shifted farther away. "I'm so sorry," she said. "I'm not used to…um…"

"You don't have to apologize," he told her. "But it would be helpful if you didn't cuddle me like Nicolas's teddy bear for the next few nights."

"Five more nights," she reminded him.

He nodded, painfully aware of the time frame. "Let's just try to get through one day—and night—at a time," he suggested.

She sighed. "This whole thing has gotten so complicated."

"On the plus side, I think your parents are starting to like me."

"My parents *do* like you," she confirmed. "My grandmother described you as very hot, Tia Deanna used words that made me blush and my sister and cousins all think you're incredibly handsome and charming."

"So why don't you sound happy?" he asked her.

"Because I didn't expect them to like you quite so

much," she admitted. "They're all going to be so disappointed when we call off our engagement."

He lifted a hand to brush her hair away from her face. "I really put my foot in it, didn't I?"

"I appreciate what you were trying to do," she said. "And truthfully, it's not just about the engagement. They'd be equally disappointed to hear about our breakup even if they never thought we were planning to get married, so I guess it's really my fault for coming up with the pretend boyfriend idea in the first place."

"At this point, instead of assigning blame, we should focus on getting through the rest of this trip without crossing that line we said we weren't going to cross. Unless—" his tone turned hopeful as another thought crossed his mind "—you want to renegotiate the terms of this agreement."

"Or we could say there's been some kind of crisis at Adventure Village and you have to go back," she suggested as an alternative.

"What kind of crisis would make me abandon my fiancée at her parents' thirty-fifth anniversary celebration?" he asked. "Because I don't think a shortage of paintballs or a malfunctioning laser vest would suffice."

"Maybe a family emergency," she began, then immediately shook her head, horrified by the words she'd spoken. "Ohmygod, no. I didn't mean— I can't believe that thought even came into my head. And I didn't mean a *real* emergency, just that you could make something up."

"Isn't making things up what got us into this situation in the first place?" he asked her.

She sighed again. "You're right. I just wanted to get you out of this increasingly awkward situation."

"I'm not going anywhere. Except—" he pushed back the covers and climbed out of bed "—to take a very cold shower."

Chapter Fourteen

Though much of Alyssa and Jason's time was spent with her family, helping to prepare for the big anniversary celebration that was the purpose of their trip, she was pleased that they'd managed to slip away on a few occasions so that she could show her seven-day fiancé some of the local sights.

They'd toured a Southern California winery, visited a local art gallery and even spent a whole day with Nicolas. Alyssa told Jason that she wanted to give Cristina and Steven some time to themselves—which was true, but he quickly figured out that her nephew was her excuse to make a trip to Disneyland.

Today she'd brought Jason to Laguna Beach so they could watch the sunset from the sandy shores. As they walked hand in hand on the beach, she found herself reflecting on the time she'd spent with him over the past several weeks and everything she'd learned about him.

He was thoughtful and kind and surprisingly sweet.

Yeah, he had a bit of a sarcastic edge, and an unreasonable aversion to green vegetables, but in so many other ways, he was practically perfect.

So how was it that no woman had snapped him up?

Of course, she knew the answer to that question: he wouldn't let himself be snapped up.

He was the perfect boyfriend in the moment, because that was all he wanted. Maybe he'd done a good job playing "family man" with Nicolas, but that was only for a day, and she knew better than to let her mind wander too far down that path. Thinking about long-term plans with Jason would be a heartbreak waiting to happen.

Still, she found herself wondering. "Have you ever had a serious girlfriend?"

"That's a strange question for a woman to ask her fiancé," he noted.

"Fake fiancé," she clarified. "And I'd argue that it's the kind of information a woman should know about the man she's pretending she wants to marry."

"Sure, I had a couple of serious girlfriends in the past." He slid an arm across her shoulders. "But only one fiancée."

She rolled her eyes. "I'm trying to have a real conversation with you."

"Am I preventing that in some way?"

She ignored his question to ask another one of her own. "Have you ever been in love? And telling a woman you love her for the purpose of getting her naked doesn't count."

"I've never had to lie to a woman to get her naked."

She had no doubt *that* was true. All he had to do was look at her and she got so hot, she was ready to strip down for him. "That doesn't answer my question."

"Personally, I think people put too much stock in the word *love*," he said.

"And I think you're avoiding the question," she countered. "But I'll rephrase it—have you ever been in a relationship with someone you thought you would spend the rest of your life with?"

"No. Maybe." He reconsidered, then shook his head. "No."

"Tell me about the maybe," she urged.

"Melanie Lindhurst. I met her in college. We were together for a few months, and there was a brief moment when I imagined she was the one."

"What happened?"

"I realized that being with one person for the rest of my life meant never being with anyone else and decided that wasn't for me."

She immediately shook her head. "There's got to be more to the story."

"I was twenty years old, and there were more hot women on the Berkeley campus than the entire population of Haven. I wasn't ready to limit my options."

"I agree that twenty is young to be thinking about 'ever after,'" she said. "But I also know that you're not nearly as shallow as you pretend to be."

He scoffed at the idea. "Why would I pretend to be shallow?"

"Maybe to ensure that no one expects too much from you," she suggested.

He was quiet for several minutes before he finally responded. "Melanie liked to talk about the future, weeks or even months and years down the road, as if it was a given that we'd be together. And I didn't have the same faith that everything would work out the way she wanted it to."

"Why not?" Alyssa asked gently.

"You've met my parents," he reminded her. "They're hardly an example of wedded bliss."

"You don't think they're happy together?"

"Their marriage just seems a little…hollow," he decided. "And definitely not something I want to emulate."

"Every relationship is different."

"I get that now, but I had a limited frame of reference back then, and when Melanie told me she loved me—I panicked."

"Do you ever think back and wish you hadn't panicked?" she asked him.

"No."

"Then maybe you didn't love her," she suggested.

"Maybe I didn't, but it felt real at the time."

His admission made Alyssa feel better about her growing feelings for him. The more time she spent with Jason, the more she liked him. Despite his reputation as a ladies' man, he was attentive and thoughtful and his kisses…

Just the memory of those kisses was enough to make her knees weak.

But what he said made perfect sense. Since they'd embarked on this trip to California, they'd barely been apart from one another. It was understandable that the physical proximity would intensify her feelings for him. No doubt her emotions only seemed so huge and real right now because of the situation they found themselves in.

But she was optimistic that, when they went back to Haven and their normal routines, those feelings would fade. And in the future, after she'd fallen truly and deeply in love, she would no doubt look back on this moment and acknowledge that "it felt real at the time" but was, by then, just a pleasant memory.

The day of the anniversary celebration, Jason was recruited by the men to help set up the tent and chairs in the backyard, so he went over to Renata and Miguel's house with Steven, while Alyssa and Cristina stayed back with Nicolas to get ready for the party.

Alyssa had packed her favorite little black dress for the occasion. It was a sleeveless halter style chiffon with a cascading panel that made her feel feminine and sexy. She paired it with high-heeled black sandals that added three inches to her height and finished the look with crystal teardrop earrings.

When she'd finished pinning up her hair and had added a light touch of makeup, she decided to see if her nephew wanted to play Go Fish before they had to leave for the party. She found him in the kitchen snacking on one of the cupcakes his mom had made for the dessert table. He jumped down from his booster seat when he saw "Tia Lyssa" and ran to hug her.

"Nicolas, no!" his mother said.

But she was too late.

The little boy had already pressed his face—smeared with white icing—against the front of Alyssa's black dress.

"Oh, no," Cristina said when she saw the unmistakable evidence of her son's affection on her sister's skirt.

Nicolas wasn't quite sure what he'd done wrong, but his big brown eyes grew even bigger as they filled with tears.

"It's okay," Alyssa said, wanting to reassure both of them. "I'm sure it'll wipe off."

But it didn't. In fact, dabbing at the white streaks only made more of a mess.

"I'll pay to have it cleaned," Cristina immediately offered.

"That's not necessary," Alyssa said.

Because they both knew the cost of cleaning the dress wasn't the issue—it was that there was no way it could be cleaned before the party.

"Okay, let me get Nicolas washed up, then I'll see what I can find in my closet for you to wear."

A few minutes later, Cristina entered the guest room with an armload of dresses.

"I only need one," Alyssa couldn't resist teasing.

"But we need to figure out which one is the best one," her sister said.

"Anything that fits is fine."

Cristina shook her head. "You never did like to play dress-up, did you?"

"And you always loved to put on fancy clothes and shoes and paint your face with Mama's makeup," she remembered.

"Good times," her sister agreed with a smile. "Having you here reminds me of those times."

"It has been fun."

"Aside from my son destroying your dress, you mean?"

"Nicolas didn't destroy anything," Alyssa assured her.

"Can you tell how much he's missed you?"

"Not half as much as I've missed him. And you."

"I've missed you, too," Cristina said. "But I can see that living in Nevada has been good for you. Or maybe it's Jason Channing who's been good for you."

Alyssa managed a smile, ignoring the twinge of guilt that jabbed in her belly because she was lying to her sister.

Cristina had always been the one person she could be completely honest with. When she'd been frustrated by endless medical appointments and the limitations her parents put on her activities, her sister was the one she'd talked to. Cristina had listened with understanding and without judgment, and she'd offered encouragement when Alyssa started running. In fact, Cristina seemed to understand—maybe even better than Alyssa did herself—that running was a way of proving that she was in charge of not just her body but her life.

But if Alyssa told her the truth about her relationship with Jason now, Cristina would be appalled to realize that she'd made her little sister share a bed with a man who not only wasn't her fiancé but not even a real boyfriend.

"What about this one?" Cristina asked, holding up a sheath-style dress.

"It's red."

"And?"

"I don't wear red."

"Why not? This would look fabulous on you."

Alyssa eyed the slim jersey knit. "I doubt I could even squeeze into it."

"Give it a try," Cristina implored.

So Alyssa took off her icing-smeared garment and tugged her sister's dress over her head.

"Well," Cristina said, "I don't think I'm ever going to be able to wear that again."

"Am I stretching it out?" Alyssa reached for the hem to pull it off again.

"No." Her sister touched her arm, halting her actions. "Because it looks a lot better on you than it does on me."

Alyssa chewed on her lower lip as she looked at her reflection in the mirror. "I think I should try the gray one."

Cristina shook her head. "No," she said again. "I'm not letting you hide in the background."

"Mom's eyes will pop out of her head when she sees me in this dress."

"Probably," her sister acknowledged, a slow smile curving her lips. "But so will Jason's."

Alyssa picked up her necklace, fastened it around her throat.

"I can't believe you still wear that," Cristina said.

"Why not?"

"It was kind of a tongue-in-cheek gift," her sister said.

"It's a beautiful necklace."

"I wouldn't have bought it if I didn't think so, but I didn't intend for you to use it as a shield."

"What are you talking about?"

"Honey, the necklace does absolutely nothing for that dress. The only purpose it serves is to cover up the part of your barely visible scar that peeks over the top of the dress."

"You know how Mama is about my scars," Alyssa said.

"I do know," Cristina agreed. "But that's her problem, not yours."

"Jason once said almost the exact same words."

"Obviously your fiancé is a very wise man."

He *was* wise, but he wasn't really her fiancé.

But, of course, she didn't say that to her sister.

Jay could understand why it was so hard for Alyssa to deceive her family about their relationship. The Cabreras were genuinely warm and welcoming people, and the more time he spent with Renata and Miguel—and especially Valentina—the more uneasy he felt about the lies.

If and when he got married and had a family, he hoped—

Whoa! He severed that thought as soon as it began to form.

Marriage?

Family?

Neither of those ideas should be anywhere on his radar. Not right now, anyway. He was only twenty-nine years old and the CEO of a young start-up company. He had no business—and no desire—to be thinking about long-term plans.

So why couldn't he stop thinking about Alyssa?

It was a question that nagged at him throughout the day.

And when he returned to Cristina and Steven's house with Alyssa's brother-in-law, he wasn't any closer to an answer.

He stripped down for a quick shower and thought about the fact that they'd been together almost constantly since they'd embarked on this road trip. That was undoubtedly the reason she'd been on his mind so constantly. As soon as they got back to Haven and got some distance, he was confident that everything would go back to normal. Alyssa would be his date for Matt's wedding, but nothing more.

His conviction lasted only until she walked into the room.

"You look...wow."

Her smile was a little uncertain. "Is it too much?" She glanced down. "Or too little?"

"I'd say it's just right."

"It's not the dress I'd planned to wear," she told him. "But there was a little mishap in the kitchen, so I had to raid Cristina's closet."

"It's lucky you wear the same size."

"We don't really," she said. "I would have bought this dress one size bigger—or probably not at all."

"It's perfect," he insisted. "Although I would like to make one suggestion."

"What's that?"

"Lose the necklace."

Her hand immediately went to the misshapen heart dangling at the end of the chunky chain around her neck. "What? Why?"

"Because it takes away from the neckline of the dress."

"Now you're a stylist?" she challenged.

"I'm gonna say no to that, because I'm not sure I even know what a stylist is," he said. "But I am a man who appreciates the attributes of a woman."

"I like the necklace," she insisted.

"You like hiding your scars," he said.

"So?"

"So you're a strong, brave, beautiful woman and your scars don't in any way take away from that."

"Yeah, I heard that surgical incisions are surpassing tattoos and piercings as the new body art," she said sardonically.

"Maybe they're not art," he acknowledged. "But they're not flaws or imperfections, either. Why can't you see them as badges of courage?"

"Because I didn't do anything courageous. I just happened to be born with a defective heart that the doctors fixed for me."

"You survived," he reminded her. "And the world is a much better place with you in it."

"That was kind of cheesy," she told him.

"But kind of sweet, too?" he prompted.

She managed a smile. "Yeah."

She slowly turned to face the mirror, then took a deep breath and reached for the heart. Her fingers trembled as she worked the toggle through the hole, then pulled the necklace away and set it on top of the dresser.

He put his hands on her shoulders and let his eyes skim over her reflection in the mirror. "Wow," he said again, softly, reverently.

She lifted a hand, subconsciously rubbing the top of the scar, visible above the square neckline of her borrowed dress.

He caught her wrist and pulled her hand away.

"Look at yourself," he said. "You're beautiful, Alyssa. Absolutely breathtakingly beautiful."

"When you look at me like that, I feel beautiful," she admitted.

"Then I will spend the whole night looking at you," he promised.

"I like the sound of that," she agreed. "But maybe you could focus on the road while you're driving?"

"All right," he agreed. "But only while I'm driving."

When they got to Renata and Miguel's house, Nicolas led the way, as comfortable at his grandparents' home as he was at his own. Cristina and Steven followed their son, with Alyssa and Jason trailing behind them.

As usual, most of the activity was happening in the kitchen, where the food was going to be laid out, buffet style, for the guests to help themselves. Alyssa set the black bean salad on the table, where her mother was fussing over an arrangement of flowers.

Renata greeted each of the new arrivals, then said to Alyssa, "Is that Cristina's dress?"

Valentina, who was sprinkling grated cheese on top of a tray of enchiladas that were ready to go in the oven, glanced over.

"It is," Alyssa confirmed.

"But it looks better on Lys than it ever did on me," Cristina said as she put the tray of cupcakes on top of the fridge, safely out of reach of eager little hands.

"I have a silk scarf that I picked up in Florence last summer with touches of that same color," her mother said.

"It's too warm for a scarf," Abuela interjected, dismissing the suggestion.

"It's a decorative accessory that would look great with the dress," Renata insisted. "Why don't we go take a look?"

"Actually—" Jason surprised everyone by speaking up "—I think Alyssa looks perfect just as she is."

Her mother's cheeks flushed. "She does, of course," she agreed. "I just thought the dress could use a little...pop."

"I'd say her curves add enough pop," Valentina said, winking at Alyssa.

"Thanks, Abuela," she said. "Because I wasn't already feeling self-conscious enough."

"A woman should never be self-conscious about her attributes," her grandmother said, looking pointedly at Renata.

Steven clapped a hand on Jason's shoulder. "I think this would be a good time for us to make sure the bar's stocked."

"An important task," Jason agreed, although he looked to Alyssa as if to ensure that she didn't mind him sneaking away from the increasingly awkward conversation.

She gave a quick nod, and the two men made their escape.

"I don't like seeing your scars," Renata admitted. "Because they're a reminder of the scariest time in my life, when I thought I might lose my precious baby girl."

Alyssa took her hands. "The last surgery was more than twenty years ago, Mama."

Her mother sniffled, nodded. "I know. But that doesn't always seem like so very long ago."

"Why don't you show me the scarf?" she suggested.

But Renata shook her head. "Your Jason is right—you look wonderful just as you are."

Alyssa didn't feel wonderful—she felt like a fraud. Because Jason wasn't "hers" and nothing about their relationship was real. But as much as she wished she could dispense with the deception, she'd taken it too far to turn back now.

"You're so much stronger than I ever gave you credit for being," Renata said to her now. "I'm glad you've finally found a man who recognizes and appreciates not just your strengths but many other wonderful qualities."

"Well, he appreciates my cooking, anyway," Alyssa said lightly.

"I guess I'm going to have to tell Lucia that our hopes of a romance blossoming between my youngest daughter and her favorite nephew were for naught."

"I didn't realize she was complicit in your plan."

"All we did was put the two of you together, hoping you would connect," Renata said. "And I didn't do it because I didn't think you could find a wonderful man on your own, but because I hoped falling in love with someone here would give you incentive to move back home."

"I miss you, too," Alyssa told her mother. "But I have a good job and good friends in Haven—a good life."

"And Jason."

"Of course," she said quickly, because any woman would surely put her fiancé at the top of her list.

"But you'll get married here, won't you?"

The question reinforced the necessity of telling her mother the truth sooner rather than later—she couldn't let Renata continue to dream about a wedding that wasn't going to happen. But for now she only said, "Yes, Mama. When I'm—*we're*—ready to get married, it will be here, and I'll wear Abuela's wedding gown, like I always planned."

Her mother's eyes misted as she pictured the scene Alyssa described.

"But today is about celebrating *your* wedding," she reminded Renata, guiding her outside so the celebrations could begin.

And so her lies could stop—at least for a little while.

Chapter Fifteen

Alyssa had a lot of reasons for moving to Haven, one of which was to escape the constant comparisons to her sister. By the time Cristina was twenty-six, she'd been married for four years and had a two-year-old child. Alyssa had simpler dreams, at least in the short-term—and she needed some time to figure out what she wanted for her own life before she could share it with someone else.

And yet, celebrating her parents' thirty-fifth anniversary, watching them interact together and listening to their stories, she could see the benefits of having a partner to share the good times and the bad. Someone to laugh with and lean on, to plan with and care for. Growing up, she'd taken so much for granted. She hadn't appreciated the special closeness her family shared until she'd moved away. And while she wasn't necessarily in any hurry to walk down the aisle, she knew now that she did want what her parents had and what Cristina had found with Steven.

"Everything okay, honey bear?" Jason asked, returning from the bar with a glass of wine for Alyssa.

"Aside from you calling me 'honey bear,' yeah," she said and offered him a smile in exchange for the wine. "I was just counting my blessings."

"You are a lucky woman," he agreed. "You have a wonderful family, good friends and a handsome and adoring fiancé whose mother made him take dance lessons as a kid."

"Really?"

He offered his hand. "Shall I prove it to you?"

She set her glass of wine on the table. "Show me what you've got."

Though his brain had cautioned him to avoid close physical contact, Jay knew there was no way to maintain the illusion of their relationship without a few turns around the dance floor. And after sleeping in the same bed for the past five nights, he didn't think a dance was anything he couldn't handle.

But the music was soft and seductive, and she fit perfectly in his arms, almost as if she was meant to be there. Dancing with Alyssa, he felt as if everything he'd ever wanted was literally within his grasp.

He immediately chided himself for the ridiculous notion, but the idea continued to nudge not just at his mind but his heart.

"Who's that in the flowered dress?" he asked, turning Alyssa around so she could see the woman in question.

"That would be Lucia."

"Diego's aunt," he said, connecting the dots. "Now I know why she's been shooting daggers at me with her eyes."

"Didn't you meet her at the potluck?"

"I missed that pleasure," he said drily.

"Well, she was extremely disappointed—my mother's words—to learn that I was planning to marry someone other than her favorite nephew."

"So maybe you are glad that I'm here," he suggested.

She tipped her head back to smile at him. "There's no *maybe* about it. I *am* glad you're here."

"Then let's make sure Lucia knows it," he said and lowered his mouth to hers.

Of course, the moment their lips touched, he forgot about Lucia and Diego and the hundred-plus other guests. In that moment, there was only Alyssa, and he'd never wanted anyone more.

Maybe their relationship had started as "plan B," but over the past few weeks, everything had changed. *He* had changed. And the feelings that filled his heart when he was with her were deeper than anything he'd ever felt before.

Their reasons for agreeing to this charade were in the past. Now he was focused on the present—and looking to his future with Alyssa.

They were up early the next morning to head back to her parents' house for an early breakfast before they started the return trip to Nevada. Alyssa had enjoyed visiting with her family and she knew she'd miss them like crazy when she was gone, but she was also looking forward to returning to Haven and the life she'd built for herself there. Over the past week, Jason had played the part of the doting fiancé almost too well, convincing Renata and Miguel that he was in love with their youngest daughter and looking forward to planning a life with her. While she appreciated his efforts, that was an illusion she needed to dispel before she started to believe it.

When breakfast was over, Alyssa steered her mother away from the gathering for a private word.

"I need to tell you something before I go," she began.

Renata's brow furrowed, a familiar sign of concern. "You're not pregnant, are you?"

Alyssa felt her cheeks burn as she shook her head. "No, I'm not pregnant. I'm also not engaged to Jason."

Her mother's eyes grew wide. "You turned down his proposal?"

"No, Mama. He never really asked me to marry him."

"I don't understand."

"We've only been dating a few months," she said, because although she couldn't continue the deception of the engagement, she wasn't ready to admit that their whole relationship had been a lie from the beginning. "And although we enjoy one another's company, it's far too soon to be thinking of a lifetime together."

"Then why did he tell Diego that you'd agreed to marry him?" Renata wondered aloud.

"Because Diego didn't seem to care that I had a boyfriend and Jason hoped he'd back off if he believed our relationship was more serious than it is," she explained.

"Diego has been rather…persistent," her mother admitted. "And perhaps that's my fault. I did encourage him to pursue you—and to not give up. But all that was before we met Jason. Before we knew you were in love."

"I don't blame you, Mama," Alyssa said. "But there's also no reason to tell Diego—or Lucia—that the engagement isn't real."

"And maybe it will be…someday."

"Maybe," she agreed, unwilling to completely destroy her mother's hopes. "But that potential someday is far off."

"Maybe not as far as you think," Renata said. "In the meantime, it's comforting to know that you have such a fine young man looking after you in Haven."

"I can look after myself, Mama."

"Well, of course you can." Her mother's immediate agreement was a surprise. "But there's nothing wrong with letting someone take care of you every once in a while, as I'm sure you take care of him, too."

Alyssa hadn't thought too much about the give and take in a romantic relationship, because she'd never really been in one before. Of course, she wasn't in one now, either, but being a counterfeit couple had given her a taste of the kind of sharing that came with being in a real relationship. She enjoyed listening to Jason talk about his stresses and worries and hearing funny stories about things that happened during his day. And she realized that being taken care of by a man didn't need to be a negative thing, so long as she was taking care of him, too.

Of course, that man wouldn't ever be Jason Channing, because he'd been clear from the beginning that their bogus romance would never lead to anything real.

Returning to Haven, where he had a king-size mattress to himself, Jay thought he would finally be able to sleep. But when he crawled beneath the covers that first night back, his bed felt big and empty without Alyssa. He missed the scent of her skin, the warmth of her body and just knowing that she was beside him.

And when he finally did sleep, he dreamed about her.

He skipped his run the next morning. Though he'd been anxious to get home and back to what was familiar, he needed some distance from Alyssa, space to clear his head of the ridiculous thoughts that had taken root when they were together in California and purge his heart of the unwelcome feelings that had started to root within. Except that not being with her didn't stop him from thinking about her. Missing her. Wanting her.

He wasn't used to a woman featuring so prominently

in his thoughts. As a result, he was distracted and short-tempered at work, like an addict going cold turkey in a desperate attempt to break his habit. And it didn't work. Despite his concerted efforts not to think about her, he couldn't think about anything else.

He went running that night, determined to establish a new routine for himself—a routine that didn't include Alyssa. But damn, he missed her presence beside him.

He didn't run Tuesday morning, either, because he'd done ten miles the night before. Then he skipped Wednesday, too—opting to go into work early and stay late. And all day, she was on his mind.

When he got home, he surveyed the meager contents of his fridge in search of something to eat. He was trying to determine the age of some frozen leftover pizza when there was a knock on the door.

His heart knocked against his ribs, anticipating who might be on the other side. And again when he opened the door and found Alyssa standing there.

"I should have called," she said. "But I thought it might be better to have this conversation face-to-face."

"That sounds ominous," he noted.

She shook her head. "It's not. I just wanted to let you know that it's okay if you've changed your mind about me being your date on the fourteenth, because I can pick up an extra shift at—"

"Whoa!" He held up a hand. "Are you trying to renege on our deal?"

"No," she denied. "I'm letting you off the hook."

He pulled the door open wider and gestured for her to enter. "Maybe you should come inside for this conversation."

She hesitated, no doubt wondering why he was suddenly so eager for her company, but finally accepted his invitation.

"Do you want a glass of wine?" he offered.

"Okay," she said. "That would be nice."

He didn't think about the fact that he'd started to stock her favorite brand—he just uncorked one of the bottles and poured a glass for her, then another for himself.

"Now tell me why you think I want to be let off a hook I didn't even know I was on," he suggested when he'd taken a seat beside her at the island.

"Because you've been avoiding me since we got back from California."

"I haven't been avoiding you," he denied.

She shook her head. "We've told a lot of lies to other people," she acknowledged. "But I thought we were at least honest with one another."

"I've had a lot of work to catch up on, so I've been heading in early," he told her.

"I guess that's what happens when you take a week away during your busiest season," she remarked.

"It was my choice to go," he reminded her.

"And now you regret it."

Maybe he did, but not for reasons that had anything to do with his business. "No," he said. "I had a great time with you."

And he'd gotten so used to being with her 24/7, he'd started to feel as if something was missing when he wasn't with her. That was why he'd deliberately attempted to put some distance between them—to prove that he could. To prove to himself that he wasn't falling for her.

So far, he remained unconvinced. And the way his heart bounced around inside his chest whenever he saw her suggested something completely different.

"But now you're trying to put as much distance as possible between us," she accused. "Because the pretend dating thing started to feel a little too real."

"Maybe it did start to feel real," he acknowledged. "Or maybe it *got* real."

Her brows drew together as she considered that. "I don't want to lose your friendship, Jason."

"You're not going to."

"Okay," she said. "But if you've changed your mind about your friend's wedding—"

"I haven't changed my mind." And even if he had, his agreement with Kevin prevented him from amending their plans. "I'll pick you up at three o'clock on Saturday."

She finished her wine and set down the empty glass. "I'll be ready."

"One more thing," he said as she pushed away from the counter.

"What's that?"

"Wear something red."

She seemed surprised by the request. "There's a color scheme for the wedding guests?"

"No," he said. "You just look really good in red."

And he was clearly an infatuated fool, because after promising himself that he would put some distance between them, his resolve had crumbled in less than three days. And he was already counting the hours until Saturday, when he would see her again.

Alyssa was accustomed to dressing in subtle colors and modest styles; she didn't own a red dress and had no intention of buying one.

Until she remembered the way Jason had looked at her when she'd been wearing the scarlet-colored sheath borrowed from her sister's closet. She wanted him to look at her like that again.

She wanted him to want her as much as she wanted him.

They'd agreed that their fake relationship would end

after the wedding, but Alyssa hadn't given up hope that she might experience real passion with Jason. But first she had to convince him to break through the boundaries he'd established for their relationship, and she didn't have the first clue how to do that.

Thankfully, she did know someone who was something of an expert on human behavior. So she invited Skylar to go shopping with her to find something appropriate for the wedding, and because she hoped her friend might be able to give her some much-needed advice on how to seduce a man who'd made it clear he would not be seduced.

"When's the wedding?" Sky asked as she looked through a rack of dresses at the upscale boutique in Battle Mountain that she'd declared was the only place to shop within driving distance of Haven.

"Saturday," Alyssa confided.

"Matt Hutchinson and Carrie Morgan's wedding?"

"You know them?"

Her friend nodded. "I went to school with Carrie's sister, Courtney. And Liam actually dated Carrie a few years back. In fact, you'll probably see him at the wedding."

"Is he taking a date?" Alyssa asked.

"Heather," Sky admitted with a roll of her eyes.

"They're back on again?"

"He says no, but going to a wedding together says something else," her friend noted.

"Why is the event significant?" Alyssa wondered.

"Because weddings tend to make people reflect on their own lives—where they are and what they want. And when they realize they haven't accomplished everything they'd hoped to, they turn to alcohol and sex to feel better about themselves."

"Is this something you've researched?" Alyssa asked.

"Not specifically," Sky said. "But I've been to a lot of weddings."

She considered her friend's revelation. "Are you suggesting that guys who've reached their goals are less interested in post-wedding sex?"

"Oh, no. They want to get laid, too," Sky assured her. "But their rationale is that they've earned it."

Alyssa laughed at that.

But a long time later, after they'd finished shopping, she ventured to ask, "What do you think it means when a guy doesn't want to have sex?"

"Is there such a creature?"

"Apparently."

Her friend's gaze narrowed thoughtfully. "Are you telling me that you and Jason haven't done the deed?"

Alyssa almost wished she hadn't said anything, but there wasn't anyone else she could talk to about the subject, so she nodded in response to the question.

"I'm sure I'm not telling tales out of school by saying that your boyfriend has a bit of a reputation as a ladies' man, so to discover that he hasn't taken you to bed is more than a little surprising."

"But we're only fake dating," she reminded her friend.

"And how long has this been going on?"

"Well, if anyone asks, the story is six months. But we've only been real fake dating for three, because that started on what was supposedly our three-month anniversary."

Sky shook her head. "Real fake dating? Are you hearing yourself?"

"I know it sounds crazy," she acknowledged.

"Admitting you have a problem is the first step on the road to recovery," Sky said. "But I'm curious…during this period of fake dating, have you been fake holding hands and fake kissing, too?"

"Yes, because those public displays are a necessary part of the illusion."

"So he's never touched you behind closed doors? Never kissed you good-night when no one was watching?"

"Occasionally," she admitted.

"But he hasn't tried to get you naked?" Sky pressed.

Alyssa shook her head. "I've been waiting—and hoping—for him to make a move, but...nothing."

"So make the move yourself," her friend advised.

"You make it sound so easy."

"Men really aren't complicated creatures."

"Maybe he hasn't made a move because he's not attracted to me," Alyssa suggested.

Her friend immediately shook her head. "I've seen the way he looks at you—he's definitely attracted."

She crossed her fingers that Sky was right. Because if she didn't succeed in making a move Saturday night—or inspiring Jason to make a move—her window of opportunity would be closed forever.

"Well, now that I've got the dress, shoes and earrings, can we finally go for lunch?"

"Just one more quick stop," Sky said.

"It better be quick—I'm starving."

Her friend paused outside The Grill. "You go in and get a table. I'll be back in five."

So Alyssa did.

Five minutes later, her friend came into the restaurant and dropped a paper bag in her lap.

"What's this?" Alyssa asked.

"What all the cool kids are wearing," Sky told her.

She put down her menu and peeked in the bag. Apparently the cool kids were wearing America's #1 Condom.

"I wish I had half your faith that I'm going to need these."

"Honey, I've seen you in that dress. You don't need

faith—but you need to be smart. Of course, some might argue that wanting to get naked with Jason Channing isn't smart," she said, because apparently a Gilmore couldn't resist taking a dig at a Blake any more than a Blake could at a Gilmore. "But since you've set your sights in his direction, you should be prepared."

When Alyssa responded to Jay's knock on her door, the first thing he noticed was that she'd complied with his request. The second was that his efforts to put distance between them had done nothing to lessen his attraction to her. Because all it took was one look—that first look—and the desire he'd been trying to deny surged through his veins.

The neckline of the dress was high enough to ensure that her scars weren't visible, but the back dipped low, revealing lots of smooth, bare skin. She'd left her hair down so that the curls tumbled over her shoulders, tempting him to slide his fingers into the soft tresses, tip her head back and cover that glossy mouth with his own.

He curled his fingers into his palms to resist the urge to reach for her. Over the past few weeks, he'd had a lot of practice keeping a tight rein on his growing desire. Sure, they'd shared kisses—necessary to convince others that they were a couple, and maybe a few that weren't necessary or part of any illusion—but he'd been careful to ensure those kisses never went too far.

But he'd done what Kevin had challenged him to do—he'd maintained a relationship with one woman for more than two months. And if this was truly his last date with Alyssa, he was going to make the most of it.

He pulled her into his arms.

"Um…hello," she said when he finally eased his lips from hers.

He smiled. "Hi." Then stepped back to look at her again. "And thank you."

She smiled back, a little tentatively. "I didn't own anything red, so I went shopping. Sky helped me pick this out."

"I guess even Gilmores get something right once in a while," he said.

She huffed out a breath. "For a few hours tonight, can you please try to forget about the feud between the Blakes and the Gilmores?"

"Why?"

"Because Liam's going to be at the wedding."

"I thought he might be," Jay admitted. "Though why anyone would want to watch an ex marry someone else is beyond me."

"Liam and Carrie dated a long time ago and have remained good friends."

"I don't get that, either," he said.

"You've never stayed friends with a girl you've dated?"

He thought about the question, shook his head. "Not friendly enough to want her at my wedding."

Alyssa looked taken aback by his comment.

"Is that really so surprising?" he asked.

"What surprised me was to hear the words *my wedding* come out of your mouth without your face draining of all color."

"Ha ha," he said.

"I wasn't joking," she told him.

Considering his reputation—and nickname—her response was understandable.

But Jason wasn't that man anymore.

And tonight he was going to focus his efforts on charming the only woman he wanted.

Chapter Sixteen

The ceremony was short and sweet. The bride walked down the aisle with her father, then exchanged vows with her groom. After the minister pronounced them married, they kissed, signed the register and walked out of the church again.

At the reception, the meal was served family style, with the salad course followed by heaping bowls of pasta, then platters of thinly sliced roast beef and breaded chicken cutlets, plus bowls of roasted potatoes, green beans and baby carrots. Conversation flowed as freely as the wine, and Alyssa found herself enjoying the interactions between Jason and his friends.

After dessert—a choice of cheesecake or a slice of the wedding cake—the bride and groom shared their first dance, then the floor was opened up to the rest of the guests.

Alyssa had danced with Jason before, but being in his

arms felt different tonight. Or maybe she felt different—nervous and determined.

"What are you thinking about?" he asked, his lips close to her ear.

"I was just wondering if it was true, what Kevin said at dinner," she admitted.

"Kevin did a lot of talking at dinner," he remarked.

"I was referring to his claim that Jenny Reashore broke your heart."

He shook his head. "Not true."

"But she was the girl who dumped you before you asked Lacey Bolton to the homecoming dance?"

"Yeah," he admitted. "But we were seventeen—neither of us thought we were going to be together forever."

"So how long were you together?" she asked him.

He lifted a shoulder, as if he didn't remember.

"How long?" she pressed.

"Eight months."

"And how long were you with Melanie—that girl in college?"

"Five months."

"So your longest relationship was when you were seventeen?"

"How about you?" he challenged. "According to your grandmother, you haven't let anyone get close since your high school graduation party at the beach."

"She told you that?"

"The question is—why didn't *you* tell me?"

"I told you about what happened at the beach," she reminded him. "And that's more than I've ever told anyone else."

He was quiet for a minute, as if considering that admission. "You're an amazing woman, Lys, and I hate to think that you'd let anything that happened in the past hold you back from what you want now."

"I'm trying not to," she said.

"Good."

As the music changed, Alyssa found herself wondering if Jason's response would be the same if he knew that what she wanted now was him—and if she ever would find the courage to go after what she wanted.

They danced and they talked and they danced some more. When Alyssa slipped away to the ladies' room, Jay went to the bar to refill their drinks.

"I didn't think you'd pull it off," Nat admitted, joining him at the counter.

"You know I never back away from a challenge," he told her.

"So you've dated Alyssa for a few months and brought her as your date to Matt's wedding—now what?"

He accepted his drinks from the bartender. "Now I'm going to take this glass of wine to my date."

"There's no need to rush," she said. "She looks like she's enjoying herself on the dance floor."

He glanced over his shoulder and discovered that Nat was right. Alyssa had returned and was dancing again—with Gilmore. It wasn't a slow dance and it wasn't just the two of them, but Jay didn't appreciate the other man shaking and shimmying with *his* date. But Alyssa had requested that he forget about the feud for one night, so he deliberately loosened his grip on the glass before the stem broke in his hand.

"I understand the reasons for your proximity rule," Nat said to him now. "But sometimes there are good reasons to break the rules."

His gaze moved back to Alyssa again.

"You can thank me now," she said.

"I'm starting to think maybe I should," he acknowledged.

"Maybe? Why only maybe?"

"Because I'm not entirely sure where we go from here."

"You need me to draw you a map?"

He knew she was joking, and yet he didn't think it was such a bad idea. He was usually sure of all his moves when it came to the opposite sex, but it had been a very long time since anyone had mattered to him as much as Alyssa did. If anyone ever had.

"I think I can wing it," he said with more confidence than he felt.

"Just don't make the mistake of comparing her to any one of the legions of women who have come before," she cautioned.

"There haven't been legions of women," he denied.

She lifted a brow.

"And what is a legion, anyway?"

"A very large number," Kevin chimed in as he joined them. Then he nodded to Jay. "You and Alyssa look good together. Not just good, but happy."

"We're having fun," he confirmed.

"Maybe we'll be dancing at your wedding next."

"Bite your tongue," Jay said, though the knee-jerk response was made without heat.

"Fifty bucks says he's down on one knee before Christmas," Nat said.

"The way he looks at her, I'd wager it happens before Thanksgiving," Kevin said.

Jay shook his head. "Do you guys really have nothing better to do than bet on my love life?"

"Not at the moment," Nat said.

"Although we could go dance," Kevin said to her.

She did a double take. "What?"

"I'm asking if you want to dance with me."

"Where's your date?"

"Dancing with yours," he said. "So why should we be left out?"

Nat let Kevin lead her to the dance floor—and Alyssa began to move away from the crowd. As she drew nearer, she smiled, and Jay felt his lips curve in response as an unexpected warmth filled his chest.

Yeah, he was going to have to thank Nat for her machinations.

But right now, he had more important things to do—and dancing with Alyssa was at the top of his list.

After the happy couple had slipped away to begin their honeymoon, the rest of the wedding guests began to disperse. When Jason asked Alyssa if she was ready to go, she lied and said yes. But the truth was, she didn't want her time with Jason to be at an end.

"I guess this is where I say good-night," he said after he'd walked her to her door. But his gaze slid over her in a way that somehow melted her bones even as it steeled her resolve.

"Or you could come in," she suggested as an alternative.

He waited a beat before responding. "For a drink?"

She shrugged, trying to appear casual. But her heart was pounding so loud and fast she was sure he could hear the echo of its beat bouncing off the walls. "If that's what you want."

"What do *you* want?" he asked her.

"I don't want the night to be over," she admitted.

He glanced at his watch. "Except that, technically, it already is."

"You're right. And you probably have an early morning, so forget I said anything." She fumbled for her keys. "Good night, Jason."

He stepped in front of the door, blocking her escape. "Tell me what you want, Alyssa."

She nibbled on her lip. It was now or never. And if she didn't go for it, she'd always wonder *what if.* Maybe he'd say no, and that would be horrible and humiliating. But if he said yes... Well, she really wanted to experience yes.

So she inhaled a steadying breath and said, "I want you to break your rules—just for tonight."

"I don't know that I can do that," he told her.

"Oh." She dropped her gaze, feeling horrible and humiliated and—

He tipped her chin up. "If I break my rules, it won't be for just one night. If I make love with you tonight, I don't think I'll be able to walk away in the morning."

"Oh," she said again as blossoming hope pushed all the negative feelings aside.

"I've wanted you for a long time," he confided. "Even when I told myself that I shouldn't. But now that I know you want me, too, there's only one question remaining."

"What's that?" she asked breathlessly.

He smiled. "Your place or mine?"

Alyssa answered that question by turning the key to unlock her door. And when he followed her inside and drew her into his embrace, she went willingly, even eagerly. Her arms lifted to twine behind his head; her lips parted to welcome his kiss.

She wanted this, she really did, but now that it was finally going to happen, she couldn't help but feel a little nervous and uncertain.

Jason, sensing her hesitation, pulled back. "Second thoughts?" he asked gently.

"No," she said. Then, "Maybe."

"Can you explain that?"

"I don't want anything that happens tonight to change things between us."

"Things have already changed."

"You're right," she acknowledged. "I know you're right. I just wish you could promise me that things won't get weird."

"I don't usually bring out the toys and props the first time I'm with a woman," he told her. "Plus, all that stuff is upstairs."

"You're teasing. I hope."

He smiled. "Yeah, I'm teasing. But maybe we should go upstairs—because I don't have any protection in my wallet."

"I've got some. Um, condoms, I mean. I picked them up when I was shopping," she said, because she had no intention of telling him that Sky had bought them.

Alyssa might not know a lot about seduction, but she was pretty sure that mentioning the name of another woman—particularly a woman whose family was at odds with his—would cool the heat between them more effectively than dumping a glass of ice water in his lap.

"In that case," he said and kissed her again.

She started to move down the hall, toward her bedroom, not letting her lips break contact with his. Because as long as he was kissing her, she wasn't able to think about what was happening, which meant that she couldn't focus on all the doubts and insecurities that usually reared up when she got close to someone.

She felt as if they'd been moving toward this for weeks, maybe months. Even when she'd told herself they were just friends, she'd wanted more. Wanted this. Through months of fake dating and their seven-day engagement, the pretend stuff had stirred real desires. But she'd been certain it was all one-sided, until the morning she'd awakened in his arms and discovered he was aroused.

Of course, a lot of men, particularly those in their sexual prime, woke up with erections. But Jason had seemed to credit—or maybe blame—her proximity for his condition. As if he wasn't just aroused but aroused *by her*. And that was when the first seeds of this seduction plan began to take root in her mind.

His hands skimmed up her back now, making her shiver. He found the zipper at the back of her dress and inched it downward. The straps slid off her shoulders and she instinctively lifted a hand to hold the bodice in place.

He caught her wrist and drew it away. "No more hiding, Lys. Not from me."

The fabric fell away, revealing the scarlet lace bra that—along with the matching bikini panties—cost half as much as the dress.

He tugged the zipper the rest of the way, and the dress slipped over her hips to pool on the floor at her feet, leaving her clad in only red lace and three-inch heels.

He swore softly, reverently. "It's a good thing I didn't know what you were wearing under that dress when I picked you up, or we never would have made it to the wedding."

"I'm happy we got to see your friends get married," she said. "I'm even happier that you're here with me now."

His fingertip traced the lacy edge of her bra, skimming over the swell of one breast, dipping into the hollow between them, then back up again. He reached behind her with his other hand, deftly unclasping the hook and discarding the garment. Then he hooked his fingers into the sides of her panties and tugged them over her hips, then down her legs. When she was completely naked, he stripped away his own clothes, then eased her back onto the bed.

She closed her eyes to better absorb the myriad of sensations that assailed her as his hands and lips moved over her. She'd never been touched like he was touching her. Had never imagined that she was capable of feeling so much. And every time she thought there couldn't possibly be more, he proved otherwise.

She'd read books, she'd seen movies, but none of that had prepared her for the exquisite sensations that ricocheted through her body, sparking new wants, igniting new desires. His hands were strong and sure as they moved over her, knowing just where and how to touch her.

He cupped her breasts in his hands, his thumbs stroking lazily over her nipples. His touch triggered an unexpected response between her thighs, making her throb and ache. Then his mouth replaced his thumbs, and as he suckled at one breast, then the other, the ache intensified.

As his mouth continued its sensual assault on her breasts, his hands moved lower, skimming her sides, sliding over her hips, arrowing toward the juncture of her thighs. He continued his leisurely exploration, sucking in a breath as his thumbs slowly traced the narrow strip of hair that was all that remained after her French bikini wax.

His thumbs parted the slick folds of skin, exposing her most sensitive core to his gaze. His touch. His mouth.

Her head fell back as his tongue stroked over her.

Slowly. Gently.

Then faster. Harder.

She tried to draw in a breath, but there was no air— there was nothing but sharp, shocking pleasure.

She curled her fingers in the sheet, bit down on her lip. His hands slid under her bottom, holding her in position while he did unexpectedly wicked and wonderful things to her with his mouth, while every dip and flick of his tongue drove her closer and closer to the edge of oblivion.

For the first time in years, she had cause to worry about the condition of her heart. She'd never felt it beat so hard and fast. She didn't know that it could without leaping right out of her chest or at least cracking a few ribs.

But she didn't ask him to stop. She didn't want him to stop. And then the wonderful, glorious sensations built to a crescendo of light and color that exploded inside her like Fourth of July fireworks. A seemingly endless grand finale that left her breathless and weak.

She closed her eyes as delicious shudders rippled through her and he slowly made his way up her body, dropping leisurely kisses along the way. On her belly, her navel, the hollow beneath her breastbone, the pale scar between her breasts. And her heart, having slowed to a more natural rhythm, stuttered.

"Okay?" he asked.

Her lips curved. "Much better than okay."

"Good."

He kissed her throat, then the underside of her jaw, then her lips.

"Is it my turn now?" she asked.

His laugh was strangled. "No. Not tonight."

"Why not?"

"Because it's been a long time since I've been with a woman and I'm already doubting my ability to last more than three minutes."

"But you've already given me so much more than I expected," she told him.

"Then your expectations were way too low, because we're not even close to being done yet."

As he was talking, he tore open a square packet and covered himself with a condom. He nudged her legs apart and positioned himself between them, and everything inside her trembled with anticipation. She wasn't just eager now but desperate for the fulfillment she instinctively knew he could give her. She wanted to feel the hard length of him inside her, stretching her, filling her.

He rose over her, bracing his weight on his forearms as his lips brushed hers gently and his erection nudged her soft flesh, testing, teasing. The ache inside her turned to need, and she drew her knees up and dug her heels into the mattress. "Now," she said. "Please."

He didn't make her ask again. In one deep stroke, he pushed into her. She gasped at the shock of the intrusion as he broke through the barrier of her virginity. He stopped moving. In fact, he went totally and completely still.

She knew that she should say something, but there were no words to express what she was feeling. No words to describe the unexpected thrill of feeling him buried deep inside her, of the glorious sensations that battered her from all directions.

Instead, she let her instincts take over, lifting her hips off the mattress, pulling him deeper, urging him on. He swore through gritted teeth as he gave up the fight for control and let her desire—and his own—carry them both toward the pinnacle of pleasure.

Chapter Seventeen

He rolled off her and onto his back, fighting to catch his breath and struggling to figure out what the hell had just happened. But it was difficult to think when his brain cells seemed incapable of the most basic functions.

"What the—"

Alyssa winced at the expletive he used to complete the sentence.

Jay didn't care. He said it again. And again.

"Don't you think you're overreacting a little?" she interjected as she shifted away from him, dragging the top sheet with her.

"No, I don't think I'm overreacting." He practically shouted the words at her. "My God, Lys—you were a virgin."

She didn't cower from his anger. In fact, she squared her shoulders and faced him defiantly, wearing nothing more than the bedsheet she held clenched in a fist between her breasts. "So?"

He found his briefs in the pile of discarded clothing on the floor and yanked them on. "So you should have told me."

And he should have known.

The clues were all there, if he'd bothered to take the time to piece them together. But when she'd invited him into her bedroom, he'd been focused on the finish line to the exclusion of all else. He'd not only taken her virginity, he'd done so with little thought and even less care, and the realization burned in his gut.

"Why?" she demanded in response to his claim.

He couldn't believe she would have to ask such a question. "Because that's not the kind of information a guy wants to discover *after* he's irrevocably changed the status."

"You're making this into a bigger deal than it is," she said, clearly unconvinced by his argument.

"It *is* a big deal."

She shook her head. "You don't understand."

"Explain it to me," he suggested.

She took a minute to wrap the sheet around herself before perching on the edge of the mattress. "All my life, I've been handled with kid gloves. There were so many things I wasn't allowed to do, so many experiences I missed out on, because my heart was fragile."

He scowled at that. "You told me your heart was fine."

"My heart *is* fine," she said. "But no matter how many doctors said exactly that, my parents refused to believe it. As a result, I led a very sheltered life.

"Yeah, I dated some, but whenever I started to get close to somebody—close enough to tell them about my surgeries, to prepare them for seeing my scars—their romantic interest inevitably gave way to a morbid fascination, and it was suddenly all about a birth defect that had stopped being relevant to me a long time ago. No one ever treated me like I was normal—until you."

He could hardly dispute what she was saying. He had no experience comparable to hers.

"Maybe it wouldn't have made a difference," she continued. "But maybe it would have, and I didn't want to take that chance. I was tired of feeling like a freak because I was a twenty-six-year-old virgin."

His fury was justified—she'd deliberately withheld important information. But it was difficult to hold on to his righteous anger in the face of the hurt and frustration he heard in her voice. "You're not a freak, Alyssa," he told her. "You're an incredibly smart, sweet, sexy woman."

"I was a twenty-six-year-old virgin," she said again.

"You're not that anymore," he pointed out.

That earned him a small smile. "I'm sorry I didn't tell you."

"Are you?" he wondered aloud.

"Well, I'm sorry that you were mad I didn't tell you," she clarified.

"I guess, under the circumstances, I can kind of understand," he agreed.

"But I wasn't only afraid that you'd treat me differently," she admitted now. "I was afraid…"

He sat on the edge of the bed, beside her. "Tell me."

She took a minute, as if to find the words she needed to express her feelings, then let them out in a rush. "I was afraid if you knew about my lack of experience you wouldn't want me."

He lifted a hand to her face, gently tipped her chin up so that she had to meet his gaze. "Apparently you're not as smart as I thought you were."

Hers showed confusion.

"How could you possibly think I wouldn't want you?" he asked, his tone softer now.

"I know you've had a lot of girlfriends," she said. "Girlfriends who undoubtedly had a lot more—"

He touched a finger to her lips, silencing her. "Let's keep this between you and me," he suggested.

"I don't want you to feel responsible for me…because of what just happened. I knew what I was doing when I asked you to stay," she said. "I didn't do it to try to turn a pretend relationship into something real."

"I'm feeling a lot of things," he acknowledged, "but responsible isn't one of them."

"What are you feeling?"

"Right now, looking at your sexy body wrapped in nothing more than that sheet, I'd say that 'aroused' is at the top of the list."

Her eyes widened. "Does that mean… Can we do it again?"

He chuckled softly. "Oh, yeah," he said. "I think it's safe to say we can do it again—"

A smile curved her lips.

"—but maybe not tonight."

The smile faded. "Why not? I've got a whole box of condoms."

And damn if that reminder didn't make him want to use every last one before the morning sun peeked over the horizon. But despite her evident enthusiasm, and his own eagerness, he had to remember that her body had been untouched and might be feeling more tender than she realized.

"Because I don't want to hurt you any more," he told her.

"You didn't hurt me," she said. "There was a brief twinge—and then there was nothing but pleasure. I want you to make me feel that way again."

"And to think that I once questioned your ability to negotiate," he mused ruefully.

Her lips curved again. "Does that mean you'll come back to bed with me?"

He didn't know how to deny her what they both wanted, so he didn't even try.

Alyssa hadn't expected any more than one night.

Especially when she saw how angry Jason was after the first time they'd made love, she didn't think anything she said or did would allow him to forgive her. But she was starting to realize that being a woman was a powerful thing—and she was enjoying wielding that power.

She knew that a woman's first time wasn't always pleasant. More often it was awkward and painful—and it didn't always get better after that.

It had admittedly taken her body a little while to adjust to the intrusion of his, but that little bit of discomfort had been eclipsed by the pleasure he gave her, both before and after. That first experience had been wonderful. Certainly she hadn't expected that it could get any better than that.

She'd been wrong.

Shockingly and fabulously wrong, as he proved to her night after night.

In the mornings, they resumed running together—although they sometimes got a later start, opting to begin the day with a different kind of cardio workout before they laced up their running shoes and hit the pavement.

Now Jason wasn't just her running partner, he was her friend and her lover.

She had a lover.

The knowledge made her giddy.

The memories of what he could and had done to her in the bedroom made her even giddier.

She didn't let herself worry about the future or even try to define their relationship because she'd never been happier than she was with Jason.

Every morning that Alyssa woke beside him, she was grateful for everything she had. She'd hoped for one night. A few hours to finally rid herself of the virgin label that chafed like an ill-fitting bra. A few hours to feel desire and desired, to experience passion.

That one night turned into two and then three. Then days became weeks. She was on summer break from school but continued to work at Diggers' and picked up additional shifts when they were offered. If she had to close the bar, Jason would meet her there, unwilling to spend even one night apart from her. Alyssa didn't complain.

She did wonder about the changes that would come along with the end of summer—when he had more free time and she had less. So far, their relationship had been mostly fun and games—which was, she knew, the only kind of relationship he had.

But with every day that passed, every minute they were together, her feelings for him continued to grow. She loved being with him. She loved his company and companionship. She loved the intimacies they shared—the way he made her feel when he touched her and kissed her, when their bodies moved together.

But even though she knew she was teetering on the edge, her heart precariously balanced, she held herself back from falling in love with him. She was smarter than that, stronger than that. And when he decided it was over, she would be grateful for the experience he'd shared with her.

She wouldn't be picking up pieces of a broken heart.

Three weeks after Matt's wedding—after the first night he'd spent with Alyssa—Jay finally acknowledged that his life had drastically veered off the course he'd set. But it hadn't happened that night. No, it was a process that had started months earlier—the first night that Alyssa kissed him.

It was crazy how much he wanted her. Never stopped wanting her. His friends weren't wrong in claiming there was a pattern to his relationships, and this romance should have run its course long before now.

But Alyssa was unlike any other woman he'd ever known. She was interesting and fun, beautiful and passionate, and he couldn't bring himself to contemplate the end of their relationship. He didn't want to imagine a future without her in it.

That was when he finally recognized the truth that had been staring him in the eye for weeks. Alyssa was more than a temporary girlfriend, fake fiancée or current lover—she was the woman he loved.

Now he just had to convince her to give their pretend relationship a real chance for a happy ending.

On a Sunday afternoon, two weeks before the end of summer, Alyssa was weeding the flower garden in the backyard when a shadow suddenly blocked out the sun.

"Diego, this is a surprise." She hadn't heard a single word from him since she'd left California, so his appearance here now was definitely unexpected.

He smiled. "I was in Reno for a friend's wedding and decided, since I was in the neighborhood, I'd stop by to see you."

"Reno is two hundred and fifty miles away," she noted. "That's hardly in the neighborhood."

"It's a lot closer than Irvine," he pointed out.

"True," she acknowledged, wiping the dirt from her hands on the thighs of her jeans. Her hair was on top of her head in a haphazard ponytail, strands falling out around a face bare of makeup, and the scoop-neck T-shirt she wore dipped low between her breasts.

A few months earlier, she might have worried about her appearance. She certainly would have tugged at the neckline of her shirt to cover her scars. But being with Jason had helped her be a lot more comfortable in her own skin and a lot less concerned about the judgments of others.

Still, she couldn't deny that this situation made her feel awkward and uncomfortable. She hadn't invited Diego and she certainly didn't want him here, but she could hardly turn him away without at least offering him a beverage after he'd come so far to see her. Unannounced and uninvited, but still...

"Can I get you a cold drink?" she asked.

"I'll have a soda, if it's not too much trouble," he decided.

"Have a seat." She gestured to the arrangement of wicker furniture. "I'll be right back."

She hurried inside and grabbed a cola for Diego and a bottle of water for herself. Then she took a few extra minutes to slice some cheese and set it on a plate with some crackers. Not that she wanted to encourage him to stay, but his family was close to hers and her mother would be appalled if Alyssa didn't offer some basic hospitality. Then she added some grapes to the plate, because her grandmother's lessons about presentation were as deeply ingrained as her mother's about manners.

"It's a long drive from Reno, and I thought you might be hungry," she said, setting the plate down along with his cola.

"I didn't realize I was until you put that out," he said.

She sipped her water while he snacked and shared some of the highlights from the wedding he'd attended.

"What are your plans now?" she asked when he'd put his plate aside. "Are you staying with your cousin in Elko?"

"No. I stopped at the Dusty Boots Motel and booked a room on my way into town."

"I spent a few nights there when I first came to Haven. It's not fancy, but it's clean and, until Liam Gilmore gets the old Stagecoach Inn open, it's the only local option. Plus, the diner does a decent breakfast, so you can fuel up before you start back in the morning."

"I was actually thinking I might stay in Nevada for a few more days," he told her. "I didn't get to see much of Haven—or you—on my last visit, and I'm hoping this time will be different."

"Oh…um, I guess I could give you a quick tour of the town," she offered.

"Or a not-so-quick tour," he suggested hopefully.

Alyssa capped her water bottle and set it on the table as she considered what to say to him—and decided that, since subtlety hadn't worked, she'd have to be blunt.

"Diego, if I ever said or did anything to mislead you, I sincerely apologize," she said. "And if my mother gave you any hope of a romantic relationship between us, I'm sorry about that, too. You're a terrific guy, really, but I don't have any romantic feelings for you."

He frowned at his cola. "This is because of that Jason guy, isn't it?"

"Even if I wasn't with Jason, I wouldn't be with you," she told him, trying for a gentle tone to dull the sharp edge of her words.

"I've been in love with you since I was fifteen," Diego admitted.

"I believe you might have had a crush on me—"

"It's more than that," he insisted. "I dated other girls, of course, but my heart has always belonged to you—even if you didn't know it. And when Renata invited me to the New Year's Eve party, I knew that she wanted us to be together as much as I did."

Alyssa couldn't deny that was probably true, at least at the time, so she focused on the present. "But it wasn't what *I* wanted. It's *not* what *I* want."

"You want Jason," he said bitterly.

She wanted to make her own choices and live her own life, but if Diego needed a scapegoat, she wasn't going to belabor the point. She just wanted him to go away so that she didn't have to feel guilty about putting that wounded look on his face.

"When you were in California for your parents' anniversary party, he told me that he'd asked you to marry him," Diego continued. "And that you'd said yes."

She nodded, not claiming the proposal had actually happened, but confirming his summary of the conversation.

"I commented then—and can't help noticing now—that you're not wearing a ring on your finger."

"Which isn't a big deal to anyone but you."

"If he's dragging his heels, that should be a warning that he's not committed to the idea of marriage—or to you."

"He hasn't been dragging his heels," she said. "We're just not in a hurry to start making plans."

"What aren't we making plans for?" Jason asked.

Alyssa started at the sound of his voice.

She'd been so focused on trying to make Diego see the futility of his romantic dreams that she hadn't heard Jason's truck pull into the driveway.

"Your wedding," Diego said in response to the question.

Jason moved over to where she was seated and bent to brush a light but lingering kiss on her lips. She knew it wasn't a gesture of affection so much as a brand of possession, and the Neanderthal display should have put her back up. But as always happened whenever Jason kissed her, she melted just a little.

"I was thinking a Christmas wedding," Jason said in a conversational tone. "But Alyssa wants to wear Valentina's wedding dress, and the alterations might take some time."

She was surprised that he knew about her desire to wear her grandmother's gown, but that knowledge finally seemed to convince Diego that Jason was committed to his supposed bride-to-be despite the absence of a ring on her finger.

"You will be the most beautiful bride," Diego said to Alyssa as he rose to his feet. "And I sincerely hope you only cry tears of joy on your wedding day."

"He has a point," Jason noted when the other man had gone.

"About what?" she wondered, shocked that he'd agree with Diego about anything.

"No one is ever going to believe that we're planning to get married unless I put a ring on your finger."

"Because we're not actually planning to get married," she pointed out.

"But maybe we should," he said.

She stared at him, wary and a little concerned. "Did you fall off the rock wall and hit your head today?"

"I'm not concussed or brain damaged," he assured her.

"Well, that's the only explanation I can think of for those words to have come out of your mouth."

"How about this one—I've fallen in love with you," he suggested.

Chapter Eighteen

Maybe she was the one who'd hit her head, because she was certain he hadn't just spoken the words she'd heard. "Are we having a hypothetical conversation?"

"No, Alyssa. I'm trying to tell you that I have real feelings for you, and I think—*I hope*—you have real feelings for me, too."

She did. Of course she did. But his declaration was as unexpected to her as Diego's visit.

"I want to end the pretense and be with you for real," he continued. "I want to marry you for real."

"Ohmygod." It was a good thing she was already sitting down, because the bones in her legs felt as if they'd completely melted away.

"I was expecting a yes or no answer," he told her. "Preferably a yes."

"This wasn't supposed to be real," she felt compelled to remind him.

"And yet this entire charade was more real than any other relationship I've ever had. My feelings for you are more real than anything I've ever felt for anyone else."

She'd never expected to hear him say those words. Words that filled her heart with so much unspeakable joy she felt as if it actually swelled inside her chest.

Except that this wasn't what she wanted. She'd moved to Nevada to be independent, and she was finally starting to get the hang of it. She wasn't ready to fall in love and build a life with someone else—not even the man she suspected she loved already.

"You said that our fake relationship wasn't going to turn into anything more," she reminded him. "You *promised*."

The desperation in her tone was Jay's first clue that this wasn't going to go as he'd imagined. "I didn't plan to fall in love with you," he said patiently. "It just happened."

"Then maybe you can fall out of love with me just as spontaneously," she suggested.

"I don't think so," he said, ruefully acknowledging that any illusions he had of her throwing herself into his arms and professing undying love were nothing more than that.

"You could at least try."

"I don't want to try. I want to be with you."

"What happened to not wanting to emulate your parents' marriage?" she asked.

"I'm not worried about that anymore. Not with you." He took her hands, linked their fingers together. "What are you afraid of, Lys?" he asked gently.

"Marriage is a promise. A commitment." She shook her head. "I can't."

He released her hands and leaned back against the rock wall bordering the patio. "You're serious," he realized. "You're actually saying no."

"I have to. I'm not ready for this," she said. "Not right now."

His wounded pride urged him to walk away. No way in hell was he going to beg for scraps of affection. But his pride was no match for his heart, demanding that he hold on to hope. "When?"

She looked at him, her eyes filled with anguish and tears. "I don't know. And I'm not asking you to wait for me—that wouldn't be fair."

"You're right," he agreed. "But I'm not going anywhere, Alyssa. Because I love you, and I know now that real love doesn't just go away. So when you decide that you're ready to share your heart—and your life—I'll be right here waiting for you."

Alyssa went back to California for a week before school was scheduled to resume. She needed time away from Jason, and not just distance but perspective, to help her get her head on straight—and she desperately needed to get her head on straight. Because it didn't matter where she was or who she was with; she was always thinking about him. And, of course, the whole time she was in Irvine, she remembered her last visit—with Jason.

She didn't like to think that it might be her heart rather than her head that was the problem. But she couldn't deny that she missed him unbearably.

Still, she was sure she'd done the right thing. Whatever she was feeling now was only temporary. They'd both been caught up in the play—like actors who fell in love while working together on the stage, only to find those feelings fade when they went their separate ways.

When were the feelings going to fade?

When was she going to wake up and not miss him?

Three days later, when she still didn't have the answers to those questions, she went to see her sister and confided, "Jason asked me to marry him."

Cristina, who'd been as hurt as she was disappointed to learn her sister's engagement was a sham, paused with her cup of coffee halfway to her mouth. "For real this time?"

Alyssa nodded. "But I said no."

Her sister's brows lifted. "Why?"

"Because it seemed a slightly less terrifying option than saying yes," she admitted.

Cristina sipped her coffee, considering. "Do you love him?"

"How would I know?" she asked. "I've never been in love before."

"So you don't think anyone who falls in love only once can ever be sure that it's real?"

"Of course not," she replied. "But even if this is real, I'm not ready for it. I've only just started to live my own life."

"And you think being in a committed relationship with a man who loves and respects you will somehow jeopardize your independence?"

"I don't know," she admitted.

"Okay, let me ask you this—do you think I'm less myself since I married Steven?"

"Of course not. But you've always been brave, strong and independent, able to tackle any obstacles in your path."

"And you think you've been scared, weak and dependent?" her sister guessed.

"I have been," she insisted. "Isn't that why you encouraged me to move away from Irvine?"

Cristina shook her head. "I encouraged you to move away so that you could see the truth—that you're every bit as brave and strong and independent as I am. Maybe even more so, because you've overcome obstacles I've never had to face."

Alyssa swiped at a tear that spilled onto her cheek. "I'm not brave—I'm terrified."

"Of course you are. Because love is terrifying. And wonderful. And I'm so happy for you."

"I told him no," she reminded her sister.

"And when you go back to Haven, you'll tell him yes," Cristina said.

Alyssa didn't believe for a minute it could be that simple, but for the first time since she got on the plane in Elko, she felt a tiny blossom of hope unfurl inside her heart.

She'd been gone for five days.

And in those five days, Jason had received no communication from Alyssa. Not a phone call, not even a text message.

Of course, he hadn't contacted her, either.

But he'd picked up the phone so many times he'd lost count. And he'd started numerous text messages, only to delete each and every one before sending.

He'd already put his heart on the line—there wasn't anything more that he could do. He didn't want to pressure her. And he definitely didn't want to come across as a pathetically needy guy who couldn't accept that the woman he loved didn't love him back.

Because he didn't feel pathetic or needy—he just felt empty, as if there was a great big gaping hole in his life where she used to be.

Okay, maybe that was pathetic and needy. And when the knock sounded at his door, he jumped up to answer it, grateful for any interruption of his unwelcome thoughts and uncomfortable reflections.

Then he opened the door, and she was there. And his pathetically needy heart immediately filled with hope and joy, though his wounded pride and wary mind urged caution.

"You're back," he said and immediately felt like a fool for stating the obvious.

She nodded. "Have I come at a bad time?"

He had no idea what time it was, and he didn't care. All that mattered was that she was here. After five endless days, she was finally here.

But of course, he didn't say that to her. Instead, he responded with a shake of his head. "No, it's not a bad time."

She smiled, though it wavered a little. "Good, because I've been waiting for five days to tell you something and I don't want to wait even five minutes more."

"Do you want to come in or say it in the hall?"

She walked through the open door and into the sitting area, but she remained standing, so he did the same.

"For a long time, I honestly thought my damaged heart was incapable of falling in love," she confided. "Then I met you...and suddenly I was feeling all kinds of things I'd never felt before. And the more time we spent together, the more those feelings grew. I knew I was starting to fall for you—and it was the most exhilarating and terrifying feeling in the world. But I didn't want to go splat, so I held myself back.

"And maybe I was doing just fine, living my own life, but you showed me what it could be like to share my life with someone. With you. And I wanted that so much that it scared me. Because I didn't let myself hope that you might ever feel about me the way I felt about you, and I was certain the only thing that would be worse than never experiencing love would be trying to put together the broken pieces of my heart.

"You once told me that I was brave, but I'm not. I'm a coward. I was willing to walk away from the possibility of what we could have together rather than risk having my heart broken."

"You're here now," he pointed out.

"I'm here now," she agreed.

"And now that you've taken the first step, the next one should be a little easier," he said encouragingly.

But Alyssa was still wary. "The next one's not a step. It's a leap."

He held her gaze, and she could see the feelings in his heart reflected in his eyes. "I'll catch you," he promised.

And because she knew that he would, she leaped.

"I love you, Jason Channing. I didn't plan for this to happen—I didn't even want it to happen. But I trust now that my feelings are real and not going to change, and I don't want to spend even one more day without you. So, if you still love me—"

"I still love you," he assured her.

And the unwavering conviction in his tone made her smile come a little more easily this time.

But he wasn't finished yet. "These past few days without you have been the loneliest, emptiest days of my life," he continued. "I was perfectly content before you came along. I didn't want or need anything else, until you showed me how much better everything is when we're together.

"There was a time when the prospect of spending the rest of my days with one person made me panic. Now the only thing that scares me is the prospect of spending even a single day without you beside me. You are my everything—for now and forever."

She hadn't expected such an outpouring of emotion, but his words filled her heart to overflowing. "In that case, I would like to say yes to your proposal," she told him. "Because there's nothing I want more than to marry you and build a life with you—for now and forever."

He turned away from her then and made his way across the room to his desk. "I still don't have an engagement ring," he said as he opened the top drawer. "And Carter will no doubt curse a blue streak when I leave him in charge of Adventure Village again, but I want to take you to New York to pick one out."

At his mention of a ring, the last of the weight that had been sitting on her chest was lifted, allowing her to tease, "They don't sell engagement rings anywhere in Nevada?"

"They don't have Tiffany's flagship store in Nevada," he told her. "Plus, I know you've always wanted to see New York City and I'd really like you to meet Brie."

"I'd like that, too, but I don't need a piece of jewelry to…" Her words trailed off when he handed her the flat velvet box he'd retrieved from his desk.

"It's not a ring," he said again. "But maybe you can wear it as a symbol of my love for you until we get a diamond."

She took the box from him and carefully opened the lid to reveal a perfectly shaped heart pendant on a delicate gold chain. "Oh, Jason. It's beautiful."

"I'm not asking you to get rid of the necklace your sister gave you, but I'm hoping you'll wear this one sometimes and know that this is how I see your heart—whole and perfect."

"My heart's not perfect," she told him. "But I promise that it's yours. For now and forever."

And when he took her in his arms, she knew that her imperfect heart had finally found its perfect match.

* * * * *

COMING SOON!

We really hope you enjoyed reading this book. If you're looking for more romance, be sure to head to the shops when new books are available on

Thursday
14th June

To see which titles are coming soon, please visit
millsandboon.co.uk

MILLS & BOON

MILLS & BOON

Coming next month

REUNITED AT THE ALTAR
Kate Hardy

Cream roses.

Brad had bought her cream roses.

Had he remembered that had been her wedding bouquet, Abigail wondered, a posy of half a dozen cream roses they'd bought last-minute at the local florist? Or had he just decided that roses were the best flowers to make an apology and those were the first ones he'd seen? She raked a shaking hand through her hair. It might not have been the best idea to agree to have dinner with Brad tonight.

Then again, he'd said he wanted a truce for Ruby's sake, and they needed to talk.

But seeing him again had stirred up all kinds of emotions she'd thought she'd buried a long time ago. She'd told herself that she was over her ex and could move on. The problem was, Bradley Powell was still the most attractive man she'd ever met – those dark, dark eyes; the dark hair that she knew curled out-rageously when it was wet; that sense of brooding about him. She'd never felt that same spark with anyone else she'd dated. She knew she hadn't been fair to the few men who'd asked her out; she really shouldn't have compared them to her first love, because how could they ever match up to him?

She could still remember the moment she'd fallen in love with Brad. She and Ruby had been revising for their English exams together in the garden, and Brad had come out to join them, wanting a break from his physics revision. Somehow he'd ended up reading Benedick's speeches while she'd read Beatrice's.

'I do love nothing in the world so well as you: is that not strange?'

She'd glanced up from her text and met his gaze, and a surge of heat had spun through her. He was looking at her as if it was the first time he'd ever seen her. As if she was the only living thing in the world apart from himself. As if the rest of the world had just melted away...

Continue reading

REUNITED AT THE ALTAR
Kate Hardy

Available next month
www.millsandboon.co.uk

LET'S TALK
Romance

For exclusive extracts, competitions
and special offers, find us online:

f facebook.com/millsandboon

◉ @millsandboonuk

🐦 @millsandboon

Or get in touch on 0844 844 1351*

For all the latest titles coming soon, visit
millsandboon.co.uk/nextmonth

Want even more
ROMANCE?

Join our bookclub today!

'Mills & Boon books, the perfect way to escape for an hour or so.'

Miss W. Dyer

'Excellent service, promptly delivered and very good subscription choices.'

Miss A. Pearson

'You get fantastic special offers and the chance to get books before they hit the shops'

Mrs V. Hall

Visit millsandbook.co.uk/Bookclub
and save on brand new books.

MILLS & BOON